THE REMAINS OF LOVE

Zeruya Shalev

Translated from the Hebrew by Philip Simpson

B L O O M S B U R Y
LONDON • NEW DELHI • NEW YORK • SYDNEY

First published in Great Britain 2013
This paperback edition published 2014

Published by arrangement with The Institute for The Translation of Hebrew Literature

Bloomsbury Publishing Plc
50 Bedford Square, London WC1B 3DP

Bloomsbury Publishing, London, New Delhi, New York and Sydney

A CIP catalogue record for this book is available from the British Library

ISBN 978 1 4088 3657 6

10 9 8 7 6 5 4 3 2 1

Typeset by Hewer Text UK Ltd, Edinburgh
Printed and bound by CPI Group (UK) Ltd, Croydon, CR0 4YY

www.bloomsbury.com/zeruyashalev

THE REMAINS OF LOVE

A NOTE ON THE AUTHOR

ZERUYA SHALEV was born at Kibbutz Kinneret. She is the author of three previous novels; *Love Life, Husband and Wife* and *Thera*, a book of poetry and a children's book. Her work is critically acclaimed and internationally bestselling. Shalev has been awarded the Book Publishers Association's Gold and Platinum Prizes four times, the Corine International Book Prize (Germany, 2001), the Amphi Award (France, 2003), the ACUM Prize twice (1997, 2005), the French Wizo Prize (2007) and the prestigious Welt-Literature Award (2012). *Husband and Wife* was also nominated for the Femina Prize (France, 2002). A feature film of *Love Life*, produced in Germany, was released in 2008. Her books have been translated into twenty-five languages. She lives in Jerusalem.

A NOTE ON THE TRANSLATOR

PHILIP SIMPSON was born in Yorkshire in 1952, and grew up in East Anglia. His published translations include *The Lover* by A. B. Yeshoshua, *Where the Jackals Howl* by Amos Oz, *From These Men* by Shimon Peres and *A Guide to the Perplexed* by Gilad Atzmon, and he has also contributed to the *Oxford Book of Hebrew Short Stories, New Women's Writing from Israel* and *Contemporary Israeli Women's Writing*, among others. He lives in rural north Norfolk.

BY THE SAME AUTHOR

Love Life
Husband and Wife
Thera

Chapter One

Has the room really grown in size, or is she the one who has shrunk? This is after all the smallest room in a minuscule apartment, but now, as she is confined to her bed from morning till evening, it seems its dimensions have expanded – it would take her hundreds of paces to reach the window, hours by the score, and who knows if she will live long enough. The remains of life, that is, the last remnant of the portion of time allotted to her, in some absurd fashion feels like eternity – being in such a state of immobility, it seems it is stretching away into the infinite. The truth is, she is already withered and wizened, as light as a ghost, and the slightest gust of wind would be enough to blow her from the bed, and it appears it is only the weight of the blanket that stops her hovering in the void, and it is also true that any breath could sever the last thread in the spool that connects her to life. But who will do the breathing, who will even take the trouble to breathe in her direction?

Yes, for many years to come she will be lying here under her thick blanket, seeing her children growing older, her grandchildren turning into adults. Yes, with sour indifference they will condemn her to eternal life, because it seems to her suddenly that even the act of dying requires some effort, some vitality on the part of the future deceased or of his environment. Personal attention is needed, a degree of anxious commotion, like the preparations for a birthday party. Even dying requires a measure of love, while she is no longer loved enough, and perhaps not loving enough, even for this.

It's not that they don't come: almost every day one of them visits her apartment, sits down in the armchair facing her, apparently enquiring after her health, but she senses the old grudges, notices the glances at the watch, the sighs of relief when their mobiles ring. All at once their voices change, becoming vigorous and full of life, dredging up throaty laughter. I'm at my mother's place, they finally inform their interlocutors, with sanctimonious rolling of the eyes, I'll be in touch as soon as I leave, and then they once again turn their hollow attention to her, condescending to ask questions but not listening to what she has to say. And she for her part retaliates with tiresome answers, reporting in detail exactly what the doctor said, reeling off the list of medications before their glassy stares. Which of us is more repelled by the other, I by you or you by me, she wonders, turning them into a single entity, her two children who are so different from one another, although it seems it's only in her presence that they have succeeded in uniting, and that only recently, addressing the elderly mother who is confined from morning till evening to her bed in the little room, detached from the force of gravity.

The room is cramped and square, its only window overlooking the Arab village. On its northern side is an ancient writing desk and to the south a wardrobe where her clothes are stowed, those colourful clothes that she will never wear again. She was always drawn, a little shamefaced, to vivid colours, irrespective of styles: a long and voluminous kaftan-blouse, a dress drawn in tight at the waist, a pleated skirt – to this day she doesn't know what suits her best, and now she never will. Her eyes wander to the oval coffee table that her daughter forced her to buy many years ago, weeping bitterly although she was already a big girl. You people forced me to move into this repulsive apartment, and even then you gave me the smallest room, so you can at least buy me something I like. Stop crying, she scolded her, everyone's looking at you, but of course she gave in, and four hands carried the table which turned out to be exceptionally heavy up the stairs to this room which was her room, where it was dumped in the centre, its new and elegant lustre showing up the shabbiness of the other furniture.

And now this too has seen better days, it has absorbed time into itself and faded. But the packets of tablets hide the oak wood, full and heavy: medications that cure infections but give rise to allergies, medications to combat allergies, tablets to stabilise the heart-rate, and painkillers, and tablets to lower blood-pressure which weakened her so much that she fell and hurt herself and since then has found walking a struggle, and sometimes she longs to pile them all up in a colourful heap and plant a medical garden in her bed, sort everything according to colours and use them to design a little house, red roof, white walls and green lawns, Dad and Mum and two children.

What was all this, she asks, and she's no longer asking why it was the way it was, nor what was the meaning of what was, but what it really was, and how did the days progress to the point where she arrived in this room, in this bed, and what were they filled with, those tens of thousands of days that clambered over her body like ants on a tree-trunk. It's her duty to remember and she can't remember. Even if she exerts herself and gathers together all her memories like old-fashioned notes in a card-index and pins them together, she will succeed in assembling only a few weeks, and where are all the rest, where are all her years? What she doesn't remember will no longer exist, and maybe it never existed in the first place.

As if in the wake of a disaster, the obligations laid on her now at the end of her life are the struggle against oblivion, the need to safeguard the dead and the missing, and when she looks again at the window it seems to her he is waiting for her there, the lake that died before her very eyes, the misty lake and the swamps surrounding him, soft and steaming, generating fields of papyrus plants tall as a man, launching migratory birds into flight with an emotive flurry of wings. That's where he is, her lake, in the heart of her valley, a depression running from the lower slopes of Mount Hermon to the hills of Galilee, squeezed by the fists of petrified lava. If only she could manage to leave her bed and make it to the window, she would get to see him again, and she tries to sit up straight, to gauge the distance with her eyes, her glance veering from the window to her aching legs. Since she fell, walking has seemed to her a rather dangerous form of levitation, but he's there, waiting for her to look, as anxious as she is. Get up Hemdi, she hears her father urging her, just one more step, one little step.

She was the first child born on the kibbutz, and they all gathered in the dining hall to see her take her first steps. It seems that all the longings for younger siblings left behind in foreign parts, for their own childhood which had been cut short by a stern ideology, for the love of parents whom they hadn't seen since they got up and left, some angry and some broken-hearted – all came together in the dining hall that had only just been built. With sparkling eyes they watched her, urging her to walk, for them, for their elderly parents, for the brothers who had grown up in the meantime and within a few years would be destroyed, and she was flustered but eager to please, standing on her unsteady legs holding her father's hand, were his fingers already smelling of fish or was that only later, and she put one trembling foot forward at precisely the moment her father released her hand, and all those present cheered and whooped and applauded her, a quite terrifying cacophony, and she fell flat on her back and burst into tears under the blue and stubborn eyes of her father, who urged her to get up and try again, to show them all that she's growing up, just one little step, but she lay on her back, knowing this was a gift she couldn't give him, knowing he would never forgive her.

And after that she refused to walk for two whole years, until the age of three she was carried around like a cripple, although tests revealed nothing and they were considering taking her to a paediatrician in faraway Vienna. Children born after her were already running around and only she was lying on her back in the playpen, gazing up at the top of the pepper tree, with tiny red balls like pills adorning its branches, whispering to her, and she smiled at them. Only they did not exhort her, only they accepted her immobile presence, whereas her father wouldn't give up the fight, and pursued by guilt he carried her in his arms from doctor to doctor, until a specialist in Tel Aviv finally declared, there's nothing wrong with her brain, she's just afraid of walking. Find something that will scare her even more.

Why scare her more? her father asked, and the doctor replied, there's no other way. If you want her to start walking, make her more scared of you than she is of walking, and thereafter her handsome father would wrap a towel around her, hold the end of it like a halter and try to make her walk in front of him, hitting her hard when she refused. It's for your own good Hemdi, he used to wheeze, choking at the sight of her face swollen with weeping, so you'll be like all the other children, so you'll stop being afraid, and it seems that doctor's advice was sound, because after a few weeks she was already walking unsteadily, her body smarting from the beatings, her consciousness frozen like the consciousness of a small wild beast, in a cruel process of training, far from achievement, far from happiness, dimly aware that even if she succeeds in walking, even if she succeeds in running, she will still have nowhere to go.

Far from happiness, far from achievement, yet all the same it seems to her this morning she has somewhere to go, to the window, Hemda, to see your lake, the one that whispers to you. If I have come to you, he whispers, if I have gathered together all my greenish waters and the fishes and the vegetation and the migratory birds, if I have succeeded in reconstituting myself in a hill town opposite your window, despite the horrendous effort invested in my relocation, won't you get out of bed and walk to the window to see? And she answers him with a sigh, just a few weeks ago I was still pacing the corridor with halting steps, why didn't you come then? Why come now of all times, after the fall, and it isn't only you, since time began things have arrived too late or too early, but he sends her a moist blast of air and whispers, for decades I've been joining drop to drop, branch to branch, wing to wing, just to appear before you again, to see you, come to me, Hemda, come to the window. And she shakes her head in bemusement. What were all those years and what were they for if they have left no register behind, if at the end of the day a little girl is left, longing to bathe naked in her lake.

With crooked fingers she tries to peel from her skin the nightdress that she received once as a present from her daughter, received with some resentment. She always looked askance at her presents, although they were agreeable enough and generous, and she always hit out at her daughter at these of all moments, when she was eager to give satisfaction. Open it, Mum, she would urge her. I spent hours going round the shops to find something you like, go on and open it, check the size, you'll like it. And she would tear the superior wrapping paper, fingering suspiciously, because the soft feel of the fabric, the unfamiliar smells it exuded, the sights hidden behind it, the landscapes through which her daughter walked without her, all these things aroused her to sudden anger, and she was mumbling, thank you, Dina, really you shouldn't have, crushing the empty wrapping, surprising even herself with the intensity of her unease. Does the giving of every small gift engender so much guilt, alongside the wish for absolute and unlimited giving? Take me with you, she wanted to say to her, instead of bringing me souvenirs of your separate existence, and Dina would look at her with a chagrined expression, don't you like it, Mum?

I love it, love it too much, was this the right answer that was never spoken, loving too much or too little, too late or too early, and then she would put the fabric back in the wrapping and hide it in the wardrobe, and only after some time, when the affront was deeply ingrained and beyond repair, too late for that, would she wrap herself angrily in that forgotten present: sweater, scarf, nightdress checked with grey flowers – who ever saw a grey flower? – and she's trying to extricate her arm from the sleeve that has stuck to her when her eyes fall unexpectedly on her exposed bosom; her nipples are grey flowers, bowing their heads at the edges of the flattened breasts, withered and drooping. Her fingers suspiciously probe the folds of skin and she remembers the youngest of her grandsons, how they sat him on her knees at a festive meal a few months ago and within moments he'd spilled a glass of water over himself, and when she pulled his shirt off he suddenly stretched out his bare arm and inspected it with wonder, as if seeing it for the first time, moving it up and down, fingering and licking, and then moved on to a frenzied groping of the soft skin of his stomach, delighting in the contact. This was a virginal love dance, a hymn to self-love, if indeed the mentality of the toddler could grasp the fact that this body was his own, if indeed her mentality today is capable of taking on dominion over the drooping body. No, it still seems to her that old age is nothing more than dirt that has stuck to her over the years, or a transient sickness, and the moment she reaches the lake, the moment she bathes in its water, her body will be cured like the flesh of the Syrian general who bathed in the Jordan seven times and was cured of his leprosy.

Come on, Hemda, put your foot down on the floor, lean against the wall and stand up straight, beside the bed your stick awaits you but you don't need it, you need only me, as in those days when you were a wandering heron, looking for shelter among the papyrus-beds. Do you remember how you used to swim naked in the winter, diving into the freezing water which scalded you like fire, until you fell ill and your father wouldn't let you carry on, but still you used to sneak away to me from time to time, throwing your clothes on the shore, and one time he came and found you there and ordered you to get out of the water, and when you emerged and he saw you were naked he ran away and after that he stopped looking for you there, so just the two of us were left but something was missing.

And where was her mother? Time and again it was her father who tried to twine her hair into braids with clumsy hands smelling of fish, it was he who forced her to walk and run, and climb on the roofs of the kibbutz like the other children. She couldn't keep up with them, while they were leaping like monkeys from roof to roof, she felt faint with fear and refused to try, until he appeared on the scene, blue eyes fixed on her with a look of menace. What are you more afraid of, the jumping or me, life or death, and she climbed with an effort, cursing him and weeping, stupid, stupid ass is what you are, I'll tell my Mum everything.

But where was your mother? her daughter asks when she deigns to listen to her stories, familiar to the point of nausea but still surprising, disconcerting anew every time they are repeated. You grew up without a mother! she tells her mother with an air of satisfaction, and Hemda protests, no, you've got it all wrong, I loved my mother so much and she loved me, I never had any doubts about her love, but Dina isn't giving up, since a whole chain of enticing inferences derives from this declaration. You grew up without a mother so it's no wonder you don't know how to be a mother, and it follows from this that I didn't have a mother either, and even my little girl is suffering from this. Don't you see how the absence of your mother, who you're not even angry with, has affected us all?

You've got it all wrong, she shakes her head at her. I wasn't angry with my mother because I knew she was working hard. She worked in the town and came home only at weekends, and even when she went away for a whole year and came back and I didn't recognise her, I thought she was a stranger who'd murdered my mother – even then I wasn't angry with her, because I understood she had no choice. You people and your anger, you and Avner and the whole of this deprived generation of yours, what good comes of all these complaints? But sometimes it seems to her she too is angry, a terrible, murderous anger, directed not at her parents only, not at her father who was so devoted to her in his own hurtful way, or at her mother who was always busy, but at them, at her children, and especially at this daughter of hers, whose hair is already turning grey.

Only yesterday, she plaited a braid in her black and curly hair, her fingers as clumsy as her father's fingers in her own hair, and now it is lank, metallic, and her daughter doesn't dye it as most women of her age do, with the excuse that this grey mane of hers is the best frame for her girlish features, and it seems to her, to Hemda, that even this is intentional, it's only to punish her that her daughter is mortifying herself, only to prove that those childhood days were fatally flawed, and to this end she will neglect herself, starve herself, turning more skeletal from year to year. And her own daughter is a good deal thinner and smaller than her. They are progressively diminishing themselves, the women in this family, and apparently in another two or three generations they will be obliterated, while her son will go on expanding, so much so, she sometimes has difficulty recognising the rotund, balding man, with his heavy panting, her handsome son who inherited rare blue eyes from his grandfather, and sometimes she looks at him with a shudder, because it seems to her that this man murdered her son and is living in his stead, sleeping in his bed, bringing up his children, precisely the same suspicions she once had towards the stranger, the woman who returned from America many years before and ran to kiss and hug her, claiming she was her mother.

All the kibbutz waited for her on the lawn, to greet her on her return from that extended mission, and only she hid in one of the trees, a little monkey after all, looking down on the tense expectation that was absolutely impersonal; which of the children remembered her mother if even she had forgotten her, and which of the adults was really expecting her, besides her husband and a handful of relatives. In fact most of them were jealous of her, especially the women working long hours doing turns in the kitchen, the children's houses, vegetable garden, sewing room, barn, storeroom, in blue working clothes with blue-veined legs, while only she, Hemda's mother, wears elegant suits and sits in some office in the town, and sometimes even this isn't enough for her and she goes away on some assignment, on whose behalf, God only knows. Yes, all these words she heard while hiding among the branches, and even if she didn't hear, she guessed, and if she didn't guess she thought them for herself, since it wasn't her they were expecting but a breath of fresh air from the big world, hope, sweet memory – all those things being brought supposedly by the woman now extricating herself from the dark taxi. Who was she? Even through the branches she could tell this wasn't her mother. The long lock of hair had disappeared, the face was full and pale, the body clumsy. Miserable and bemused, she jumped down from the top of the tree, no one saw her escaping from there, running as fast as she could and as far as she could, to the lake.

You're not my mother, she would shout finally when she returned to her parents' room and stood facing her, and the strange woman would look at her sadly, her eyes fixed for some reason on the perky incipient breasts of a twelve-year-old, covered by a grimy blouse. My poor darling, how neglected you look, she would say, as if she herself hadn't been doing most of the neglecting, and at once she would try to placate her. I was sick for a long time, Hemda. I was laid up in the hospital and that's why they cut off my hair. I had a kidney infection and my face swelled up, and Hemda searched in that face for the familiar scars of chickenpox, two tiny craters between chin and cheeks. You're not my mother, she declared again, disappointed, you have no scars, and the strange woman fingered her chin, I have scars, you just can't see them, here they are, and Hemda burst into tears, where is my mother? What have you done with my mother? – and at once she fastened on her father's scrawny thighs, don't touch him, don't do to him what you did to my mother, he's all I've got left now, and the first nights she used to writhe on her bed in the children's house and see in her mind's eye how the stranger, the woman who swallowed her mother, was now chewing her father's thighs as if they were roasted chicken legs, sucking the marrow from his bones, and soon she would tuck with relish into her meagre flesh too, perky little breasts and all.

Two breasts, two thighs, two parents, two children, and in the middle she herself, more obsessed with her dead parents than with her living children. A son and a daughter were born to her, a pair of children, the expanding mirror-image of the couple who created them, while the third pair in the family, she and her husband, always seemed to her like a transit station between two capital cities, and now when she places her feet on the floor, still cold although outside the air is blazing, she sees them there before her, the first couple, her father in blue working clothes and her mother in a white silk blouse and pleated skirt, the braid adorning her head like a soft royal crown, and they stand on the edge of the lake and smile at her, pointing with their hands towards the calm water, the colour of milky coffee.

It's late, Hemda, time to wash and go to sleep, they say, pointing to the lake as if it's a wash-bowl meant only for her, look at how dirty you are, and she hurries towards them, out of breath. If she doesn't get a move on the lake will disappear again, the young parents will disappear, but her legs are heavy, sinking into the sticky mud. Mum, Dad, give me a hand, I'm drowning. Tentacles of viscous mud wrap around her waist, drawing her body into the depths of the swamp. Mum, Dad, I'm choking.

Crawl on your stomachs, she remembers the instructions of the nature studies teacher when they went out to look for swallows' nests and the mud attacked them, enfolding their legs. Her mouth, open to scream, is filled with compacted earthy mush and she's choking. Give me a hand, but her parents stand and watch her without moving, smiles on their lips as if she's putting on an entertaining show for them. Can't they see she's sinking, or do they want her to disappear? Her body lands heavily on the floor underneath the window. It seems she's been taken from this place, as the entrails of the mud eagerly digest her ankles. How welcome she is in the depths of the earth, she has never felt so warm a welcome, but she's still struggling, trying to hold on to the legs of the table, the time hasn't come yet, too early or too late, the time hasn't come yet, and with the last remnants of her fading consciousness she crawls to the phone. Crawl like crocodiles, the man shouted, otherwise you'll drown. Her parched throat is blocked. Dina, come quickly, I'm suffocating.

Dina is standing motionless before the kitchen window, gazing in astonishment at the pine needles that have joined together, interwoven, stretching out to her like empty hands, begging alms. She has taken the eggs, the grey dove. Only last night, before going to sleep, she peered again at the window sill and saw the eggs gleaming at her from the darkness of the nest like a pair of benevolent eyes, and at once the dove appeared and covered them with her body. Warmth wafted towards her from the body of the dove, gentle tranquillity, sweet memory. What could be simpler, just sitting like that, without moving, for hours upon hours, eyes alert but body still, all gathered together, concentrating on the objective. She has moved the eggs from here, flying away in the darkness of night with a white egg in her beak; she laid it in a different nest which she prepared in advance, and came back to collect the one left behind. Was it her insistent staring that scared the bird away?

What a strange pain, she mumbles as the phone rings on, what a stupid, unnecessary pain, to stand like this, in gloomy reverence, as if before a desecrated tomb, confronting the stack of pine needles, which yesterday was a house of miracles and today is a meaningless agglomeration, and she holds out her hand to the tiny cradle and crumbles it. The spring breeze will disperse the twigs in a moment, and no trace will be left of the life that for a whole week was so vibrant here, filling her with a strange emotion: two eggs in the nest, one egg unhatched.

Why did she take them? she asks aloud. More and more she's been hearing her own voice recently, surprisingly loud, especially when there's no one else around, her thoughts emerge from her throat unrestrained and it's the voice that exposes their nakedness, their embarrassing simplicity. Must buy milk, she hears herself announcing with solemn intensity, as if talking about a national assignment, or I'm going to be late, or where is Nitzan? It seems this question has been heard again and again in the void surrounding her, and it isn't so much where is her only daughter located at this particular moment, because there are still simple answers to this one: she's at school, or at a friend's house, or on her way home – but where is her heart, which all through the years has been close to hers and is now alien to her, beating against her vigorously and aggressively. How can even the most natural of loves turn into disappointed love, she wonders, following the child with yearning eyes, trying to tempt her with those treats that in the past elicited cries of sweet delight from her: come on, Nitzi, let's bake a cake together, come on, let's go to the cinema, have you seen there's a new pizzeria just round the corner, fancy a pizza? But now she meets a look of sulky indifference and a cold voice answers her, some other time, Mum, I've no time just now, but time for her friends, she has plenty of that, because straightaway she's making arrangements with Tamar or with Shiri, disappearing as if escaping from her, and Dina watches her go with a frozen smile, trying to hide the hurt. What a strange pain.

Leave her alone, let her grow up, Gideon scolds her, anyone would think you wanted to spend time with your mother when you were an adolescent, but she doesn't answer; her answers to him are left unspoken, roaming around in the void of her belly and finding no outlet. It isn't the same thing at all, my mother actually preferred my brother, my mother was never a pleasant companion, with those depressing stories of hers about the lake, she always saw only herself, she didn't know how to be a mother, she learned too late.

Two eyes, again she hears her voice breaking the silence, coarse as the voice of the dumb, two precious stones, diamonds that gleamed from the window sill as if from the floor of a dark mine shaft, why did she take them, what scared her away? The guttural wail of a cat answers this question, drowning out the ringing of the phone with another hot, hairy flame, squirming between her legs. Where have you been, Rabbit? she greets him ceremoniously, filling his bowl with dried titbits, where have you been and what have you done? But he's in no hurry for his brunch, lingering between her bare legs, nuzzling her warmly. That's the way he goes and circulates between the three of them as if trying to bind them together with his tail, to imprint on her skin the heartfelt wishes of her daughter and her husband, to imprint on their skin some desiderata of her own, because lately it has seemed to her that this cat, this overgrown tom erroneously named Rabbit – with his white fur and long ears he should really have been called Hare – is the last remaining cause that unites them, like a child of old age preserving a faint echo of the family, besides possessions, of course, the furniture, the walls, the car, the memories.

Because she has noticed recently that almost every approach to her daughter begins with a memory. Do you remember how we used to play in this garden? We loved staying here after dark, after everyone had left, and there's Bar's house, do you remember when you went there for a sleepover but called us in the middle of the night and asked to be taken home and after that she didn't invite you again? You remember how I used to take you to the crèche and afterwards we'd buy ice cream here? Why does she need so much corroboration on the part of her daughter, what difference does it make if she remembers this detail or another, and it isn't all these things that she wants to remind her of, but their love. Do you remember that you loved me once, Nitzan?

Where did it suddenly spring from, this moment in which the balance between memories and desires is shattered? No one has prepared her for this, neither books nor newspapers, neither parents nor friends. Is she the only woman on earth who feels this at such an early stage of life, and without any disaster visible to the eye, the first to feel that the pan of the scales laden with memories is overflowing, while the pan of desires is as light as a feather, and focused entirely on restoring something that used to be.

Enough, she says, enough of this already, you hear me, Rabbit? Enough, but the cat isn't giving up, latching on to her with devotion, pricking up a sinewy tail as if presenting her with an abstract of all the anticipated summer heat. This is unbearable, she says, all at once it has become too hot, just a moment ago it was winter, and now in one day it has turned to summer, without stages, without transitional seasons, what a lost, desperate country, always going from extreme to extreme.

Because the smell of the overnight bonfires is still weighing heavy on the sweltering air, how hard it is to breathe and perhaps there's no need for it, recently it has seemed to her even the smallest of tasks is too complicated for her, and perhaps it's her motivation which is no longer strong enough. Once, when Nitzan needed her, she used to breathe frantically, stealing oxygen from the mouths of passers-by, but now that the girl is distanced from her, hurting her deliberately, she has no interest in oxygen, let others breathe it. What an unpleasant age, she sighs, forty-five, once we would have been dead at this age, we would have given up raising children and expired, liberating the world from our presence, the prickly presence of women no longer fertile, husks devoid of charm.

We're not answering, Rabbit, she informs him when he leaps up on to the marble worktop in the kitchen, for all I care they can carry on calling until tomorrow, I don't have the strength to talk to anyone, but when he paces with majestic slowness towards the window sill and sniffs with satisfaction the empty space left behind by the dove eggs she understands – someone left the window open in the night despite her clear instructions; this is the one that destroyed the nest, the rabbit, or rather the cat, and when she peers out, to her dismay she sees broken shells on the pavement below, and a repulsive gunge, the remains of life.

Gideon, she yells, I've been telling you all week, don't open the kitchen window, but he went out some time ago, his old Leica hanging round his neck like a child's lunchbox, and an extra camera slung from his shoulder, wandering about restlessly, eyes darting, relentlessly seeking the unique combinations which define reality for him. Did she really say this? For a moment she hesitates, maybe she only intended to say it, and again the strange pain between the ribs, the anger aroused again. Two little embryos once resided in her nest, two precious stones, and only one of them hatched, her Nitzan, a tiny but healthy baby, while the other didn't survive, turned into repulsive gunge, and nobody was to blame for this, but all the same she insisted on blaming, especially herself. Was this down to her preference for the girl? Was it their anxiety in the first weeks of pregnancy which drained the young creature of the will to live? How are we going to cope with this, tell me, he used to sigh, he had only just been sacked by the paper, and he was shutting himself away for hours in his improvised darkroom, and emerging from there grim-faced, as if disaster had struck: two parents, two embryos, all at once, what's going to happen, who's going to bring them up, who's going to bring us up? For hours they used to lie on the sofa, staring at the walls of the cramped apartment, what's going to happen, we need to find a better apartment, need to find work, need to take out a loan. The list of obligations grew longer, intensifying the helplessness. A menacing nihilism emerged from within her in those days, meeting his own in a dark alley, until one day he packed a small bag and left, I need time to recuperate, he muttered at her, as if this was a blow that had landed on him, and she thought he would return that evening or the next day, but a few days later he called her from Africa, and when he finally returned he had in his knapsack some exclusive shots which turned him overnight into a celebrity photographer, while in her hidden nest there was just one egg.

Can thoughts kill, can wishing for failure engender disaster? She wanted to be left alone in those days, with two tiny creatures clinging to the walls of her womb like snails on a tree-trunk, and most of the hatred she directed at him, at the male. Could she have been otherwise, probably not, but neither could he. In the first years she was so busy with the baby she was almost incapable of imagining in herself the existence of another creature, but the more Nitzan grew, the more he haunted her, the child who wasn't born, the child who gave in too easily, and sometimes at night when she came to tuck Nitzan into bed, it seemed to her she could hear someone else breathing in the room, a sound wafting between the toy shelves, and in the daytime she used to see him cavorting alongside Nitzan as she played – his hair the colour of honey, as rich and abundant as hers, his eyes brown-green like hers

– and when she painted, and when she read, and when she wept, but now that Nitzan is moving further away from her he isn't receding, he always was a sweet child, considerate, silently obeying her repressed wishes.

What are you waiting for, have another child, her mother used to urge her, Nitzan needs a brother or a sister, and you need to back off from her a bit, and she would reply scornfully, really, Mother? The way you backed off from me? You should know, they call that abuse, not backing off. Deep down inside she knew her mother was right, and still she hesitated, she so much enjoyed devoting herself to her daughter and giving her all the things she herself never had, to say nothing of the obstinate refusal of Gideon, and she always believed it wasn't too late, there was still plenty of time to convince him. Now and then she would try, we have another opportunity for happiness, Gideon, come on let's do this before it's too late, but he would recoil at once, how do you know this would be happiness, it could be precisely the opposite. We're doing all right as we are, why spoil it? Why risk what we have for the sake of something unknown?

What kind of a world do you want to bring another child into? he would chide her, as if she had expressed some exceptional and outrageous request, you have no idea where you're living, join me on one of my trips and you'll get to know this land, they're not all sitting in comfy apartments talking about happiness, there are people for whom a kid just means an extra mouth to be fed, and she wondered why this was relevant: was a child that they brought into the world destined to steal the rations of another child, and again she would back down, afraid of pressurising him, afraid on her own account of change. Weren't they doing all right like this? Yes, it was good, too good perhaps, bringing up Nitzan without competitors – unlike her experience of growing up driven by jealousy and hatred directed towards her younger brother – and the girl flourished, surrounded by love, why endanger what is for the sake of something unknown? Yes, it sounded convincing, and it almost convinced her, but in her training college which had turned over the years into a university, the students had different ideas, and when she stood up in front of them and lectured on the expulsion of the Jews of Spain they laid sensitive hands on their tumescent bellies, and they didn't seem to be risking their happiness, on the contrary they were boosting it, and recently she has begun to suspect that they were right, she was the one in the wrong and it was too late to make amends. She of all people, supposed to be teaching them, had not read the book of life correctly, since the Nitzan of today isn't the sweet and loving girl she once was; the quick-tempered girl who slams the door of her room in her face, the door of her heart as well, is hardly going to console her with her very existence for the children she didn't bear.

Don't get worked up about her, they tell her, be glad that she's daring to kick out at you, that's exactly the sign that means she's growing up right, she needs to get away from you but she'll be back, and in the meantime make the most of the extra free time you're going to have, you might finally get round to finishing your doctoral thesis. They all have words for her, Gideon, her mother, her friends, all of them offering her words from moving lips, like remedies for an embarrassing disease, but what is she going to do with them? Can she cradle the words in her arms, take the words out for walks when the air cools down a bit, show them the moon and the stars? What a strange pain this is, peeping out between her ribs as if they are the bars of a cage, she's cultivating it and it is certainly well-nourished, developing nicely; within a short time it has turned from a tiny snail into an oppressive and demanding creature, impeding respiration and arousing waves of nausea, stopping her concentrating on her work, not allowing her to perform the simplest of tasks, even answering the phone, which apparently has been ringing for the past hour. She's become so used to it that it seems to her to be emerging from inside her own head, through the ears and into reality, the ringing of alarm bells because there is no point to words, this is an era of sound which is starting now, with the remains of her life, it is she who is ringing out to the world, it isn't the telephone, because when she finally approaches it nothing is heard.

The receiver is cold for some reason and when she lays it on her breast, a torrent of blazing heat rises from within and she clenches her lips – it seems if it escapes from her throat there will be no way back, fields will burn, forests will blacken, houses turn into charcoal, an unbearable heat will sweep the globe, consuming all at once those she loves: Nitzan sleeping over at a friend's house, her body thin and frail, Gideon on his travels, photographing the relics of the Lag Ba'omer bonfires which burned out before morning. And for that reason she must not release the torrent raging inside her, she has to keep it trapped in her lungs, so it burns only her. She gave them so much, the two of them, over the years, and now it seems this is the last favour they will ever ask of her, and even if this is bound up with the total cessation of breathing she will take it on, prove to them her devotion, by the kitchen window I shall burn like a torch of memory, by the kitchen window I shall weep, and when they return they will find here on the floor a broken shell, repulsive gunge, the remains of life.

Only this morning before he left she tried to delay him by the door, I have a pain, Gideon, and he asked coldly, with a minimal glance in her direction, where does it hurt? In the heart, she said resentfully, aware that this pain was inferior by comparison with pains of the body that merit instant recognition. And he, predictably, snorted with impatience, what's been the matter with you lately? Get a grip on yourself, be glad that you're healthy, that we're doing OK, look around you for a moment and say thank you.

Thank you, she says now, thanks to you for the support, really, but what did she expect? For years he's been remote, immersed in his own concerns. Was there ever any basis for the belief that now, when she needs him, this will change? Is he the one she really needs? Again that pain in the innermost kernel of her being, crumbling from within like a diseased tooth. I'm sick, she says to the silent telephone receiver, I need help, I've lost something and I don't know if I'll ever find it.

What will she call this thing, that has bound her to the tumult of life like an embryo attached to the feeding tube, years upon years, although recently it seems that a hard-hearted midwife has cut the cord with sharp scissors, as if to say, Mazaltov, you're born, but she knows this isn't birth, it's extinction, sudden excision of the purpose of life. Her thumbs whiten on the telephone receiver which is making its voice heard again, but she doesn't reply, putting it to her breast, her lips are clenched and she isn't breathing, only she knows how dangerous her respiration is. And her brother Avner counts ten rings and cuts the connection and then leaves her a message on her still inactive mobile. Mum's had a fall and she's unconscious, he tells her angrily as if it's her fault. She's in casualty. Come as soon as you hear this message.

Avner never liked being left alone with his mother. Even now, with her mouth sealed, albeit by an oxygen mask, and her arms lying motionless alongside her body, her eyes closed and consciousness flickering, he's afraid of her, perhaps she'll stretch out her wrinkled arms to embrace him, perhaps she'll try to kiss him with her parched lips, perhaps she'll embarrass him by bursting into tears, Avni, my boy, I've missed you. Almost every visit she greets him with a complaint, where have you been, I've missed you. And when he tries to reassure her, I'm here, Mum, she asks anxiously, but when will you come again?

I'm here, be happy that I'm here now, he reminds her again, but she isn't letting go. I see so little of you, and I miss you. Even when he's sitting facing her she's missing him, even when she sees him she perceives only the empty space of his absence. Milksop, mummy's boy, the children in the kibbutz used to tease him when she lingered at his bedside, reluctant to leave him, or when she came looking for him in the garden, calling his name in her high, somewhat strident voice, Avni! Where are you? His face was flushed with shame when her cry was treated as an alarm signal, danger, time to hide, go to the shelters, and already the children were imitating her before his crimson features. How embarrassing to be loved so much.

What a topsy-turvy world, he sighs, and what a perverse invention is the kibbutz, which has become the natural habitat of cruelty and lies, where all sensibilities are trampled down, especially for the males. Masculinity is a perverse invention too, since sometimes it seems to him that for years he's been living underground, and not only he but all men, like war criminals afraid of exposure, like state's witnesses, they all unwittingly wasted the best years of their lives, and not to realise some lofty target or other, but just to survive.

In recent years it seems the stress has eased a little, when half of your life is behind you discipline starts to waver, as with an apprenticeship when the end is approaching, and then it happens that men become more feminine and women more masculine, but now in confrontation with her it is aroused again, his old tension, seeing the wreckage of this person who brought him into the world, the last witness to his infancy, his delicacy, his loneliness, his heartbeat, the whole nightmare of concealed emotions, his great shame.

A flowery sheet covers her tiny body, and she used to be such a big, clumsy woman, in colourful and tasteless garments that she started to wear by way of contrast after leaving the kibbutz. Like a crumpled robe her skin has sunk, wasting away to nothing around her bones, wafer-thin and mottled, and he peers furtively at his own hands, inspecting his skin. How meagre is the dignity left here, how cruel the transformation, only with us is it so, since in animals old age doesn't create such a radical change. They become a little slower, and the sheen of their fur is dimmed, and yet they remain themselves, whereas this old crone, whose hair is sparse and whose chin is sharp and whiskery, whose lips have disappeared into the void of her mouth, her dentures smiling at him from the top of the closet, has changed beyond recognition from the big-limbed woman who used to search for him in the grounds of the kibbutz, calling his name as if only he could save her from some terrible disaster that was about to engulf her. Avni, Avni! Where are you?

Where has all the flesh disappeared to, he wonders, confronting the hollow skin of her arms when she holds out her hands to greet him, the skin hanging from them like bat's wings. People grow smaller, it emerges, grow steadily smaller, and the space they take up in the world is reduced, likewise the space that the world takes up in them, and unconsciously he strokes his stomach, which has expanded recently, and then withdraws his hand as if it's been burned because, it seems to him suddenly, that is where her flesh is hiding, all the flesh that was hers has migrated in recent years into his body, a kind of vengeful enchantment that his mother has succeeded in casting as a means of cleaving to him at the end of the day, just as she carried him in her womb so she has forced him in her last years to bear the flesh that has peeled off her, and so the world is not diminished, since their combined weight is unchanged.

What a scary idea, he grimaces, seeing an involuntary spasm pass over her face, like the spasm on a baby's face which is mistaken for a smile, what nonsense, it is all the fatty foods that the Bedouin are feeding him there, in their tents, brass plates heaped with yellow rice, and hot pittas and strong cheeses, sometimes even strips of mutton, seeking to show him their gratitude with the dishes that they serve him, whole sheep of gratitude are bleating inside him, flocks of them, trying to silence with their voice the echoes of the old disdain.

What an anarchic place, he glances at his watch and sighs, he's been here an hour and no doctor has come anywhere near, an hour has elapsed and there's no sign of his sister. Not that he's at all eager to see her, the arrogant face that has grown leaner in recent times, the unfriendly stare, but he wants to get out of here and this is the only way. Excuse me, he tries to attract the attention of one of the nurses, what's with the doctor? How much longer will he be? But she rebukes him as she walks past him. It will take as long as it takes, believe me, the doctor isn't playing cards now or drinking coffee, and he falls silent, chastened, lowering his gaze to his stomach. Just a few years ago, he had a different kind of prestige in public places, and even if they couldn't identify him by name, his face would provoke some reaction. I know you, they would say, flashing hesitant smiles at him, and sometimes memory brought clarity, ah, I saw you on TV yesterday, you're the attorney who works for the Bedouin, right?

Not only for the Bedouin, he would correct them pedantically, for anyone whose rights are being trampled on, and immediately he would be rewarded with appreciative looks, and it was only his wife who never missed an opportunity to mock him. Champion of the rights of man, she sneered, Robin

Hood no less, and what about my rights? In her eyes, he was always in the wrong.

What anarchic times these are. Only yesterday he returned humiliated from the courthouse. He was appealing for an order to restore the situation as it had been before, and the judge sent him packing without even looking at the documents. The petition had expired, she declared, the facts had already been decided on the ground and there was no way of changing them. When he left the building his forehead was burning, and he could barely drag himself to some bar to relax a little before confronting Shlomit and the boys. So much effort going to waste so easily, but how foolish it was, really, seeking an injunction to restore the *status quo ante*. Is there any such possibility on the face of the earth, to put things back as they were before?

Even under the former dispensation the situation had been intolerable: ramshackle tents alongside the winding road to the Dead Sea, a few corrugated iron shanties. These were no longer proud shepherds roaming the desert with their flocks and living lives of freedom, moving in the summer to Shechem and in the winter to the Judean Desert. There was freedom no more, there was penury instead, territory shrinking and people forced to live like gypsies on the fringes of towns, cleaners and sanitation workers, thieves and ghosts, and he sits among them and eats, and can do precious little else.

Hemda Horowitz, he's awakened suddenly from his reverie when a man's voice calls his mother's name, as if inviting her up on the stage. Yes, he hurries to answer, as if his name has been called. He stands up from his seat for some reason, that's my mother, he explains, and the doctor glances at him without interest. Tall and handsome, younger than him, his look proclaiming an unbridgeable distance. What's happened, he asks, and Avner finds himself detailing, as if pleading a case in court, the entire sequence of ailments affecting his mother in recent years, but the doctor interrupts him, what happened this morning?

She contacted me, although I bet she tried my sister first, he adds unnecessarily. The call was a total blank, I mean she didn't say anything, but I heard her breathing and when I got there I found her on the floor by the window, and for a moment I was afraid she wasn't alive. I called an ambulance straightaway. She was already unconscious although somehow she managed to dial my number before collapsing. He's speaking on her behalf, and it seems to him it's the judge who's listening to him now, peering at him from behind the doctor's back, trying to trip him up. Did you really hurry there? she sneers. You didn't stop off on the way, not even for a moment, to drink an espresso perhaps? And when you saw her lying there by the window you didn't feel the slightest twinge of relief, a warm infusion that spread through your body, much to your shame, and after calling the ambulance you didn't by any chance get into her bed, cover yourself with her blanket, bury your face in the pillow, saturated with her smell, and you didn't for the first time in years shed a tear, although it wasn't for her you were weeping?

Embarrassed, he wipes the sweat from his brow as the doctor walks away, giving rapid instructions to the nurse as he goes. What is this, what's happening to me, he glances around furtively, afraid that the expression on his face, his tone of voice, his posture – all these are betraying him, and the whole of this assemblage, doctors and nurses who aren't drinking coffee and aren't playing cards, patients and their visitors, technicians and maintenance staff, all are watching him and they know that sitting there in their midst, at this very moment, is a son who doesn't love his mother.

Through the curtain which is only half closed he notices a man of about his own age who has also been brought in here, stretched out on the narrow bed with eyes closed, breathing heavily, and a woman with her straight back turned to him, wrapped in a glossy red satin blouse, pulling up a chair and sitting down beside him, in a hurry to hold his hand. Concealed behind the curtain, he peers, fascinated and alarmed, at his mother's new neighbours, because it seems to him suddenly that through them reality is transmitting its dire warnings to him, hailing destruction, the end of all flesh! It isn't that he doesn't know that people of his own age and even younger fall ill and die, and yet he has never seen this with his own eyes, and he always felt protected from death by the very existence of his mother. Now he feels a pang of fear at the thought that his mother might be going to the world hereafter some time in the next few hours, leaving him without so much as a morsel of the supposed protection that she has provided. A man without parents is more exposed to death, he thinks, and for a moment he longs to turn to his neighbour and check with him urgently, find out if he still has parents, and he peers at the pleasant, yellowing face, drawn to the eyes, which open suddenly, and their expression is young, clownish almost, as if he's only pretending and in a moment he'll get up and walk out of the building, arm-in-arm with his statuesque wife.

Is this really his wife? Their gestures are still fresh, without the ennui that accumulates over the years between partners in a couple, like dust on furniture that hasn't been moved often enough, but on the other hand, they are about the same age, an observation that makes interpretation a little difficult, since it seems to him that new love in mid-life tends to involve an age-gap, like for example that between him and the young intern who's waiting for him now in the office, and when he sees her in his mind's eye he sighs, wiping the sweat from his brow again. Anati, who introduced herself straightaway by her nickname, and he blurted out, Avni, although nobody except his mother and his sister called him that, and since then her pretty lips have launched his childhood name into the ether unabashed: Avni, the client has arrived, Avni, the office is trying to contact you, and all in good heart and without ulterior motive, arousing in him heavy and sad desire, sacks of desire he carries on his back like a weary porter, and she doesn't even notice.

Strange, once the heat of passion would have put a spring in his step, whereas now it's an infusion of lead into his bloodstream, forming clots of blood that roam around the body and threaten its survival. Is he really lusting after her, Anati, with the full body which she actually finds rather tiresome, the prim coiffure and the lovely eyes? So predictable, the lawyer and his junior clerk, and yet this had never happened to him.

Through the curtain he hears soft speech, a melodious laugh, almost devoid of anxiety, sees his neighbour's yellowish hand reaching out to the woman's dark hair, smoothing it slowly, and when she turns towards him Avner catches sight of her aristocratic profile, and he sees her laying her head on the man's chest, her fingers skimming the length of his arm, until it seems that it was a mistake that they were ever summoned here, to this abode of pain and sickness, when they should be relaxing now in a manicured garden, white wine in their glasses, or packing a suitcase for a short and enjoyable break, and suddenly he feels that it's his duty to warn them urgently, open their eyes and get them out of this place before it's too late, you've found yourselves in a poisoned cottage, and the witch will turn you into soup, or plead on their behalf in the assizes that determine the fate of bodies, but when the doctor approaches them and he forces himself to eavesdrop on their conversation it becomes clear to him that he's left it too late: for three days no morsel of food has touched those lips, pains in the stomach are intensifying, and a reverential fear takes hold of him when he realises that here, right beside him, a man is ebbing away, at an awesome rate, and this man, suddenly he feels a powerful and devastating empathy towards him; this man is loving and being loved in a real moment, even as he is consumed like newspaper thrown into a brazier to keep the fire going, while he himself, Avner Horowitz, has never loved or been loved, and yet no one pities him.

Take me instead of him, he wants to say, because this man, this sick body, contains within him a living love, and his anticipated death, like the death of a pregnant woman, is the very embodiment of perversity, and already he's ready to lie down on the lean body as if to protect him from the explosives of fate, but very soon his sorrow for this couple is tempered by sorrow for himself and for his sons, especially the youngest, who will not remember him at all, even for Shlomit, and he imagines her directing a petulant glance at him, why are you giving in so easily, why aren't you fighting? And already he's wondering whether sentences of life and of death are really entirely separate, perhaps it is specifically the one who has known love who is entitled to depart from this world peaceably, whereas the one who hasn't is required to stay and complete his education, and perhaps that's why the couple beside him are behaving with such serenity, as if there is no contradiction between love and death, as if they complement each other. But who will take pity on the woman, no longer young, whose beauty radiates to him through the curtain, and what will become of the love with which she is loved, where do they dwell, the loves that live on after the deaths of their practitioners, and it seems to him that if he prays and implores with all his might, perhaps this curtailed love will migrate to him, as his mother's flesh was transferred to him. She's lying motionless before him, with the arrogance of one who has reached a ripe old age and is fully entitled to be a burden, when all the efforts and the essence of life are directed towards clinging to life, and after struggling a little with the notion of sacrificing his body, he finds himself ready and willing to sacrifice her body, to cast her flesh into the fire blazing beside him and add a few years of life and love to this man, who is still smiling sweetly, almost apologetically, and still going up in flames.

Don't worry, you'll soon be feeling better, he hears her whisper, and nods gratefully, as if the encouraging promise had been addressed to him, you'll soon be feeling better, don't worry, but how can he not worry when he has no way out. For years he's been wrestling with the same questions, what am I doing with this wife, what am I doing in this job, what am I doing in this country. Until not so long ago he still believed that if you do what's required of you, you make the world a better place, but recently it has seemed that a kind of legal principle has been lost, something which, even if never proved, was at least intelligible: false steps lead to disaster, the right steps may be your salvation. More and more he has been feeling that the forces beneath the surface are much stronger than the logic that once regulated them; if there was an opportunity it has been lost, but perhaps there never was one.

I'm trapped, he wants to tell the woman in the red satin blouse. At twenty-three I found myself married to the first girlfriend I ever had, to this day I don't understand how I was seduced into that. For many years my work was a refuge but recently I've lost the strength, the hope, but the man beside me still has hope, it turns out, because in a low and pleasant voice he says to his wife, I know, and for a moment it seems that this knowledge of his is set to confound what the doctors know, what the research and the statistics say, I know there's no cause for concern, I know I'll soon be feeling better.

Resplendent on his finger is a thin wedding ring, identical to his wife's ring, and both of them sparkle on their hands as if they married only yesterday, and their eyes sparkle too. Is it the proximity of death that enlivens their love, or is this indeed a newly wed couple, plucked at the very outset? Even if they aren't young, it seems their love is young, and already he's trying to construct their story: for years they lived in isolation until they met in miraculous fashion, or alternatively, two families were dismantled to form this brief love that is being curtailed before his eyes. His heart has always been in the theatre, and if he hadn't taken it on himself to fulfil his father's dream and study the law, he might well have found himself there, and now he consoles himself with the delusion that these two partners are merely hollow ciphers awaiting the biography that he will invent for them, but then he sees the woman turn her head and wipe away a tear with the ringed finger, and in the process her eyes meet his. It seems she is noticing him for the first time, although he has been moving the curtain aside, gradually but persistently, eager to cancel absolutely the partition between them, and it wasn't out of interest that she turned to face him but in an effort to hide the sudden onset of weeping, restrained indeed but visible to the eye, and she raises her shoulder to wipe away the tears on the fabric of the short sleeve, and when this doesn't work she bends down and dabs at her eyes with the hem of her blouse, in the process exposing a smooth midriff, and on the blouse there is a rapidly spreading stain, the moisture of tears blended with black mascara. Avner takes from his pocket a somewhat used tissue, the one that absorbed his bizarre weeping this morning, in his mother's bed, while she was stretched out on the floor by the window, and holds it out with a shaky hand to the woman facing him. She tries to smile at him gratefully, but her lips tremble, and after thoroughly mopping up her tears, almost damaging the delicate skin under her eyes, she tucks the tissue into the pocket of her trousers and turns to the invalid's bed, her back to him, and he stares at her and thinks wonderingly of their tears blending on the paper tissue, of her piercing, sharply focused pain meeting his own, inexplicable pain.

And if I were the one about to die, with my wife sitting beside me, he wonders, in our case too would the approaching end generate such tenderness? Apparently not, since already he could feel in his flesh the intensity of the anger that would flood the corridors of the hospital like a mighty whirlpool. His anger at her for not letting him break free from her until the last day, anger at himself for always yielding in the end, and even when he imagines her and not himself on the deathbed, his anger is undiminished, since both her illness, if she were to fall ill, and her death, if she were to die, would be directed against him, to destroy what remains of his life with bitter memories and guilt, with untimely orphans. Yes, as far back as he could remember, he had always been trapped, at too young an age he was tied to her, and it didn't occur to him that this first love for a diminutive, short-haired girl, which was in essence youthful curiosity and a confused inclination to find a refuge from his mother, would turn into a trap in which he would flutter all his life, unable to escape or to adjust; sometimes he almost managed to extricate his body there but always left one or other of his body-parts trapped in remorseless pincers, even if it were only the nail of his little finger – the pain would still be unbearable and liberation impossible.

The deep, seemingly eternal sleep of his mother, the whirring of the ventilators and the ringing of telephones amid the coughing and the mumbling, gradually lull him into a state of soothing inertia, as if all these mechanisms are designed to protect him. He leans back and covers his eyes with his arm and apparently slumber takes hold of him, since when he wakes with a start a little while later, the curtain has been removed altogether and the bed beside him is empty. The lean man, with the yellowing skin and the winsome smile, and his beautiful and aristocratic wife, are no longer there, they were his neighbours only briefly, it has turned out, and although his tears are in her pocket he has no idea who she is or where they have gone.

Did he die just a moment ago, give back his soul to his maker, whereupon his body was immediately disposed of, or had he been admitted to one of the wards? Perhaps their love had defeated the disease, and he rose unexpectedly from the bed and they walked home arm in arm, leaving him traumatised by the premature parting, for which he was entirely unprepared. He had been convinced that long hours were still in store for him as their neighbour, as is typical of casualty wards, hours in which he would succeed in finding out their names, their business, their love story, and now he is afflicted by such a deep sense of lost opportunity that he beats his forehead with his fists, as he used to do as a child in moments of frustration. You've missed it again, you've gone wrong again, you thought you had time, you thought that even someone whose days were numbered would wait for you. That's the kind of person you are, dozing while more opportunities pass you by, and although it isn't clear to him precisely which opportunity he's lamenting, what those two partners could have taught him, he stands up sadly from his seat and moves to the bed beside him, maybe there's some scrap of information left there that can help him. But the chart attached to the bed is blank, nothing has been left on the sheets, and he wanders among the patients looking for the nurses, until he catches sight of one some distance away and summons her with energetic gestures, as if his mother needs her urgently. Tell me, he tries to smile when she approaches him, perhaps in spite of it all she'll remember him from his television appearances, the patient who was in this bed, have they admitted him to one of the wards? And she replies, I'm sorry, I'm not allowed to divulge any information. Are you a relative of his? And he says, no, but I lent him a book and I have no idea how to find him. And she whispers, they went home, you'll find them at home.

Then that's a good sign, isn't it? he tries his luck, but she answers dryly, I don't know, there are people who like to die at home and some who prefer hospitals, and already she's walking away, leaving him stunned and aghast. People like to die at home! What a cruel expression, as if it's about something mundane, like diet or accommodation. Are you out of your mind? How can you say anyone likes dying? he wants to reprove her, as if she were one of his interns, caught expressing something in slovenly style, but of course she's gone, leaving him beside the empty bed, and he sits on it with some diffidence, smoothing the sheet with his hand the way the woman in the satin blouse caressed the bony forearm, and when it seems to him no one is watching he lays his back on the mattress, followed by his thighs and his knees and finally his feet, black courtroom shoes and all.

Before his eyes he sees with a kind of transparent, dazzling knowledge, how they will get into their car; slowly and cautiously she will settle him down in the back seat, sit down at the wheel and flash him an encouraging smile via the mirror, driving gently, as if she's transporting a day-old infant, and he sees how they will arrive at home, and she will lead him to their bed, the bed of their lovemaking and the restful sleep that followed it, and the days that lie ahead of them he sees as if he has already faded and died once, in a different past, the heavy twilight hours, neither day nor night, as if they are already detached from the processes of the sun, the grief of the departure of souls he sees, a dance without movement, a song without sound, and when he lies on the narrow bed, keeping watch from there over his mother, who is stretched out beside him, over his empty chair, he whimpers again, but he has nothing to wipe the tears away with because his handkerchief is in her pocket and they fall from his eyes and are absorbed by the sheet, and he has no one to hide them from, since no one is looking at him, and all the time he's scanning the corridor, maybe he'll see her again, maybe she's left some document behind here, perhaps she'll return to give him back his tears and he'll be capable of eliciting from her mouth the end of the thread that will help him to follow their fate. For a moment he is jolted by the sight of a red radiance, a fleeting distant phenomenon that vanishes, leaving behind it a mirage-glow, and again he sits up with pounding heart when a female form appears, rapidly approaching his mother's bed, but it isn't her. The tall and lanky woman in the black blouse and the narrow skirt, also black, naturally, is his sister Dina, two years his senior, and although he has been waiting for her all morning so he can escape from here, he closes the curtain that separates them and before she notices him, he lays his head on the pillow and pretends to be fast asleep.

Chapter Two

Dina knows she has to hurry; at this age anything can happen. In a single moment people depart this world, and even those who have hung on there year after year may suddenly collapse, like guests outstaying their welcome at parties, harassing the hosts and then slipping away abruptly and discourteously without a goodbye or a thank you, with no pause for leave-taking, no opportunity to forgive or to ask a final question, nor to appease, gratify or compensate, and yet when she finds herself in the hospital lobby it isn't her mother she hurries to see. Instead of heading for the cold sterility of the casualty ward she makes her way to a building set back a little from the others, surrounded by lawns, where heavy-bodied women pad around slowly but with faces full of longing, where the smell of blood is blended with the smell of milk spraying from swollen breasts and the whiff of delicate baby skin meeting the air of the world for the first time; the smells of life, which changes in an instant, hang back and make way with reverence for the new kings of glory, and this is where she wanders about, feeling awkward, peering into the rooms, pretending she's looking for some new mother, but her empty hands and grim expression undermine the camouflage. She walks down a long corridor, eyes darting about, looking for the room where she herself gave birth, sixteen years ago.

It was the last room, she remembers, the one closest to the hills, and beside the window she lay, suckling her winter baby while the flakes of snow began to fall on the treetops, and when Gideon arrived in the morning he found them by the window with its veneer of misty vapours, and he smiled with feeling and kissed the pair of them; they were so close together that one kiss was enough, and then he raised the camera that was hung round his neck and shot them wrapped in the viscous mist, her face beaming at him beside the face of the sleeping baby, and since the fixed space between them was filled precisely according to the baby's proportions, this picture which still hangs opposite their bed dazzles her every morning with the brightness of the snow that was quick to melt, blurring her with the touch of the violet vapour. Usually there's nothing to be seen there and it's only in rare moments that pale figures emerge from the gloom like ghosts, like two ancient souls given the right to be born again, one in the arms of the other.

This is the room. She stands wavering in the doorway, thinking that is the window, those are the hills, that is the last bed, where a girlish figure is lying on her back covering her face with her arm, her hair a shade of chestnut brown. Look at this thin arm, reminiscent of Nitzan's arm, but that's impossible, Nitzan's in school now, she remembers with relief, as if only this fact serves to refute the notion, since for one scary moment it seemed to her that in the gulf that has recently opened between her and her daughter a full-term pregnancy could easily be fitted, along with clandestine birth and the whole process from beginning to end. With quick steps she approaches the bed, just to be sure these are foolish thoughts that she'll be ashamed of straightaway: Nitzan is at school now, her body as slim as ever, Nitzan has never known a man, Nitzan wouldn't hide such a traumatic thing from her, but all the same this body is familiar to her, that posture, frozen and intense, and she whispers, excuse me a moment, and it's only then the young woman moves her arm and cries out in a astonished voice, Dina? What are you doing here? And Dina nods her head at a loss for words; after all what can she say to her? Relief at finding this isn't Nitzan has turned to acute embarrassment in confronting her student, who has indeed since time immemorial reminded her of her daughter with her slender physique, and despite this or perhaps because of it her presence arouses unpleasant tensions in her, and the girl herself, Noa, adds to these tensions with her excessive argumentativeness in class, veering between lack of interest and overstated, tiresome involvement.

In recent weeks she's been absent from class, to Dina's relief, and someone had indeed reported that she was on pregnancy leave, another detail that had slipped from her memory, who could count their pregnancies anyway, and here she is, on her bed, making it seem that all the hundreds of women who have occupied this bed since then have been erased completely, and before she can find words to explain her presence in this place Noa smiles at her and says, it really touches me that you've come to see me, and Dina tries to smile back at her, blending truth and lies, my mother was admitted to this hospital, and I heard you had given birth, so I dropped by for a moment to see how you are, and when Noa repays her with somewhat overplayed interest in the state of her mother's health, her embarrassment increases, because she doesn't know what state her mother is in. Perhaps at this very moment she is breathing her last, perhaps even calling her name, wanting to say goodbye to her daughter, who for some reason prefers to sit at the bedside of a woman in the maternity ward, an acquaintance but certainly not a friend, and she decides to cut short this unplanned visit. You know what, I'll come back to you later,

I've left her alone and I'm not comfortable with that, and to her surprise she sees disappointment on Noa's face, as she says, stay with me for a while seeing that you're here already, and you haven't even asked about the sex of my baby.

Oh, sorry, Dina apologises hastily, I'm so confused this morning, boy or girl? Noa grins, as if she's played a trick on her and caught her out, a boy *and* a girl, she announces, twins, and all at once the repulsion and the attraction intensify beyond endurance, because she can't wait to escape from this place, take to her heels and run, without salutations, without goodbyes, race down the corridors and push aside anyone who stands in her way – and simultaneously, at this very moment she longs to go to the young woman's bed, clasp her to her bosom and never let go.

Tell me, did you feel strange too after the birth? Noa whispers suddenly, looking round to check that no one's listening, it's the opposite of what I expected, I was so happy to be pregnant and now I feel my life is over, and babies disgust me, they look to me sort of uncooked, like raw meat, did you feel like that? And Dina stands and faces her entreaty with a heavy heart. Don't worry, Noa, it happens to lots of women, the days following childbirth are hard and turbulent, it will be all right, I promise you, but when she looks into the eyes moistening before her she sees deep gloom, as if she were on her knees and peering into a well, and she says, if you don't feel better in a few weeks go to the doctor, it could be postnatal depression, and he'll give you some medication and you'll be fine. I didn't feel that way but it happened to my mother after I was born, she blurts out the words that surprise her too, much more so than her interlocutor, because they were never expressed aloud, the thought was never even explicitly thought, but now, confronting the two dark pools she knows, an intense knowledge that needs no explanation, not that any explanation is possible at the moment, or ever will be.

Her strength exhausted, she flops down on the empty chair beside her mother's bed. Her brother has only just now slipped away, apparently, because his scent is still around and it seems she should have fumigated the seat before sitting down, the scent of a man who's trying too hard to blur the traces of his body, smothering himself with heavy, suffocating sprays. No one on their kibbutz in those days had heard of perfume for men, and only Avni made himself a laughing stock with his concoctions and his meticulous coiffure. Sometimes she suspected he was secretly dowsing himself with the toilet air-freshener. How dare he desert his post before she arrived, she wonders, but at the same time she isn't too upset by his absence; this way there will be no need to pretend, to hide the tempest of the soul that has an embarrassing source, not the murmuring of the mournful heart confronted by the elderly mother stretched out before her, her nightdress torn as if she's been cruelly raped and her bosom exposed, mottled with white pock-marks like the love-bites of the angel of death, her toothless mouth agape in constant complaint alongside the detached oxygen mask. She takes in the alarming sight impatiently, as if since time immemorial her mother has been exposed to her in her clumsy latent ugliness; she has always seen her like this, even when she was young and healthy, dreamily walking the paths of the kibbutz.

Nausea rises in her throat when she examines the pockets of withered skin, imagining her lips licking this skin, groping for the nipple. Even if decades have passed since then these are the same lips, the same nipple, barely covered by the rags of the nightdress with its pattern of grey petals. This is the nightdress from Venice, she recognises it suddenly; she bought it for her at least ten years ago and she's never worn it before, and the memory of that trip at once brings a surge of acute pain. Did something start there with its consequences extending to this very morning, did she resign herself there to something she perhaps wasn't supposed to resign herself to?

They left little Nitzan with her mother; this was the first time they travelled without her, and it seems to her now it was there that their lives diverged into different alleyways, since she longed to revive and restore the early times of their love, longed for all those signs of romance that surrounded them in such abundance. Most of the couples around were busy with one another, between the boats and the doves, the canals and bridges, but Gideon was busy with them and not with her, running to and fro in agitation with his camera, aiming it like a whip and pressing the shutter again and again. Maybe I'll offer the paper a series of loving couples in Venice, what do you think? he asked, and she said, sure, what a wonderful idea, trying to hide the affront, because he noticed every other detail but not the new dress she was wearing at dinner that evening, or the glossy lipstick she bought before the journey.

What do you expect, it's the way of the world, she tried to console herself, as they sat face to face in the restaurant and he was looking over her shoulder. With Nitzan at her side she found it less irksome, but there without her the days seemed intolerably long, and the obligation to enjoy this place turned for her into torture, and what she really wanted was to go home. The beauty of the city sprawled on her heavy and menacing as she tried, even from this distance, to follow the girl: now she's waking up, now she's going to the nursery, now she's coming back. A deep grief, a feeling that they would never meet again, took hold of her as she walked beside him among the palazzos, and it wasn't the glories of the sites she saw but the children of the tourists passing by her, trying to endure the sight of a child when her daughter wasn't there, her ears alert to their voices. It seemed to her they were calling to her incessantly, not by the name her parents gave her in childhood but the name given her by her daughter, Mum, Mum, the children bleated to her in their clear voices, Mum, look how high I can jump. Mum, I'm hungry, tired, bored.

At the end of the day this is a disappointing city, she said to him when they returned to the hotel on the last night, a narcissistic city that exists only in the eye of the beholder, there's no gulf between the place and its image, no truth waiting to be revealed, just what you see, it seems that if the tourists stopped coming it would sink and disappear. Sounds of laughter rose from the piazza below, and for a moment she felt they were mocking her for her words, you too need to be looked at, you're sinking too, and he opened another bottle of wine, I've got so used to photographing ugliness that I really don't care, he said, what's wrong with a little beauty? How well she remembers that night, the tickling of wine pouring down the throat, the dim and scary sense of mirage, even when he took her in a loving embrace, even when he snuggled against her and fell asleep at once, his hand resting on her stomach. Reliefs of winged babies hovered above her in the corners of the room – was he there too, their lost baby, gazing at them with plaster eyes, and she hastily covered their naked bodies with a blanket. It was only the morning after, their last day there, that she relaxed a little, hastily buying a present for her daughter and putting a lot of effort, and nervous energy, into finding a present for her mother, as if there was anything on the face of this earth that could satisfy her, compensate her for this unsavoury sequence called her life, and now as she probes the soft material over the humps of her mother's bony knees, she wonders why this of all mornings she chose to wear her forgotten present for the first time, to be ripped apart in a panic by the medical team in their efforts to resuscitate her, and left looking like the shirt of a mourner at a funeral.

In her childhood she didn't often see her mother in her sleepwear, and in her innocence she thought she went to bed in her simple daytime clothes, and one time, when she fled from the children's house in the middle of the night and her mother opened the door to her, she was astonished to see her swathed in soft and attractive fabric, and for a moment she thought this was sophisticated evening dress and she'd stumbled into a secret party going on behind her back. Even now the feel of the fabric arouses a painful longing in her and she hesitantly extends her other hand and caresses again and again the hem of the nightdress, almost leaning over her mother's bare knees, and anyone looking on from the sidelines would be convinced it was the raddled skin of her legs that she is caressing with love and devotion, refusing to be separated.

Avner overhears the questions of the specialist doctor, who is casually writing up his notes on the life-story of Hemda Horowitz, almost eighty years of age, a widow plus two, the names of the medications she is receiving and her medical history, and it seems Hemda is herself listening to the data that Dina is passing on with an air of crass and imperious boredom. But it's really the events of this morning that the doctor is trying to extract, not wanting to leave a single moment unaccounted for; how much time elapsed between the raising of the alarm and the arrival of the ambulance, he asks, needing to establish to what extent the supply of blood to the brain has been compromised, and it's for this reason that the old lady is hitched up to weird and wonderful machines which tell more about her than she could ever tell about herself. But this specific question the older daughter can't answer, and the son who knows is keeping silent, hidden behind the curtain. Wasn't it always like this, he wonders, they inhabit the same space but their personalities are entirely different: Dina the serious, the responsible one, trying to be a useful member of society but incapable of carrying it through, while he's the one ducking his responsibilities, hiding at a time when only his evasive presence has the potential to relieve anxieties, whether he likes it or not.

Half an hour passed, he wants to say, a precious half-hour, but then her life is full of hours, with their halves and quarters, and the essence of things no one can decipher: how she came to be born to pioneering parents in the middle of the first half of the twentieth century, such a dreamy girl, strange and eccentric, who never managed to adjust to kibbutz life although she was born and raised there, how she married their father, that lonely foreign youth, whose love turned to hatred and his dependence to resentment, and how she succeeded in achieving nothing, living always on the negative side – a wife who didn't love her husband, a teacher who didn't like teaching, a mother who didn't know how to bring up children, a storyteller who couldn't put anything into writing.

For many years it seemed the kibbutz was to blame for all this, that only when she left would her real life begin, but even when she finally succeeded in extricating her family from there and moving into a small apartment in a housing project on the fringes of Jerusalem, the process itself sapped all her strength and she failed in the attempt to be born again; it was death that awaited them there, not life, since their father couldn't stand it and within a few years he fell ill and died, and he remembers now the fearful rage that was aroused in him that summer, when the three of them were left in the sweltering apartment, when he realised it was too late.

Because of you I missed out on the chance of knowing him, your aversion to him was forced on me too, how hard it was coming to terms with the knowledge that he would never know his father, not ever, but did he know her, had the decades that she lived on after his father's death helped to deepen their acquaintance, and does he have any interest in this now, when his sister is energetically pushing the wheeled bed towards the examination rooms? Furtively he rises from his bed, like a patient who has enjoyed a miraculous recovery behind the curtain, without medical intervention, and follows her progress from a distance, keeping a safe space between them. If she sees him he'll pretend he was looking for her, and if not he'll be spared the need to conduct a tedious conversation, while at the same time proving his dedication, being there and ready to jump in if the need should arise, like a male predator keeping a close eye on his family from a distance while going in search of prey, and in the meantime he'll scour the ward for other families, or not so much families as couples, one couple in particular to be precise, for whom he's searching so earnestly he almost loses sight of his sister, chasing after every sparkly fabric that he sees; in fact it isn't the woman in the red top that he's longing to see but the man at her side. He wants to hear his voice, find some excuse to conduct a conversation with him; in places like this brief and unexpected relationships are forged.

As he advances towards the main exit he realises that if he had indeed been discharged, it would be beyond the strength of the man to make it to the car park, and thus he would be forced to wait for his wife, sitting by the exit, and that is where the thread should be picked up. It seems to him for a moment that he's spotted his swaddled form on one of the benches, but when he quickens his pace towards him, he has no choice but to pass close by his unconscious mother and his sister, who is leaning on the side rail of the bed and looking at him in bemusement. Hey, Avni, she waves at him, where have you been? I thought you'd gone without waiting for me. He says, what a thing to say, I've been here all the time, I just went down to get a drink. His eyes are straining to see what's going on in the lobby, and she says, wait here a moment, I need the toilet, and at once she disappears as if she can't bear his company. So he's trapped, wondering whether to abandon his mother for a moment and hurry to the door; what can happen, at the most they'll miss their slot. But all the same he doesn't dare leave the open-mouthed old woman unsupervised and he makes his mind up and takes a firm grip on the bed, pushing it in front of him and using it to clear himself a path, almost at a run, like an orderly taking a patient for emergency surgery, to the hospital lobby, and all of this to prove how right he had been, or how mistaken, not hurrying there at the outset but instead stretching out on the vacated casualty bed alongside his mother, because there's no doubt the man was sitting here and waiting, but now all that is left for him is to watch as he is led carefully towards the gold Citroën driven by his partner, an incurable case turning his back on all the doctors and medications, all the questions, hopes, inquiries and demands, gathered in to a place where the last words are said, a dance without movement, a song without sound. With bitterness in his heart he stares at the back of the receding car, then goes out into the sweltering air as if retracing the last footsteps of the invalid on his arduous journey, and already he's hurrying distractedly across the car park, rummaging in his pocket for his keys, when he remembers to his horror that he's left his unconscious mother in the lobby, and he runs heavily up the incandescent ramp, arriving out of breath at the place he left just a moment ago, to be meticulously checked out by the concierge as if he's a newcomer.

No one has touched the bed, he's relieved to see, as if the bed with his mother in it has become one of the regular fixtures of the hospital, planted in the floor like those benches in the sitting area, but from the end of the corridor his sister is running towards him, and on her face is the expression he's so accustomed to seeing on the face of his wife, a blend of disgust, rejection and anger, and she pants at him, are you insane? Where have you been? I've been looking for you all over the hospital, I thought something had happened. And he too is still panting, confronting this paragon of forthright self-righteous femininity, and he looks down and mumbles, I met a friend here and I went outside with him for a bit, why are you making such an issue out of it, and they're standing facing each other on either side of the bed, with the body that brought them together back then binding them now whether they like it or not, but also erecting a partition in its typical fashion – when his downcast gaze meets the upward gaze of his mother, a surprisingly clear look, excited, almost ecstatic.

Daddy? her toothless gums mumble at him, and he looks around him in embarrassment, as if it wasn't to him that the syllables were addressed, as if expecting to see there the legendary father whom he never knew, rising from the dead and hurrying to take his elderly daughter in his arms, but she fastens her eyes on him and repeats, Daddy? – extending to him the apologetic smile of a child trying to evade punishment, her hand reaching out for his and he recoils, Mum, it's me, Avner, and Dina's here too, he adds, urging his sister to back him up, to help him draw their mother with a chain of words into their world, but his mother ignores his words and beams at him in wonderment and joy, nothing can destroy her happiness, the undiluted happiness that he sometimes identifies on the face of his youngest son, the absolute embodiment of all delights, her fingers avidly caressing his arm, I've missed you, she whispers, it's been so long, I was afraid you weren't coming back.

Over the rail of the bed he sees his sister breathing heavily, her dark eyes moist, and she clutches her mother's other hand, this is Avner, he isn't your father, she says in her authoritative tone, as if standing in front of a class, we're in the hospital, you had another fall, do you remember? But the old woman rejects her words angrily. Leave me alone, I didn't ask you, she says, let me be alone with him, and she shakes off her daughter's hand and holds his arm with a vigour which reminds him for a moment of the healthy-bodied woman she once was.

We need to take her back to casualty, and talk to the doctor, he whispers, it seems there may be some damage to the brain after all, and they move along the bustling corridors, a middle-aged mother and father and their geriatric baby, who suddenly bursts into tears, with a plangent wail like a siren, rising and falling, her crumpled face awash with tears. He never saw her like this, and really it's no wonder, after all he didn't know her as a child, and listlessly he goes on dragging the bed with its squeaking wheels. Mum, relax, he mumbles, everything's going to be all right, you'll soon be feeling better, unconsciously repeating the dubious promise that he heard through the curtain just a little while ago, and he looks for a little encouragement in Dina's face. Just a moment ago she was there, pushing the bed along from behind, her curls shading her brow, her long fingers, like the talons of a bird of prey, caressing the bed rail, and suddenly there's no sign of her.

With pounding heart Dina hurries to her car, eyes smarting. It's wrong to feel offended by children or by the elderly, she knows that, but these are specifically the ones she feels offended by, by her daughter and by her mother, who totally negated her existence, holding on to the arm of her brother while pushing her away brusquely. If it were possible to attribute this to old age or to the fall, that would certainly be some mitigation, but old age or the fall has only given prominence to what she has always known, what her mother has tried to hide from her until this morning, when it was no longer possible to pretend; her feelings like her exposed breasts, revealed in all their shameful ugliness.

Ferocious heat enfolds her limbs when she leaves the air-conditioned corridors, and she sighs, these heatwaves of early summer, from year to year they become harder to endure. It seems to her that her flesh is scorched, and sizzling audibly, and she looks in alarm at her exposed arms, surely this is inconceivable, it's just the intense heat of the hamsin season, it will pass soon enough, any woman of her age recognises this. I'm going out now, my darlings, I'll be home soon, she hears the young woman beside her trying to reassure her impatient children. Another half-hour if there are no hold-ups, she sends the promise via her mobile, and Dina glances at her with envy, how she misses that sensation, knowing someone is waiting for her at home. Enjoy it, she wants to whisper to the woman who is going to the car in front of hers, enjoy it even if gets tiresome sometimes, it won't last for ever, and she takes her own mobile out of the briefcase, she needs to talk to Nitzan, to hear her voice, it feels like weeks since they met.

I'll be home soon, dear, she whispers into the phone, but the girl doesn't answer, and yet it seems to her, to Dina, that it's her she's returning to, getting into her car and driving impatiently, as she used to when Nitzan was small, hurrying home when classes were over, the knowledge that her daughter was waiting for her coiled around her like a rope, a noose to which she gladly proffered her neck. Sometimes she used to run along their street, really run, a little shamefaced, how much meaning there was in every step. Mum! You're home! The little girl would leap up to greet her, taking her by the hand and insisting on showing her the marvellous things she had been doing, little treasures of happiness she would find among the wooden bricks, among the furry animals and the tattered books, and even when Nitzan was a little older, turning into a serious and grown-up girl, she would run to meet her from her room, telling her stories, showing her pictures and exercise-books. How nice it was coming home, even if she was tired after a long day's work, even if what awaited her was another white night of work to be checked and marks to be awarded. How she longs for such pleasure, and suddenly it seems to her it's still in her hands, she can again be that woman who is awaited with love. Nitzan must already be at home, perhaps she'll open the door to her and fall into her arms, and she will feel how a candle that was extinguished in her has been relit, and she will gladly cook a light meal for the two of them and they will sit together in the kitchen. You see, I don't need much to make me happy, she explains aloud, just talking with the girl in the kitchen, feeling I'm needed by her, not loved necessarily, just needed.

The first moment of an encounter dictates the way it will continue, she says aloud, I shall go into the house smiling, as if I've had good news, turn to her with some light banter. How absurd this is, I'm preparing for a meeting with Nitzan as if we were talking about something fateful and crucial – and this is my daughter, my bones and my flesh, but the absurdity doesn't put a smile on her lips; rather it plunges her into a depression that she tries to alleviate with simple decisions, peering in the interior mirror and smearing on lipstick, blackening the eyes with a make-up pencil. Nitzan is waiting for her, of that there is no doubt, even if she doesn't know it she's waiting for her, so she'll go into the house with a smiling face, no hint of reproof or petulance, and that way she'll get her back.

There's her satchel thrown down in the lobby, beside it a superfluous sweater that she forced her to take yesterday, giving off a barbecue smell of charcoal and incinerated potatoes, those are her sandals, and she herself must be in her room. Nitzi, she calls out in a sprightly voice, would you like something to eat? And when the girl doesn't answer she opens the door of the room, and the smile that she prepared in advance remains in place, her lips drawn tight, when she sees her daughter's naked back laid motionless on the exposed chest of a fair-haired boy, his eyes closed. On the single bed they are huddled together, clinging to each other like twins in their mother's womb, and while she dithers in the doorway, stunned, the boy's eyes open and scan her awkwardly, and then in response to the smile that has congealed on her lips, a smile is transmitted to her over her daughter's back.

Taking small steps she moves out of there, her gaze fixed on his face, and without turning her back on him, as if this were a holy place, she retreats stumbling to the kitchen and stands again by the window, her elbows on the cool marble. With shaking hands she washes her face in the kitchen sink, full as it is of dirty utensils, her hair dipping in a greasy frying-pan, and while it's still shedding fetid liquids on her blouse she goes back there, clutching the door-frame and peering in, her eyes scanning the short legs of the bed, the colourful sheet decorated with figures from fairy tales, the feet lying side by side, like two pairs of twins, her daughter's slender ankles beside the boy's thighs, and her cut-off jeans against his flanks, her smooth and milky back, her angular shoulders, her arms hugging his chest, while his arms are laid now at the sides of his body and his eyes are closed again, as if the vision that he saw, of a grey-haired woman staring at him in horror, was a marginal interlude in an otherwise pleasant dream, but even with his eyes closed it seems to her he's watching her, and even when his lips are closed it seems to her, with the same crazy certainty that she identified this morning in her mother, he's repeatedly mumbling, Mum.

Gideon, she whispers from the bedroom next door, putting the phone to her lips and he's tense at once, has something happened? She says no, everything's fine, forgetting even to mention her mother's admission to hospital, but Nitzan, she adds and hesitates, wondering how to dress it up for him, Nitzan is here with someone, they're asleep in her bed, it's so strange . . . She tries to steer him cautiously towards the simpler extreme of the experience she's had, and Gideon chuckles, oh, yes? Great, so she's finally bringing him home, I told her she could take the initiative and not wait for him, and Dina seizes on this scrap of raw information, hard to chew though it is. What, she told you she had someone? She didn't tell me anything, Gideon says. She met some guy called Noam not long ago, a friend of Shiri's brother.

Shiri's brother? she repeats irritably, then he must have done his army service, at least five years older than her, is that acceptable to you? she sneers, hiding behind the tiresome details which aren't the main issue for her; she knows precisely how old he really is, after all he's Shiri's twin. In the background she hears Gideon telling someone, I'll be with you in a moment, it's Dina, pronouncing her name in a somewhat meaningful tone. Who are you with? she asks, feeling suddenly suspicious, and he replies, I'm in the middle of a photo shoot, Dini, is there anything else? and she adds, yes, my mother's in hospital, she fell over and knocked herself out, and this time he sounds more alarmed than she is, demanding to know the details. I'll call in there on my way home, he promises her, although this isn't the promise she was hoping for.

Oh, Gideon, she sighs, putting down the phone and stretching out on the bed fully clothed. The warm breath that she detected in his voice arouses longing in her, and a sour taste in her throat as if she's been drinking something contaminated, a drink she put a lot of time and effort into preparing, what a waste, and already too late, and it seems she herself doesn't know what she's referring to: too late to fall in love with each other, too late to bring a child into the world, too late for new life, but this contamination, wasn't it always there? Oh, Gideon, if only we could start again, I'd do everything differently.

Like a blank canvas the past is spread out before her, giving itself into her hands. It's forbidden to start on this, she knows, but still she goes ahead and devotes herself to this dangerous game of hers, as when she was a child, lying on her bed in the children's house and imagining the life awaiting her, the future that would set her apart from the kids all around her, who didn't read books, weren't as gifted academically as she was, but now this turns into torture, to go back and imagine with such precision what could have happened and didn't happen, and her fault alone. Here she is, sitting with Orly and Emmanuel in the university cafeteria as almost every evening, keeping their secret faithfully; it doesn't even occur to Emmanuel that she knows and on the face of it he loves and admires the pair of them in equal measure, his two teaching assistants, his star pupils. He's comfortable sitting between them, mocking the students who pass by them with reverent expressions on their faces, inventing nicknames for them and imitating their halting speech, his eyes twinkling wickedly under the silver quiff, and as she's choking with laughter a morsel of sandwich sprays from her mouth on to the collar of his nicely ironed shirt, and he reassures her, it doesn't matter, we're like a family here, and Orly grins, Dina doesn't know what a family is, she grew up on a kibbutz, and Emmanuel says, there isn't anyone among us who doesn't know, everyone learns at his own pace.

He was then exactly her age now, Professor David Emmanuel, eminent historian, did he too realise it was too late? Or did he still not understand anything, since from his point of view all of this could have carried on if she had not curtailed their future with one sentence, three futures that were closely intertwined; she bit the hand that caressed when for a moment it stopped caressing. That evening too they were sitting there after a day of teaching, as a violent rainstorm lashed the city, threatening to drill holes in asphalt roads and stone roofs. At once she sensed that something wasn't as it had been the day before yesterday, since Emmanuel was pale, running a cold and blowing his nose incessantly, turning the end of it red, and Orly was quieter than usual and refusing to eat, and no wonder, after all she knew what he was going to say. Alas, girls, he sighed, you wouldn't want to be in my shoes just now, and when they looked at him quizzically he wiped his nose again and coughed. I've been given an impossible task, he said, I have to choose one of you, our team is shrinking, only one of you can have tenure here for the coming year.

Why was he looking only at her, why was Orly looking down? The din of the torrential rain was deafening. I've chosen Orly, he said in a cracked voice, I'm sorry, Dina, I think she is more suitable, but I'm sure that within a few years there will be a vacancy here for you as well, and she stared at them, stunned, while Orly's eyes sent her a desperate appeal, don't reveal the secret that I told only to you, but the resentment wrapped around her throat, the resentment of the less-loved daughter. It isn't fair, Emmanuel, she mumbled, I know you.

Did she say, I know you are lovers, I know you are having an affair, or did she perhaps say, I know she's your mistress, seizing the opportunity to offend her too. It wasn't fair, nothing about this was fair, and that was all she knew for certain when she fled and ran to the bus-stop, and there she encountered the dean of the faculty, who greeted her with a smiling face. I read the article you published about the holy child of La Guardia, he said, a brilliant piece of research, I very much hope you will settle in with us here, you have so much to contribute, and she muttered, that's what I was hoping too, until this evening, and she boarded the bus in a hurry, she'd already said too much, but he pursued her and finally sat down beside her, asking her to explain why her hopes had been dashed.

Unrestrained the words cascaded from her mouth, she told him everything, she turned informer, and thereafter she didn't go back there, despite offers and appeals, and even these faded away as the days passed, and although the two of them left at the end of the academic year – Orly vanished as if the earth had swallowed her, and there were rumours that she had gone to study abroad on a bursary arranged for her by Emmanuel, and he himself left for a university in the south, apparently leaving the field open for her, if you're really so well suited come and prove it – she refused to return to the history team, even when someone else, a woman younger than both of them and far less talented, took advantage of the confusion prevailing in the faculty. In her forbidden moments, when she allows herself to play this game, the three of them are still there and their futures still ahead of them, when the rain stops, and when spring bursts into flower, and when summer is shining, year after year, as it could have been if she hadn't ruined everything, even burying her own aspirations under heaps of rubble.

And Gideon was definitely on her side then, until his patience snapped. What are you demanding of yourself? he asked her, bemused. They are the ones who did you an injustice, you had an obligation to expose it! How could he promote Orly when he was having an affair with her, and leave you behind even though you were much better qualified? He just wanted to keep her close to him so she wouldn't betray him, don't you see that? That's enough, Dini, stop punishing yourself and go back to the university, you're wasting your talents.

But she was no longer sure of this. How do you measure talent anyway, maybe Orly really was better qualified after all, and when she stood before a class the following year, in the training college where there was a warm welcome for the distinguished refugee from the history faculty, and lectured on the causes behind the expulsions from Spain her voice was softer and less vigorous, and the words which in the past had flowed from her throat packed tightly together in impressive sequences began to sound haphazard and deflated.

A dry breeze of defeatism hovered there, which she was incapable of negating, even though in the first years she hoped that the transition would enable her to devote herself to bringing up her daughter, to enjoying her more, without the pressures of academic competition. But with the passage of the years Nitzan needed her devotion less and less, and the competition that she so much hoped to get away from was rampant, so it turned out, even among the defeated, and was more virulent than ever, especially with all the new regulations; as a result of these, if she doesn't complete her doctoral thesis some time soon, the thesis that she began back then, eighteen years ago, under the supervision of Professor David Emmanuel, there won't even be a place for her there.

For some reason she always goes back to that evening when the course of her life was changed, and it's only from there that her consciousness moves to other focuses of pain, older and deeper, but again and again it seems to her that everything is determined from there, even events that happened years before then, as if there's no early and late, only late, like that day when it became clear that her embryo wasn't going to survive any longer. Gideon was still in Africa then and Orly accompanied her to the clinic for the tests, her face flushed as she regaled her with personal anecdotes, how Emmanuel invited her to his house for a Sabbath meal with his wife and children, who were already treating her as a big sister, and when he took her down to drive her home, believe it or not, right there in the parking space, in front of his house, he pounced on her, and at that moment his wife came out with the rubbish, what luck, she didn't notice them, imagine it, Dina, and Dina imagined it, her hands on her bloated belly, a worrying tingle in the loins. You wouldn't believe how beautiful he is when he's making love, suddenly he goes wild – but now it was her turn, the turn of the doctor to inform her, to console her, he simply stopped developing, this happens a lot in twin pregnancies, and it's better when it happens at this stage, you're young and healthy and you can have many more children. But she wasn't interested in many more children, and she didn't even feel grieved; after all, she wasn't a mother yet and only mothers know what grief is, and she went out of there to Orly and her stories. The thought of Emmanuel's face leaning over her in the parking space she found more disturbing than the lone silhouette in her womb; no longer two pairs of wet ears but just the one pair listening to her secrets in the watery inner space, and now it seems to her again that all these things were connected, that if that rainy evening she had restrained her resentment, two children would be waiting for her at home today, and she sees them holding her hands, surrounding her with the wall of their love, built by four hands. She sees them growing up, her burgeoning breasts and his first moustache, her pelvis expanding and his voice changing, but when she recedes he stays; he always was a considerate, conciliatory child, obedient to her unspoken desires, and now he comes bounding out of Nitzan's room and stands before her, with his bare and smooth chest, with his awkward smile, and she leaps up from the bed, just what the doctor advised her not to do, as the room turns dark and spins around her, but unlike her mother, who lost consciousness some hours before this, her consciousness clears miraculously as she falls, when she sees her daughter, roused urgently from her sleep and not pausing to put on a blouse, bending over her. She stares at her so acutely that it seems it's her internal organs she can see, the fist of the heart, the twin lungs, the earthy clod of the liver, the delicate tracery of the intestines, as she saw her that day, visible inside her belly in shifting patches of light, but when she turns her eyes to the doorway, to the steadily darkening silhouette, a child, she will hear herself saying aloud, where have you been all this time?

Chapter Three

What is left for us in the evening of our days other than the visions that linger in our mind's eye? So much has been taken over the course of the years, loss after loss, and all in the natural process of things; we must not complain. Even the one who has amassed wealth will die penniless, take her for example, Hemda Horowitz, who was born too late or too early, definitely not in a time and a place that suited her, but in a time and a place that demanded of her more than she was capable of giving, while what she offered they rejected with disdain. To jump up on rooftops they demanded of her, and to leap from roof to roof as if there were no yawning gap between them, to run across oscillating bridges, along railway tracks suspended in the air above river gorges, to fish in the lake on cold and pitch-dark nights, while she wanted to impress them with words. So many stories she had which were never put into writing; all of them she knew by heart, in miraculous fashion, but when she tried to tell them the children used to mock her flowery style, her implausibilities – that's impossible! they used to upbraid her, the minority who condescended to listen, there's no such thing as a lake that talks!

Because it was the secrets of the lake that she whispered into their disbelieving ears on winter nights, when the winds whistled around the isolated children's house, snatching everything that stood in their way, all the stories that the lake told her of what he had seen with his eyes and heard with his ears, tasted with his tongue and probed with his fingers. He told her about the fishing-boat inlaid with gold buried in his depths, and asleep on its deck the girl who drowned, whose weeping is sometimes heard at night, Mummy, she cries, help me, Mummy, and about the man who searched for the loved one who was forbidden him among the reeds, and whispered of his love in the ears of the migrating birds, until he lost his wits and the marshes swallowed him, and even from under the ground he went on talking to her and his throat filled with mud until he died again and again, and about the woman who longed to bear a child and bathed every day in the waters of the lake to be purged of her barrenness, but the lake said to her, I shall be your son, I shall be your infant, and he dowsed her with water that filled her womb and distended her belly until she gave birth to a water child, a tiny wave disappearing amid his brother waves.

Even her father, who so loved reading, was hostile towards her stories, this is no time for stories, Hemdi, he would sigh, it's a time for action, and the Jews have contributed enough stories to the world; only her mother, on her short visits, would listen to her with eyes closed as if hearing sweet music, write this down, she would urge her, you can't remember it all, but she did remember, she cleared a lot of space in her head and remembered, not leaving room for anything else, until she had no regular words left in her. When they asked her a simple question she would open her mouth to give a simple answer, but only stories emerged, like steam from a boiling saucepan when the lid is removed, and anyone who came too close would be scalded. It's a fact that they all kept their distance, except her father, who would grip her hand and drag her after him, fuming. You have to answer to the point, you have to answer them in their language. In a group every nonconformist is miserable, why do you always need to suffer? Sometimes she thought he was going to drown her in the lake, or drown the lake in her, and years later when she heard her father energetically backing the scheme to drain Lake Hula, in opposition to the other veteran fishermen, although she was already a grown-up married woman by then she couldn't rid herself of the idea that this was nothing but delayed revenge on the entity that had robbed him of his daughter and destroyed his educational project, which was no less valuable in his eyes, and as it was to turn out over time, no less a failure. But he wouldn't live long enough to realise just how foolish the project had been, and perhaps this was the very reason why he didn't live long, because when the work of draining the lake was finally finished and the whole farm went wild over the territory which had been cleared, which did not repay them with the same alacrity, her father was the first to recognise the terrible mistake and the first to pay a personal price, which did no one any good.

She remembers him restlessly pacing the open expanses, suspiciously fingering the dry, peaty soil, prone to overheating, walking among the kibbutz members like a morose prophet, until one morning he didn't wake from his sleep, and when she came to visit him at the end of the day, heavily pregnant as she was, he was already as cold and stiff as a marble statue, on his face the anger and disappointment that were turned on her in the early days, when she refused to walk. She stood frozen by his bed, and it seemed to her that again his hand was held out to strike her, because again she was the one unable to walk and he was the one hitting her, from his bed and from his death, and again this wasn't loss of control but an unbearably sad compulsion, and she put her hands on the folds of her belly which was racked with pain, how regular its beats, every second minute she groaned, falling on her bed as then and trying to uproot from her inner self the pain of his beatings and the pain of his love, the pain of his life and the pain of the death of the dearest to her of them all, and when they found her there it was almost too late, and by a miracle they managed to make it to the hospital just in time, and she gave birth to Dina, much earlier than planned.

The birth of her first-born daughter, the death of her father, the capitulation of the lake, all these together were congealed in her consciousness into a complex and suppurating knot. The motherhood and orphanhood which were bound together with a fateful and cyclical bond left her so confused that it seemed to her in those days that her dead father needed her more than her living daughter, desperately needed her forgiveness, and she would sit for hours beside his freshly dug grave, her breasts leaking milk that quickly dried, and on the way back she was looking for the lake, believing that if she searched well enough she would find him, it couldn't be that he had disappeared completely, that his mighty and supernatural presence had been nullified by the hand of man. All that he had done was restrict himself, not in dimensions but in appearance, and henceforward he would be like a god, revealing himself only to those worthy of it, and she was certainly worthy, who could be more worthy than she, and so she used to walk among the new fields of wheat with the fire lurking in their depths, while he waited to appear before her with all his winds and his smells, his waters and his secrets, and all this time laid on a bed in the children's house was one baby born prematurely, hungrily sucking her thumb, a baby who instead of bringing consolation and blessing as is the normal way of babies, seemed to be in the grip of a curse and waiting for some sorcery that would lift the curse, and bring her mother back to the world of the living and to her.

And waiting too, as silent and disappointed as his little girl, her Elik, lean and handsome and foreign-looking, precisely what she was attracted to when he arrived on the kibbutz with a group of boys and girls from Europe who filled the familiar space to overflowing with their strange expressions, with their unfamiliar accents, with their stories about snow and cherries, forests and trams, stories which, like candy spiked with drugs, aroused forbidden longings among the grown-ups, while the children reacted with superior scorn, but she was drawn to them and in particular to him. It seemed that even in their circle he was an outsider, refusing to strike roots, wandering alone at the edge of the highway as if waiting for a visitor who never arrived, and only after they became acquainted did she discover that he was indeed waiting with dedication for his beloved parents, who put him on a ship and bade him a tearful goodbye, promising to join him in two to three weeks, as soon as they had the papers they needed. But a year had passed and not a word heard from them, and yet he went on waiting all his life, refusing to grow up without them. Not until his parents were approaching the age at which people are expected in the normal way of things to go and join their ancestors, and he himself was close to the age of discretion, not until then did he give up hope, and when this desperate flame was extinguished, his grip on the world faltered and he soon fell ill with the disease that would kill him.

Is this the true story, she sighs, until the last moment she will be telling herself stories, only herself, after all no one else is interested in her story, and is she entitled to condense her husband's biography into such a small space, with a few sentences that are pleasing to her ears? And maybe it wasn't for his parents he was waiting, but for her, and maybe not for her but for another woman, another life. It was his misfortune to turn up on her kibbutz, his misfortune to fall into her arms, fair and sensitive-looking, shorter than her by a head; she wasn't worthy of him. It soon became clear to her that in her heart her father had already taken up residence, despising any display of weakness, and this time she was the one forcing a helpless creature to walk along railway lines suspended above a chasm, she had no patience for him, she derided his longings, the sentimental memories repeating themselves; salty tears pricked her cheeks but she couldn't wipe them away when she was lying underneath him, clamping her thighs together. She always loved looking at him but recoiled from his touch, the exuberant and flustered touch of an adolescent, grateful for the briefest of moments.

How clear it was that he couldn't help her in those days, and yet she still had hopes. She used to visit him in the kibbutz secretariat, and find him glowering among piles of papers; he wanted to study law but the kibbutz wouldn't authorise it, they said they needed an accountant, not a lawyer, and he would look up at her in his most persuasive manner and say Hemda – even her name he had difficulty pronouncing – soon we'll go and visit the baby, she's developing so nicely, and she would nod sadly, yes, let's go and visit poor little Dina. In her memory the birth of her daughter and the death of her father were bound together like a single blow, so that sometimes she tended to believe it was the birth that hastened the death and not vice versa, and there were moments when she saw her father being born out of her while her daughter lay as still as a marble statue, and how could Elik with his bruised consciousness grasp the smallest part of all this if he even had difficulty understanding her language? He came without a single word of Hebrew to her of all people, with her lavish and high-flown style, he whose life ended there in the port of Hamburg, and she who always felt her life had not yet begun.

And where was Mother? Her beautiful mother, always busy, and again incapable of perceiving her distress; of course she couldn't do that, after all she had lost her beloved husband, bearing her grief with pride and coming and going, looking at her with that air of tolerant curiosity, like then, when she returned from her long trip and noticed her budding breasts, but where was your mother when he rousted you from your bed on black and rainy nights and dragged you crying and kicking to the fishing boat? As strong as a man he wanted you to be, stout-hearted and bold-spirited like him. Is that why he reconciled himself so easily to his wife's absences, letting him mould his daughter as he pleased?

How heavy the oar was in her hands, when he showed her how to hit the water with it. Get away from here, fish, get away, she wanted to shout. This is just a trick, don't believe it, because that's what they used to do then, beating the water with oars to scare the fish, which would dive deeper in their fear, straight into the net spread out down below, but the fish are the children of the lake and he's going to miss them, she thought, feeling the pain of the bereaved lake, who was losing more children every night, and sometimes she feared his vengeance, lying at night trembling, terrified, in the dark children's house, convinced that at any moment his grieving waters would rise and sweep away the buildings of the kibbutz and drown their inhabitants, and only hundreds of years from now would the relics of their bones be found, like the elephant's tusks and ancient human bones that had turned up in the marshes nearby.

He forced her to go out fishing, he forced her to eat the miserable fish, how powerful was the anger building up in her body, though she never dared be angry with him for any length of time; now and then she would be seized by a momentary wrath which changed at once into deep trust: he must know what he's doing, it isn't possible that he doesn't know. He was a wise and responsible man, their conscience and their compass, how could he be wrong? His premature death curtailed their separation and left her close to him, but finally she had been given an opportunity to defy his authority, and that is why he has returned to her suddenly, sitting beside her bed and looking at her with his lovely blue eyes, and she shakes her head at him in a rage, holding out her arms to him but not to embrace him, to hurt him is what she wants, to revenge herself on him, my father, it's still hard for her to express her grievance which turns at once into a thin whimper, how could you dare mould me in the image of another person, how could you dare leave me like this, suspended in the air between heaven and earth, incapable of being the girl you wanted me to be and not the girl I was destined to be.

She sees before her the two girls: one of them tough and resilient, knowing no fear, and the other timorous, dreamy and lazy, and between them she herself, except that her limbs are splayed in the space between the two of them, before they collide together with the contrary force of attraction and repulsion, and how will they coalesce in the form of one girl who is whole, firm and enduring, and she's so tired of this dizzy dance which has been going on for decades, more than her father's years, more than her mother's years, more than her husband's years, so exhausted, and only one thing she has the strength left to do, the strength of her love and her wrath, to hold out her hands to her father's attractive neck and squeeze it in a slow strangulation that will drain the last surge of will-power remaining in her and leave the two of them lifeless.

Her arms catch him off-guard as he bends over her, trying to bring his ear close to her lips and to detach some intelligible words from the howls that come gurgling up from the throat like bitter vomit, how quickly has her innocent joy turned to discontent, and as he's trapped between them, the old aversion to her touch is aroused in him. He's suddenly so close to the bony clavicle, the empty chest, but to his surprise the enfolding movement doesn't turn into the familiar, needy embrace, but focuses on his neck with an intensity he didn't know existed, accompanied by angry moans, and out of the fog of excessive proximity to her skin with its wrinkles and blotches and the vapour from her mouth it dawns on him that his mother is trying to squeeze the life out of him, stopping him from inhaling or exhaling ever again. For a moment he is prepared to commit himself into her hands, revelling in the first helplessness like a baby in his mother's arms, for punishment or for mercy, surprised to discover how much he prefers her strangulation to her embrace.

Her muscles, which have leaped out from their hiding-place, tighten a ring of fingers around his throat, which is pulsing vigorously and he closes his eyes in pain and bewilderment, like someone tempted to play a dangerous game with a child and finding that he is the stronger of the two. In the kibbutz pool he used to compete with the other children to see how long he could keep his head under the water, and he always won, and only his sister Dina could defeat him sometimes. What lungs you must have in your family, the children used to laugh, the lungs of a hippo, but he knew, as she definitely also knew, although they never talked about it, that it wasn't a question of inflating the lung; it was all about a life force inadequately developed, a dark attraction to self-destruction, an attraction that he senses now in its full intensity as his head sinks down on his mother's chest and his mouth drips saliva on her torn nightdress.

How did you dare, how did you dare, her voice is growing in volume and the words strike him with an awesome inner conviction, you ruined everything, left me with no prospects, her toothless gums belt out her snarls in full, undigested and unchewed, you were wrong! You weren't right! she growls underneath him, her eyes screwed up with the effort. Why do I need to drive a tractor? Why do I need to catch fish in the lake? I was afraid, afraid, why did you force me? You were wrong, she repeats. No father should be allowed to get things so wrong and make his daughter a failure too. Her words surround his neck, tightly gripped in her hands, the air in his lungs is diminishing, as if he were already sinking, heavy and lifeless, to the bed of the lake. I am the drowned boy, brother of the drowned girl. Is he breathing at all, does he still exist? It's obvious he could extricate himself but he doesn't do it, it seems he's even making an effort to help her in the fulfilment of her last wish, as if obeying a law of nature, what could be more right than the one who gave life being the one who takes it back.

In the swooning mists he remembers the smile of the man who lay on the adjacent bed, and tries to smile back at him. You and I, he thinks, have been fighting with the same energy, and now we're both standing down, because with standing down comes a happiness sharp as a needle, a cruel happiness which no sadness in the world can overcome, and I feel it migrating from your body to my body and I'm prepared for it, at the moment of your death it will come to me and then I shall die too, but now rapid footsteps are approaching their bed, and he is impressed – apparently the white-gowned nurse knows his name and the name of his mother, Avner! Hemda! What's happening here? she scolds them as if trying to separate two brawling children, her hands too stretching out to reach his neck, to prise away the bent fingers clutching it. Let go of him, Hemda, she shouts, and the old woman obeys, flustered, don't be cross with me, Mother, she whimpers, he's the one who got it wrong, he wasn't right! You always cared about each other more than about me, and Avner lifts his head slowly from its resting-place on her wasted bosom, as if waking from sleep, and to his astonishment, recognises his wife. What are you doing here? he mumbles, as if her presence in this place is beyond all imagining, at this moment it belongs exclusively to him and to his mother, and she's still incensed. Dina asked me to come here and relieve you. Why didn't you tell me?

She looks suspiciously at him and at his mother, who has suddenly fallen silent, as if trying to interpret the scene that has just been curtailed, and Avner peers at his wife angrily, again she's extricated him without checking that he really wants to be extricated, the way she did it back then, in their youth, again from his mother's arms, and again that amalgam of grudge and gratitude that he felt towards her even then, although nothing is left now of the slim short-haired woman who offered him a temporary and apparently comfortable refuge which turned into a final refuge, just his grudge against her. How heavy this grudge of his had become in recent years, how heavy she had become too, thighs and hips and nape, short neck; a thick-fleshed woman has swallowed up that young lady, wrapped her in a crumpled and stained white blouse, why wear white if you can't protect your clothes from dirt?

As the air flows again in his throat, almost against his will, he is filled with a prodigious hunger, and he straightens up and probes his neck. He longs to get out of here and to breathe savagely, to escape to another life, a life not yet lived, overlaid with virginal beauty, after all it wasn't death he was rescued from, but submission; it wasn't her hands he was delivered from, but his own, and he coughs, his throat is dry and his neck still throbbing vigorously. She's really confused, he apologises on his mother's behalf, she thought I was her father, as if such an episode were a routine occurrence between a daughter and her father. For some reason it's important to him to keep this incident under wraps, the physical intimacy between him and his mother that he hasn't experienced in years, arousing ancient memories of their love, and when he looks at his wife with her reddening cheeks, he knows that again a moment of good will has been lost. She hurried here to be by his side, disregarding tiresome calculations, she was hoping to support him and again it turns out she is superfluous, and again he is to blame, again they are creating the same feelings for each other. Is there a way out from this accursed circle, and is he really interested in getting out; perhaps there's no point in making an effort, in drawing her close to him and embracing her round the waist and thanking her for coming, there's no point in inviting her to drink coffee with him in the cafeteria nearby. He glances at his watch and says drily, I must dash to the office, I have an important meeting, stay with her here until I come back, all right?

Without another glance at her or at his mother he's out of there, his hands still probing his neck as if trying to loosen a tight collar, or perhaps change ties, feeling a surge of excitement as he passes the bench where that man was sitting, his short-term neighbour, before being taken to the car, gilded like a royal carriage; there can't be many cars like that round here, and suddenly it seems to him nothing would be simpler than locating a gold Citroën in the biggest city in the country, and in a state of agitation he walks on under the ferocious sun of early summer, which is likewise stretching out incandescent fingers to massage his neck.

He loves this path leading to his office, the combination of elegance and squalor; to reach it you walk between piles of broken bottles and empty crack-cocaine bags, with smells of urine and dog faeces, and suddenly before your eyes the building is revealed in all its antique glory, revealed and at once disappearing again, on account of two ugly extra storeys tacked on to the top of it. He is like this too, at least in his own eyes: the handsome and debonair young man to whom the years have added storeys, suspending a repulsive stomach from his midriff, sticking puffy bags under his eyes, and plucking out his smooth, black and glossy hair, a kind of cruel joke: let's see how you cope with a different façade, and he's already almost giving up; how wearisome is this daily struggle, and how little depends on it, and who is it for anyway, after all Shlomit and the boys accept him as he is, they don't have much choice, and only at certain moments, like now in the doorway of the office when he stands watching his intern, does he believe it would be possible to peel off all of these things with a single accurate touch.

How he loves to stand in the doorway when she hasn't noticed him, to look at her as if her image is projected on a screen and impossible to touch, and hence his attempts at closeness are not so different from the efforts of his younger son to touch the colourful images that he sees, but the truth is he doesn't want to touch her, touching is such a crude and simple thing. She moves through her little domain stiffly, and when she turns her back the broad line of her bra appears, constricting her back, and beneath it the gathered folds of her flesh, but she doesn't know, and her not-knowing touches his heart when he is party to a private secret hidden even from her.

Until a year ago he had two interns in his office, and it seemed to him sometimes, especially when he was on his way in, that this was what coming home should be like, so much

more pleasant than returning to Shlomit and the boys. Wasn't this his true home, wasn't this his real family, single-parent father to two grown-up, talented girls? He enjoyed supervising them, and even when they made mistakes he wasn't too censorious, and the fact that they were replaced every year or so didn't impair the sense of family but even deepened it, since even in a family it really makes no difference which of them are the practical souls; it's a question of what functions they are required to fulfil.

Lately his work has contracted, and so he has been forced to make do with one intern, becoming a single parent father to a single daughter, and at the beginning he was reminded now and then of his first-born son Tomer and his long years as an only child, and it was only after Yotam was born that he understood how tiresome they were, but it seems the two of them are accustomed to this restricted frame, and he really doesn't need an extra intern, and he's happy with her enthusiasm, her seriousness and her maturity, and it's only her choice of nickname that irritates him sometimes, Anati, it has such a childish ring to it, and yet she's so wise and so quick on the uptake, what does she need with any extra letters.

Attorney's office, good morning, she answers the phone, no, he hasn't arrived yet, his mother's in hospital, I expect he'll be here before midday, have they blocked your application again? I'll tell him to contact you at once. Her face lights up on hearing of the fresh injustice and she hurries to record all the details in her notebook, and when he sees how well the office is functioning without him he feels a pang of acute sorrow, yes, in the same way the world will function without him one of these days, full of injustices, desperate phone conversations, blouses buttoned up to the neck, mothers and sons, nothing will be diminished. Likewise the world will function without

the man he met this morning, if you could call this a meeting, as he didn't notice him at all, just gazed at his wife with his last vestiges of strength, as if trying to imprint her features in his memory, so now he will also try to memorise the sight of those delicate lips despatching words into the receiver, and those animated fingers avidly recording the contentious details. Outside the window their ugly ailanthus tree is flourishing, the tree that he learned to love, an urban survivor that can hold on anywhere. There's no such thing as an ugly tree, Anati said when he apologised on behalf of the tree, his regular joke, and suddenly he wakes up with a start, as if he's overslept and held up an urgent assignment, and he says to her without preamble, Anati, I need your help. It seems to him that if he involves her in this strange project the strangeness will be cancelled out, that if she and not he contacts the vehicle agency and asks who has bought a gold-coloured Citroën in the last year, this unavoidable mission will become a natural part of his world, and she looks up at him and says Avni, how is your mother? as if trying to re-arrange his entry here. Suleiman is looking for you, she adds, he's on his way here now, and barely has she spoken his name when he appears, as if he too has been hanging back and watching them, expecting an official announcement.

Many years have passed since they met almost by chance, as Suleiman was trimming the ivy at the entrance to their building, and when Avner acknowledged him he was tentatively asked if he was the lawyer who lived here; the neighbours had told him a lawyer lived upstairs and Avner, who had only just completed his studies and was already regretting his choice of career, confirmed this in a faint voice and at once found himself listening and volunteering to help in a small issue, a biblical-style dispute taking place at the end of the second millennium, the case of three shepherds

whose flock had been confiscated on the grounds that they were operating in a closed military sector, and the huge indemnity that had been imposed on them for the return of their livestock. It was his first case and it dragged on for nearly two years, a minor case which became a big one and went all the way to the Supreme Court, in which he was able to prove that the order for closure of the area had not been properly presented, and not only did he succeed in getting their money back with interest, he also ensured that their right of residence would be recognised in law, and since then members of the Bedouin clan, Suleiman included, had tended to credit him with higher powers. But now Avner sees disappointment and scepticism in his face as he says, did you see that the application has been rejected? They've served us with a demolition order on the school, and at once he pats his stomach and adds, you've put on weight, Horowitz.

Don't worry, that was to be expected, he says hurriedly, so we'll lodge an appeal, apply for an interim injunction to delay the demolition, would you like some coffee? And Suleiman says, no, I must be moving, I have no time. Despite his immaculate attire, his striped shirt and light linen trousers, despite his shaved cheeks and the pen gleaming in his breast pocket, he exudes involuntarily the smell of the clan, the pungent smell of fire and dust. Another appeal? How many are we allowed? he complains bitterly, it's about time a solution was found, and Avner sighs, believe me I'm doing everything I can, how did you manage to get here?

I came here for medical tests, and I'm running late, maybe I'll come back afterwards, he says and already he's going, lithe and athletic, and Avner sits at his desk exhausted, staring at the files that surround him, files full of documents, documents full of words, so many words on this impasse that's a matter of life and death for them, so many words about structures illegally demolished and rebuilt without licences, when building with licences is impossible, files crammed with documents about wretched utility buildings erected in the desert, ramshackle prefabs, appeals upon appeals, this frightened country of his fighting every symbol of permanence, attributing menacing significance to every toilet seat, is it possible to make war on fear without creating fear? Is defence possible without attack? If there was an opportunity it's been lost, but more and more it seems to him there never was.

These crammed files give him an overview of the deceptive geography of this land, a double, triple geography, Hebron both far and near, Gaza both far and near, files in place of people of flesh and blood, since most of his clients are barred from access to his office, and with a sigh he rubs his neck, which is still painful, how many appeals? For long years he has fought against the stronger parties: the state, the army, security services, he has fought over territory and compensation, over flocks of sheep and mud huts, over hovels and toilet seats, because that's where the dignity of mankind is found in the line of fire: the dignity of sixteen-year-old Khaled, who worked for a stonemasonry contractor until a crane dropped a tombstone on his back, and since then he's been paralysed, and because he was working there illegally the contractor refuses to have anything to do with him, and the family dare not complain because in the meantime he's employing his younger brother, and who's going to fight to get him some compensation; and who will care about Halla, due to be deported to Jordan in contravention of the basic right of the individual to marriage and family, and about the three children who were playing with an unexploded mortar shell and were fatally injured, and who will defend the interests of Suleiman's oppressed community, the free spirits of the desert, the Bedouin who were once proud nomads and are now shovelling shit on the urban fringes? Few are prepared to represent the powerless, and the most brilliant brains put themselves at the disposal of the most powerful; how tempting it could be to represent the government, the banks, the wealthy of the land, but when you put on the gown and perform in the Supreme Court, you feel strong in the very act of speaking up for the poor and the downtrodden against mighty forces and even getting the better of them from time to time, and you're no longer powerless, even though in recent years your successes have been fewer, and he remembers the disappointment on Suleiman's face; is it he who has grown weaker, or is the state getting stronger, meaning that it's weakened and for this reason is defending itself all the more vigorously, and he shifts his gaze from the files to the tree that is flourishing confidently as if winter will never return. Anati, I need your help, it's really urgent, he repeats, because it seems to him suddenly that if he succeeds in locating the car and thereby the couple who travelled in it, perhaps he may also succeed in delaying the demolition order in the High Court.

The tiles are still cold from the winter that has only just left, and when they meet her incandescent back they emit a soft hissing sound; it seems to her she is wreathed in vapours when she opens her eyes and finds beside her on the floor the delectable body of her daughter, leaning over her; a sweet smell of summer fruits wafts from her hair, and her arms in their wrapping of thin silky skin enfold her neck, and her touch is unbearably delightful. Mummy, Mummy, she whispers in her ear, and Dina tenses up, afraid to move so much as a fingertip lest the charm fade and her dream end abruptly. A pitiable whimper rises from her throat, the whimper of a dog meeting his master after a long separation, since such a heavy weight of longing assails her that she doesn't know what to do with it, absolute bliss and facing it its destruction, like two sides of the same coin.

High above their heads hangs their first picture, and she remembers how she loved it when Nitzan sneaked into their bed on Sabbath mornings, and sometimes she would gaze at the picture and say earnestly, I want to be a baby again, I want to be this baby who's just been born, and Dina was alarmed; has the girl been reading her thoughts, after all that's what she wants too – though it's shameful to admit it, she wants to bear Nitzan again, bring her up again.

But why? she would ask her, feigning innocence, and Nitzan would reply, because it's easier when you're small, and she in her customary manner hurried to reassure her, my darling, it's a lot more fun being grown-up, think how interesting your life is now, how many things you can do now that you couldn't do before, and Nitzan used to insist, but I didn't have the problems then that I have now, that was what she called the distress she suffered when confronted by disloyal friends, by nasty conspiracies; she used to tell her all about them in detail and Dina listened and encouraged, how she enjoyed these intimate conversations with her serious, grown-up daughter, and suddenly here in her arms is a painful reminder of what she used to have and has lost, the supreme pleasure of close proximity, skin to skin, cell to cell, as the ground is close to the tree planted in it, its roots entwining in the depths while it grows and flourishes.

Mummy, don't cry, the girl breathes into her ear, you fell over but everything's all right, Dad said you'd be all right, and in the meantime I wasn't to call an ambulance, how are you feeling? And Dina shakes her head, how hard it is to distinguish between reality and fantasy when they use the same language. Surely these are words of reality: Dad, ambulance, everything all right, and at the same time how dreamy is the inner sensation, just as it is when she's playing her imagination games, immersed in memories of a past that never was. What's needed is a special language for fantasies, as there are parts of the body designed exclusively for love; all this mixing up always seems to her mistaken, an amalgam of secretions and pleasures, and she smiles at her daughter with closed lips. Nitzan is so sensitive to smells, the lightest puff of vaporous breath is liable to repel her.

But why be immersed in a past that never was? The one that they had, the two of them, was fine and satisfactory, side by side they flourished, she lacked for nothing, she had all she needed in the love of her only daughter before she turned her back on her, and although she's well aware of all the theories about the need for separation, and knows this is a process through which the girl must pass on the way to constructing her identity, and there is no denying her love, it is firm and enduring even if it's hiding behind a barbed wire fence – in spite of all this she can't help grieving for her, and now with Nitzan kissing her cheeks and pleading, Mummy, say something, so I'll know you're all right, she smiles dumbly, what can she say, for years things haven't been as all right as this, so happy in other words, as at this moment, on the floor at the foot of the bed, and at the same time it's clear to her that if she only admits it her happiness will be taken from her within a few minutes and then it won't be all right any more, absolutely not. She hugs her daughter and it seems to her that the ceiling above their heads is rolling back like a stone placed over the mouth of a well, and the sky appears, not the caustic sky of the beginning of summer, but with winter clouds soft as a blanket covering them, and snowflakes gathering around them with a soft sigh. So wondrous is this moment that she must hide it as she used to hide her few treasures in the children's house, hide it even from her daughter, her own flesh and bone; how despicable it is to be worrying the girl like this, pretending she hasn't recovered in order to enjoy more of her favours.

Mummy, she hears the slightly childish voice, wake up, say something to me, I don't know what to do before Dad arrives, and she opens a cautious eye and peers at her daughter; her hair covers her face when she bends over her, her skin is light, almost transparent, and her eyes soft behind the thin glasses that emphasise her vulnerability, and her distress is so obvious that she's forced to comfort her, don't worry, Nitzi, she whispers, I'm all right, I felt giddy for a moment but it's passed now.

I've brought you some water, the girl beams, come on, drink it, I'm so glad you're getting better, I was really worried, and as she's making an attempt to sit up and sipping the water, she hears a rustling sound from the next room and all at once the vision returns to her, sweet and horrific, of how they lay entwined on the narrow bed, skin to skin, cell to cell, and she asks cautiously, is he still here? And when the girl hesitates she goes on to ask, what's his name? Where did you meet? And at once she regrets it, why waste a precious opportunity on superfluous questions, after all she knows who he is, his name is Noam, and they met at Shiri's place, but the girl who is sitting facing her cross-legged looks at her with a strange expression and asks, who?

Nitzi, she emits an embarrassing hiccup, there was someone with you in the room just now, wasn't there? I came into the room and saw you asleep, and Nitzan shakes her head, no, there wasn't anyone, and Dina turns her gaze from the girl to the ceiling, where the bulb has died in a lampshade slightly charred at the edges, like the pupil of an open eye that doesn't see anything, to the window that is closed for some reason, building up the heat like a stove, to the wardrobe with its sliding doors open and inside it clothes arranged in meticulous order, Gideon's handiwork. Helplessness, as demeaning as madness, takes hold of her, familiar in its substance but not in its intensity, yes, you can cast doubt on the vanities of speech, after all our experiences are as clay in the hand of the potter, the fruit of our imagination or the fruit of the imagination of the creator of the world, what really is the difference? She saw what she saw, with the eyes of the flesh or the eyes of the spirit: they lay embracing on the narrow bed, limbs intertwined, and already she's prepared to leave the question unresolved, to accept the girl's version as a way of preserving their intimacy, and she grins, so it seems I was dreaming, I dreamed I saw you in your bed, embracing a handsome young man who looked remarkably like you, but the girl stares at her with an enigmatic look that alarms her; what's happening here, is the barrier between reality and imagination disintegrating, or worse, is it her daughter who's disintegrating; if indeed she did lie to her, then it's more than a lie, it's almost sadism, and she peers at her daughter fearfully, as if she's just detected in her the first symptoms of a terrible disease, degeneration of the heart muscles. She sits facing her with legs crossed, her back leaning against the frame of the bed, her face sealed, on her body an old pyjama top that she put on in a hurry, inside-out, again she's wrapped up in herself, and Dina lets out a sigh; where has it gone, the simple closeness of touch and speech, and will it ever return? She sits down beside the girl, facing the wardrobe, is there really nothing left from all those years?

At a loss she sneaks a glance at the mirror on the door of the wardrobe, which contains her daughter, the high arch of the feet, the thin ankles, all of her still girlish, airy, alongside her friends, heavy as women, and all of her hard to decipher, as if she's returned to the mute days of babyhood, when it was necessary to guess her needs and her troubles according to signs, and now she's looking for signs again, but it seems Nitzan is misleading her deliberately, and as they sit in silence side by side opposite the open mirror-doors, and the room swelters in the debilitating heat of early summer, and between them a question is suspended, it seems to Dina that her daughter has been replaced by a mysterious visitor, the exterior remaining as it was but the interior changed utterly, like a building with its façade preserved and behind it renovations in progress, and when the door of the wardrobe suddenly starts to sway, to move from side to side, she's already prepared to concede that the earth is shaking too, and she's losing her grip, except that in this case the quake is accompanied by a throaty yowl, and emerging from there is the cat known as Rabbit, squeezing through the narrow aperture, gurgling loudly and bringing a smile to their lips.

My Rabbit, Nitzan coos at him, digging her fingers into his fur, you little fool, did you get shut in the wardrobe? That's exactly where you liked to sleep when you were a kitten, she reminds him, isn't that right, Mum, he used to sleep in this wardrobe? And Dina confirms this gratefully, as if acknowledging a shared memory is bringing them closer again, and she too caresses the white fur. Her fingers touch her daughter's fingers and she recoils as if foreseeing her recoil, but to her surprise her daughter takes her hand, her throat too emitting feline gurgles sounding like the beginning of a laugh that Dina is already responding to gladly, hoping that she's about to say, how could you believe me, Mummy, of course there was someone with me, and she stretches out her other hand to hug her daughter, whose back is heaving with that strange chuckle, growing in volume and growing in clarity.

What's up, my darling, she draws her closer, why are you crying? Tell me, I'll help you. Again she's carried away by the legendary might of motherhood, which aspires to solve every problem, to eliminate every pain through the power of love and devotion, sacrifice and conjecture, and the girl is gathered into her embrace, a fragile egg in the nest of her arms, her breathing abrupt, body shaking, Mummy, she says, panting the staccato syllables, I don't know what to do.

About what? Dina asks, tell me and I'll help you, but the creak of the apartment door silences their voices, and already he's there on the threshold of the bedroom, with the erect stance that's typical of short men, the camera swinging on his chest, what's happening here, girls? His voice is distant and faintly critical, as usual drawing a distinction between him and them. And they stare at him as if caught misbehaving, keeping from him a whingeing female secret that's of no interest to him anyway.

I'm already OK, she says hurriedly while the girl disentangles herself from her arms. I fainted apparently, she says. Yes, so I was told, do you want me to take you for a check-up? His feet are planted in the doorway and he doesn't approach her, as if he's looking at her through the lens of his camera. No, what's the point, she says, having difficulty repressing her anger, even when his intentions are good he's a nuisance, she's only just taken the girl in her arms and here she is slipping away, and at the same time she senses his anger at being summoned home prematurely and to no purpose, seeing that her condition isn't serious enough to justify this sacrifice. His presence makes her uneasy, like the presence of a stranger, his arrogant expression, his solid body. How handsome he is still, even more so than before; middle age suits his small, almost childlike facial features, his greying hair sets off his tan, and behind the spectacles his brown eyes are curious, almost challenging.

Once she loved looking at him, his beauty was hers too, but in recent years they have been separated by some silent movement like the shifting of continents, and now as she sits on the floor and looks up at him the pain between her ribs intensifies and she wants to pull him to her, wants him to sit beside her on the floor so he'll pay attention to her distress, your reserve is making me ashamed of feeling anything at all, and as she's still staring at him in silence rapid footsteps are heard in the hallway and the sound of the front door closing.

Nitzan has gone! she cries and leaps up as if intent on stopping her, but again the dizziness swirls around her, the beating of the wings of black birds pushing her down on the bed. Gideon, call her, she's going! And he looks at her as if she's out of her mind. What's the matter with you? She isn't an escaped prisoner and you're not her jailer. So what if she's gone, she'll be back, but Dina shakes her head, you don't understand, she's gone without telling me something important, at long last she wanted to confide in me, she's in distress and I don't know why.

You're not supposed to know, he grins, she isn't a kid in the nursery who tells you everything that happens to her, she has a life of her own, and that's lucky for her and for you too, and she protests, you're not listening to me, Gideon, something strange was going on here, she lied to me and then regretted it, or she didn't lie, I really don't know if she was here with someone or not. Again she tries to stand up, holding on to the wardrobe, her hand on the mirror, confronting the solid profile of a pale woman, with dishevelled hair, and when she goes from there the damp imprints of her long fingers are left behind. Although her head is still spinning and her knees quaking, she makes her way with purposeful tread to her daughter's room.

Mysterious and provocative, the bed with its disordered sheets confronts her, and she stares at it with wide-open eyes, trying to recreate the scene that she saw, if she really saw it, how they lay embracing, skin to skin, cell to cell, clinging to each other like twins in their mother's womb. Did she lie to her? Of course she lied, it's inconceivable that she could have seen them only in her mind's eye and the readiness of her daughter to lie to her, to make her doubt her ability to distinguish between imagination and reality, it's so cruel, and she can't attribute such cruelty to her daughter without feeling acute and truly unbearable sadness, and she falls upon the girl's bed, sniffing it like an animal, firm in her resolve to prove that she told her the truth.

The smell of a bonfire rises from the thin blanket that was tossed aside; she looks for signs on the sheet, on the pillow, what will the inanimate objects tell her, what can be learned from one crease or another, from the strand of blond hair that you seize upon suddenly, needing to check the length, since the colour of their hair was identical. A desert wind blows out the belly of the curtain above the bed and she's suddenly scared, is someone hiding there, is that where the truth is concealed? You're sick, he whispers to her and grins, you always were, but now it's impossible to hide it any more, compressed air is breathing syllables of dust and despair over her, you're sick, you're sick, and only then does she notice her husband standing behind her in the doorway; did he hear the words too, or was he perhaps the one who spoke them? How detached his expression is, lips stretched into a contemptuous leer, what are you looking for there, virginal blood?

Without answering she lays her head on the pillow and covers herself with the blanket, that's the way Nitzan lies here, the violet chiffon curtain behind her, before her eyes the door and beyond it the house with its bright and bare walls, almost without pictures, because Gideon prefers the shadows that the trees cast on the walls, its sparse furniture, only what's really needed; the house is simple and clean, almost ascetic, almost stylish. This is how Nitzan lies here night after night, what does she see, what does she hear, does she know how much prodigious effort went into creating light beside her, as in northern countries, where the populace fill their houses with candles; this is what she's been doing for sixteen years, lighting little candles for her daughter, watching the flame like a hawk, making sure it doesn't blow out in the wind. I'm cold, Gideon, she hears herself whispering, and at once corrects it, I'm hot, why did she say cold when she meant hot, and why did she call on Gideon? Well, there's no point in trying again, but here he is approaching her, sitting down beside the bed, listen, he says, without looking at her, you need to take care of yourself, it isn't an easy age, I've been reading about it; there are women who have difficulty coping with the menopause and you have difficulty coping with everything, but to her surprise there's no criticism in his voice, only complicity, and she straightens up slowly, his words drawing her closer to him with gentle strings. You've been reading about this? She's amazed, almost grateful, and he says, this is no laughing matter, Dini, this is a serious business, not long ago I heard of a woman who killed herself on account of menopausal depression, a woman leading a perfectly orderly life, married with three children, you need to look after yourself, perhaps that's what Nitzan was trying to tell you, you should be caring for yourself now and not for her.

Because of that she lied to me? she asks, resting her cheek on his knee, she said there was no one here in bed with her, but I know there was, look. She holds out a sweaty fist to him saying, this is his hair – but her hand is empty, the evidence falling away from her piece by piece, and Gideon grins, his hands immobile at his sides, not caressing her hair. So what if she lied? Why are you making such a big deal out of it, everyone tells lies, don't you tell lies sometimes? And she says, who, me? Not really, not to people close to me. Her face flushes when she remembers the lies she had told just this morning to that student of hers in the maternity ward – what a strange, unnecessary encounter that had been – and she rubs her cheek against the stiff material of the jeans. You're taking this very lightly, as if you tell lies all the time.

Not all the time, only when there's no choice, he says, but she feels his thigh muscles tensing and her heart thumps, where were you, really? And he says, I was doing a photo shoot in the Negev, and she looks up at him, so how did you get here so quickly? I drove fast, Nitzan scared me, when you drive fast, you get there quickly, but she's staring at him in sudden doubt. Again her face is covered in sweat, hot vapours flood her chest, the interior of the skull, any moment now they will bore a hole in her cranium and black smoke will rise from there like the genie from the bottle. Days upon days he has been wandering the roads without her, sometimes accompanied by other photographers, journalists, some of them female, are you lying to me too? And he gazes back at her with the enigmatic look that she saw in the eyes of Nitzan. Of course, all the time, he chuckles, and the smile deepens the distortion of his features, giving them an expression of eternal mockery, and she pulls him to her although this isn't what she wants; but what she does want, she only wishes she knew. To eradicate the pain is her desire, to excise it from her body and flee from it, to run light and ethereal in empty streets, to restore to herself distant knowledge that has been lost, certainty that has dissolved, curtailed hopes.

Without opposition and without passion he stretches out on his back and she drapes her limbs over him, this is the way

I saw them, she whispers, she lay on top of him, they were really connected, her head on his chest, and this was strange because they were half clothed and half naked, and they looked like twins, not like a couple, and he sighs, it makes no difference, Dini, you weren't supposed to see this, you weren't supposed to interpret this, and again she wonders if he's only pretending not to understand her, as once they used to understand each other well, but all this is unimportant now, because she has a more urgent question for him, and not for him exactly but for his body, lying under her stiff and motionless. Oh, Gideon, she sighs, how foolish it is to ask questions of the body, because it's a liar too, like her body which desires not him but distant knowledge that has been lost, certainty that has dissolved; it's certainly not this deceptive intermingling that appeals to her now, nor the calm and confident manner in which he has been taking possession of her body for close on twenty years, nor his cheery sigh of ecstasy, because it's at precisely that time, when he's responding to her, that she's assailed by sadness, how hollow are these familiar motions when then there's no new life at the end of them; even if this life isn't destined to materialise there would still be the possibility, glowing with a precious light. If only we could have another child, she whispers in his ear, why didn't we do that when we still could, what a waste, we had treasure and we let it rot.

Anyone would think you were sterile, he complains, still panting, you're a mother, what difference does it make, the number of children you have? In Europe one child is quite enough, it's only here that everyone overdoes things, as if more means better, and she protests, I'm not talking to you about ideology but about desire, I so much want to bring up another child. Their bodies are still fused but again that abyss is gaping between them, they have surely left it too late, and there's no point in reviving the old argument, which led to wherever it led, and no point in laying blame. She wasn't determined enough, his opposition was stronger than her aspiration and now it's too late, and their bodies, still together and soon to be separated, are no longer capable of creating life, just moans of transitory pleasure; although apparently everything remains as it was, in fact an awesome change has taken place between them in recent years, and they're still negotiating the terms. Their one-off coupling has lost its vitality, for ever and for always, but this doesn't prevent other life combinations, of him with another woman, for example, someone to whom he might appeal, and his advantage over her, even if he doesn't exploit it, enrages her again and she asks, who were you with when I called you?

A new correspondent from the paper, you don't know her, he replies and straightens up, moving her off him, and she asks, how old? And he says, I have no idea, thirty maybe, and suddenly her jealousy of this woman flares up, not for travelling today with her husband to the Negev, if that is really where he went, and not for being fifteen years younger than her, but because she is capable of realising the one thing that she longs for herself, and as she lies here alone, hearing her husband turning on the tap in the shower, and the powerful jet of water that is washing her body from his body, she wants to extricate herself from the bed and join him, standing by his side under the hot stream, the way they used to do things years ago, and melting away the pain, but an icy chill grabs the tips of her fingers, spreading up from her toes, and she pulls the blanket over her; suddenly her teeth are chattering and her body is heavy and cold.

With an effort she opens her eyes and tries to move her stiff limbs, seeing him standing facing her with wet hair, buttoning his denim shirt. You're awfully pale, he says, maybe you're sick, there's a nasty virus going round, causing nausea and giddiness, and she doesn't respond. She really wants him to go, how strange that his presence intensifies her isolation, but he hesitates, when are you teaching today? he asks, maybe you should cancel, and then he remembers, so what's happening with your mother? And she stirs herself, embarrassed, how could she forget so absolutely?

Chapter Four

Again he tries to ram the spoon into her mouth, forcing her to drink the sweet lake water, and again she's sprawled among the reeds, surrounded by yellow water-lilies. The sun melts her limbs and they dissolve into the muddy, loamy soil, and he goes down on his knees and dips the spoon in the water of the lake, and then pours the liquid into her gullet. Drink, Hemda, drink, we have to drain the lake, spoonful by spoonful, until the water is all gone.

But I don't want to drain the lake, Daddy, I love the lake, she protests, trying to keep her lips sealed, and he rebukes her at once. What has love to do with it? We need this land to grow wheat and barley on it, apples and avocado. There are obligations and there are loves, he says, and obligations take precedence, so drink up, Hemda, and she groans, but I'm only little, how can I drink a whole lake? and he says, gradually, there's no need to hurry, we have all our lives ahead of us.

So all my life I'm going to be lying here like this, while you give me water to drink with a spoon? She's horrified, is that what I'm going to do with my life? And he replies, pensively, perhaps not all your life, just until it's dried up. The faster you drink the faster it will dry up and you can start to live. What a hopeless task, but in fact no more hopeless than other tasks that he imposed on her, crossing rickety bridges, driving a tractor and digging ditches. The way he stood behind the tractor with arms outstretched when she was afraid to go any further because of the gorge lying in wait for her at the side of the track. I'm not moving from here, he announced, if you put it in reverse, you'll run me over! And she drove on, her hands shaking on the wheel, her mouth gaping with fear, and now too she opens her mouth wide to do his bidding, swallowing the water of the lake which is sweeter than the way she remembers it. She was always a little disappointed with the taste. The words fresh water had such a promising sound, but in fact there was only brackish water in the lake at that time, not fresh at all, and she planned to steal bags of sugar from the dining hall and sweeten the water with it, but she didn't have the nerve, and it seems someone else has done this for her in the meantime, because now the taste is heavier and more concentrated than she remembers, and her father says, well done, Hemda, well done, have another little drink. Why does his voice suddenly sound feminine, feminine and hoarse like her mother's voice?

Mum's here too! she exults, opening her eyes wide to see her, but closing them again at once, lest the rare and precious vision dissolve, having to compete with another vision, that of her daughter-in-law Shlomit sitting beside her, a cup of tepid tea in one hand, and a spoon in the other, and she wants to return to the tall reeds, the white flowers adorning their heads like locks of hair, that's where she belongs, not in this place whatever it may be, she has no idea – that's where she belongs. How short are the days of childhood, and yet there's no end to them; only with her death will her childhood be sealed.

What a shame, she sighs, discovering that her parents care more for her than her children do, more than her husband; they are alive and vivacious, dispensing fear and love, exploiting every chink in her consciousness to bring her back under their control, and confronted by them her Elik is falling away, and she forces herself to remember him now. The smells of the hospital lead her unawares to the last years of his life, how bitter he was, his jealousy more ferocious than ever, because it seemed it was only then he found the logic, her health as opposed to his sickness, her lengthening life as opposed to his imminent death.

He seemed timid and bashful, but at home in their company he would periodically explode into terrible rages, especially after they left the kibbutz and for the first time were four people living in one house, a family in other words. In the tiny pocket-sized apartment in the housing project overlooking the Arab village that straddled the ridge, when he was working unwillingly as a clerk in a local branch of the bank and she, deprived of the protection of her kibbutz, sometimes felt that the three of them were being held hostage by a dangerous invalid, or to be more accurate, the two of them, she and Avner, since Dina was always beyond his reach, out of the danger zone; a fraternity of the deprived united them and has lasted until today, years after his death.

How he used to attack her beautiful boy when he stood in front of the mirror, adjusting his hair. Out having fun again? he would scold him. Sit down and study, or nothing will come of you in the end! Only yesterday you were out at the cinema, today you're staying at home, and she would stand like a lioness between him and her son, what are you talking about? He hasn't been out all week, you leave him alone, and at once the familiar arguments erupted, and Avner would flee the family home with tears in his eyes, receding in the distance, and at weekends escape to his girlfriend on the kibbutz, and sometimes she would come to them on a Friday afternoon, short and crop-haired, exhausted from the long journey.

Against her will she accepted her, the living partition between her and her son, hoping he would find a more impressive partner than this one, or better still remain hers exclusively for a few more years, but Shlomit wasn't giving up so easily, to this day she has held on to him with her fingernails, with her arms that have thickened, with her children, especially the older one, so like her, and when she opens her eyes cautiously, slyly, and sees her there beside her, firm and enduring, again the old forgotten grudge wells up in her, and she stretches out her hand and pushes the spoon away, sneaking a glance at the stain left by the liquid on her daughter-in-law's white blouse. Where's Avni, she wants to ask, or more to the point, where am I, but no question is heard, although she feels her lips moving above the ignominiously empty gums, her tongue sliding over them again and again, searching for the lost teeth, the lost years.

Really lost? How much anger poured out of her after his death, sitting hour after hour by the window and fuming, like the peat that burned perpetually in the depths of the marshes, what a betrayal, a husband who leaves the world too early or too late, abandoning her to the last age, children who slip away from her as they grow up, and this city, Jerusalem, where she so much wanted to live a new life, and now it stands before her indifferent, locked and bolted, almost hostile in its dangerous fringes, live in me if it matters to you, love me if it matters to you, but don't ask anything of me. Unlike the absorbent and vibrant entity that is the kibbutz, which both snatches away and bestows, she found the city non-negotiable, repelling all expectations and accusations, putting them back in her arms like her dead husband.

But what stopped you living, what stopped you making new acquaintances, finding new work, after all you weren't that old, it was just your stupid pride; the daughter of kibbutz aristocracy, a queen voluntarily exiled from the far and mysterious North, what does she want with teeming neighbourhoods, young families mainly and their children running up and down the stairwells where the smell of fast cooking hangs, fried sausages, burnt rice, meat cutlets, and their dissipated lives, billeted in cramped apartments above her and beneath her and on all sides.

Why don't you go out now and then? her children used to nag her, you can't go on like this, sitting by the window all day, the landscape isn't going anywhere, you have nothing to watch over, until she started to pretend, and when she heard them coming in she would immediately sit down with the notebook in her lap, the notebook she inherited from her daughter, and now she sits up in alarm, the notebook, she tries to say, don't touch my notebook, as it's suddenly clear to her that she'll never go back there, never again sit by her window, staring at the ridges that mask the towers of Bethlehem, and she sees them coming mournfully into her apartment and rooting through her possessions, opening drawers and closets as if searching for the abstract of their experiences, and how great will be their joy when they suddenly find the old notebook hidden in the linen closet, and how great their disappointment when they open it with an air of reverent awe and find that it's empty.

Yes, this is all that's going to be left behind from her decades on the face of the earth, an empty notebook, since she never dared write one word in it, as this word, the first one, would need to be single and unique, a princess of words the like of which had never been written; this word must embrace all the sounds she heard and the sights she saw and the smells surrounding her, the rustle of the east wind stirring the thicket and the cries of the fish caught in the net, the smell of the papyrus huts of the Arabs on a sunlit day, and the dignity of the herons nesting in the reeds of the marsh, the chatter of the women mending the fishermen's nets with their young fingers, the sound of the cracking of barbel eggs which stick to the stones of the river, the growl of the catfish recumbent on the floor of the lake, lying in wait for the small fry, the eye-catching courtship colours of the males at the start of the spawning season, the grunting of the wild boars, and the smell of the sudden smoke rising from the ground, the sight of the waves broken by the wind and turning on their foam-covered backs, the beauty of the clouds above Mount Hermon which foretell the approach of rain, and the bemusement of the cranes returning in the autumn and not finding the lake. Such a heavy weight she imposed on this one and only word that it sank, plummeting like those metal ingots that were found on the bed of the lake after it was drained, and it seems to her suddenly that maybe now she could try, a last attempt, not to mention a first, without words, just to hold her notebook close to her body, pressing so hard it penetrates beneath her skin, to dry up her milk and her blood. Is this not a sacred obligation, to keep a record while it is still possible, as the sole survivor from the disaster, and she waves her hand at her daughter-in-law, catching sight of her suddenly, some distance away, the notebook, she shouts, bring me my notebook, but Shlomit carries on receding, she's already turned into a tiny dot on the landscape alongside the dwindling lights of the kibbutz, because a storm is brewing, an east wind shakes the boat, yellow water-lilies move about as if life has been breathed into them, their heart-shaped leaves spread on the surface of the water, tens of thousands of green hearts, and the thickets are stirring.

All the children had already gone to their beds that stormy night. She too was dead-tired when her father dragged her to the boat. Are we fishing on a night like this, Daddy? It's so cold and rainy, but he scolded her, don't be such a weakling, Hemda, you think people don't eat in winter? He wrapped her little body in a fisherman's rain-cape, and dragged her after him. There were four men in the boat, one at the oar and one with the net, and she a wet bird in the bows. The wind whistled in their ears as they spread the net on the pitch-black waters, and the marker-corks bobbed in a long line above the surface of the lake. It isn't your turn to sleep yet, her father, the skipper, growled at one of the crewmen, dozing over the oar. Hemda, take over from Yosef for a bit, but rowing was such hard work. Sometimes they rowed two men to an oar, and here she was by herself, her face sweating from the effort despite the cold, while jets of rainwater ran off the cape and under it her limbs were shaking.

The lights of the kibbutz had vanished completely, violet flashes sharp as thorn pierced Mount Hermon and the rain intensified, foaming the surface of the lake, night birds screeching in the distance, and she leaned over the side of the boat and whispered, flee you tilapia, flee you catfish, although she knew that only a net crammed with colourful booty would put a smile on her father's lips, and then perhaps they would return in the last watch to the jetty, singing lustily, God will build this land, God will build Galilee, content to unload the nets, sit in the dining hall and wait for fried fish, and she would grab a slice of bread with jam and run to the school, wet and tired and stinking of fish.

But it's only one of these nights she wants to tell her notebook about now, and about the ringing of the bell, made from an empty gas cylinder with a metal bar for a clapper, a means of informing the fishermen of the night's events on the shore, and that night the bell rang out loudly, telling Yosef of the birth of his first-born son, and Yosef pleaded to be allowed to return to the jetty to see his wife, but her father refused categorically. We can't stopping fishing in mid-shift, he rebuked him, you'll see her in the morning. Yosef obeyed him, clenching his lips, restrained and disciplined man that he was, one of the founder-members of the kibbutz, and that night of all nights the fish outwitted them, and the nets came up as empty as they had been when they were cast.

Fishing is a riddle, said her father as the bell rang again and again, as if again and again the baby were being born, and when they landed in the morning, the empty nets in their hands, they were met on the shore by a group of comrades, bare-headed, who took Yosef by the arm and led him to his tragedy, to his son who lost his mother a few hours after leaving her womb, to the body of the young wife whose life was cut short by a rare post-natal complication, and Hemda wept profusely before the pale face of her father, it's all because of you, she shouted at him, if you'd let him come back perhaps this wouldn't have happened, and her father grabbed her arm and walked quickly to the dining hall, his lips quivering. If only he had shared his pain with her, if only he had said the obvious, I didn't know, I couldn't have known – but instead he snapped at her, you don't stop a job halfway through.

At breakfast he didn't eat anything, just poured himself cup after cup of scalding tea, and she watched him as he walked to his room, swaying slightly, the typical gait of fishermen, whose bodies expect the ground to move, and he was the veteran among them and the oldest of them, he taught them all to fish, everything that he learned from the Arabs in the early years he taught his younger comrades. She didn't go to school that day; shivering from cold and exhaustion she hid among the bushes under his window. If she had heard one sigh she would have gone in and tried to console him, but a heavy silence rose from the room, which remained dark all that day, and in the evening at sunset, when they all accompanied the young mother to her grave, he came out of there and walked to the jetty, without assembling the rest of the fishermen, without taking a basket of food and drink. With a heavy heart she watched his boat receding, doesn't he know how dangerous it is, going out fishing alone at night, has he forgotten the Arab gangs, poachers who lie in wait for unwary fishermen? Daddy, she shouted to him from afar, Daddy, come back, and all night she tossed and turned on her bed, sure she would never see him again, hating him and loving him, overwhelmed by pity and anger. Murderer, she was mumbling, tasting the word with her tongue, murderer, who told you you had to be tougher than God?

At the start she used to watch the orphan child, who grew up before her eyes like a monument under construction, like living testimony to the passage of time, to pain that doesn't pass. She would see Yosef walking with him in the gardens in the afternoon, both of them lean and slightly stooped, a gloomy and isolated pair. How deep is orphanhood, how strong is widowhood; these words that she knew from books absorbed the likeness of these two, and in her imagination her mother would adopt the child to atone for what the father did, and perhaps even she herself, though she was only twelve years old that night, could turn into a mother for little Hanan, named after his mother Hana, because deep in her heart she believed she too deserved a part of the blame – if she hadn't been in the boat perhaps her father would have been less severe. He was so intent on her education, on the personal example he set her, and she was afraid for years that the ghost of Hana was going to pursue her until she too died in the throes of childbirth, that would be justice, but when she held baby Dina in her arms for the first time, it was her father who lay before her, breathless and lifeless.

What kind of a deceptive plot, bereft of forgiveness, is she trying to tell her notebook, disaster following in the wake of disaster. So much had been taken over the years, and it was in the shadow of disaster that they grew up, generations of children on the edge of the lake; is that why they loved it so much? Since time immemorial ominous-sounding surveys had been conducted there. Engineers from the central areas visited them regularly, their faces full of importance as if they were taking part in something big and decisive, and carrying sophisticated measuring gadgets. This had been going on for years, and the children who changed with the years would watch them anxiously, what are you doing with our sea? Are you really going to drain it? But why?

Her father loved to tell her the stories he heard from the Arab fellahin about the giant Nimrod who lived in the high stronghold named after him, Kalaat Nimrod, the biggest fortress built by the Crusaders in the Land of Israel, with his massive physique and heroic persona: at every meal Nimrod devoured mountains of food and diverted a river into his mouth. Seated on the top of the ridge he could stretch out his hand to the sources of the Jordan and draw his water from there, but with his prodigious strength he dared, to his misfortune, to raise himself above Allah and to fight him with his bow and arrows, and Allah dropped blood from Heaven on his arrows, early in the morning and at dusk, and finally he sent to him the tiniest of his creatures, the mosquito, to punish him for his blasphemy, and the mosquito flew up his nose and penetrated his brain.

Every day the mosquito would come out to rest on the knees of the heroic giant and return to its residence in his brain, and Nimrod's eyes were losing their sight, until he became sick of his life and commanded his servants to cut off his head and replace it with a head made of gold, and since then every year a great swarm of mosquitoes has risen from his grave and spread across the marshes of the Hula Valley, and she saw the giant Nimrod in the form of her father, and sometimes when her father was dozing in the bows of the boat in the light of dawn, she was convinced that in his sleep the Arabs had cut off his head and placed a golden head on his shoulders, hence his vicious temper, and the moment his genuine head was returned to him, she would feel his love once again.

Did she ever really feel it? From such an early age she was expected to learn to read the signs of love through harshness and unreasonable demands; of course if he didn't love her he wouldn't have invested so much effort in her education, he wouldn't have laid such expectations on her and he wouldn't have been disappointed by her again and again, no, she's shaking her head now like an angry toddler, the fact is that his love for her mother was something else. Stop it, Hemda, you're upsetting your mother, he used to scold her when she tried to share her troubles with her Mum, even during the war when she'd been wounded in the leg by a piece of shrapnel and was distraught with pain and fear it was the same rebuke: stop it, Hemda, can't you see your mother's crying?

So many species of fish, so many species of love, of pain, of holding on, even now she can't let go, like the male tilapia whose mouth is full of fertilised eggs, his future offspring, and for this reason he can't eat for months on end, so her throat is filled by her father and her mother, and until she can manage to open her gullet and accommodate her offspring, she lays her eggs and gets as far away as she can, and only later does she search for them in the undergrowth, among the boulders, running on the lawns of the kibbutz and shouting, Avni, Avni, where are you?

Between his office and the law courts, between his mother's house – she's returned in the meantime to her bed in the little room facing the window – and his house, between the two boys: the younger one, cheerful and precocious, and his big and clumsy older brother, so like Shlomit, Avner roams the streets in his car, the list of addresses nestling in his pocket, the list that Anati succeeded in getting for him from the vehicles agency with astonishing and heart-warming guile, and the task is proving harder than he expected: in subterranean car parks, at roadsides, in private parking spaces, roofed and exposed, gold-coloured cars have been left, dumb, their seats upholstered in leather or fabric, souvenirs laden with significance, like the first pairs of shoes hanging from mirrors, and they are closed and sealed, their secrets hidden from the eye, and he proceeds slowly along the crowded city streets, holding up the traffic, chasing every flash of gold that dazzles him, accepting with resignation the hoots and the insults. Where are they now, where is their abode, perhaps they came from a different town anyway, perhaps they went back to the hospital, where without knowing it they shared with him a rare moment of beauty and pain that gives him no rest, and at night when he can't sleep he gets out of bed and goes into the children's room; is that man too standing now by his children's beds, in the gathering gloom of the imminent end, sending them into a long life without a father? Is he seeking to be with them now as long as is possible or does he find it hard to endure their presence, wrapped up in his pain, as his own father was, and he imagines him walking at dusk in a big and fragrant garden, among laden fruit trees, golden medlars and plums, and ornamental trees with blossom just starting to fade, a nervous smile on his gaunt features, but why is he so eager to see him again, he can't be his friend any longer, the ways things are, and anyway he hasn't been in the habit of making friends in recent years; it would be more accurate to say, he never was.

He was never that fond of them, of men that is, and these last few years he hasn't even bothered to pretend. Men of his own age depress him, and the younger ones arouse his envy and that depresses him too, and in fact the whole human race is appealing to him less and less, the oppressors and the oppressed alike, and yet despite this he goes on committing himself to these searches, going out of the office when the sun is setting, scouring the streets of the city, he's never explored this city as thoroughly as he does now, in the grip of a gloomy obsession. Since he arrived here in his youth he's had no leisure to get to know the place, too busy adjusting to the humdrum routine, so it became his city without any effort on his part to make its acquaintance; he had no qualms about leaving it to others to ponder its true nature, to attribute intentions and qualities to it, so long as it remained in his eyes an arbitrary collection of streets, his home in one of them and his office in another, the Supreme Court here and the District Court over there, and it's only now that for the first time the details coalesce into some kind of fateful whole that includes him at its centre, into a blurred sense of mission, and although he has nothing to say to this man or to his family he needs to locate him; just at the very time when all the others are hurrying to their homes, to their children and their suppers, he finds himself loitering, turning eastward and passing his mother's house at the moment the light in the window goes on, and he notices the blacker than black head of the new carer who's been assigned to her, popping up and disappearing, and then he passes his sister's house too, paying her an imaginary visit. Is that Nitzan standing there in the lobby, making an animated phone call, her mobile concealed by her flowing locks of hair, so it looks as if she's arguing vociferously with herself? He never warmed to the girl, that small body uttering adult thoughts from such an early age always repelled him, and she for her part never showed any interest in him and his family; his children were a nuisance to her, and it seemed she and her parents had created a kind of closed and exclusive unit which needed no one, least of all him.

Hey, I'm the only uncle you've got, he wanted to say to her sometimes, we're family, although the conversation he was really after wasn't with her but with her mother, I'm the only brother you've got, why do you reject me, what have I done to make you so angry with me, but who has the energy for emotional exchanges, and anyway it seems everything that could be said has already been said to the point of exhaustion, and they won't find new words in middle age, and besides there are always more urgent things to do, like loitering generously outside his own house, giving his family a portion of his time. The shutter to the balcony is closed and yet it seems he can hear his younger child crying so he knows he should turn off the engine and go up to them at once, but his task hasn't been accomplished yet, and perhaps this is the evening it will happen, and anyway his presence won't do them any good at the moment, when all his attention is directed towards something else, something more pressing. He wants to appear before them relaxed, to enjoy them and have them enjoy him, not cause them disappointment when he comes in, especially Tomer, who treats him to looks of resentment and yearning that invariably give him the urge to get out of there at once.

There are people who go home happy, he thinks in wonderment, as if this is the first time the possibility has occurred to him, and he tries to classify his friends and acquaintances, pausing for a moment over his wife: to which category does Shlomit really belong? It's hard to distinguish in her between love and duty, between competitiveness and preference, sometimes it seems to him that her sole motivation is the need to prove to him how superior she is to him; her victory is already assured but she isn't giving up. Again he hears Yotam weeping, who knows what Tomer is doing to him this time, despite the gap between them, nearly ten years, he's consumed by jealousy that intensifies from day to day. Yes, he will leave the car straightaway and go up and take the wailing infant in his arms and caress his sweaty curls; Daddy, Daddy, the little one will whimper, and once again he'll be taken aback, Daddy? He finds it so hard to see himself as father to a baby. This sudden pregnancy and the miracle baby who emerged from it seem to him entirely separate from him, and to the same degree from Shlomit too, she who looks older than her age and when she pushes the pram alongside the young mothers could almost be taken for their mother, and therefore he feels this isn't a case of routine parenthood, but a kind of custodianship of the child which has been entrusted to them, a child who was born too late but fortunately for him doesn't realise it yet, too busy demanding attention to his constant needs.

The party's over, kid, and it wasn't that good to start with, now they're clearing away the disposable tableware, discarding the left-over food, stacking the chairs, and it's out of your hands, kid, you can't put back what's been done. Already the guests have left, the booze has been guzzled, the short-lived jollity has indeed faded, there isn't much left, believe me, for your sake we'll go on pretending, but one day, and it won't be that far away, a bright boy like you will find out for yourself, and then what?

What will happen then, he sighs, turning off the engine and resting his forehead on the wheel, nothing will happen, for a long time now he's stopped believing in external, extreme events, these do happen apparently but not to him. With him it's a case of moderate progress and moderate decline, with no steep gradations on the way, from two interns in his office to one, from courtroom victories to compromises and from there to lost cases, and already he's out of the overheated car, in a moment he'll go in and comfort the little boy, sit for a while with Tomer, help him with his homework, but the door which just a moment ago was locked is opening again with a loud screeching sound, not yet, too early to be swallowed up by their evening routine. He'll be back soon enough and now he'll try again, and maybe tonight it will happen.

How hot it is tonight, and the hours of darkness bring no relief; if he has a garden he's sure to be out there now, sprawled on a chair with all strength exhausted, staring at a moon as slender as a lash falling from the eye. On just such a night his father departed this world, and of course it's obvious that he hasn't seen him since then, and obvious though it is, he still can't come to terms with the notion that in more than twenty years he's had no contact with his father, not that he ever spent much time in his company. What a bitter yearning would rise from his gut in the first years when he remembered him, the reproaches that could be heard as far away as the mountains, why did he upset him so much? Apparently, they were two lions, one young and the other fully grown, but in fact they were more like sheep lost in arid wastes, in a neighbourhood under construction on the edge of the desert, generating housing projects as sharp as teeth, disfiguring the ridges. Unlike his father, he doesn't give his children a hard time, he never shouts, preferring to retreat before some truth escapes from his mouth, something that can't be taken back, to go away as he is doing now, leaving Shlomit alone for yet another evening, and he's swallowed up by the traffic streaming westward as if that's where he lives, to the estate that was once a small village and still has only tenuous contact with the city; it seems to be hiding from it in a graceful sort of way, with its charming and colourful houses, resisting annexation.

For years he's been trying to convince Shlomit of the advantages of moving here, especially after the second child was born and their house became cramped, but she has always been vehemently opposed to the idea: it's too far, she can't cope with all the travelling, it's hard enough the way things are now, she complains, as if it's his fault, and she may have a point there; while he's in the office until late in the evening she's the one who has to do the fetching and carrying, but there's something offensively self-righteous and spiky about the way she states her case. It always seems to him a vital ingredient is missing from her sanctimonious assertions, precisely the ingredient that would induce him to listen to her, rather than just hear her. What a shame she doesn't want to live here, because now as he's descending into the throbbing heart of the little settlement, he's filled with nostalgia for a forgotten youth, guiding his car slowly along narrow and twisting lanes, the way he used to ride on a little donkey, looking in the darkness for a home that would suit him, and in time, or perhaps the very next morning, he won't remember which he saw first, the gold-coloured car parked in a private space or the bereavement notice which had been pinned up on the gatepost two days earlier, presumably, since the funeral took place yesterday, the funeral of Rafael Allon, buried in the Mount of Repose cemetery, before the grieving eyes of his parents Yehoshua and Miriam, his wife Elisheva and children Ya'ara and Absalom, whose names are picked out in black under his name, and he steps out of the car with quaking knees and stands before the notice repeating the name again and again in an awestruck tone: May your memory be blessed, Rafael Allon, rest in peace, Rafael Allon. Black on white I take my leave of you before I even got to know you, and it seems to me now I haven't missed a bigger opportunity than this in a lifetime of missed opportunities, as I missed out on a father and missed out on love, and coming face to face with your explicit name my heart aches, and he peers around him to be sure there's no one there, and then he stretches out a hand and caresses the name of the deceased, the names of his widow and his orphans, and at the end of the list of mourners he adds in transparent letters, in the secret code of hot and sweaty skin, his own name, Avner Horowitz.

When he hears women's voices, muffled syllables approaching the gate, he hurries to find refuge in his car, turning on the radio and pretending to be holding a conversation on his redundant mobile, his heart thumping painfully. From the radio speakers scrawny arms of sorrow are held out to him, like the arms of the man who has now acquired a name, at the very moment of losing his life, Rafael Allon, how lean he was and at the same time, how much weight was carried by his presence, and he angrily probes his own arms, crushing the viscous flesh. In his childhood he used to pinch himself until his eyes filled with tears and his skin was covered in livid blue fingermarks, and when his mother saw the lesions and exclaimed in horror he would claim that other boys had done this to him, but he refused to betray their names, and now he finds himself groaning as if the sounds penetrating the void of the car are trying to subdue him. How are the beloved snatched from the bosoms of those who love them most, what a cruel parade is mounted every moment while you are busy with your own concerns, trying to control the minutest of details. Look, people are leaving and passing by your window, two women of indeterminate age, evidently just friends of hers, of the widow Elisheva, and already their car is leaving the place, the beam of its lights exposing you for a moment, and moving on. Poor Elisheva, they will surely be saying, how is she going to cope without him, how well she cared for him, and the children still so young, how sad, and he imagines her sitting among the mourners, erect and elegant, more beautiful than all her friends, does she wipe away a tear with the hem of her blouse, exposing for a moment the smooth skin of her midriff, and he's so eager to see her again he gets out of the car and tries to move round to the side of the house, to catch the voices behind the impervious gate.

From a garden nearby the barking of dogs is heard, or perhaps from their garden; in estates like this one it's impossible to feel safe without a dog, and you can't feel safe with all these dogs running around, perhaps their overcrowded suburb is preferable after all, and again you're caught in the lights of a car and you pretend to be hurrying up the street. On your left is a dark wadi with a smell of rapid decomposition rising from it, the smell of vegetation defeated by the sun, almost as sharp as the scent of blossom that wafts in the wadi during the short-lived spring.

Standing behind a slender pomegranate tree he peers at the new mourners getting out of their car, a young group, friends of the children apparently, and one of them weeping bitterly; is she the daughter's best friend? From far away he hears the hum of the city but the wadi is deep and appealing and it seems to him that different rules apply in there, and he approaches the edge and sits down on a warm slab of rock, the tides of grief shattering on his back, and he shakes, hiding his face in his hands and sighing a bitter sigh.

What a tragedy, not yet fifty years old, he hears a voice behind him and for a moment it seems to him he's the one being talked about, and he turns to face a heavy-bodied woman, her red-dyed hair fading and dishevelled, wearing a broad tunic over tight leggings and carrying a dog-lead, and she half-asks, half-declares, you're from the faculty too, and when he nods hesitantly she asks, have you just come out of there?

No, I'll go there some other time, he mutters, I'm not close enough to the family to go in on the first day, and she says, this isn't the first day, the funeral was delayed because it took some time locating the son in South America, and Avner can't conceal his surprise. Really? So when did he pass away? And she says, exactly a week ago, last Monday, don't they keep you informed in the faculty?

No, I've only just come back from abroad, I wasn't here, he says hurriedly, while struggling to digest the new information. It was last Monday that he saw them, did he breathe his last that very day, or perhaps it's a different man altogether, even if their cars are identical? The city is big and crowded and full of dead people. If you're finding this hard I can go in with you, she's quick to offer. I come here every day, bringing cake or a pastry, today I haven't had time yet. She lets out a loud whistle and a black dog, resembling an overgrown jackal, comes running out of the wadi. He bares his teeth at Avner, who stands his ground, though with some trepidation.

It's all right, Casanova, calm down the pair of you, she grins while fastening the lead to the collar, as if they were dim-witted brothers locked in combat. He means no harm, and nor do you, I hope, *yalla*, let's go, and Avner is taken aback by her mannerisms; she was definitely born on a kibbutz, reminding him a little of his wife with her unmediated brusqueness. It's as if she has him too on a lead; passing by his car he knows he could still extricate herself from her grasp, mutter a word of thanks and get out of here before he's rumbled, but he waits beside her obediently until the gate is opened, adjusting his appearance, tucking his shirt-tails into his trousers, smoothing his hair, what if she recognises him? What will he say to her, how can he explain his presence? A spasm of embarrassment grips him as he follows the red-haired neighbour and her dog along the narrow driveway, fringed by flowering jasmine bushes with their strong, sweet and intoxicating scent.

But perhaps all this is about someone else entirely, another family, perhaps that man is still alive, saved by the power of the love that he gives and is given in return, after all she said to him quite plainly, soon you'll be feeling better, and already he's concentrating on a vivid hope, but in the crowded lounge he immediately sees the portrait of the deceased on the table, and recognises the delicate smile, which confirms for him that he's come to the right place, his grief is appropriate.

It had happened that very day apparently, on his last day he saw him, a dance without movement, a song without sound, and all his frantic scrabbling around the city with the object of seeing him again happened after his death, and he leans against the wall and lets his neighbour remove her protection from him, immersed as she is in animated conversation with a diminutive woman, her hair close-cropped and carrot-coloured, a hard set to her features, square and tired. He looks around him and searches for her, the elegant profile, the pale face framed by black hair, don't worry, soon you'll be feeling better, she promised him, was she referring to his imminent death, and he definitely heard the promise and it was he who shared their last hours with them, a chance witness to their love, and was it really chance?

When he doesn't spot her he glances at the upper floor, perhaps she went to lie down for a bit. His glance moves up the stairs which presumably lead to the bedrooms, lingering on the floor with its trim of soft pastel colours, and goes back to scouring the lounge, the light sofas, the big window overlooking the garden, daring to inspect the assembled company, all gathering together in groups, most of them around his own age, just so long as no one recognises him. His glance passes again over the face of the neighbour, and immediately drops down, but she's already remembered him, to his dismay. I've brought you a foundling, Elisheva, she jokes and points to him. He's from the faculty. He was hanging around outside, too scared to come in, and he finds himself, his mind in a whirl, moving forward and extending his hand and mumbling words of condolence in the ears of the widow who has just lost her husband and who bears absolutely no resemblance to the woman he saw beside the deceased exactly one week ago, in his last hours, and he knows his face is flushing bright red as if he is the one lying to her, and lying is precisely what he's doing now, claiming brief acquaintance at some international conference, and then he drops her hand as if talking is too much of an ordeal for him, and slips out into the corridor. Much to his relief the bell rings again, and a great tide of mourners comes streaming in, and already the widow is hearing the sincere condolences of others, the ones who genuinely and innocently knew her husband, unlike him, although in a sense, he thinks as he's groping for the way out, he knew him better than all of them.

As he walks to his car it seems to him the black jackal is stalking him with teeth bared and he quickens his pace, having difficulty recognising his own among all the cars that have arrived in the meantime, and when he finally spots it he fumbles for his keys. They were in the pocket of his trousers, or perhaps he left them on the boulder at the edge of the wadi, he hurries there and for a moment the wadi is lit up by the lights of a car, which passes by the house of mourning but doesn't stop, and he stares in bemusement as it seems to him he recognises the restrained, aristocratic profile, but she keeps on going, where to exactly? Does this track connect with the main road? And again he's scrabbling anxiously in his pockets; his fingers find a small hole in the side of one of them, could the keys have fallen through it, without him noticing? Only the switched-off mobile is there, inspiring a little confidence, and he contacts the taxi firm, and gives the address of the house, but walks down the road, not wanting to come across that woman and her dog again, and already he isn't sure which of them he's more afraid of; in fact in his eyes they have fused into a single entity, a gigantic red-haired and slovenly jackal with the woman's raucous voice emerging from his throat.

More cars climb up the narrow ascent, so narrow that if a car comes in the opposite direction, one of them will be forced off the road and into the wadi, and when he nervously scans the new arrivals it seems that in every car the driver is a woman with elegant profile and black hair, and he strains his eyes but to no avail, since the next lights he sees belong to the taxi that's coming to get him out of here, and he takes his seat in silence in the back, agitated and sweaty and unaware of the questioning glance of the driver. Where to? he asks and Avner hurriedly gives his address and then changes his mind, what's the point of going home just to pick up the spare keys and come straight back here. The children will be disappointed and Shlomit will attack him as if all his actions are designed to hurt them, and her in particular, and Anati has a set of keys too, just to be on the safe side, and he contacts her, trying to adopt a casual tone.

Are you at home, Anati? Do you still have my car keys? So I'll drop round and pick them up, OK? I lost mine. Remind me of your address, that's fine, it's right on our way, but in the silence that prevails after this, he hears again and again the words that came from his mouth, as strident as the voices that come crackling from the taxi's radio-phone, and it seems to him that a secret and extensive network is listening in to his words, deciphering their secrets, and the network has been joined both by the late Rafael Allon and by his living lover who mourns for him in secret, and now he too, in an almost haphazard phone conversation, has tied his destiny to their destiny, in a thoroughly arbitrary but well thought-out sequence, presided over, as always in fact and almost without her knowledge, by his mother, who can no longer tell the difference between left and right, past and present, in what is left of her dying consciousness.

Wait for me here for two minutes, I'll be back straightaway, he tells the driver, who has pulled up outside an elongated housing development somewhat resembling a train, and he wanders among the entrances; where do the numbers start from, that's always the question, especially when you're in the middle and don't know which way to turn. Are you actually retreating when you think you're advancing, or is it vice versa? Once he lived with Shlomit in a similar project not far from here, and he remembers that even then he used to come home embittered, identifying her with the ugly building and the filthy staircases, even then she was bound up in his consciousness with the anger of lost opportunity, although they were still at the beginning of their lives together, with the option of multiple changes of apartment, and multiple changes of partner. Why was he so quick to commit himself, and by the same token, why so quick to lament the loss of his life, after all the two of them were younger then than the girl who opens the door to him now in the full bloom of her clumsy maidenhood.

For the first time he sees her body without the carapace of the stiff office clothes that she makes a point of wearing, in a red cotton dress speckled with black dots, giving her the appearance of a massive beetle, and it seems that without the harness of her tight garments her body is spreading out in all directions, doubling its bulk with every movement, and she greets him with an apologetic smile, I was just about to contact you, I can't find them, I'm sure they're here but I've no idea where.

That's not so bad, I'll help you search, he says hurriedly, noticing the red moistness around her eyes and eager to reassure her, but when he follows her to her room he's taken aback; never in his life has he seen such disorder: piles of clothes on the floor, shoes, books, papers, and he scans the room in utter perplexity, there's underwear scattered around too, knickers, bras, tampons, a riotous glut of bodily references devoid of any modesty but also devoid of eroticism, and she's quite unabashed, trampling on clothes and other stuff with her bare feet, rummaging among them and tossing them around her, as if the bundle of keys is likely to be found in the cup of a bra or the toe of a sock, and as he's wondering how he can really be of any assistance to her, should he be picking up clothes too and throwing them in all directions, hooting is heard from the street, and he remembers the taxi that's waiting for him out there. The two minutes are up, and he knows he should say to her, leave it, it doesn't matter, I'll pick up my spare keys from home, and this is indeed what he says as he's dashing down the stairs, but instead of opening the door of the taxi and getting in, despite all his desires and inclinations, and giving his address, he goes to the driver's window and pays and doesn't even wait for change, but runs back into the building and pounds up the stairs, panting when he reaches the door, which is still open. The driver's already gone, he gasps with the last of his breath, he didn't wait for me, and she straightens up, looking him in the face and blushing. Has his transparent lie caused her to blush, or is it a transparent lie of her own, as she's now holding out her closed fist to him in a childish gesture. I've found them, she announces.

To push her gently until she stumbles and sprawls on a heap of clothes with her spongy flesh, her dress pulled up to reveal simple cotton underwear, her eyes closed, eager to give satisfaction, he's not the one she was waiting for but still, he's here, to fasten his lips on the strong shoulders, on the heavy breast whose slightly lugubrious profile is clearly visible through the speckled fabric. To strip off her blouse, he's ready for that too, also to rub his skin against her skin, his age against her age, his grief against her youth, he wants to wallow in her body parts until they comfort him; her lips will comfort his lips, her fingers his fingers, her bones his bones, since it seems he's trapped in the void that the deceased left behind while he was still alive and he doesn't know how to get out of it, the void to which jasmine bushes lead the way with their sweet and heavy and intoxicating scent, this void which like birth and death cannot be apprehended, as if he's been bewitched by the deceased in his last moments, and only a counter-spell can save him, and only if he's comforted can he comfort others, the widow and her children and especially the lover who has no one to comfort her, and the desire is so strong that he has to cling with all his strength to the wooden doorpost lest he be swept towards her on a raging tide, because between him and her stand blocks of air as solid and motionless as corpses, planted in the floor, and if he approaches her he will be forced to push them aside too, Shlomit and the boys and even her, the secret lover.

So many times this has almost happened to him and at the last moment he's grabbed the lintel, or the handle of the door, or his briefcase; any substantial object symbolised in that moment the stable life standing in the way of ruin, it seemed the slightest movement would bring about total collapse, and he takes the car keys from her hand. Any chance of a glass of water? he asks with parched throat, it's terribly hot outside, and she hurries to the kitchen; did he really perceive disappointment in her face, what does she want, what does she want from him? The glass isn't clean but he represses his distaste and drinks, naturally at home he would have rinsed it again and again; why is it that he, who takes cleanliness so seriously, is always coming up against women to whom that kind of pedantry is anathema, and he hands her the empty glass. Thanks, he says, I must be going, but to his surprise she urges him to stay. Like a beer? she offers, looking suddenly like a little girl afraid of being left alone in the house.

A beer? he asks as if she's suggesting something exceptional, OK, if you're having one too. He glances into the fridge which she's opened and which looks to be in surprisingly good order, sits down at the kitchen table and wipes sweat from his brow. The sun which set some time ago is still attacking the roof of the apartment on the upper floor, its rays penetrating through the thin concrete and fixing on his forehead, and she puts a bottle in front of him and sits down, and again he notices the redness of her eyes, as if she was weeping bitterly before his arrival, and he asks, are you all right, has something happened?

He really doesn't know much about her, she only came to his office two months ago, after taking her degree with distinction, intent on specialising in human rights cases, although she's had offers from much bigger practices. With clients she's compassionate but practical and in her free time she joins every demonstration going, all instances of injustice and iniquity get her adrenalin flowing, and now as she smiles awkwardly he notices for the first time that her front teeth are remarkably small, giving her smile a somewhat frugal look.

I'm just a bit confused today, she says, her voice becoming almost childlike, I wanted to give you something, and when she rises and leaves the kitchen he imagines she'll be leaning over the piles of junk in her room, which suddenly seem to have a kind of charm for him in their absolute freedom, something not at all perceptible in her movements, but she comes back at once and hands him an envelope. This just came today from the printer, she says, you're the first, and he opens it and takes out a sheet of stiff brown paper, printed with simple letters, a few letters, some names, a date, a place, and he's so surprised his brain can't cope with what's written there, and it's hardest of all to figure out what it has to do with her.

What is this, who's getting married, are you getting married? he asks, almost in shock, and she nods joylessly. It came today from the printer, she repeats, as if this will account for her gloom, and he recovers enough of his composure to say, Congratulations, Anati, that's wonderful news! He wonders if he should shake her hand or embrace her, and as he's sitting and she's standing before him either of these actions would seem a little strange, so he examines the invitation again, and notices the single name under her name, the parents of the bride amount to just one father, whereas the groom comes equipped with both parents, as required, and already he's concentrating on this detail and the painful imbalance it will create, marring the entire event. What happened to your mother? he asks, remembering how assiduous she had been in asking after the health of his mother when she was in hospital, and she says, she died when I was eight years old. She sits down facing him and wipes her eyes. I don't know what's happening to me, when I saw the invitation I was so flustered, suddenly I realised it was sort of for real.

Sort of for real? He's astonished by this style of speech, whish isn't typical of her, and she says, not sort of, actually for real, on the twentieth of August, Anat and Lior, but this Anat is me, and suddenly I'm no longer sure she really should marry Lior, because perhaps it's too soon and perhaps she doesn't love him enough and perhaps she hasn't loved enough yet in her life. Do you always talk about yourself in the third person? he asks, fixated as usual on the style rather than the substance, and she blushes, only when I'm alone she says, it started after my mother died, and I'd tell her all night about her daughter, I got used to it, and she takes a thirsty gulp of beer, like a kindergarten child drinking chocolate and Avner sighs, it seems no one ever loves enough, how long have you been together?

Four years now, he's my first boyfriend, she says, and I was the one who put pressure on him to marry, how strange it is, the way things change, but since we decided it's been closed as far as he's concerned, and suddenly for me it's open. How do people know what is the right thing to do? She turns her wide eyes to him, full of tense enquiry, and he grins, that's the question of questions, Anati, but there it is, we don't know, aside from a few lucky people who see everything clearly.

The invitation still in his hand, he creases the edges of it distractedly, how do people know what is the right thing to do? Does he have any role in her life at this moment, should he be warning her? And he mutters hurriedly, as if he fears he's going to say the wrong thing, listen, I married my first girlfriend and all my life I've regretted this, although I've taken no steps towards freeing myself from this marriage, and although obviously there's no knowing how a different life would have worked out. Of course, this doesn't teach you anything about your life, he's quick to point out, you can't draw a conclusion on the basis of another's experience, but if you're not sure then wait, sometimes it's worth waiting for love, even if it comes when you're already at death's door; when I was with my mother in the hospital I saw love, and it's a sight you don't forget. His hands, feverish from the confession, fiddle with the cardboard as the phone rings and she gets up to answer it, and he's surprised to hear how cold her voice is, I told you before, I want to be alone today, that's enough, Lior, stop pressurising me, and Avner perks up quickly as if the words were addressed to him. I must go, they're waiting for me at home, he says to her as she goes back to standing at the kitchen door, we'll meet tomorrow in the office, he adds almost sadly, because for a moment he finds himself hoping he'll never see her again, never see her and the agonising question on her face, what's the right thing to do, and as he leaves the building, the car keys in his torn pocket, he crushes the invitation and throws it in the overflowing bin, with its garland of little bushes of garbage.

Chapter Five

It isn't a matter of contemplation and cogitation, deciding who was in the right, she repeats, it's determined by history. It was reality that left no room for doubt. The critical hour of the expulsions drew a distinction between the traditional way of adherence to the God of Israel, in defiance of rigid official decrees, and the spiritual-philosophical way of life that led towards change of religion. The question that has been debated incessantly since the twelfth century – whether it is permitted to dabble in extra-Judaic philosophies – was resolved not by reference to the precepts of the Talmud but on the basis of personal choice. In the opinion of the sages of the expulsion generation, this choice clearly proved who was sketching out a way of life and thought that had status in Judaism, such that Judaism could exist within it, and who was showing the way towards betrayal of faith and loss of identity – but a guttural sound like the cooing of a dove interrupts the flow that is so familiar to her; year after year she's been trying to infect them with her enthusiasm, with steadily diminishing success. Is she to blame for this, or are successive generations losing interest?

Any questions so far? She turns to face the class, noticing one of the students who sits beside the window, the sunlight flooding her face and a tiny baby at her breast, making rhythmic gurgling sounds. Usually they ask her permission, and usually she doesn't object. Congratulations, Abigail, she says caustically, only just born and already he needs to know about the Spanish expulsions? Irritation flushes her face and she continues her lecture in a severe tone as if trying to scare him off, there were two sides to the crisis created by the expulsions, the crisis of those who were expelled and the crisis of those who weren't expelled. In the last years of the fifteenth century these two were combined into one deep crisis, which undermined the self-perception of Judaism as it had prevailed in Spain for hundreds of years, and demanded new solutions. Her eyes are fixed on the spectacle and the pain is thumping between her ribs: one body with two heads, one small and one large, each nourishing the other, a sight simultaneously wondrous and monstrous. The dark shadow of the nipple as it slips from the infant's mouth, the sheer delight on his mother's face, the cooing and gurgling sounds emanating from the tiny body as it fills up with milk, all these things rekindle her wrath at the young student who isn't concentrating as he should, and his mother, who is subjecting her to an unbearable experience, presenting her with sights and sounds which like the act of love itself are not appropriate in public places.

Abigail, I'm sorry, this crying is a distraction for all of us, she hears herself saying, perhaps you should make other arrangements for lectures, and Abigail starts as if she's been plucked from sleep. But he isn't crying! she protests, her lips quivering in resentment, and Dina declares, of course he's crying, it's impossible to teach like this, all these noises are upsetting our concentration. Impatiently she watches the movements of the student as she gathers up her belongings and leaves with the baby in her arms. He utters a loud valedictory cry, and Dina smiles at the remainder of the class. I'm sorry, usually I have no problem with this but today it's been really annoying, don't you think?

It seems she will wait in vain for their endorsement; how transparent she must be in their eyes, a desiccated woman on the verge of the menopause expelling a young and fertile mother from her class. In the aftermath of the expulsion there was a boost to the Messianic principle in Jewish belief, she goes on to say, not only survival of the soul but also earthly redemption of the body, ingathering of the exiles and resurrection of the dead, all of these became values of immediate significance, and a tight connection was forged between awareness of destruction and hopes for salvation. Abigail's empty chair rears up before her, flooded in sunlight, and is that a dummy that's been left in the corner of the seat, perhaps she'll pick it up after class and hide it in her pocket, confiscate it to teach the girl a lesson, but what will her students think of her, even the way things are now they're looking at her suspiciously, and she cuts the session short a little ahead of time and escapes to the staff room, hoping to meet Naomi there, and sure enough here she is, poring over an open Bible and making notes in an exercise-book.

What are you still looking for there? she smiles at her, you must know it all by heart, and Naomi raises tired eyes to her, dark bags hanging under them, I wish, it's been years since I taught this story and I don't remember it at all. What story? Dina asks, filling a cup with cold water, and Naomi says, Hannah and Samuel, I forgot just how shocking it is, how could anyone give up a child like that, especially after she wanted him so much? And Dina listens without much interest, here's another shocking story for you, she says, just now I threw a student out of my classroom because she brought a baby with her to the lecture.

You have the right to do that, it bothers me too if babies cry, Naomi says, and Dina confesses in a whisper, so her colleagues won't overhear, but that's just it, he wasn't crying, it was out of jealousy I expelled her from the room, don't you get it? I couldn't bear to see this, and Naomi lays a hand on her arm, oy, Dini, what have you got to be jealous about? This baby will abandon her in the end too, even if you have ten children you'll be left alone in the end, believe me.

Thanks, but that isn't quite the point, she sighs and sits down facing her, there's a difference between a large and a small family, there's a difference between being left alone at the age of forty-five and at the age of sixty-five, and Naomi says, of course there's a difference, but not a substantial one, and perhaps it's even healthier to get your life back at an early age and not at the last moment, look at me, by the time my brood grows up and leaves the house I'll be an old woman.

The later the better, Dina insists, wiping the sweat from her face with a paper hanky, you don't know what it's like when you want to give and you have no one to give to, when suddenly no one needs you. Not long ago I heard about a woman who killed herself because of a mid-life crisis, and I really understand her.

Take it easy, really, you're exaggerating so much, Naomi scolds her. Gideon needs you in his own way and you can be sure Nitzan does too. She's barely sixteen, you're taking too much notice of the faces she puts on, and Dina grimaces, what faces? I've hardly seen her in ages, her life is completely full, and I've no idea what's happening to her, she doesn't tell me anything.

Fine, so she's a typical adolescent, Naomi declares, but it doesn't mean she doesn't need you, you've just been shifted a little to the side, that's the whole story, she says, moving the Bible and the exercise-book apart by way of demonstration, and Dina says, I know all about that, and I've come to terms with it, I just can't forgive myself for not having another child, if I was like you and I had a young child like your Ro'i in the house, everything would look different.

What's going to become of you, you're already sounding like Hannah praying for a son, Naomi smiles. Perhaps your prayers will be answered too, but look what a price she paid, she takes a quick gulp of her coffee and gathers up her possessions, we'd better move, we're already late, aren't we? And Dina says, I've finished for today, I've had two hours of tuition cancelled, my class is ahead of schedule, and Naomi draws her close and into a sweaty embrace. Don't be upset, Dini, apparently you didn't want it enough, and you can't judge things from a perspective of hindsight, just look at the advantages. I live in a madhouse, nothing but chaos and quarrelling all the time, and you have a quiet life, that's not a small thing.

But I'm not looking for a quiet life, she protests, and watches her friend as she enters the classroom she just vacated, small and dumpy as a she-bear, and her four children are the same and so is her husband, a family of bears Nitzan used to call them derisively. What, are they having another cub? She was surprised when Naomi got herself pregnant again, four years ago, haven't they ever tired of making cubs? Of course they all look exactly the same. How lucky I am to be an only daughter, she used to declare now and then, it's more fun this way. If I get bored I can invite a friend round, and if I get tired of company I can be alone, and I have Mummikins all to myself, I can nestle against her and purr like a kitten.

Yes, that's the way things looked, and she mustn't forget, different rules applied in their small family in those days, this was separate territory, independent and proud; from their superior vantage point they looked down on the uncouth behaviour of other families, bowed down under the burden of complaints and quarrels. I'm enjoying bringing up Nitzan more than Naomi is enjoying all four of her offspring, she used to remind herself repeatedly, I have time for her, I have patience, I can give her so much, without feeling guilty for neglecting another child, and for Gideon this was definitely enough, his needs were modest, as was his talent, and it didn't occur to her that all this was bound to change, nor did it occur to her that this equable state of hers depended on the assumption that she still could, if she only wanted to, bring another child into the world, but all at once, within less than a year, like a war breaking out on several fronts simultaneously, Nitzan moved away as if they had never snuggled up together in a fluffy blanket of intimacy, and instead of the warmth that the girl had bestowed on her all those years, her body was attacked by ferocious waves of heat, accompanied by bouts of giddiness that brought her close to fainting, and as she was knocking, cluelessly, on the doors of Gideon's heart and on the doors of the fertility clinics, it became clear to her beyond any doubt that her prospects of once more attaining that harmonious fusion were nil; she would never regain the holy spark that she saw in the face of her student, that aroused her to anger and pain.

On leaving the college car park she sees her waiting at the bus-stop, still ungainly in the aftermath of pregnancy, holding with an unpractised hand a pram, a briefcase and a baby, and an extra blanket draped over her arm, and she pulls up, somewhat shamefaced, just short of the stop. Like a lift, Abigail? Come with me and I can take you wherever you need to be, I have time, but her student shakes her head, there's no need, my bus will be here in a moment, and Dina tries again, I'm sorry, it was upsetting my concentration, even if he wasn't actually crying, and Abigail clutches the baby to her breast. No problem, she says, forgiving her loftily, I won't bring him into class again.

But even when forgiven she can't let it go, feeling an obligation to accommodate the mother and baby if only for a short time in the void of the enclosed car, holding them prisoner. Let me make it up to you, she flashes her a smile and Abigail gives in finally, loading her heavy and copious gear in the boot, as if she were a refugee fleeing from a war zone.

With the baby asleep in her arms she sits down in the back and fiddles with the safety belts, and Dina watches her in the mirror while putting on speed, hypnotised by the clumsy movements, the neglect and the slovenliness, how well groomed she was just a few months ago, with fitted clothes and high heels, but now she's many times more beautiful, because there's a higher purpose to all her actions: when she eats her eating is designed to satisfy her baby, and when she sleeps her sleep is for the benefit of her baby, and this purpose, which has been gradually eroded over the years, will any substitute ever be found for it?

Where do you live? she asks, in fact ready to take her anywhere just to draw into herself this agonising experience; previously she couldn't endure it and now she can't endure the idea of separation from it. No problem, my mother lives there, and I was going to visit her today anyway, she says hurriedly, secretly despising herself. Why not be her driver, offer her your services as a nanny, and not only her, you should put up a sign in the street, responsible and experienced childminder, academic with a doctorate, almost, college lecturer, a glittering career awaits you, and as she drives down the streets with their sparse traffic, scraped by the noonday sun, watching her prisoner in the mirror, her face radiant and her breasts full and the baby asleep in her arms, an idea comes into her head, cruel but not without appeal, how she will rid herself of the young mother, throw her out of the car in the middle of the desert and be left alone with the baby, surprise the others when they come home, new baby, new life. Nitzan will coo around him in great excitement, extending warm and emotional contact to her as well, and Gideon will smile his restrained smile and raise the camera that's a permanent fixture on his chest, and they'll be so close together one kiss will be enough, and she shakes her head again and again, trying to dislodge the hum of the malign fantasy. Yes, in a corner of the mirror happiness dwells, unbearably close and distant, and she doesn't dare address it with words; what will she say to the young mother, saturated as she is in that sublime state of individuality and unity, will she ask how old the baby is, and what is his name, and how does he sleep at night? A croak of envy will escape from her throat if she opens her mouth, and how paltry are these minor details which will be forgotten anyway, does she remember the precise history of Nitzan's infancy? Only their love, when it was born and when it expired.

The lids are covering her eyes, and soon drowsiness will overtake her, it seems the baby doesn't sleep that well at night after all, this is the time to pick up speed, the desert is close by and the heat is blazing. Left at the next corner, Abigail says in a small voice, and Dina clamps her lips, feeling cheated as she stops outside the crowded apartment block, only recently built and already showing signs of decay, and she gets out, pulls the pram from the boot, like a genuine taxi driver, and hands her the rest of the gear. Thanks very much, really, Abigail says, and where did you say your mother lives? A last attempt at striking up a conversation with her unpredictable teacher, and Dina mutters, not far from here, and drives away abruptly, leaving her standing at the side of the road, watching the car receding with a grateful expression. She has no idea of the danger she has been spared.

Everyone gets the baby he deserves, she smiles bitterly into the broad face of her mother; from under the pale shadow of the brows red eyes peep out like open wounds. Shall I cradle you in my arms, mother dearest, tickle your tummy, stick a dummy in your mouth, cover you with a blanket and leave the room on tiptoe, returning very quietly a few minutes later to watch you sleeping? How can it be that you're the only one left to me, you never were mine and anyway you're only the relic of a person. A twitch of a smile appears on the clenched lips and it seems to Dina that her mother, immersed in one of her fantasies, isn't even trying to hide her malicious joy. All these years she has looked askance at her devotion to Nitzan, as if it was all aimed at her, with the object of showing her: you see, this is how you bring up a daughter, this is how you love a daughter, and how happy she will be to discover that her self-righteous daughter has gone off the rails too, even though she doesn't know exactly how. And now the carer has taken advantage of Dina's arrival to go shopping; she's entrusted her into her hands as if her hands were the safest.

How naïve Rachela must be, thinking I can be relied on, she chuckles, there's no person in the world who's angrier with her than I am. Any intruder getting into her miserable apartment to hunt for ornaments or money to buy drugs would be more merciful to her than I would, but I suppose she is safe after all, because she has nothing that I want to steal.

Again a smile rises to her mother's lips, an almost pleading smile which ratchets up the tension, and she rolls up the shutter; a strong southern light dominates the room, and she shakes the old woman's shoulder. Mum, wake up, she urges her, you'll have plenty of time to sleep afterwards, I need to ask you something, since it seems to her suddenly this is her last opportunity, as lucidity is rapidly fading, perhaps now her luck will hold. The sight of her face, locked into sleep, reminds her how she once came to her parents' room at the regular visiting time and found her in her bed, and she was so unaccustomed to seeing her asleep she thought she was dead, and shook her tearfully. Mum, you're alive, you're alive, she shouted in her ear, and Hemda opened astonished eyes and shouted back at her, of course I'm alive, why are you making such a fuss? I've got a touch of flu, that's all, and Dina was pushed away, chastened, from under the blanket. How strange and rare was the physical contact, and she remembers how little by little her mother's aversion towards her seeped into her consciousness. This was a faint physical sensation of unwillingness that she was unable to hide, although she put an arm around her, and Dina was filled with compassion for her mother, being forced to endure her company, and sometimes it seems to her she feels this echo breaking out from Gideon's body under the blanket, and she turns her back to him and cringes as if she's been hit.

In the light that floods the room, her mother's withered features look like dried fruit, windfalls from the tree, stained and cracked, but her vision is clearing and Dina sits by her bed solicitously. Are you all right, Mum? she asks with a strange intonation, lifting the blanket and climbing into the bed that was once hers, in the room that was once hers, huddled as before beside the body that has diminished beyond recognition. Mummikins, she whispers, do you remember Nitzan used to call me that? Perhaps you'd like to have this nickname too. I need help, Mum, she clutches at the body that exudes warmth, low but steady, as indifferent as a corpse and yet alive, I'm so lonely, this must be the way you felt when Dad died and we left the house; Gideon isn't dead and Nitzan hasn't moved out, but still I'm left alone. You were right and I was wrong. I should have had another baby and now it's too late. I know there are worse troubles than this, but I feel my life is over, and cautiously she moves her mother's arm and places it under the nape of her neck in a forced embrace.

Do you hear me, Mum, I want to hurry away to the kindergarten now to pick up my little boy, I want to see the happiness in his face when I come in, I want to hug him and take him to the zoo, I want to play with him and read him stories. You see, I have so much to give him, I have time and I have patience and I have love but I don't have a little boy, and I see him in the form of the child who was nearly born to me, Nitzan's twin brother, I see him so clearly, and all this time that she's pressed against her mother she avoids looking into her face lest she be repelled by a stray smile, a flat look, and so when her voice is suddenly heard she's startled, as if a third, external party has joined them, so accustomed is she to the silence of the old woman, who mumbles something indistinct, sounding like, you will find the child.

What did you say? She turns over on her stomach and moves her face closer to her mother's, despite the rank smell of the breath that she's exhaling, what child? How will I find him? He died in my womb after all, and again the voice is heard, you'll find yourself a child, but her eyes have already closed, and there's no knowing if the words were directed at her, or perhaps this was a random interlocking of their consciousnesses; ever since her return from the hospital her mother has been asleep most of the time, and hardly responding to anything, and it seems she's stopped recognising her children, although there are moments when a look of acute discontent appears on her face, apparently directed at them.

Mum, explain to me what you meant, she urges her, how shall I find him, where do you find children? But a sound of snoring trills from her throat and Dina lays her head on the pillow beside her. When Gideon snores her sleep is disrupted for hours, but her mother's snoring is somehow comforting, a last symbol of the life that still remains in her. You know, Mum, I'm so cold now that even your meagre warmth is comforting, she whispers in her big ears, the ears of an elderly elephant hanging on her skull with its sparse hair, but sometimes I'm so hot it's your cold that I need, and sometimes I think I'm going out of my mind. Not long ago I heard about a woman of my age who took her own life for no discernible reason, and although I don't know anything about her I understand her completely. I think she hanged herself, the way you hang a shirt in the closet after ironing, have you ever thought of hanging yourself? And when her mother responds with a faint gurgle she whispers, it's OK, Mum, no need for you to feel uncomfortable, it seems to me we've never had such a good conversation, I've never before got so much from you.

Despite the warm breeze blowing in from the window her teeth are chattering, and she presses against the body beside her until drowsiness overtakes her. It seems to her that her mother is whispering to her, sleep, sleep, like that afternoon when she found her sick. Sleep, sleep, she urged her in the hope of hushing her, and Dina lay down beside her and watched her as she slept, her face flushed from the illness, her thick hair strewn about her head, and she caressed it again and again until she saw her father peering in from the doorway. Dina-le, get out of that bed and hurry up, you don't want to catch something from Mum, she's running a high temperature, and he pulled her out from under the blankets, and Dina was surprised, if she was running a high temperature why was she so cold, and even now he's standing in the doorway, disrupting her sleep, did he have some hidden intention back then, when he extricated her from her mother's bed as if this were the danger zone? After all she was his in a sense; in an accord that was never openly acknowledged between the partners, Dina belonged to the father and Avner to the mother, a bad deal on both sides, and now it seems he's risen from the dead to separate them again. What's up, Dad? Is old age infectious too, is death infectious?

Oh, here you are, Rachela answers her, I was just thinking, why has she gone out and left Mum alone, and when Dina sits up in the bed a little flustered from sleep, she shows off her purchases. I've got some lovely tomatoes. I'll grate them really fine for your mother, with a little salt and olive oil, would you like some too? And Dina says, no, thank you, I really should be going, and she rises heavily, her bones aching, as if she's just caught a dose of that flu from forty years ago.

Have something to drink, you don't look well, Rachela urges her, I'll make you tea with lemon, and Dina wonders how this woman, of about her own age, could take on herself the role of her mother as she understands it, as her mother has never understood it, and already she's accepting the treatment on offer, sitting in the kitchen and watching the nimble fingers as they brew tea, squeeze a lemon and move a tomato back and forth over the grater, in a moment she'll tie a bib around the old woman's neck and feed her with a spoon like a little child. Who knows how many mouths she has already fed with these efficient fingers, which manipulate the kitchen utensils the way a pianist plays the keys, how many children she has swaddled and bathed and groomed and hugged, and for a moment she wishes she could be the child of this woman, about whom she really knows nothing; it was her sister-in-law Shlomit who heard about her from a friend and brought her to their mother the day she came out of hospital.

How many children do you have, Rachela? she asks, the appreciative smile poised on her lips, ready to hear the answer she's expecting: five? six? – perhaps even more, but the fingers freeze for a moment over the grater and then resume at a redoubled pace, rejecting the ripe tomato and starting immediately on the next in line. I have no children, she admits with taut lips, and Dina is taken aback, that's all right, she mumbles, feeling like a judge pardoning the defendant, and prays that her question will fade away. To her dismay, the shouts of the neighbourhood children returning from school suddenly filter in through the kitchen window, as if all the children they could have had, the pair of them, have gathered together for a surprise party in their honour, and Rachela sits facing her, wiping her fingers on an apron. I did have a little boy, she corrects herself in a low voice, but they took him away from me, gave him away for adoption. I couldn't care for him, I was deep into drugs at the time, and they took him away from me.

When was this? Dina asks, trying to hide her astonishment, and Rachela replies, fifteen years ago, he's now seventeen and a half. I've been working hard for years now, so that when he turns eighteen, if he decides to open the adoption file and meet me, he'll see that I've sorted myself out and he won't be ashamed of me. Have you any idea where he is? Dina asks and Rachela shakes her head, I don't know where he is and I don't know his name but I'm sure if I see him I'll know it's him. That's all I'm living for, for the moment they tell me he's opened the file and wants to see me. I've got the dresses ready, one for the winter and one for the summer, just so long as he isn't ashamed of me.

He'll be proud of you, Rachela, Dina says, laying her hand on her arm, thanks for telling me, she adds, I didn't mean to intrude, I thought it was a simple question, but apparently there aren't any simple questions, and there are certainly no simple answers, and she takes two saucers and doles out portions of the thick liquid. Like sisters we shall sit in the kitchen and eat and confide, she thinks, mysterious threads tie one person to another, mysterious threads guide our lives, like blind tramcars we roam the streets, incapable even of looking up at the sky, to see the network of cables above our heads.

In silence they sit face to face, dipping spoons in the comforting purée and raising them to their mouths like a pair of toddlers, until Rachela perks up suddenly, I must feed Mum she says, as if this were their shared mother, and Dina nods distractedly, they gave up my baby for adoption, Rachela told her, you will find the child, her mother said, and it seems to her that new tidings are flowing in her veins like an invigorating and health-giving infusion of blood, because perhaps at this very moment in this country or elsewhere a baby is coming into the world whose mother is incapable of caring for him, and all she needs to do is find him and clasp him to her heart.

The shouting of the children playing down below pricks her flesh like thorns. They're no longer bothering to call her, they're not trying to include her, how can she join in their games when she can't walk, how will she jump and run when she can't even stand on her feet? Under the pepper tree she reclines, playing with the clusters of red berries that hang from its branches. They're stooping low and it seems that any moment she'll be able to touch them, but a warm gust of wind blows them away, and she stretches out short arms, how high are the branches of the tree, it seems they will never bow down to her again, they are treacherous too, her red berries, teasing her and disappearing, challenging her from the treetops.

Is this what she does all day? she hears her mother sighing, find her a child, find her a child to play with, even a baby to lie beside her in the playpen, she can't go on spending whole days alone, but her father disagrees. She's supposed to get fed up with the loneliness and start walking. If she has company, it will perpetuate her disability.

Here's her mother leaning over her, for a moment she's very close and then she recedes, like the red pepper tree berries, teasing and disappearing, she isn't a part of the household in her life, but a guest, leaving words behind and going away. Find her a child, she repeats after her, but what does she want with children, she hates them, their whoops and cries, all aimed at her. She wants them to shut up, she wishes she were the only girl in all the world. Again she hears them mocking her, what kind of name is Hemda, it's a name for a cow, Hemda, let's hear you mooing, moo moo – fluting their lips at her. Her father so wanted her to be like the other children and yet he gave her this weird name, she moves uncomfortably within this name, not meant for her and not saying anything about her, but perpetuating a moment in which she played no part but from which she came into existence, as if it were a short letter from her father to her mother, a one-word telegram. This was their rapture, their *hemda*, and she had nothing to do with it, so why does she have to testify throughout her life to their momentary joy? How stupid the children are, this isn't a name for a cow, it's far more embarrassing than that.

What does Hemda mean? Elik asked her the first time he dared to address her, and she replied, it's a kind of ecstasy, a short-lived happiness, and he nodded seriously and repeated her name, stiffening it with his strange pronunciation, and she was enchanted by his seriousness, imagining mistakenly that as he accepted her name, so he would accept her, wholeheartedly and with dignity, even if without joy.

How hard it was in those days to salvage even a little happiness, like the futile attempt to extract a drop of honeydew from a withered flower, and that's what her Elik was: a desiccated bud, decaying before he could blossom, as she was too, and all of those around her, traumatised by the casualties of the great world war, traumatised by the casualties of the regional war, refusing to be comforted. How ashamed she was of him in those days, even at the outset of their love, and how ashamed she was of herself when she realised how thoroughly she had imbibed the values of her father, the ethos of heroism and valour. She wanted her loved one to fight on her behalf, fight for her country, and thereby expunge for her the stain of her disabled childhood, and prove to her father she was worthy, but he wandered around the farm, nice to look at and as thin as a girl with his murmuring heart while his contemporaries were at war, incapable even of grasping the horrors haunting her mind.

Because she longed to sacrifice him, and perhaps that's why she chose him, an orphan innocent lamb whose parents sent him far away to keep him safe. She shifts painfully in her bed; even if it wasn't his absolute death she saw before her eyes, but only his readiness to die for her, for her kibbutz, for her country, he wouldn't understand, stranger that he was.

Some thirty years later, did she try to sacrifice him again for the protection of her son, and this time did she succeed? When young Avni, superbly attractive with his black hair and his blue eyes, was training his body in readiness for his call-up day, returning from a run and doing press-ups on the sparse patch of grass by the entrance to the building, panting noisily, chest rising and falling, she looked on from the kitchen window, admiring his muscular back and his strong shoulders; how can I foil your plans, my dear son, after all I have no life without you – until her salvation came from an unexpected quarter, her salvation which was also her disaster. A few weeks after her son enlisted in the combat unit for which he'd been training a whole year her husband, his father, fell ill with the disease he was to die of, and suddenly she had a compelling excuse. You'll have to serve closer to home so you can spend more time with your father, who knows how long he can hang on, the army isn't going anywhere but your father is, and Avner submitted at once. Without a struggle he abandoned his greatest ambition and applied for a transfer to a base closer to home, so he could come round every evening to see his father staring into a static void, expressing no gratitude and showing no interest in him, unaware of the secret deal that had been stitched up behind his back, fading steadily but not dying, not absolutely, not even prepared to perform the single gesture which would have absolved his son from the shame of deserting his post and from the torments of guilt, and it was only a whole year after his discharge from the army that his father left this world, having forced them to make disreputable calculations of profit and loss, opportunity and advantage, and ostensibly to wait for his death although in fact they had been waiting for years to be allowed into his life.

How dark are the deals woven in the interior of the house, in the name of love and sacrifice, without contract and without witnesses, without words and without mercy, deals even Satan wouldn't have thought of, hiding behind our inadequacy we decide with an idle thought the fates of those dearest to us, and she purses her lips, refusing to submit to the laden spoon that's trying to penetrate her mouth. Never has she seen things so clearly, never before have the days of her life coalesced before her into a web devoid of pity from beginning to end, and it seems to her now her bones are cracking under the weight of consciousness. What desperate deal brought her into the world, and what deal will take her out of it, exactly as her husband was taken, and she covers her face with her hands because here he is approaching her with a metal object in his hand, leave me alone, Elik, this isn't the way things are done in the family structure, the family battlefield would be more accurate, your punishment won't come to you at the hands of the one you have injured but at the hands of the one you love most, the one on whose behalf you sinned.

But where is this loved one and where is her love for him? It seems her heart has dried up over the years and the conditions for love are no longer there, like water in the desert; even if you succeed in getting to it by some miraculous means, the sun will vaporise it in a moment. And perhaps it never was there at all, just a mirage, sweet memories that have changed their taste, as after betrayal. Can you delight in memories of love, after betrayal has become evident? Even your most beautiful memories will be stolen from you, and yet in spite of herself her lips are drawn into a smile when she sees young Avni running to meet her and she spreads her arms in welcome, the scent of freshly mown grass enfolding their embrace in an enchanted robe against the backdrop of the silvery peak of Mount Hermon. Again and again he runs to meet her with a charming smile, his legs plump, a shirt with green and white stripes on his solid body, from a distance he looks like a tiny animal springing from the ground, and she doesn't run to him to shorten the journey, he likes it when she waits for him rooted to the spot with arms outstretched as he comes closer and closer, his panting preceding him a little, until he falls into her embrace, and this moment when her arms are wrapped around him and his body clings to her wobbly body and sinks down on the lawn with its freshly mown grass, this is apparently her moment of short-lived joy, her *hemda* moment.

When she smiles some rough liquid is forced into her mouth and she grimaces, refuses to swallow, what has Elik prepared for her, has he burned the stew again, will she have to scrub the bottom of the pan and cook something else in a hurry? When they left the kibbutz and settled on the outskirts of the city with two moody adolescents, the four of them were surprised by the sudden need to eat, the daily burden that was almost alien to them, feeding four people three times a day, far from the nit-picking but comfortable ambience of the dining hall. A time for transformations, although it didn't work out well, a time for agreements, for recognitions, very nice too, or perhaps not quite so nice: this is your house, these are your children, this is your husband, he'll do the cooking, you'll do the cleaning, he'll work in the bank, you'll teach in the school, but how she hated his cooking. Gloom took hold of her whenever the four of them sat at the table confronting another mess of burnt lentils, tasteless rice; there were only a few dishes he had learned to cook and almost always he blackened the edges of the pan, and yet every evening he expected gratitude and admiration, and every evening he disappointed and was disappointed. Even Dina he used to scold when she had difficulty praising his cuisine, and she herself wondered about love, does it, like faith, transcend the mundane daily details, or is it precisely those details that inform it? If she loved him more, would she have loved the meals he served up too? After all, it was the essence of his personality that he presented them with every evening in the naïve expectation that they would find it palatable; until one day when he treated them yet again to a burnt offering she rose in fury and threw the whole dish including the pan into the bin and marched out, slamming the door, signalling to her children to join her, but only Avner followed her down the stairs, a little flustered though he was already a mature youth, and they went to the local pizzeria which had just opened and ate in silence, staring at the families huddled round the plastic tables, while Dina remained in the house with her father. He never again tried their patience with his cooking, nor did he try to bolster his status in the family in any other way and she wonders about this now when he seems intent on feeding her, surely she too, like him, is already beyond hunger and thirst. Is this their first meeting in the next world, where he's an old-timer and she's the newcomer, the direct opposite of their meeting in her kibbutz? In the world of the dead, will he exact his vengeance from her, or will he perhaps greet her with grace, hold her wrinkled hand and show her the attractions of the place, the way she led him to the lake the very first time they met? For a moment he'll be revealed before her as he really was then, with his bright boyish face, and it seems that only thus can she love him, she at the end of her life and he at the beginning of his, only thus can she see him the way he was, lonely, needy and an outsider; how quickly his loneliness turned into self-imposed isolation, his neediness into persistent demands, and his outsider status into alienation.

A shudder grips her legs when she climbs to meet him on the rickety rope-ladder, will he extend to her his white, slender hand that hasn't grown sufficiently? All of him stopped in mid-growth, as if separation from his parents stunted his physical development too, and that's why she always felt clumsy beside him, with her tall stature and her broad shoulders. At last we are compatible, she whispers to him, see how I've shrunk. When I walk beside you in the avenues of the world of the dead, between the spirits of blue apple trees with clouds trapped in their branches, we will look like husband and wife in every respect, and a second wedding canopy will be set up for us there, late compensation for the first, discredited one, back then in the long shadow of war.

It was her father who led her to that canopy, exactly the way he forced her to walk on her feet twenty years before. He always stood behind her, watching her every movement like a hawk, a blue-eyed hawk. How meagre was his faith in her and in her strengths, he was the one who said, marry him, Hemda, he's a good boy, and he loves you, as if these were the only conditions needed for a decision of this kind, and she hadn't dared say, but I don't love him, Dad, I mean I don't love him enough, how simple and almost enticing it would be, to sink into the depths of his disbelief in her, and drown all her desires in it.

Under the canopy in the dining hall on a rainy evening when it seemed the marshes surrounding the kibbutz were overflowing, threatening to sweep away the lawns, the low houses and the trees they planted to hide them from the

Syrians, she felt this wasn't a wedding but her bat-mitzvah, which had never been celebrated and wasn't even recognised in this atheistic kibbutz. It seemed to her this was an internal family event between her and her parents, and every one of the invited guests was an external element, even the bridegroom by her side, who might have been the senior invitee but was in no sense at all a member of the family.

How beautiful her parents were that evening, her mother in a cream-coloured silk dress, greying locks of hair framing her head, eyes moist and kindly, her lips with the first tiny wrinkles around them parted in an innocent smile, as if she didn't understand anything, and perhaps she really didn't understand – this wise woman, the one the leaders of the kibbutz turned to for consultations, some of them secretly in love with her, who managed complex corporations but knew nothing about her daughter Hemda, standing now under the canopy, the misery of defeat overwhelming her to the point where she longed to escape, roll up the ends of her dress and run to her lake, which waited for her in stormy spate, enclosed by bubbling swamps. This was exactly the way they had surrounded her in the dining hall when she was one year old, eager to see her taking her first steps, and she wasn't capable then of giving them the present they expected of her, and now once more they were all standing round her smiling in anticipation and she was paralysed again, again she had fallen on her back and was weeping bitterly, but this time no one could see and no one could hear, the art of concealment she had learned well over the years, sometimes it seemed to her this was all she had ever learned, perhaps only he could see and understand, her father who stood tensely beside her mother, his hair already sparse and his forehead etched with wrinkles, but his beauty still as potent as ever, anxiously watching every step she took, a menacing look in his eyes; would he take her to the doctors again as he did before, my daughter refuses to walk, my daughter refuses to love.

How great is the power of refusal, it seems only thus is it possible for her to feel the very essence of her existence, this bony entity who is named after transient joy. How strong is the refusal to love her husband, to love her daughter, who came into the world after long years of reluctance, and only when Avni was born did the internal bone marrow dissolve, and she was filled with light, with compassion, with *hemda*, a whole lake of graciousness sprang up within her, fields of water-lilies, pink-white clouds of pelicans hovering over them, but the petulance of her husband grew ever more intense, even now she recoils under the blanket, repelled by the memory. Almost every night the expectant look would rise to his face, shortly followed by the movement of the hand thumping her back, and she would mumble, I'm tired, Elik, and pretend to be asleep, her body embarrassed and recoiling from the perpetual desire that he aroused and yet undermined, what did he really want, and from whom? It couldn't be me that he longed for, persistently and constantly, and she tossed about on her bed at night, wondering if this was the way things were done in the neighbouring houses, wondering about herself, accustomed from the dawn of her childhood to the gloomy austerity of her father; he was wrapped up entirely in her but without happiness, and it seems that without realising it she has been halted there, bound to the angry face of love, for only according to the intensity of the gloom was it possible to estimate the intensity of love.

And so her desire too was never reciprocated in full, since she wanted to share with her husband her love of the boy, the moments of grace and charm, she wanted to shower him with warmth and protection, so he would lack for nothing, all her actions were directed solely to this end. What a foolish aspiration, she cringes now under the blanket, so he would lack for nothing! Seeing her son before her very eyes, walking about the world for long years in steadily decreasing circles, heavy and listless, dissatisfied, his lovely eyes vanishing into his face like a pair of dying lakes.

Chapter Six

For some reason he's in no hurry to retrieve his car, not that evening nor the morning after; he likes to see it in his mind's eye parked outside the gate like his trusted envoy, keeping watch over the visitors, arrivals and departures, silently absorbing the grief – and this of all mornings, it turns out, Shlomit expects him to drive Tomer to school, as she's running late, and he grumbles, it's not that far, he can walk it, we were never driven anywhere when we were children. Do you think it's healthy for him, hardly moving? Have you noticed how fat he's getting?

He isn't the only one round here who's getting fat, she mutters, but I'm glad to hear that you're looking at him every now and then, and before he has time to respond she asks, where exactly have you left your car? And he replies, in the garage, there was a problem with the windscreen wipers, and she's sceptical, wipers? Since when have you needed wipers in the summer? To which he retorts, quite unabashed, how else do you think you keep the windscreen clean? But I wouldn't expect you to know, when was the last time you cleaned anything? And when she tells him to shut up he notices Tomer peering in at the kitchen door, his cheeks flushed as if he's been slapped, and he approaches him and smoothes his hair, his fingers recoiling from the greasy contact. Morning, young man, he says with an effort, the car's in the garage, so we'll walk there together, and that way we'll get a chance to talk, OK? But when the boy looks up at him, utterly bemused, she cuts in, out of the question, he won't be there on time if you go on foot. You should have told me before you didn't have your car, I'd have woken him up earlier, now you hurry up and get Yotam dressed and I'll take both of them as usual.

I don't understand you, he protests, you complain that I don't devote time to him, and when I say I want to be with him, you object to that too, but she's not letting this go unchallenged: you have innumerable opportunities to be with him, his diary isn't exactly full of meetings with friends, as you know, but why should this be at the expense of his schooling? Please, pick him up at lunchtime. And he groans, lunchtime I can't do, I'm in court, and she spreads her arms in an expansive gesture as if saying, I rest my case, as if there's a jury sitting there, but he's the only one, their first-born son, his stomach bulging and his shoulders slumped. I do have friends, Mum, he mumbles, I just don't like meeting them in the afternoon, I see enough of them at school, and Avner gives him a supportive look, that's OK, Tomer, I didn't have many friends at your age either, it isn't the end of the world, and she pounces on the opportunity, even today you're hardly surrounded by friends, so who are you to reassure him?

No one at all, he says, and anyway who's talking about reassurance? He leaves her in the kitchen with the boy, as she slices a roll in two and inserts a slab of salted cheese as she does every morning; her fingers are thick and strong, nails bitten down like the nails of a child, and he thinks how these hands, with the fragments of cheese scattered over them, will soon be manipulating arthritic limbs, time to get up, move! she will bellow, urging her post-operative patients to leave their beds and take their first tentative steps, and for a moment, he feels a pricking in his heart over the lost opportunity for which they're both responsible and shame takes hold of him, as if they've been collaborating in some ridiculous petty crime, theft of cheap chewing gum or a few sweets found in their pockets, and when he hesitates in the kitchen doorway, thinking perhaps this is the time to go to her and embrace her, hugging her shoulders in the shabby nightdress, she's already yelling at him, why are you standing there? How useless can a man be! Get Yotam dressed, and he's pushed into the children's room, finding the little one sitting up in his bed with a miniature picture-book in his hand, and he's muttering to himself in a didactic tone, like a teacher testing a pupil, what's this? and at once he replies with satisfaction, it's a house, and what's this? A cat or a rabbit? He chuckles as he remembers his favourite cat, the one belonging to Dina and Gideon.

Daddy, it's Daddy! he cries out when he sees him in the doorway, standing up in the bed and stretching out his arms to meet him, completely naked; the heavy night-nappy has come adrift from its moorings and fallen on the mattress, and Avner finds himself darting furtive looks around, Daddy? Who's a Daddy? He lifts the happy body from the bed, his skin so smooth he almost drops him. How it always bemuses him, this morning jubilation, how long can you keep on going, he wonders as he rummages in the chest of drawers. Shlomit exploits his helplessness and dresses him in tattered clothes, turning him into a beggar whether he likes it or not, but today he's going to the nursery in style, in minuscule jeans and stripy shirt, today he'll be Daddy's boy, and he remembers his favourite stripy shirt, the only garment he wanted to wear in his childhood, how they mocked him for paying attention to things like this. He carries him in his arms to the bathroom and washes and caresses his florid face, then grooms his black and still sparse hair with a soft brush. You're sweet, you're sweet, he murmurs in his ear, and the little one echoes back to him, you're sweet, you're sweet, and Avner puts his lips to the warm cheek; suddenly he wants to stay like this for ever, not go to the office, not take him to the nursery, just shelter in the shadow of this little boy who is all blessing and joy. Blessing and joy, really? It depends who it's for, because now he sees the eyes of his first-born son staring at him from the bathroom door with a quizzical and accusing look, did you kiss my cheek like that, did you brush my hair as gently as that? And as if caught red-handed he puts the toddler down at once, and he utters a wail of discomfiture but then perks up and runs to his mother. What's he doing in jeans? she fumes, who dresses a child in jeans for the nursery, it's so uncomfortable, don't you ever think about what you're doing? And when he looks at his first-born son it seems to him these critical words are emerging from his throat too, how similar he is to Shlomit, with his puffy and resentful features, and he mutters, see you later, sweetie, his arm brushing the boy's shoulder as he passes by him, then he grabs his briefcase and leaves.

In a dark jacket and collar and tie he makes his way, a morning breeze calming his skin; soon the chill will melt away but for the moment it's comforting, like a wet towel on a fevered brow. Around him people are walking at an almost uniform pace, men, women and children, as if they're all the loyal employees of the same firm, and they're all on the same assignments, and he peers at the people-carriers passing by him. Yes, perhaps she's right, most of the toddlers are wearing comfortable woollen trousers, not jeans, but it isn't this that's bothering him, rather it's the feeling that has tormented him for years and he has no idea if there's anything in it, the suspicion that the lives of all these others are much better than his life.

In circles within circles this feeling has enclosed him since the days of his youth, circles growing ever tighter around him, country, city, family, wife. Was it his father's nostalgic stories about Europe, stories of snow and cherries, of grand houses with magnificent frontages and gleaming tramcars silently passing by, that instilled in him the feeling that the dusty country in which he was born and raised was only a meagre substitute for a real country, and his modest northern kibbutz was likewise a meagre substitute for a great city? And when they relocated from there, he found himself in the most remote outpost of the poorest city, and when he hitched his life to the life of his first girlfriend, he felt from the outset this was a pale imitation of a real love life, compared not only with the lives of others, but also with the life he himself could have lived.

What folly, his mouth is full of saliva and he could spit on the pavement, so intense is the repulsion, you will never know; you envy even those who are down on their luck, even that man who was about to die you envied because he got to love his wife with the full intensity of love, and now it turns out she wasn't his wife and he's already turning to dust, and still you believe his lot is better than yours. What is this? he asks himself in the voice of little Yotam, it's stupidity, it's impertinence, and again it seems to him he sees her from afar, her black hair and the sheen of her red blouse, how typical of you, chasing a mirage, looking out for a red blouse in the teeming streets, as if she's always going to walk around for you in the same blouse. How typical of you to focus on the wrapping and not the essence, the clothes and not the betrayal; the betrayal is redoubled as the grief is redoubled, for our loved ones and for ourselves, but her grief is heavier still because even what she didn't have she's bemoaning, the chance she never had to live with him, to bear him children, all the years she lived without him and all the years she will live without him, and all these cars advancing in astonishing silence and in exemplary order suddenly look to him like participants in a funeral, the endless funeral of their secret love, to which he was a chance witness, but since the moment of his presence there, seeing what he saw and hearing what he heard, a mission has been imposed on him.

His mission is secret and not yet clear to him, only when he meets her again will it be clarified, and in the meantime he'll be content with the knowledge that his car is still there, outside the house of the deceased, a knowledge that imbues him with a warm sense of belonging, as if he has struck a root, and from this root some young shoot of wisdom may spring, and already he's debating how long he can leave it there, perhaps for ever? The fact is, he doesn't really need a car; he can walk to the office, as he's doing this morning, a quarter of an hour at a brisk pace and he's there, while for the courthouse he prefers to take a taxi, and transporting the children around is usually Shlomit's job, and his visits to the territories are becoming fewer. He hardly needs a car at all, so he can leave it there permanently, and from time to time he'll pay it a visit, looking for signs of deterioration, until it's covered in dry leaves and the tyres are flat and it will turn into a kind of monument. To what precisely, he wonders, to mystical brotherhood and the sharing of destiny? To the defeat of love? Anyway, the purpose of a monument is to perpetuate the victory and not the defeat.

When he passes by the café close to his office, with its attractive Hebrew name in meticulously pointed script, he sees dozens of people silently surrounding a notice, a blazing torch depicted at the side of it, and the rest a list of names: ten young names for the ten victims who lost their lives, assassinated here two years ago precisely, and he quickens his pace and lowers his eyes so no one will recognise him, in a situation like this, pain erases all restraints. There he is, the murderers' lawyer, this has been yelled at him more than once and more than twice, defending the monsters who killed our children, although he never represented those suspected of attacking civilians unless he was convinced of their innocence, but how do you explain that to the grieving family, and he remembers that morning when Ali came to his office, frightened and desperate. You must help me, they've arrested Ibrahim!

Arrested Ibrahim? On what charge? he cried, prepared to summon up all his years of experience in the defence of the son of his Palestinian friend whom he had learned to love and admire in the long hours they spent together in military courthouses, and Ali mumbled, they say he was involved in a plot to bomb Café Sheychar, but I don't believe it, it's true he's become more extreme lately and moved away from us, but terrorism? It can't be so! and Avner said, Sheychar? his voice unsteady as if they were talking about his own sitting room. Shlomit was then on maternity leave and she liked strolling down there with Yotam, and sometimes he left the office and joined them there for a late breakfast, and the thought of his injured baby, weeping bitterly while his parents lie dead beside him – for some reason this was his immediate choice out of all the horrendous possibilities, little Yotam would live and the pair of them would die – was so painful he could hardly breathe. Sheychar, just down the road? he asked again, and Ali nodded, that's what they say, and Avner shook his head slowly, staring at him intently as if trying to imprint his appearance in his memory, and not only his appearance but also his recollection of the many conversations they held while waiting for judgments, about cases, the political situation, children. How he loved talking about his son Ibrahim, the pride of the family, studying medicine in Jordan. I can't, I can't represent him, he said finally, I'm sorry. They stood face to face, in silence, all their years of acquaintance collapsing at once under the impact of this moment, until Ali turned on his heel and went, and he hasn't seen him since.

Some time later he heard that the lawyer from Ramallah who defended the boy succeeded in extenuating his culpability in the plot, and for this reason he was sentenced to only twenty years in jail, but not long after the conspirators were arrested, another gang succeeded in carrying out the atrocity, one end of Sabbath, when he and Shlomit and the children were at home, but the café was full of young people, including the ten of blessed memory whose names are inscribed in stone, and he was going over and over the sequence of events, sometimes castigating himself for not defending the son of his friend who was facing life imprisonment. Who made you a judge? You don't know and you're not supposed to know what the judge knows and decides at the end of the day, and wasn't this youth entitled to appropriate representation like anyone else? But all the same, my priority has always been to defend human rights, not the interests of one ethnic group or another, and what is terrorism if not the most serious assault on human rights imaginable? I'm not a sword for hire, going with the highest bidder, he used to justify himself, there are lawyers who will defend anyone, but I'm not like that, for better or worse. But most of all he was worried by the fact that the incident had actually happened in the end, and it had been impossible to prevent the terrorist attack at Café Sheychar – arrests, trials, even discarding his old friend Ali, nothing had made any difference, and facing up to this tragic reality he stood helpless, as if confronting some cruel fable for children, where the outcome is known from the start, and all the ramifications and contortions of the plot are incapable of averting it, and now he quickly crosses the street; more than two years have passed since that morning, was it then he lost his belief in himself?

Sometimes when he crosses busy streets, when he looks at the toys mankind has built for itself, cars and aeroplanes, weapons and explosive charges, poisons covert and overt, static and mobile machines, he feels sorry for people who have set out to improve their environment but are incapable of improving or fortifying themselves, and are unconsciously intensifying their vulnerability; as the prospect of coming under attack becomes stronger, so the ability to defend against it is reduced, to such an extent that he's surprised every evening to realise that he still exists, that his house is standing, that since the death of his father in the final days of his youth and until the death of Rafael Allon he hasn't had to face death in a frontal fashion but only in oblique encounters that left him feeling intimidated and almost guilty.

A sigh of relief emerges from his throat when he enters the cool stairway of the building, opening the door of his office to find his intern struggling with the water-cooler, trying to change the tank and embracing it as if it's her baby. Soon she'll be having a baby of her own, he reckons, remembering their conversation with some embarrassment, unless she heeds his advice, that is, and changes her mind. How did he have the nerve to drop all those hints, suggesting to her she was perhaps making a mistake instead of reassuring her in a straightforward fashion, telling her for example, these are the doubts that attend on any crucial decision, and they say more about the personalities than about the decision.

We're going to be late arriving at the court, Avni, I called you but you didn't answer, she chides him with an intimate smile, as if they've just woken up together from a post-coital nap, and he glances at his watch, how long has the journey taken him, nearly an hour since he left home, he's been strolling along slowly as if the whole world is willing to wait for him, judges and lawyers, witnesses, plaintiffs and defendants. Sorry, I'm without my car today, he says, I left it in a garage, and she's surprised, in a garage? You said you lost your keys.

Never mind that now, he says hurriedly, we'll just take a taxi, have you got the files? The new photos? And she says, of course, everything's packed and ready, and her body too is packed in stiff fabric and he wonders how she's managed to squeeze into her clothes, a black blouse with a white pointed collar, black trousers; he seems to remember trampling on these with his shoes last night but there's no mark on them this morning, and in particular he's surprised by her resolute attitude when they chat on the way to the courthouse, it seems she has no doubts about the validity of their arguments, not in this case and not in the others, while his own resolution is flagging, and it's clear to him that if he were to tell her about Ali she would rebuke him sharply, and suddenly he's appalled by a thought that occurs to him for the first time: was it Ali himself who planned the attack on Sheychar, for the sole and exclusive purpose of proving to him that he was wrong, his son had no hand in it?

He still loves this set-up, the full panoply of the law, although he understands less and less what it is about it that he loves. Is it the meticulous order that instils confidence, where everyone has his place and his role, is it the archaic formality, of which there is no trace anywhere in this country but here, which reminds him of his father's stories, and perhaps it's the theatricality, since it's nothing but spectacle, even if crucial decisions are being taken, even if the place looks more like a school classroom than an auditorium. It's a fateful children's show that they're mounting here, disguised in black robes and indulging in etiquette from another world, rising to their feet when the judge enters, rising again when it's their turn to speak, addressing one another with honorific titles and in terms of friendship and respect, while keeping an ironic restraint, and the words leaving their mouths finally take on their appropriate weight. Here it is impossible to use them casually, since every word is recorded, and so meticulously that there are moments when it seems this is the sole purpose of the session, they are all gathered here in their robes to help the stenographer document the event, that evening in Nablus for example, during the curfew, almost three years ago, when the light was fading and a Molotov cocktail was thrown at an armoured vehicle, penetrating an aperture and injuring the patrol commander in the face and hand, and later that evening when he saw three suspicious figures fleeing the scene he gave the order to fire.

The machine-gunner has testified that he saw a figure falling and two other figures bending over the recumbent form, and even then we didn't know if we'd hit anyone, the commander is telling the court, because when you're under fire the natural thing is to lie flat, and I thought perhaps this was a trick, and how could we know in the dark that these were peace activists from Europe, and all this the judge repeats in the first person, at dictation speed, as if she herself had been present in the armoured vehicle, peering through the slit at the dangerous streets, and when Avner listens to him, the young man with the close-cropped black hair, and open-necked shirt exposing a tanned chest, he feels a resurgence of that old grudge against them, against all those who have fulfilled the dream of his youth which is no longer a dream but a sensation of failure which has remained as acute as it ever was. He was almost like them, like these men, vulnerable and lethal, but his father's illness wrecked the plan that he'd been working on for months on end, with incessant running and press-ups, lifting weights every morning. He survived seven weeks of training on the Golan before the news came through of his father's condition, and he capitulated at once, and the army seemed ready to capitulate too; that unwieldy and inflexible body adapted itself with astonishing speed to the new requirements, spewed him out of its steel guts and dumped him in a base close to Jerusalem, where he did boring clerical work, and went home every evening to a fading father who didn't need him, and to a mother who needed him too much, while his few friends and contemporaries went home only for short and infrequent weekends, and he no longer understood their language. And all of this he could perhaps have endured, if he had been convinced it was only his father's illness that had diverted him from the ways of manhood, the arduous life to which he aspired, but deep down in his heart he had doubts, then and even now: was it not his secret desire to get out of there one way or another? It didn't take him long to realise that despite the press-ups and the sit-ups, this steel crutch wasn't meant for him.

How longingly he used to look during days of training to the rifle by his side as to his only salvation; at last he had a friend after his own heart, devoted and steadfast, and he hadn't yet fully grasped the concept that the proven talent of this weapon was to kill and destroy the other person, since it seemed to him it was aimed solely at him, this was the one and only solution, and he had almost made up his mind to release himself in this way from the yoke and from the shame, from the desperate effort to fit himself into the frame, and he was only putting this off from moment to moment and from day to day, just one little squeeze, and in the silence that reigned thereafter he would perhaps find some peace for himself, since he had no other way of getting out of here, but then it happened; almost unbelievable how his mother with her acute senses was capable of reading his thoughts, of fulfilling his secret aspirations on his behalf, although sadly there was no relief in this.

He knew that first and foremost this was his failure, with his father's illness carelessly tacked on to it, and since then he has looked with fear at men in uniform and men under arms, as if they were threatening him personally, and perhaps Shlomit is right when she claims that his excessive readiness to identify with the other side is fuelled by jealousy and frustration, because now when he stands up and confronts the defendant, with every intention of subjecting him to an aggressive and closely argued cross-examination, he feels suddenly absurd in his black gown, as if he's wearing a dress, and to his dismay he realises that in his flustered state back in the office he forgot to change his flip-flops for black shoes, and when he tries to pace purposefully to and fro before the defendant, his footsteps make a squeaking and scraping sound, like a pair of millstones. He clears his throat to cover his embarrassment and manages to regain some composure, attacking the young man with a barrage of awkward details and trying to establish premeditation or carelessness at the very least. Was this the last of the daylight or darkness? Were night-vision instruments in use? How much lighting was there in the street at that hour? Did you not know about the activities of the peace campaigners, who had an office in the city? It's inconceivable that you didn't know, inconceivable that you didn't see them, inconceivable that the street was completely dark.

Only in two streets in Nablus was there any lighting, the officer replies, a peace activist from my point of view is an innocent civilian and as such I make every effort to protect him from harm, but I was sure these people were terrorists. After the incident I was in action all through the night, and the next morning, even before my own injuries were treated, I was summoned to an inquiry, and it was only then that it became clear what had happened – and at this point the counsel for the defence, with her long and blackened eyelashes and jutting chin, interrupts him and proposes to present some photographs which were taken at the crucial time and which should settle two central issues which have been controversial, the state of the light at the time of the incident and the clothing worn by peace activist Steven at the time of his injury, to which the prosecution duly retaliates, showing the judge horrific pictures of the victim, whose face has been completely destroyed.

It was dark, the commander repeats, there was no illumination which would have enabled us to identify the figures. I put on my night-vision goggles and I saw three figures dressed in black who were endangering me, the safety and welfare of the unit was my first responsibility, and Avner persists, the lighting is a side issue, Your Honour, and it doesn't always show up reliably in photographs, we know for a fact that they raised their hands and they called out in English, saying don't shoot. They were dressed in fluorescent jackets . . . Every detail takes on fateful significance, as is appropriate when dealing with disaster; the woman's red blouse, the man's yellowing skin, the last words she whispered in his ear, don't worry, you'll soon be feeling better.

When the defendant steps down from the stand his girlfriend hugs him and her fingers caress his cheeks, and Avner wonders if any woman will ever caress Steven's shattered face. He calls the next witness to the stand, and while he's asking and enquiring, asserting and listening, interrupted and interrupting, from time to time he remembers his car, parked outside the house of mourning and keeping an eye on the visitors, arrivals and departures, and the path where the jasmine bushes bloom and waft their intoxicating scent. Soon evening will come down upon them, and soon he will be there too, and he knows with a strange certainty that this evening, on the edge of the cavernous wadi or beside one of the bushes, at the end of the trail or the start of it, or perhaps leaning against his white car, which already resembles a giant boulder, one of the very stones of the place, he will see her.

What a strange childhood, Dina says, taken aback by the sound of her own voice in the empty room, enclosed by glass, what a strange age to be, the age of decay is childhood without hope, sky without moon. She has never before felt so close to the very beginning of her life, when the body was still narrow and enclosed and the mind had not yet woken up, hiding alone and almost indifferent within its shell, listening to repressed sounds, not yet connected to any other mind in that enlivening and painful linkage.

Is it there we are supposed to return to, she wonders, with what remains of our love, what remains of our strength, after the prodigious effort of raising and tending a family, after our children have grown up and our husbands have aged and our parents gone to another world, to return to that unripe, self-centred and enclosed existence, to bind up in silence the wounds of the betrayals we have suffered, the desertions we have suffered, binding and releasing, releasing and binding? But in our childhood we held in our hands a luxuriant sphere, the great and impressive sphere of the future, whereas now our hands are empty and it seems this has happened all at once, in the space of a few months our future has disintegrated and crumbled into dust.

A viscous, unfamiliar fatigue takes hold of her in the mornings, sticking her limbs together and slowing her movements, while at night her sleep is plundered by mordant chasms of wakefulness, this isn't the heavy blanket of sleep that's spread over her but a net full of holes. How strenuous the effort to sleep has become, and how will she stand up tomorrow in front of her students who are also tired; they too have nights of disturbed sleep, only they are awakened by beloved babies whereas she is awakened by the baby she never brought into the world, and she springs up drenched in sweat, her heart pounding and a blazing torch igniting in her chest, and it seems any moment a flame will emerge from her throat, a tongue of fire that will take hold in the corners of the house, and she strips off her nightie in the dark, kicking at the burning blanket, turning on the light and changing the damp pillowcase, but almost immediately her toes are quivering in the cold, and she fumbles for the clothes she stripped off and left scattered around the bed, trying to tug them out from under Gideon's body, and he wakes grumpily and slinks away to the single bed in his darkroom. When he abandons their bed the last vestige of sleep disappears from the room and again she turns on the light, pulling out a book from the shelf, but as she lies on her back and holds the book open, hanging over her is the flesh of her arms wrapped in raddled skin, and she stares at the strange sight in bemusement: what is this arm to her, reminding her of her mother's arm, and what are the powerful currents buffeting her body, boiling lava and melting snow.

When she dresses, exhausted, in the morning, confronting the scattered bedclothes, inside the bra that she's fastening she notices, nestling silently, pockets of flesh that have lost their vitality, the monthly cycle of filling and emptying, and they hang on her body lacking stimulus and sensation, almost like an internal organ you never knew existed, and she averts her gaze dismally. Of course she didn't expect to keep her youth for ever; for years she's been shadowing her mother's ageing process, but she didn't expect it to come to her so soon, and she wonders about those close to her who don't sense these transformations, treating her as if they know her while she goes on changing, but how few they are, those who are close to her; she has always preferred to be alone, with just a few people around her, and even they aren't as close as they used to be. It seems that the thing closest to her now is the house, with its four rooms and its enclosed balcony, and like her it is wondering where they've all disappeared to, because the place always used to be full of commotion in the afternoons, when Nitzan came home from school with a friend or two, and Gideon sometimes came home early to develop his pictures, dipping them in his trays, showing them to her and asking her opinion, and the mothers of the schoolfriends would stay for coffee, and her students would contact her from time to time, and now it seems to her the house is decaying, its arid rooms closing their eyes in thirst, because Gideon is coming home late, and even then he's tired and not inclined to talk, sitting down with his laptop and transmitting his pictures to the editorial team, occasionally muttering some criticism of young editors who have never in their lives been in the field and have no idea which pictures to choose, and Nitzan usually prefers to accompany her friends to their homes or to roam the streets with them, and when she returns she disappears into her room and Dina hesitates by the closed door, listening to the twittering of the voicemail and the ringing of the phone and the clicking of the computer keyboard and the giggling emerging from the room. Already she's incapable of distinguishing between a human voice and an electronic voice, and thus whole hours of the day have lost their clear and reassuring structure and turned into an extended mishmash of time, in which it's apparently possible to do wonderful things, to help the needy or develop latent talents, or alternatively do the things that are required, such as her doctoral thesis, without which her job isn't secure, but she's unable to gather her resources of strength together; they are scattered about the rooms, leaving her feeling as if she's about to faint.

You're sick, she says aloud, almost with malicious satisfaction, you're sick, in the end you'll be like that woman who hanged herself, and she scours the house, wondering how you carry out something like that, it seems that even for suicide talents are needed that she doesn't have, practical creativity, resourcefulness and determination. Her gaze wanders over the light fittings, the taps, the lintels, here's the stool that Nitzan used to climb on to brush her teeth, that could come in handy, and she shakes her head in an effort to dislodge this dreadful thought, and yet she can't let it go.

You remember you told me about a woman who killed herself? she asks Gideon, how exactly did she hang herself? He doesn't remember anything about it, his life is packed with one-off encounters, random information, I've no idea, Dina, why are you so interested, did I say she hanged herself? But he doesn't wait for her answer, he's too busy. It isn't easy competing with younger photographers, to run from demonstration to funeral, from military operation to government session, and search once again every time for the special angle, and he's never satisfied, even when he wins prizes and recognition, and he'll always be worried, always hoping to find tomorrow what he didn't find today. It isn't her his interest is focused on, but his camera, and although this is the way it has been for ever, it has irked her more and more in recent times; still, she can console herself with the thought that she doesn't need close and cloying love, didn't she tire of the calm and gentle man who was then at her side, and choose Gideon instead?

He admired her wisdom and that was why she thought him stupid, he was besotted with her and that was why she recoiled from him, he wanted to marry her, he wanted a big family, he surprised her with gifts and on top of everything else he was tall and handsome, and she ditched him in a moment, at the party she went to with him, on an unfenced rooftop in Jerusalem, where she met the short man with the camera slung round his neck, with the childish features and the sardonic look, and he said the most predictable thing to her. That's what Gideon was like, not trying to impress, but with a tone to his voice that embellished the words and imbued them with extra significance, so much so that he seemed to be deriding any interlocutor who failed to understand him fully.

Are you new in town? he asked her, or something like that, and she admitted to this at once, although it soon became clear that in fact he was the new one in town, and this was his party, a kind of housewarming, if this tiny penthouse apartment could really be called a house, and when he said to her, you're invited to stay after the others have gone, she grinned, taken aback, hadn't he noticed she was with a partner? She stayed close to Eytan most of the evening but began watching Gideon intently, would he issue the same invitation to other girls, and she was especially surprised that he didn't take a single photograph, as if he didn't think them worth it. He walked among his guests with dignity, drinking incessantly, not dancing much, and when she finally saw him dancing with an unfamiliar girl, long blonde hair and a tiny miniskirt, she felt a twinge of jealousy as if he had betrayed her, and all this time her Eytan was whispering endearments in her ear, filling her plate, and turning in the course of one night into a millstone round her neck.

Two and a half years they had been together. Her father went into hospital alongside his mother, they died almost the same day, and it seemed a covenant of orphans had been sealed between them then, a seal that no one could break, but how easily it was broken, as things turned out; the day after the party it was broken, when she climbed the sixty-four steps and stood panting before Gideon's door at the very moment it opened and the blonde came out, her hair wet; the breath knocked out of her, Dina started to retreat, blushing like a beetroot and almost fainting from embarrassment, and to her dismay she heard his voice behind her, hey, why are you running away? And when she turned to face him like a trapped animal, there was a sudden flash of light from his camera, flooding her anguished features.

Come up, he said, leaning on the rail, did you leave something here last night? and she mumbled gratefully, yes, my sunglasses, and he grinned, are you sure? You come to a party in the middle of the night wearing shades? And she said, yes, just imagine it, I hate the light. Then how are we going to live together? he said sadly, I'm addicted to the light, and she smiled, taken aback but her confidence returning to her in a reassuring current, driving white cells of identity through her veins; look, she has an existence of her own, she has a name, qualities, preferences, she doesn't like light, for example.

So it seems we're not going to live together, she replied, I'll just collect my glasses and go, and at that moment she believed with total sincerity that she had really left her sunglasses here, and she followed him to the roof and searched for them among the empty beer bottles and the full ashtrays, while in fact they were perched above her forehead, and all this time he was walking behind her and photographing her, wearing only his underpants, surprisingly strong and muscular, and it was only when she came across a mirror hanging on the wall in the corridor that she noticed her glasses hovering above her scalp, and she didn't even manage to murmur, this is my spare set, or my boyfriend lent them to me, before he gently removed the sunglasses from her head and the camera from his chest and stood facing the mirror from behind her, peeling off her long grey dress, her bra and panties, and because he was slightly shorter than her, his reflection in the mirror was virtually invisible to her and it seemed her clothes were being removed by themselves, but then she felt the sudden shock as the portals of her body were invaded and she saw her shoulders heaving and her breasts shaking and the astonishment on her face, she had never before seen her face during the act and now it seemed she couldn't do anything but look, though it was a taboo, almost like incest, seeing her eyes open wide in a kind of ecstasy she never knew she was capable of feeling, lips parted and longing to be kissed, and her whole expression that of a woman submitting in the archaic and almost demeaning sense, a woman whose body opens before a man, and a stranger at that, who has just dismissed another woman.

Her breath misted the mirror when he uttered a sigh of intense and subversive delight, and tears filled her eyes, and it was only then that he appeared in the mirror behind her. Don't cry, sweetheart, he whispered. In time he would call Nitzan that, but he didn't ask why she was crying, and if he were to ask, how could she explain it? To her surprise, he gathered her to him and laid her head on his shoulder and his skin had a sour and enticing smell of pine needles, the heavy pines that surrounded his roof, which today enclose her tiny study, and he said, don't be sorry, whatever you want you can have, take your time, I'm here, showing her with a few simple words that her situation was clear to him, committing himself easily as if the words had no value, or perhaps the opposite, giving her a rigorous and surprising present, whatever you want you can have. How did she know what she wanted, she didn't even know him, did he whisper that to the girl who was there before her? And when she went home that evening she found Eytan waiting for her in the kitchen, slicing vegetables for a salad, and she held his hand and told him in a trembling voice what had happened that morning, and he shook his head again and again as if not believing, Dina, Dina, he mumbled repeatedly, and that night he packed his possessions and left, and she wandered sadly around the empty house; it seemed to her her father had died again and she was left alone with her mother, and once more she had only herself to blame, since the photographer on the roof wasn't renowned as a high achiever, he wasn't capable of absorbing the pangs of grief and regret, and of course he had no interest in finding himself in constant competition with another man who loved her unconditionally, although after less than a year he married someone else, so apparently he didn't really love you that much, although you can be sure this was only a sign and symptom of the scale of the crisis he was going through, and maybe the four children he has brought into the world since then with his rich American wife in a settlement in the Jerusalem hills are likewise sign and symptom of his love for you, who knows, and you found yourself with a stranger, someone you've never been able to figure out to this very day, you couldn't have guessed at his coolness and insularity, and on the other hand his devotion; the rare moments of intimacy between the two of you are still more precious to you than the abundance that others could offer.

Because in the end, as she discovered, she too was suited to this style of life, living beside him but not with him, especially when Nitzan was there to enliven and console, but now as she sits at her laptop on the enclosed balcony surrounded by pine needles, she knows that for the first time since the moment on the roof of his house, a decision stands before them, and that all their love and hate, their friendship and their rivalry, their happiness and pain, are piled up on one pan of the scales, while on the other for the first time there is a heavy and menacing aspiration, an aspiration which apparently came from nowhere but is deeply rooted in her essence and in her secrets.

Because only this can breathe life into her, put back into her hands the miraculous sphere of the future, only the thought of that baby who is waiting for her far away, and yet the whole idea seems to her so far-fetched she doesn't try to put it on a practical footing, it's like those fantasies of childhood that have no limit because they have no validity, and she sits and stares at her computer in her transparent study, your watch-tower, Gideon used to jest, because from there she looks down on birds and treetops and clouds and solar thermals, on all those who don't need her; her desk is piled high with exam papers she's supposed to be marking, what a strange child-hood, she says again. Her mobile rings and she hears Nitzan's voice. Don't wait up for me, Mum, the girl announces, I'm staying over at Tamar's place tonight, she's got the house to herself, is everything all right with you? she asks unexpect-edly and Dina replies hastily, yes, of course, why?

You've been acting a bit strange lately, Nitzan says, but at once her voice is swallowed up by the hubbub of the school, and Dina replies with an effort, strange? How? – not wanting to overload the thread of the conversation with her issues, or pressurise her only daughter the way her mother pressurised her, but Nitzan's already moved on, so I'll be back at midday tomorrow, OK? She's impatient to join her friends who are calling her, perhaps she'll tell them where he disappeared to, the boy who slept beside her in her bed. Well, enjoy yourself, Mum, you can have a romantic evening with Dad, she chuck-les. And Dina says, thank you for that, my dear, although the conversation is already over, and she rests her head on the pile of exam papers, her eyes smarting, and the air-conditioning wafts a gust of hot wind in her direction; her watchtower heats up easily and is inundated by the dust of the desert, although its windows are closed.

Yes, a romantic evening is in store for them, and what is she going to say to him this evening, find me a baby because that's what my mother muttered in her sleep? Or will she quote the words of Rachel to Jacob, give me a child or else I die? Anyway she hasn't the faintest idea what it involves, how you go about it, where you start, and all at once she shakes herself and attacks the computer, how easy it is these days to garner information, and a lot more besides; in the space of a few hours she meets more people than she's met in the whole of her life, people who, like her, are longing for a child, who give themselves strange and sometimes ludicrous nicknames, and yet they take themselves absolutely seriously, and expect to be taken seriously by others, and here they are readily sharing with her their life-stories and aspirations, and especially the problems they have had in foreign and alien countries, confronting devious and venal authorities and unwieldy bureaucracies, and they are ostensibly powerless but bursting with hope, and although they are apparently strangers to her, they feel so much closer than her husband and her daughter, than her mother and her brother, and it seems to her suddenly that a generous and overflowing heart beats in the body of the computer, which until now has served her for the purposes of her work alone; she reads and reads breathlessly about men and women, together or individually, who haven't managed to bring a child into the world, and yet have found that the world is full of children, although the way to them is long and arduous, full of pitfalls and miracles, and so they have taken a child from the world and given him a home, and their stories describe a love affair like no other, a sense of destiny and a deep bonding of souls.

This woman for example, who calls herself Izdarechet, at this moment living completely alone in a remote village in the Ukraine, and waiting long days for an invitation to see the little girl allocated to her, and all her friends are sending her messages of encouragement and hope, although they have never met her, telling her about their experiences, about listless, dispirited children who came to life, a new light in their eyes, and all at once her mother's arid words take on a disturbing substance, yes, this is possible, it lies within the scope of reality, which is the reality of her new brothers and sisters, in this fellowship to which she now belongs, these people who have clasped an abandoned child to their bosom, even if most of them are younger than her, even if most of them have no children of their own, they understand her heartache, and she's so absorbed in reading that she doesn't notice the darkness coming down, or his entry into the house, until he approaches her, standing in the doorway of her study, in shorts that expose powerful legs and a faded T-shirt; he always puts on the first thing he finds in the wardrobe, deliberately downplaying his appearance but still managing to look stylish.

I see you're finally going back to your thesis, he smiles at her with satisfaction, it really is about time, and she hastily turns the screen off. I've got a million exam papers to mark first, she mumbles, I'm fed up with this burden at the end of every year. If you'd stayed at the university your teaching assistants would be marking the exams for you, he reminds her, you've got to go back there, unbelievable the way you let that mistake destroy your career, and she protests, that's enough, Gideon, it's over, I've no prospect of going back to the university.

I'm sure you could if you wanted to, he persists, you don't value yourself highly enough, as soon as you have your doctorate they'll be running after you, and she grins, I don't doubt it, but in the meantime do you feel like eating out tonight? Nitzan's sleeping over at Tamar's, and he says, I know, I just spoke to her, and immediately he adds, I'm really not in the mood for going out, and she rises from her seat unsurprised, this is the normal response, fine, so I'll fix something for us here. A surge of vitality rises in her, she must succeed tonight in drawing him into her still hazy scheme; the beginning is unclear but the end is love.

Optimistically, she puts a bottle of white wine in the fridge to cool and slices green vegetables, she'll serve cold yoghurt soup, appropriate in the current temperature, and omelette well seasoned with herbs, he likes simple food, as does she, and this time she won't be upset by Nitzan's absence, since he is the only one she needs this evening, his agreement to breathe new life into their little family, to give it taste and hope, and when he comes into the kitchen the upper half of his body is bare and she notices for a moment how much he's aged, greying tufts of hair on his chest, and his attractive full lips have thinned a little recently, but she won't let this trouble her just now, and the child won't mind either, better a middle-aged father than no father at all, and he inspects her with an air of satisfaction, a little patronising, you look so much better, he says, I've been telling you for years to get to grips with your thesis, I knew it would do you good, and again she's surprised to hear he's been looking at her at all, even if his conclusions are completely wrong.

With a thin smile she sets the slightly rickety wooden table on their balcony, an evening breeze from the hills wafts into her face with a conciliatory touch, lending significance to every movement, as it seems to her this very night she has conceived, by the power of thought and desire alone, and therefore this night is different from all other nights, the spirit of God hovers over it, and she pours wine into the glasses, ladles the yoghurt soup into dishes and slices bread. She loves to watch him eating, his movements elegant and measured, and Nitzan is the same – unlike her; she still snatches at her food as if she's having to share it with twenty other children, and now she looks at him pleasurably and asks, so where have you been shooting today?

I was in that hostel for the children of migrant workers, real sweeties they are, and it's disgraceful the way they're being treated, and she can't believe her good luck, it seems this is the signal she's been waiting for, the green light to broach the subject with him, but how to begin, she hasn't had time to plan properly, to mould her words into a really persuasive set of arguments. She takes a hasty gulp of wine; her face is drenched in sweat and she wipes it with a red tissue that disintegrates on her cheek and leaves thin red strips behind, resembling scratches.

Gideon, listen, she has to sound rational, responsible, and not flaky and obsessive, the way she probably looks now with her face flushed by sudden heat, and he looks up at her, what's the problem? he asks, but there's no curiosity in his face, only fatigue and perhaps a touch of fear of what's coming, and she smiles tensely, no problem, everything's fine, I've just had a thought, an aspiration I should say, I've suddenly realised what we need to do to have a really good life, but she's already grinding to a halt, as it seems to her that the yoghurt and the carefully sliced vegetables are climbing up her throat and threatening to spew out of her mouth in disgust – what a lame sentence! And evidently she isn't the only one who has this impression, since he says in a chilly voice, but we're doing all right, I am anyway, more or less, of course it's all a matter of expectations, you're not planning to drag me to a holistic self-help workshop or a Buddhist meditation class or something like that? And she breaks into forced laughter, perish the thought, she hastens to reassure him, although it occurs to her that photographing one variety of unconventional workshop or another is just the kind of original idea that would appeal to him, and he's probably already regretting the loss of the opportunity.

Listen, Nitzan's already a big girl, she tries again, but this statement in itself is enough to bring tears to her eyes, as if she had said, Heaven forbid, Nitzan is ill, or worse still, Nitzan is dead, and she continues in a tearful voice, the tissue drenched with her sweat now dabbing at her eyes, and you know how sorry I am we didn't have another baby, but suddenly I've realised perhaps this is for the best, because this enables us to do something even nicer, do you hear?

I've always told you one child is quite enough for me, and I'm glad you've realised it's for the best, he nods while she flinches as if she's been hit, and then she stands up and moves across and sits in his lap, laying her head on his shoulder, needing a comforting touch. You don't understand, Gideon, she whispers, it's suddenly clear to me what we need to do. I know this will seem crazy to you at first but when you think about it you'll see how wonderful it would be for all of us, and he shifts uneasily on the weather-beaten chair, what on earth are you talking about? he asks and for the first time she's having to confront the explicit words, not the disjointed words floating around in her mother's room, not the silent words on the computer screen, and she hesitates for a moment and says in a low voice, I want to adopt a child.

What? he roars, or perhaps it only seems that way because his mouth is close to her ear, and immediately she jumps up from his lap, or perhaps he's the one who pushes her off, and so he's looking up at her from below, the lenses of his glasses flashing with astonishment, adopt a child? Where did that idea spring from? You're not normal, Dina, are you kidding me? And she sits down facing him, where has her incisive intellect disappeared to when she needs it most, why can't she state her case with the same fluency that she deploys when explaining the background to the Spanish expulsions, and she says, listen for a moment, why are you reacting so aggressively, we have only one child and she's growing up, a few years from now she'll leave home, and I feel I've got a lot more to give, I love being a mother so much, so why not rescue a little child who doesn't have a home, and rescue ourselves as well, put some meaning into our lives, instead of growing old and empty, don't you see how wonderful this could be?

Not in the least, he retorts morosely, I don't need rescuing and I'm sorry to hear you're so afraid of being left alone with me in the house after Nitzan leaves, you're just talking bull-shit, I don't know what's come over you suddenly. It's nice to know you love being a mother, but when Nitzan grows up that isn't going to stop, she'll still need you. All right, I know how much you've enjoyed being Nitzan's mother, but how do you know you'll love a child who isn't yours, with all kinds of problems that you've never had to cope with? Adoption is a minefield, I've heard some real horror stories about adoption, a friend of the son of my editor killed himself not long ago, just eighteen years old, an adoptee from Brazil, you have no idea what kind of hell they went through with him, is that what you want, to turn our lives into hell?

You're always telling me about suicide cases, she mutters, bemused by this unexpected onslaught, are you trying to plant that idea in my head? She chuckles hurriedly, to show she's only joking, although the heated conversation is grieving her to the marrow of her bones, and he says, you're completely crazy, Dina. Obviously I'm not against adoption in certain cases, but you need to know it's a mad gamble, only people prepared to handle huge problems can take this on themselves, and I know you're not looking for problems. You're looking for happiness, he declares bitterly, and you won't find it there. Take a lover if you're bored with me, that would be a lot simpler all round, believe me.

How can you say that, she gasps, lips quivering, what do I want with a lover? I want to bring up another child in part-nership with you, I want us to be as happy as we were when Nitzan was born, a child means new life, new meaning, especially if this is an orphan who would otherwise stay in a children's home, and he interrupts her, leave it, Dina, you're just spouting clichés. You have no idea what's involved, there are more parents than children in this equation, demand exceeds supply, so don't kid yourself that you're rescuing anyone. If you don't take the child someone else will, hopefully someone who can provide a home in a normal and less dangerous country.

You're wrong, I would be rescuing, she insists. I believe we have so much to give a child, I'll rescue him even if someone else would have taken him, we are experienced parents, our economic situation is stable, he'll have a wonderful sister, and I'll have plenty of time to devote to him.

When they sack you from the college because you haven't got your doctorate you'll have plenty of time, I don't doubt it, he sneers, but you don't take on a child to pass the time. I understand people who want to be called Mum or Dad, but you already have a daughter, don't you see the difference? You're a mother, and you should be content with that and not want more than you have. You're just going through a midlife crisis, and in your typical way you've chosen a very original direction, so get this into your head, he leans towards her over the empty wine glasses and soup dishes, a kid won't make you any younger, a kid won't compensate you for the mistakes you've made, you can't take a poor kid and load him down with crazy expectations which have nothing to do with him. In short, Dina, instead of trying to relive an old happiness that will never return you should come to terms with what you have and see if you can find a focal point in this life as it is, understood?

How can you speak with such finality, she protests, her hand massaging her aching ribs, you're taking the easy way out, saying I've gone mad and you're not even trying to examine this, and he interrupts her again, there's nothing to examine, your motives are all screwed up, and you know what, even if they were impeccable, this still wouldn't suit me. I have enough love in my life, I feel like a father even though my daughter has a life of her own, and I'm not young any more, you're forgetting I'll soon be fifty-five and the last thing I'm interested in is running after a child who isn't mine. Anyway, what would we have in common?

And what do you and I have in common, she wonders, staring with hatred at his lips as he sets out his arguments fluently; it seems to her he's never before spoken so volubly, and ironically he was better prepared for this conversation than she was, what do you and I have in common, really, and she gets up angrily from her chair, longing to pick up the glasses and dishes and hurl them down into the next door neighbour's back yard, to hear them shattering on the paving stones, but no, she's not going to let him break her down that easily. I'm not giving up on this, Gideon, she says, knowing her lips are trembling, the fragments of the paper tissue still clinging to her face. She knows he's convinced she's gone out of her mind and there isn't even a smidgeon of compassion in his heart, I'm going to do this, I can't let go this time, and he gets up and stands facing her, you need urgent treatment, Dina, you've gone completely crazy lately. Don't go thinking I haven't noticed it, I just didn't think it would go this far.

How easy it is for you to accuse us of insanity when our aspirations contradict yours, she declares scornfully, although deep down in her heart she isn't sure that so many women would actually be standing beside her in this particular case, and he looks at her coldly, you know what? Maybe you're right, I really shouldn't be analysing your mental state, so I'll just tell you what I feel: this does not suit me. I'm not interested now in bringing up a small child, you can't force this on me.

And to add substance to his unspoken threat he stands up and walks out, in one moment; it seems to her he hasn't even paused to put a shirt on his bare chest or shoes on his feet, he just disappears in a flash, while she's carrying the quivering tableware to the sink, leaning over the taps, and she stares at the empty balcony, at the empty chair, she hasn't even heard the door slam, so perhaps he's still in the house after all, but what difference does it make, really, the question isn't, where is Gideon at this moment, but what is she going to do now he's made his position clear, what will she do with the remains of her love, the remains of her life.

Chapter Seven

The smell that pursues her, the smell streaming in through the open window and flooding the apartment, clings to the sheets and the skin, the smell of fire and dust, the smell of the peat burning perpetually in the depths of the marshes. How could they ever have believed that agriculture would work in the place? Fields of cotton they wanted to plant there, wheat and barley, sugar-cane, didn't even the specialist brought in from Holland say, nothing will come out of that peat, only dust and permanent fire. It will oxidise at an accelerated rate, he warned, it will dry out, it will petrify, it will subside, it will combust spontaneously under the ground and burn for weeks on end, however hard you try you won't manage to dowse the fires.

What had always happened there in the past was the rare miracle of water and fire clinging together, intertwining amid the fans of the papyrus, until the water disappeared and the fire celebrated its victory over the land as it subsided further, like a malicious laugh rising from the belly of the earth, sending them all fleeing to their homes, to close the windows, although there was no defence against it. Year after year their food was impregnated with the smell of the burning peat, the loaves and cakes they baked, the clothes they wore and laundered, even the babies born to them, especially her Dina, who had a lengthy and miserable birth, and sprayed around her without knowing it the smell of the fire, the smell of the mistake, the smell of the incinerated dream.

And it was this smell that drove her from the kibbutz in the end, at an unsuitable age, in conditions that didn't conform, too late or too early, but how naïve she was to think she could get away from it; it has found her in the end, it has chased her this far and day by day the fire is drawing closer to her, in the belly of the blazing earth they will lay her body, her heart will blend into the heart of the earth, like it she has dried out, petrified, subsided, like it she has disappointed, after all she, she and no other is the peat bog which is no good for anything.

Close the window, she tries to shout, but only a hoarse croak emerges from her throat; the smell is heavy and as tangible as a hand grasping her neck, it seems to her that a strip of fire is racing towards her from the foothills of Mount Hermon, the kiss of fire destined for her alone, year after year it has been on her trail, searching her out from house to house, any moment it will find her, now that she can't walk; her steps always were faltering. How can you possibly walk with confidence when under your feet a constant battle is raging, years of warfare with no decisive result, until her father died and the fire defeated the water. How high the flames rose after his death, cavorting around the sterile plains, sending up clouds of viscous smoke; get him out of there, he's burning, she used to run to her parents' room shouting, the fire is getting close to Dad and we must get him out of there, and her mother would look at her with a pained expression, relax, Hemdi, the fire won't reach the cemetery, nothing's going to happen, she sighed, anyway the disaster has already happened.

How do you know what's going on under the ground? she would whimper, you have no idea! And her mother did her best to reassure her, calm down, your father's soul is with us, and nothing else matters. What a strange phenomenon is a mother without a father, indeed what a strange phenomenon is a mother, but she was a mother too, here comes Dina's Mum, the nursery staff used to proclaim whenever she entered the children's house in the Kibbutz and she always imagined she heard sarcasm and censure in their voices, because her baby was invariably uneasy in her presence, embarrassing her with her screams in front of the other mothers, choking when she tried to feed her, spraying the white liquid in all directions, and the smell that emanated from her surprisingly swarthy skin was the smell of fire.

Close the window, she pleads, Dini, Avni, have they left her alone, and where is that woman with the black and glossy hair, who reminds her of her nanny in the first kibbutz, Shula, she remembers the name, which of them is called Shula? Close the window, but the room is dark and silent and she takes short breaths, beating her head on the pillow. If only she could get out of here, if only she could make it as far as the window, but she's so weak and her legs are painful, she can't even sit up. The phone is beside her and she grabs it, pressing digits at random as if it were a mysterious chest with a combination lock, a treasury of deliverance tucked away in it, but how will she get the right number, and what is the right number anyway, and since when has her daughter's number been the right one.

I'll call her in my heart, she mumbles, my Dini, because the memory of a rare moment reverberates in her consciousness: the early rain was falling, wild and stormy, and she took the baby with her to her father's grave, no one saw her when she ran out of the children's house, and she sat panting on the new, wet basalt slab, clutching the baby in her lap, stroking her hair as she told her the story.

I was the first baby born on the kibbutz, she told her in a whisper, and they all gathered together in the dining hall to see me walking. With sparkling eyes they looked at me, encouraging me to walk, and I was scared but I wanted to please them. I put one foot forward at the very moment my father let go of my hand, and everyone shouted, a terrifying sound, and I fell down on my back and for two whole years I didn't walk, and they wanted to take me to a specialist in Vienna, until a doctor in Tel Aviv told my father, she's just afraid to walk, make her more afraid of you than she is of walking, and suddenly a faint smile appeared on the baby's lips, and under the high and prominent forehead there was a wise and attentive look, and she told and told, holding her tight, interlocking rib to rib so it was impossible to separate them, until the baby let out a treacherous wail which betrayed them at once, and suddenly she was surrounded, her husband and her mother and the nanny, and they snatched the wet and shivering baby from her, as if she had done her some harm, and after that she wasn't allowed to spend time alone with her, not that she wanted to do that anyway; she had lost faith in her, they had both lost faith in each other, since then that look had never returned to her daughter's eyes, only doubt and unease she found in those eyes, with their lightening colour.

She doesn't love me, she would whisper secretly, my baby doesn't love me, and now she clutches the pillow and raises it slightly, little Dina, she whispers, my poor little one. The pillow is bulging too much and she makes an effort to give it the right shape, to narrow the waist, and a soft rustle wafts towards her through the pillowcase, a barely perceptible movement of life, and she presses it to her bosom. My baby, she wails, as if she hasn't seen her daughter since then. They reprimanded her sternly, snatched the infant from her and walked away, what was she supposed to have done, so what if the baby was a little wet? The rain treated them kindly, the rain put out the fire, soothed the body of her father laid under the slab, so many stories she wanted to tell her little daughter, so many corpses of stories have been buried inside her, my baby, help me.

How could I help you if I was a baby? She recoils on hearing the cold voice, drops the pillow and strains her eyes in the darkness of the room, has she arrived? Did she hear her calling to her in her heart? But why has she come in such a hostile mood if she's responding to the call in her heart? How long have you been here, Dini? She tries to grope, to get a grip on details, but her daughter isn't interested in details, since that evening their wishes have ceased to be compatible. I'm always here, Mum, she says, don't say you didn't know, and Hemda chuckles awkwardly, again the bitter way she says Mum, as if this is an honorific title she doesn't deserve. That's exactly the way the nursery staff used to greet her, here comes Dina's Mum, forcing her to confront a whole convocation of ponderous women kneading their babies like lumps of dough with their experienced hands, to confront Elik, who was just waiting for the opportunity to rise above her, to prove himself better than her, and it's a fact, the baby did smile at him, never stopped smiling, and she moved further away from them, taking her pupils out on long walks, telling them the stories of the lake instead of teaching them about the natural world, sitting for hours on her father's grave in the little cemetery and all of them staring at her anxiously as if she'd gone out of her mind, but she showed them when her Avni was born, she showed them what motherly love was all about. How easy it was to hold a baby in her arms, a strong and healthy male after a frail and lifeless girl; the touch of female skin has always repelled her and she found it hard to understand how a woman can give birth to a woman. Surely a woman should bear a man and a man should bear a woman, what a shame this isn't the way of the world, even seeing a woman suckling a baby girl is difficult for her, and she averts her gaze as if it's a perversion.

And to think she nearly gave up on him, alienated in equal measure from her swollen belly and from the toddler dogging her footsteps and she was hoping for a miracle. She bathes in the water of the lake and the belly is detached from her body and floats on the surface of the water and turns into a great fish, and here she is running to the summit of Mount Hermon, wallowing in the snow until the belly is torn open and subsides slowly, rolling away like a snowball, but then the little girl would hold out her arms to her and she would pick her up angrily as if she was the one who made her pregnant and all of this was her fault, and it seemed to her this was a pregnancy that would go on for ever, a sterile pregnancy with no birth at the end of it, how sterile in her eyes were the fertile years.

But just when she despaired of miracles the true miracle happened, something she had never considered or imagined, although it was as it turned out the most common miracle on the face of the earth, bringing tears to her eyes even now, since after the noisy flurry of limbs at the birth silence reigned, and when she opened her eyes she found beside her a solid and stalwart creature with rosy cheeks, staring at her calmly through half-closed eyes.

Hypnotised she gazed at him, people came and went and yet she remembers only him, and the serenity between them, as if a spectral voice had come down from heaven and declared this was the soul destined for her, and although in this face opposite hers there was no outstanding beauty – it was creased and flushed from effort – she couldn't take her eyes from it, and apparently he felt the same way, as his eyes didn't shift from her face, narrow and dark and sweet, like little raisins, they watched her, and she put a finger to his cheek, she was so weak this was the most she could do, and tears of sudden plenty flowed from her eyes.

And suddenly she's alarmed: had her memories been spoken aloud, had they reached the ears of her daughter, sitting in the armchair in the darkness and keeping silent, for years she has been denying this, as if it were a secret love affair, you love him more, you always loved him more, her daughter had been throwing at her the whole of her childhood, and she was constantly denying it, trying to take her in her arms, but a faint physical revulsion welled up in her when confronting the new female limbs. Who is putting this nonsense into your head? I don't want to hear this any more! Was this Elik? She always found it hard to believe he would betray her so blatantly.

I was young, my father had died, and you weren't an easy child, it took us time to get used to each other, but she never managed to say these simple words, only a fervent denial intended to cancel out absolutely her daughter's resentment, and now she strains her eyes in the darkness, are you there, Dini? she asks, did her daughter hear the ancient memory emerging from her mouth in explicit words, a confession that will destroy what remains of the closeness between them, and she hastily emits a nervous laugh. You won't believe it, she says in a jesting tone, I dreamed about a baby, I dreamed a baby was born to me, and I loved him, she adds with emphasis as if describing an extraordinary thing, but the armchair facing her is silent, perhaps she's gone to sleep, perhaps it's the nanny sleeping there, and perhaps there's no one there at all, as in the children's house when she was ill, moving an empty chair close to her bedside and laying a blanket on it, and in the delirium of fever she would see her mother sitting facing her, worried eyes fixed on her and on her lips a thin smile of self-control.

I'll be all right, Mum, don't worry, she used to mumble, because her father was always telling her, you mustn't upset your mother, you mustn't worry Mum, and to this very day she doesn't understand why, she only well remembers what a hard test childhood illnesses were for some of the parents: some of them couldn't stand it, and would creep into the children's house at night, and the young Hemda liked the thought that her mother was watching over her in her sleep, and even if there was doubt she preferred it to negative certainty, but now when she coughs, trapped and constrained by the smell of fire, she finds it hard to endure the doubt, Dini, she scolds her in a loud voice, why didn't you close the window?

The window is closed, Mum, she hears her voice, just like your heart, and she recoils in shock, that's enough, Dini, what do you want from me? I received much less from my mother and I loved her so much, I never doubted her love, why are you blaming me all the time? But her daughter interrupts her, what do you want from me, all I said was the window's closed.

What's the time she asks, morning already? Lately she's been almost enjoying the time that enfolds her, without reservations or boundaries, and she walks in its wide open spaces as if in a giant orchard, plucking a sweet fig, a plum warmed by the sun, melting in the mouth, freer than she has ever been before, and it cancels for her benefit the rigid rules of early and late, it was or it was not, turning a blind eye to minor offences. A time criminal she has become these last weeks, and in the midst of her misery she's happy and in the midst of her loneliness she's surrounded by people, inviting in whomsoever she pleases, a guest in the midst of her life she visits herself at the staging posts of her time, loitering as long as she chooses, but now, confronting her daughter she has to get a grip, she always had difficulty sleeping in her company, her presence inspires unease in her, and when they left the kibbutz and started living together it was the most embarrassing problem imaginable, a mother who can't sleep because her daughter is in the next room.

It seemed to her she was testing her remorselessly, trying to read her thoughts, invade her dreams, eavesdrop on words spoken in her sleep, and now again she has to gather the bones of memory into one body, one time; what is the time, she asks, but no voice answers her voice, and only a blast of oppressive heat is transmitted to her from the silent armchair, fingers of fire are approaching her, so familiar to her that her breath is knocked out of her when the blanket moves and someone squeezes into her bed, everything has already happened and it seems it will never stop; in their children's house, when the nannies were in a deep sleep, the nocturnal wandering would start. Sometimes one of the girls terrified by a nightmare, sometimes a child younger than her who needed protection, and sometimes there were those hazy, breathless visits that left a sticky stain on the bedclothes, but the body pressing against her now is hot and bony, and it seems all it wants from her is to be swallowed up in her and to swallow her, to be born in her and give birth to her, oy, Dini, she sighs, don't cry, why are you crying? And her daughter clings to her as if digging into her skin, help me, Mum, he doesn't want the child.

What child, she doesn't dare ask, so frail is her trust in her memory and so afraid is she of being caught out, and therefore it's preferable to keep silent and deduce one thing from another and be content with cautious questions, why doesn't he want that? And Dina wails, he says it's madness, he doesn't want a child, he doesn't need a child, he's fine as he is, do you think it's madness, you think I'm off my head? How crowded is her grave tonight, she sighs, it seems to her that for years she's been laid out in the dark covered with clods of earth, and now the grave is opening, shafts of light pierce her eyes, and a violent blast of air invades her nostrils, they're throwing in another corpse alongside her and covering it, and now it will be crowded for ever, until eternity her daughter will be whispering feverishly in her ear, don't run away from me, give yourself to me one last time, don't go running again to your father and your mother and that lake of yours, and she holds out a hand to her daughter; the ground wallows between them heavy and muddy and she must dig a hole to reach her, very gradually she digs, of course the two of them are buried here for ever, and of course she too was accused of madness in those years, that was the way I greeted you, my dear daughter, but they were wrong, it wasn't madness, the very opposite.

And if he leaves me, she asks, do you think he's going to leave me? And Hemda sighs again, they all leave in the end, the child leaves too, but it makes no difference, you're a mother, you need a child, it's a simple story, because suddenly she sees her as a little child holding a baby in her arms and running away from her, and she chases after her in alarm, be careful, Dini, you'll drop Avner, support his head, she ran so fast on her scrawny legs, and when she finally caught up with her and grabbed the baby from her arms, the girl wasn't letting go, she held on to his feet and shouted, this is my baby, I'm his mother, I'm his good mother, and she stood before her grieved and agitated, as at this moment. You are a good mother, she says, it's a simple story and don't let anyone complicate it, a mother needs a child, how calm the baby was in her arms, how he enjoyed the chase. Where did you want to take him? she asked when she got her breath back, and the girl replied, to his house, he wanted me to take him home, and Hemda asked, where is his home, and she replied, in the cemetery, in your father's grave.

But when he stands facing his car, with two parking tickets stuck to its front windscreen and hand-shaped leaves speckling its roof, he wonders where it came from, this absurd confidence that she's really going to appear before him this evening.

Because only now, in the purple twilight, does he notice how close his car is to the gate of the house of mourning, almost blocking access to it, undoubtedly arousing surprise and indignation; he must get away from here before members of the household notice him and try to find out what he's up to, and what's he doing here anyway, not only is he bringing no benefits to them, he's actually doing harm. It's obvious to him that he can't do them any good, but he still believes there is one soul he can help, and with all his fibres he seeks to compensate her for the gift she gave him, and longs to console her but doesn't know how, because when he gets into his car and drives away in haste, powering up the steep incline and stopping on the edge of the wadi, he realises how flimsy his prospects are of ever meeting her again, least of all in this place, even if he locates the grave and visits it every day, even if he makes a point of participating in all the memorial events. A hidden grief has been imposed on him, more closely hidden than his own, and he leans his head on the steering wheel, seeing how all his efforts so far have only taken him further away from what he saw in his mind's eye; his bourgeois exegesis of the scene behind the curtain has been utterly invalidated. This wasn't the leave-taking of a couple living in the full bloom of love but stolen moments of love, capable of sweetening a little the taste of death, and he has no idea what he's supposed to deduce from them about his life and his death, and he turns on the wipers and stares at the water spraying the front windscreen, tracing transparent semicircles, and it's only now he realises how close he's come to the edge of the wadi and he shudders when he steps out of the vehicle and sees one of the wheels already teetering on the brink.

Uneasily he looks around, drawing into himself the smells of sage and rosemary and the tantalising whiff of burnt straw, stumbling when he treads on the dry pine cones scattered on the ground, gilded by the setting sun. Where is she now, where is she mourning; he remembers how she wiped away her tears with the crumpled paper hanky he offered her, and a delicate twitch danced on her cheek when her tears mingled with his tears. Does she have a family too, a husband and children from whom she must hide her grief, and perhaps she's already separated from her husband and her grief is exposed but there's no one to comfort her, and he leans against a fig tree with its tangled branches and fruit still hard, big leaves drooping like the ears of a chastened dog, and stares at the sun as it lingers on the ridge, drawing the colours of the hills down into the wadi.

It's been years since he found himself face to face with the sun, just the two of them, and he sticks a straw in his mouth and sucks it like a cigarette; the sweet taste of dust spreads through the void of his mouth, is this the taste of death? The wadi is deep and dry, with a rocky heart, is this what it looks like? Look, the sun has disappeared behind the ridge in the reddening west, so it seems a fire is burning beyond the hill and only the sparks are managing to climb up over the ancient terraces, turning pale as they ascend. To his surprise he notices that even after sunset the sky is still clear, and for the first time it occurs to him that in reality there is no link between the disappearance of the sun and the disappearance of the light. Where does the darkness come from, he looks around him as if expecting a black ball to come rolling down from the hills, colouring everything in its path, or is it from the treetops that the darkness emerges, since they are already blacker than black.

Two sweaty boys run up the steep and narrow path, reach the end and turn round, their footfall echoing loudly, and he walks down in their wake, noting a flowering bush with a crop of little honey-apples, and he plucks the sticky fruit eagerly, biting into it cautiously and quick to spit it out, is this the taste of death? The darkness rises from the earth to the sky, he establishes with certainty, not the opposite as he thought until now. On the peaks of the ridge opposite the lights are coming on like beacons, and with them the sounds become sharper, the crying of a baby, people parting company, cars receding, and when he hears loud barking followed by reprimands in the hoarse voice that's so familiar to him, he tries to find a hiding-place and disappear from sight, but too late, as she's already standing there facing him, and for some reason she seems glad to see him.

I was sure it was your car down there, I told Elisheva, she announces with satisfaction, and he's embarrassed, I lost my keys, I had to leave it here, and he asks hurriedly, how is Elisheva? The neighbour sighs, she's having a hard time, but it's going to be even harder when the seven days of mourning are over, so I was glad to hear about the memorial day that you're organising for him, it's good for the family to attend events in his memory, and he asks tensely, when is the memorial day? And she says, the thirtieth of the month, that's also thirty days after his death, aren't you taking part?

No, I'm in accounts, he mumbles, where is it taking place? And she says, they don't keep you informed in your faculty, do they, and he grins, that's right, I'm always the last to be told anything; he's torn between the impulse to prolong the conversation until she divulges some extra information, and the fear that the longer the conversation goes on, the more likely it will become that his deception will be exposed, and she shakes the lead in her hand, Casanova, come here, now! I'm fed up with chasing after you! The shadows of the trees sway at their feet in the thin breeze and for a moment it seems the trees themselves are moving. Yes, yes, life races by like a shadow, she says, it feels like only yesterday they moved in here with their young children, what a family, so much love, I never saw anything like it, for fifteen years we were next-door neighbours and I didn't hear a single argument going on in that house. God knows how she's going to get over it, poor thing.

They say it's easier to get over the loss of a good marriage than the loss of a bad one, he finds himself offering some lame consolation, although I've never been convinced of that myself, what is there to miss about a bad marriage? But the neighbour declares, that's actually quite logical, you come out of bad relationships with a sense of lost opportunity, you eat your heart out thinking of what you didn't do, you feel anger and guilt, and there's no longer any chance of putting things right, no chance at all, she stresses in a menacing tone, as if she's been sent to warn him, and Avner recoils from her outstretched finger, retreats and turns to his car, still poised precariously at the edge of the wadi.

I must make a move, he says, give my regards to Elisheva, we'll meet in happier times, he adds and at once regrets it, and she corrects him pedantically, we're going to meet at the memorial day, and he nods hastily, yes, of course, but before he can get into his car a black and elongated shadow comes bounding towards them from the wadi, panting heavily, almost knocking him over as it barges in front of him and springs into the car, sitting in the driver's seat, and she laughs, he loves car journeys, this dog, come out of there, you silly thing, you're not going anywhere.

Rafael used to take him out with him sometimes, in the car or on foot, he really loved dogs, and it was he who gave us Casanova, isn't that right? she adopts a childish, simpering tone and addresses the dog, who puts his paws on the wheel as a spittle-flecked smile appears on his gaping muzzle. They had a bitch that whelped and he was one of the litter, and after the bitch died Rafael decided he didn't want another dog, but he used to take Casanova out for trips almost every day, didn't he, puppikins? And where did Rafael take you? she asks the dog. Elisheva used to worry, sometimes he'd disappear with him for hours, that was the kind of man he was, a real angel, even a dog he was incapable of disappointing, imagine it, even when he was really ill and weak from the treatment he insisted on taking him out from time to time, isn't that right, Casanova? Didn't you love going on trips with Rafael? Where were you going? And they both turn their attention to the dog, whose black beady eyes are fixed on the front windscreen, his mouth open, and it seems that any moment the revealing words will emerge from there, and Avner trembles as if the honour of the dead man is being impugned between them unknowingly, and he glances at his watch and exclaims, I must make a move, my wife and my children will be waiting for me, it's nearly supper time. Suddenly he's proud of this pairing, my wife and my children, and he enjoys throwing the words into her face as if saying, the deceased isn't the only one who had a wonderful family, maybe I have one too, maybe I have one and I don't know it, maybe this evening I'll find out, because when she pulls the hairy creature out of there with some effort, leaving his smell in the void of the car and the imprint of his fur on the seat, reverberating in Avner's ears are the warnings he heard, and he drives fast, escaping from the mountain settlement and heading for the city centre.

She isn't going to be found, he's never going to see her and he'll never hear their story, and perhaps it's better that way, as their secret love can no longer be salvaged, nor can the grieving family, but perhaps his own family still could be, if only to make it easier for him to lose it, so he won't be tormented by the grim sensations he's been warned about, you feel anger and guilt and there's no longer any chance of putting things right, no chance at all, and he pulls up at an oriental bistro by the roadside and buys fresh pittas, hummus and tehinna and onion salad, Shlomit will be glad to be spared the bother of cooking supper tonight, and he drives on at speed, hooting and overtaking a car that's being driven very slowly and veering from side to side on the ascent. For a moment it seems to him he sees her sad face reflected in his rear-view mirror, no wonder she's driving erratically, but at once he loses her as she's overtaken by other cars and he's not going to stop at the side of the road and wait for her, he'll carry on to his home, since this is what the dead man wanted to say to him, look to your home, as long as you have a home, and he thinks of him crossing the wadi with the big and exuberant dog, perhaps she lives not far from there, in one of the houses on the ridge opposite which light up in the darkness, and from this vantage point she could watch the daily routines of his life. With this urgent excuse of walking the dog, did they succeed in meeting, until he could no longer walk? And what did they do then, did the dog drag him to the door of her house where he collapsed, exhausted, to be transported from there to the casualty ward, and where was his wife Elisheva that morning, which was apparently the last morning of his life, and which of them was at his side when he gave his soul back to the creator of the world; he realises he'll never know the exact sequence of events, and even his detailed analysis will remain dubious, dependant on changes of mood. Is the vision he saw behind the curtain sending him in search of a love he never experienced, or sending him back home to Shlomit and the children, to try sweetening the mush of their shared lives with the berries of his understanding of death, as it seems to him the void of his mouth is full of them, berries which have a concentrated taste, salty and sweet at the same time, like the honey-flavoured fruits that grew on the bush, and when he locks his car he notices a gold leaf stuck to the windscreen under the wiper, an autumn leaf in midsummer, and he runs it delicately over his cheek and tucks it into his shirt pocket, and its touch, cool and pleasant like the touch of a caressing hand, remains on his face when he goes into the house, his hands full of greasy packages.

It seems to him he's the bearer of good tidings but they carry on as normal, not appreciating the magnitude of the moment, and even the little one, sitting in the corner of the lounge and engrossed in his box of toys, ignores his arrival; a smell of cigarette smoke wafts into the house from the balcony, Shlomit hasn't been weaned yet from her telephone cigarette, and he follows the smell and sees her leaning on the balustrade with her back to him, unaware of his presence. Yes, you're right, she's saying, but it's a simple enough story, I'm not sleeping at night for worry, the wind breathes life into her hair and her nape is exposed for a moment, fleshy and yet attractive with a few stray black strands, and when he puts his hand there she turns sharply, Avner, you startled me, she rebukes him, how long have you been standing there? What's going on? She probes her nape as if she's been stung, is that motor oil from the garage you're smearing on me? And he shows her the bag, I've brought some food, and she hastily says into the receiver, I'll get back to you, looking at him with indignation, the same blue eyes that once turned to him with love and admiration.

What beautiful eyes your children will have, they used to say to them in their youth, since both of them were endowed with a generous sparkling of blue eyes under dark eyebrows, but Tomer has to be content with the pale brown eyes of his grandmother Hemda while Yotam scans the world with eyes that are bluish but small and slightly slanted, so different from Shlomit's wide-open look, which used once to transmit to him so many heartfelt emotional messages, but for years now has been aggressive and damaged, and now it seemed to him he detects contempt as well, when she rubs her neck and then sniffs her fingers in disgust, as if there's no one more pedantic than her in matters of cleanliness, and he puts the bag, oozing grease, on the balustrade, precisely where he will find it tomorrow evening, after the sun has ruined the food, and yet he will open every single packet and sniff, deriving pleasure from the repulsive smells, an act of mordant self-deprecation, as if from the start he brought his wife and children a meal unfit for consumption.

Who were you talking to? he asks, reminding himself of his father, who in his later years was jealous of his mother and whose suspicions were aroused by every one of her phone conversations, and she says, to Dafna, why? And he says, just asking, as this wasn't really the question he wanted to ask her; he wants to know what it is that's worrying her so much, and why she can't sleep at night, and why she recoiled from his touch, but as the prospect of a sincere answer seems unrealistic he prefers to leave the clarifications for a more favourable time, and just asks, where's Tomer, and she replies, in his room staring at the computer as always, where else could he be, staying with friends? And yet again her voice is censorious, how long will she go on pinning her son's problems on him?

When he turns towards his son's room he sees three dirty plates, stained with the remains of salad and egg-yolk, on their round dining table, apparently they've already eaten their supper without him and why not, really, he's home late again, already nearly nine o'clock, and he goes into the children's room; on the computer screen frenzied figures are rushing about, but his son's back is as still as a rock, even his hands are laid motionless on the desk, and this contrast sparks a sudden fear in him, as if everything is topsy-turvy and the artificially generated images have sucked from his son the very spirit of life, and he stands behind him and lays a hand on his son's shoulder. The T-shirt is too tight for him, accentuating his bulging belly, and this annoys him, what's going on here, in his time there were no overweight children, not in his kibbutz or the neighbouring kibbutzim, maybe one who had a genuine medical condition, but most of them were running around incessantly, not allowing hollow figures to do all their moving for them, and he hears his angry voice emerging from his throat, what's happening to you, Tomer? Is this what you do all day? An unpromising opening sentence for an evening of playing happy families, and he regrets it at once, peering around to be sure Shlomit hasn't heard, where is she, anyway, has she gone back to continue her conversation on the balcony, but his son undoubtedly heard it, as his shoulder twitches uneasily under his touch and he moans as if he's been hit, leave me alone, Dad.

It's because I'm your Dad that I'm not leaving you alone, he retorts sagely, because I care about you and I can't bear to see this decline, and his son replies bitterly, oh, you can't bear to see it? Then just don't look, and Avner tries to moderate the tone of his voice, hey, that's no way to talk, listen to me, Tomeri, we need to sit down together and think of healthier ways you can spend your time. I still don't know why you left the karate club and Tomer shoots him an accusing look, why? Because I wasn't any good and the other kids laughed at me! This was a look he inherited from Shlomit, as if Avner's responsible for each and every one of his problems.

So what if you weren't any good, he growls at him, it wasn't the Olympics, and you were only in the beginners' class, you're supposed to be there to learn and improve! and his son protests, but they were all better than me and I didn't like it! But his father isn't letting go, I didn't like it! he repeats scornfully, since when did everything have to be liked? You do what's necessary, even if you don't like it. So why don't you join some other club, judo or football, what's wrong with that. Anything's better than what you're doing now, and here she comes, homing in, she won't miss an opportunity to attack him and defend her son. From which standpoint are you speaking, precisely? she hisses, her venomous voice preceding her body into the room, anyone would think you're working out every day or taking care of your body, look at that paunch you've grown these last years! And Avner breathes heavily, his fists pressed into his stomach; he must not lose control, not be like his father.

What's wrong with me trying to prevent him making my mistakes, his voice is heating up, he's still a child, he can change, and why are you defending him all the time? Don't you see how much damage you're doing to him? You're making him feel weak, needing his mother to defend him, and worse than that, you've got him thinking his Dad is some kind of monster he has to be protected from. Your brain is deteriorating too! he adds, and this is obviously a step too far, since Tomer gets up from his seat and shouts, his face swelling up, leave me alone! Stop arguing about me! I'll jump off the balcony to make you stop arguing about me! And Shlomit hugs him, there there, it's all right, darling, we're not arguing about you, we're arguing about ourselves, and he whimpers in her arms like an overgrown cub, you never argue about Yotam, and Avner remembers with a shock that Yotam has been left in the lounge unsupervised and he hurries away to find him, but he's not quietly nestling by his box of toys, maybe he went out to the balcony and climbed on the balustrade and he runs out there and calls his name, finally finding him sitting in the bathtub surrounded by smiling plastic ducks, and he's smiling too but his smile is anxious, Tomeri crying, he says sadly, Tomeri bad? and Avner is quick to deny this, putting on a childish voice, no, Tomeri not bad!

Tomeri not bad, the infant repeats thoughtfully, then Daddy bad? he launches another question, a turbid soap bubble, and Avner replies emphatically, no, Daddy not bad! Again the infant repeats it with relief, but this leads to a conclusion ten times more worrying, then Mummy bad? And Avner says no, absolutely not, Mummy not bad, but all of this fails to reassure the canny little boy, who needs to identify the rotten apple, and he makes one final attempt, then Yotam bad? And Avner holds out his arms and hugs his little shoulders, almost squeezing into the bath beside him fully clothed, as his heart goes out to him and he says again, what a thing to say, no and no! Yotam isn't bad! No one in our family is bad!

And when the children are finally asleep he'll find her stretched out on the sofa in the lounge, after the little one has been imprisoned in his bed, submitting with surprising obedience, as if trying not to spoil the effect of the litanies of reassurance, so carefully put together, and after he has sat for almost a whole hour at the bedside of his first-born son, who was lying on his back with a blanket pulled up over his head, with only the movements of the blanket showing that at intervals he was inserting his index finger in his nostril and from there to his permanently open mouth, and Avner laid a hand on his shoulder and apologised again for hurting him but also repeated his assertion that this was only because he cared for him so much, he loved him and worried about him, and finally he suggested the two of them go out running every evening, although there were no decent routes in their suburb. You know what, I have an idea, he came alive suddenly, we'll go to a different area and run there, because I know a wonderful route; in his mind's eye he saw the two of them climbing up the narrow asphalt road, sweating and feeling purified, alongside the wadi exuding the scents of straw and dust, sage and rosemary. We'll leave the car in the parking space at the bottom and run to the last house and back, what do you say, eh? He slaps his son's shoulder enthusiastically and tries to pull the blanket off him, while the boy hastily removes the finger from his nose. And Avner is a little taken aback by the sight of the face revealed to him, he was more comfortable when he lay there covered up, and he's shaken when he remembers the threat that neither of them dared to address directly, I'll jump off the balcony to stop you arguing about me, and immediately he bends down and kisses his brow with clenched lips. An unpleasant smell rises from the blanket as it's rolled back, something reminiscent of an unventilated and mouldering tent, and he thinks of his son a few years from now, years which will pass in a flash, in pitiless army encampments, grinding his teeth in the effort to keep up, issued with webbing and helmet and rifle, surrounded by shouted commands and humiliations, without a mother to protect him and cater for all his needs, and that's even before the real war starts, and how will he cope with that? His head is weighing so heavy on him, he suddenly flops down on the chest of the bemused child.

Are you all right, Dad? his son inquires cautiously and Avner perks up at once: it will be many years yet before that happens, six at least, and he tries to take comfort in this, no point in worrying about it now, and he leaves on a cheery note, so good night, sweetie, we've decided to go for a run tomorrow evening, don't forget, and he turns out the light and walks a little unsteadily to the corridor, looking around him. Where is she now, and how great is the effort required of him when he tries to do the right thing, it isn't logical, having to extinguish three fires every evening, it wasn't supposed to be like this, and again he thinks of the dead man when he was still alive, when he was still healthy, was he too forced to wander like this between his wife and his children? Probably not, a wonderful family, the neighbour said quite clearly, and he accepts her testimony at face value, although things concealed from her have been revealed specifically to him; in wonderful families things happen naturally, without the expenditure of so much effort.

What do you expect, you're the one who started it, he knows she'll say if he dares to complain, and perhaps she's right, at least in certain cases, that venomous heat of hers must testify to correctness, or at least to a strong inner conviction that he himself finds it hard to feel in relation to family matters, and perhaps in judicial matters too he's already lost it, and he remembers the testimony of the platoon commander. Just a few years ago he would have confronted him with the superiority and aggression expected of a defender of humanity, making him ashamed of the most natural impulses such as zest for life and love of country, whereas today he mumbled, consumed by doubts, quibbling over details of lighting as if he were an electrician, dragging his flip-flops back and forth while swift-footed justice danced between one body of evidence and another, leaving behind clouds of dust, and he goes hurriedly into the lounge, trying to catch the tail-end of an item on the television news, it seems it's precisely his petition that's been mentioned, or perhaps he's again imposing his internal world on reality; in the past the media used to deal with these issues all the time, but in the nature of things interest has waned.

What was that? he asks his wife, stretched out on the sofa, and she says, I wasn't paying attention and immediately turns off the set, the news has already moved on to the next item, a fire somewhere in the north, and he wonders how it is that his presence curtails her routine activities: a phone conversation nipped in the bud, the TV silenced, all the gadgets that she operates around herself are muted, for no good reason really, after all she's keeping quiet enough herself, or so it is until she flashes him a malicious look and says, I won't let you do to him what you've done to me.

What have I done? he asks, taken by surprise, what are you talking about? And she says, I'm talking about what you've been doing to me all these years, making me feel I'm not good enough for you, not beautiful enough, not clever enough, don't you see you're doing precisely the same thing to him? And he sits in the armchair facing her, staring at her bare feet, the only segment of her anatomy which seems to have retained something of the delicacy that was there before, her small and narrow feet are being forced to bear the weight of an increasingly cumbersome body and yet they are still beautiful; he's filled with compassion for them and he wants to take them in his lap like little puppies and caress them.

Are you listening to me at all? she says, all the time you're yelling at him and humiliating him, but he's starting to grow up now and he needs the support and presence of a father to help him turn into a man, not criticism, it's as if all the time you're saying to him: I was expecting a higher achiever than you've turned out to be! Don't you realise how much damage you're doing to him?! And Avner take a deep, heavy breath, you're exaggerating a bit, aren't you? It's over-protective, what you're doing; when he's in the army are you going to run after him like this, defending him? And she utters a derisive snort that dilates her nostrils, what has the army to do with it? What's the army to him?

You'd be surprised, he says, just how quickly the years pass, and at once he adds, I believe it's my duty to wake him up when he's obsessed with shit, eating it or watching it, that's how I show him I value him and I'm not giving up on him, and you don't back me up in this! But his voice sounds to him weak and defensive, as in the courtroom this morning – when justice abandons you, you stay abandoned – and he tries to formulate an attack, why don't you take a close look at what you're doing, he's caught up now in the flow of his words, becoming more and more convinced, you're the one creating distance between us when you defend him against me as if I'm a monster, that's the worst damage, you're not only weakening him, you're also depriving him of a dad, the only dad he has! he adds from the heart, unnecessarily, as if all the other kids can choose from a range of dads. What did I say to him, anyway? he presses on, there was no need for you to intervene! You're the one who's incapable of abandoning the symbiosis between you, and you're prepared to sacrifice me for the sake of it, and worse than that, your beloved son too! And she leaps up from the sofa as if stung by a scorpion, I've heard enough of this rubbish! You're confusing me with your psychotic mother! I have no interest in keeping him for myself, on the contrary, I just want the two of you to be closer. He feels his stress levels rising; now she's thrown his mother into the fire, excellent combustible material in all conditions, soon to be followed into the flames by his father.

Your fancy declarations don't impress me, he snaps at her, what counts is what you do, and the way you stand by him and oppose me is destructive and absolutely unnecessary, and why bring my mother into it? She had good cause to defend me, as my Dad's aggression towards me in those years was extreme. Today I've no doubt it was connected with his disease; he had a brain tumour and it changed his personality completely.

Then perhaps you've got a brain tumour too, she suggests with an ugly smile, gathering her legs into an oriental posture, her thick thighs exposed as her dress rides up, and he stands before her trembling with rage, how unloved am I, if he only dared he would put a hand to her mouth and wipe that smile from her lips, how unloved am I, and he turns his back on her and goes out. Where will he go now? He longs to sit for a while on the balcony, to breathe the air of a cool summer evening, one of the unique pleasures that this city has to offer on a lavish scale, but the iron shutter is already closed and if he opens it the boys might be woken up, and he strips in the dark bedroom and goes into the shower with a towel round his waist, as if afraid of being exposed to her in his nakedness, and only when the water streams over his shoulders does he let go of the towel and it falls to the floor of the shower and absorbs the scalding water that seethes with disappointment and hatred. What's the matter with her, how has she become so malicious, it seems to him her heart is sprouting poisonous weeds, and is this just down to neglect? He sees himself uprooting them with a firm hand, one after another. Perhaps you've got a brain tumour too! She's prepared to sacrifice his health on a whim, just so she'll be seen to be in the right, and he remembers his father standing before him and yelling, shorter than him but bristling with anger, like a spiteful cat that doubles in size, out having fun again? Done your homework yet? Nothing will come of you, nothing, nothing is what you are, and one time when he stood in front of the mirror and combed his hair, how handsome he was then, even he himself recognised this and he smiled at his reflection, and then the angry face popped up behind him. You Nazi! he yelled at him, and Avner turned to face him, stunned. You're crazy, he mumbled, I've got a crazy dad, what do you want of me? And at once his mother appeared from the kitchen, get out of here right now, she shouted at his father, brandishing the big wooden spoon in her hand, if that's the way you talk to your son you're not living here any more, and his father wasn't giving in that easily, how do you intend to support your family if I'm not living here? You can't go on dreaming for hours by the window and scribbling in your notebook.

I'll get by very nicely without you, she replied, I just want you out of here now, but it was the son who went, packed a few clothes and travelled to the kibbutz, to Shlomit, who caressed and consoled him, and it was impossible to imagine then that twenty-five years hence she would be using this pain against him in such a shameful fashion, just as it was hard to believe it was his father's hidden disease that made his responses extreme. Could it really all be blamed on the tumour? It's a fact he never attacked Dina, it was only him he envied, begrudging him his youth, his beauty, his mother's love, and he punished him for all this by denying him his love, and again he remembers his mother's stories about fishing in the lake, how they used to trick the fish with a trawling net, a double net with crude and tight mesh, and any fish making a heroic escape from the first net would immediately be caught by the second.

The water gathers up his tears and sweeps them away into the convoluted drainage system of the building, spoilt kid, mummy's boy, again he hears the scorn of the children and he tries to suppress his weeping, crushing the slippery bar of soap with his hand, and when he starts meticulously soaping his body his paunch protrudes between him and his genitals and thighs and feet, so he can't see the lower segment of his body at all, as if it were suspended in space, out of reach, and giddiness attacks him, and he leans against the wall of the shower and pinches his flesh angrily. It's as if his stomach is nothing but a tumour that has attached itself to his body, and he remembers with jealousy the slim build of the dead man on the last day of his life; his yellowing skin hung on his face and yet he was beautiful and boyish, this is the slimness he aspires to and he's going to get it, he swears to himself, and at once an extra oath is added, he's going to leave her, he's never getting any closer to this woman, and it makes no difference how upset the children will be, no difference that the little one is so little and the bigger one is just starting to grow up, there's no good time for separations and he can't do this any more, he wants to be loving and loved, like the deceased on his last day, and before he sees in his mind's eye the packing cases filling the house and the misery of his sons, he turns off the hot tap and turns on the cold, surprising himself with this courageous act and all his flesh tingling.

But when he emerges, treading on the cold and wet towel and wrapping himself in another, she's already in their bed, wearing the nightdress he bought her one birthday, its blue colour has faded to yellow following repeated laundering and inadvertent over-exposure to the sun, her eyes peer at him over the binding of an open book, and he hurriedly gets into the bed, turns his back on her and pulls the blanket over his head as his son did, next he'll be furtively picking his nose. How sharp the sense of smell becomes when there's no partition between you and your body, although he's only just soaped himself he senses an unpleasant smell rising from him, heavy and pungent, thus he apparently lay stinking in his mother's womb day after day, and thus he will stink in his grave, and when he feels her finger on his back through the blanket he freezes like a trapped animal, if he plays dead perhaps he'll be left alone.

Leave me alone now, he moans, I don't want to talk to you any more, and she grins a throaty grin, who said anything about talking? Her breasts are pressed against his shoulder, I'm sorry, Avner, maybe I was exaggerating a bit, I'm just worried about Tomer, I'm not sleeping at night for worry, and instead of being beside me you're against me, and he moves the blanket down from his face, I'm not against you, it's you who's against me, he mumbles, you're not giving me a chance, you attack me as if I'm the enemy of humanity, and she presses against him, so why don't we both make an effort, OK? For Tomer's sake. He listens to her dubiously, what exactly is she suggesting, sexual intercourse for the sake of the child? Why not for their own sake, since when have adults not been allowed to make an effort? And more than this, he wonders what signals her body is sending him, does she really want him or is this part of the deal, how demeaning for him and really for her too, it's been months since they did it. When was the last time? Her birthday or his, whichever came later, suddenly he can't remember, long ago sex had lost its routine presence and turned into a bourgeois ritual, like a bottle of champagne that's opened on special occasions although no one particularly likes the taste, except that year when she wanted to be pregnant with Yotam, then every morning she was chasing up the mysteries of her ovaries, and the need for precision dictated their sex lives for almost a year, and although they were both practical and not romantic by nature, in the spirit of the entire process a kind of serenity dominated them then. But once she got what she wanted it seems she lost all of it, and although he felt as she did he held this as a grudge against her, and even now her body annoys him, like his own body in fact, and not only on account of its weight but also its weightlessness, and therefore the breasts that are pressing into his back seem to him like envoys without power and without attraction, and he mutters coldly, I'm bushed, good night, and in silence she gathers her limbs together and moves to the other side of the bed and within a few minutes she's fast asleep, as always, so much for her claim that she isn't sleeping at night. Her steady breathing has accompanied his insomnia for years, a kind of family curse shared by him, his mother and his sister Dina, almost the only thing that unites them.

There were years when he found in her healthy sleep a blessed balance, and years when he envied and hated her for this, and the further they grow apart, while she is subsumed so far as he's concerned into some multitude of blurred faces that isn't him, her sleep no longer affects him, one more person who sleeps easily, it's only by chance that this miracle happens in his bed specifically, and he leaves the bed with a sigh and goes to the children's room, does he have the strength to walk out on her, has he not left it too late?

The night-lamp with its Mickey Mouse ears and silly smile lights up the face of Yotam, sleeping with mouth open and knitted brows, whereas Tomer is beyond the range of the faint rays and his face is dark, as if their beds are located far apart in different geographical zones. Was he really expecting a different kind of child, did the boy's resemblance to Shlomit alienate him from him as their relationship soured, or was it the resemblance to himself? He didn't take pleasure in him, didn't take enough pleasure in him, while Shlomit was quick to possess him avariciously, turn him into flesh of her flesh.

With a heavy heart he leaves the bedroom and switches on the light in the kitchen, realising how hungry he is; his big stomach is hollow, besides a tasteless croissant in the courthouse cafeteria he has eaten nothing all day, but he'll get over it, he's not going to give the stomach what it's demanding, he'll punish it and starve it, subdue it with a firm hand, and he bends down and drinks lukewarm water from the tap, drinking and drinking until the void is filled and then dragging his tired legs to the bedroom. Through a crack in the shutter the beam of the street-lamp filters in and a thin ray of light rests on Shlomit's neck, emphasising the contrast between her soft white skin and her curly black hair, the texture of pubic hair, and he fumbles distractedly with her neck, his other hand going to his awakening penis; it seems the hunger has migrated from his stomach to his loins, hunger for a chunk of fresh and oily meat, attractive even in its hairy ugliness, as a surge of vibrant lust unfamiliar to him impels him to leap suddenly on her neck and bite it angrily, desperately, like a dog mounting an unknown bitch beside a refuse dump, and before she can let out the howl of pain and protest that will instantly kill the illusion, he puts a hand over her mouth, which smiled the most repellent of smiles at him only a little while ago, crushing her lips with his fingers, and with the other hand he guides his penis, stiffened by resentment, between her thighs, drawing a fierce delight from the disgust that her body arouses in him, and all this time his teeth are locked on her neck as his body rises and falls over her, her hair filling his mouth until he feels close to vomiting, but still he doesn't give in, his eyes darting around tensely to be sure no other dog is approaching, because the moment he releases the neck the humiliating sensation will dissolve, his last grip on life, and he goes up and down like a hill-climber, running on the steep and narrow path alongside the wadi, with its warm and perfumed exhalations, and he's gasping and panting, in his mouth the strange and sticky fruit he plucked from one of the trees, the shape of a honeycomb and tasting salty, until he stumbles suddenly and falls into the depths of the wadi, his body crashing on the rocks, and there they attack him at once, shedding his blood, cutting off his head, what a devilish relief, he isn't the hunter but the prey, and she isn't the bait but the naked trap, and a renewed wave of hatred towards her washes over him as he pushes her away abruptly and retreats to the side of the bed, breathing heavily.

He never attacked her like this before, and he's embarrassed between the sheets, although at the same time he relishes the sudden sense of freedom, is this manliness, is this how real men feel, devouring many women, firing their rifles? Did that platoon commander feel this way, after he shot and injured the peace campaigner, is this how they all feel, that nothing will stand in their way from now on and for ever, that the universe lies at their feet? How nice it will be to wake like this in the morning, with a sensation of wondrous intoxication, how nice it will be to fall asleep like this now, but here comes her voice breaking through the darkness, and it's bland and matter-of-fact, as if her neck hadn't been gripped by his teeth just a few moments ago, tearing open the webs of sleep and bringing him back to this part of the world: to his country, to his city, to his family, because she says suddenly, as if they were engaged in a casual midday conversation, tell me, have you spoken to your sister lately? And he replies in a whisper, overawed by their voices, overawed because they have a whole language at their disposal, not just grunts and groans, no, I haven't had occasion to, why?

She's gone off the rails, his wife declares with satisfaction, you wouldn't believe it, I called in this morning to visit your mother and found Dina in her bed, snuggled up against her like a baby, it seems I woke her up because she was totally confused, and she looked frightful, she adds, getting down to the detail, she was always jealous of his sister who, she claimed, looked down on her, you must talk to her, and he asks testily, now? At two in the morning?

Of course not, she grins, it really isn't that urgent, I just wanted to tell you before I forgot, and he mutters, great, so you told me, and he's cursing her inwardly, wondering why she saw fit to open her mouth and drive away the sleep that's finally cooperating with him. This is just what he needs now, his sister's woes, and anyway who knows what's going on with her, they live so close to each other but hardly ever meet, each of them dubious about the other, defending his or her choices, each of them disappointed by the other. He refuses absolutely to think about her now, about his stuck-up sister, with her annoying didactic rhetoric, her cold and aloof husband and the daughter who's too skinny and too smart, an irritating family, he sighs, and already his anger is veering towards his sister, since it seems to him it was she who sprang upon him suddenly from his wife's throat, to rob him of his sleep tonight.

Chapter Eight

In the morning the rays of sunlight creep in with the cruel cunning reserved for this room which was once her room, and it seems that thirty years haven't elapsed and she's still a young girl with all her life ahead of her, time enough to destroy her meagre fortune. How she hated the mornings in this room and the invasion of the rays that pierce her eyes, knives of light slicing her sleep thinly, until she's forced to wake up to transparent reality, dazzled and flustered. What's the time? she sits up in alarm, I'll be late for school, why didn't you wake me? It seems any moment now she'll find her father standing at the little mirror in the shower room and shaving off the bristles of the day that's passed, and her mother in the kitchen, washing the dishes from the day that's passed, but she's in no hurry to leave the bed, her limbs are tangled up in knots that she can't untie, her neck trapped between her shoulders and nausea rising in her throat, and when she tries to move her head on the axis of her paralysed neck she notices the body beside her, the old woman lying motionless on her back like a mummy, her skin covered with a kind of dark wax and her mouth open, and she too gapes beside her in bewilderment, how did you get here and how long have you been here, a girl scared in the night and creeping into her parents' bed, but your father's been dead a long time and your mother's old and you yourself are on the cusp of the age of decay.

You sat on the balcony and drank what was left of the wine from the meal, the bottle that was fuller than you expected was steadily emptied, you waited for Gideon and perhaps you slept on the balcony, but how did you drive here, and how long ago was that, and how is it that no one's looking for you, as if you never had a family, you're even more isolated than your mother, and when she turns to look at her again she's shocked, there's no sign of exhalation from her mouth and nothing going in, no movement reverberating in her body. She's dead, I smothered her without knowing it, like an inexperienced mother with a day-old child, perhaps I killed her on purpose, I pressed the pillow down over her face, avenging myself on her, on Gideon, on Nitzan, on Avner, and she made it easy for me and didn't even struggle. After all, if I don't even remember driving here, who knows what else I did and I don't remember. She feels her heart wandering between her ribs, soon it will burst and fall silent and thus the two of them will be found at the end of the day in one bed without a living breath between them, a mother and daughter who never shared a single moment of grace, and she tries to stabilise her breathing, putting a tremulous finger to her mother's arm. You're alive, please be alive, she implores, amazed at how hard it is for an inexperienced person like her to distinguish between death and life, because suddenly she hears a faint rustle exhaled by her mother's nostrils, and when she presses against her the old woman opens her wrinkled eyelids and mumbles, what's this, what was all that?

Go back to sleep, everything's all right, she whispers, gratefully laying her head in the hollow of her shoulder. Her mother's bones are so brittle, they are liable to crack under the weight of the heavy skull deposited on her, but she wants to keep it there for ever, the fear of loss cancelling out all partitions, and she embraces the old wax doll in her arms, the shell that has been emptied and can therefore be filled with any content, according to changing needs, which lately have become brazen and embarrassing. In a moment she'll fasten her lips to the nipple and try to suck from there the taste of life that she has lost, let me drink your grey milk, Mother, give me life, until she forces herself to abandon this and escape from the bed, with the musty smell rising from it, put her feet on the floor and walk away, with aching bones and heavy nausea, away from here, this room is no longer her room and the bed is no longer her bed, midday already and she has no idea what's happening at home. When did Gideon return and where did he go, is Nitzan at home, is the cat's bowl full or empty, and she washes her face in front of the small mirror in the bathroom, only her forehead and her eyes and the bridge of her narrow nose are visible, a reminder of the days when her mother was taller than her, a reminder of the differences in dimensions and status within the family as reflected in the positioning of the mirror; ultimately it wasn't satisfactory for any of them, and yet it didn't occur to them to acquire a larger mirror which could accommodate the faces of all four of them.

Oval coronas surround her eyes and her hair is dry and unruly, and when she stretches her body, her sunken cheeks are revealed and she passes her tongue over her lips, and the tiny wrinkles dancing around them, and anyway this mirror was always tough on faces, as if prophesying the future and anticipating its arrival, and now she lingers before it, washing her face again and again in cold water, as if this is the way to smooth her skin. In years she hasn't scrutinised her face with such painful thoroughness, look at yourself, are you really going to push a pram down the street? With this crease between your eyes, and the fatigue behind them? This isn't for you, this is for your students with their radiant skin and fresh faces, even when they're tired; as for you, even when you're not tired the lights in your eyes have gone out, and she dips her head in the basin under the tap, wetting her hair, brushing her teeth with a finger, be content with what you have and say thank you, Gideon was right, what presumption, what madness. Will a young child make you younger? The opposite, he'll just emphasise your age, will he make you calmer? The opposite, he'll just intensify your fears, and it isn't fair for the kid either, getting middle-aged parents who may not have time to bring him up at all, not to mention the difficulties you can expect if a child is damaged or scarred, will you be ready for that too? Have you any idea just how much effort is needed?

Her hair is dripping water on her shoulders and she puts her hands on the sides of the basin, fighting another wave of nausea, and when a sour whitish liquid leaps from her throat she bends over the toilet bowl, her finger thrust into her gaping throat, just as it was then, some thirty years ago, when her girlish face was reflected back to her in the stark marble sides of the pedestal, with the thin trickle between them, and all kinds of weird and wonderful foods made their way from her throat to the throat of the bowl, from her tormented gut to the gut of the toilet.

In those days there was no name for such phenomena and they were never discussed, and as a result it never occurred to her that she had secret allies, somewhere in the world there was at least one other girl going down on her knees before the toilet bowl after almost every meal, especially if she overdid the eating, and any slight deviation from the norm was excess in her eyes, not to mention the wild and unruly diets designed from the outset to lead to this result: fresh bread with chocolate spread, ice cream and halva and cake, all the foods not even to be contemplated by a girl with expanding thighs and bulging stomach, decadent meals that could only be snatched when there was no one else in the house, with pounding heart, and a tense look from the window at the entrance to the neighbouring house, to be sure she wouldn't be disturbed, and immediately after this the bending of the already aching knees, and the finger down the throat, and the slimy cataract gushing from her mouth in a violent stream, leaving behind it a sour taste in the void of the mouth and on the tips of the fingers, and she'd stick her head under the tap, scrubbing her hands with soap and her lips as well, putting a little soap into the mouth, sprinkling herself with her father's pungent shaving lotion, as her mother didn't possess so much as a single phial of perfume in those days. But sometimes it simply didn't work, sometimes the gloop stuck to the stomach and refused to climb up the oesophagus, and then the finger would roam around the mouth, damaging the delicate uvula, and nothing came up but bloody saliva, and in the meantime some member of the family would have returned home and would be pestering her, come out of there, Dina, you can't monopolise the bathroom for hours on end, there are other people here, but not one of the people living alongside her in the tiny apartment asked himself or herself, or her, no one gave any thought to what she was actually doing in there, no one knew how deeply trapped she was in the disorder she had developed, how loudly the toilet was calling to her all the hours of the day and the night, no one realised this was the only time she was happy, when the gunge poured from her mouth, leaving the stomach empty and the body purified.

Hey, come out of there, Dina, they would go on urging her until she stood up with difficulty, stumbling to her bed with painful throat and bloated stomach; a sadistic disco dance in progress in her gut, ice cream cavorting with halva, bread with chocolate, and all of them maliciously joyful. She writhed on the bed, wishing there were some newly invented but simple operation, akin to abortion, a scraping out of the stomach with a long spoon shaped like a ladle, even without anaesthesia, just so long as it got rid of everything in there, until she turned into a creature unencumbered by a physical body. She had to try again later, when they were all asleep, she'd drink a lot of water and sneak into the bathroom, to the toilet bowl that was waiting for her with open mouth, how hard it was to find privacy in a crowded apartment house with hollow plaster walls and one shared toilet, and yet no one ever noticed her distress.

What were they so busy with, she wonders now, washing her hands over and over again with the cheap soap; Nitzan must be home by now, and she is hypersensitive to smells, but what was it that preoccupied her father and her mother and stopped them noticing her, each of them huddled in a corner and licking wounds while she was harming herself every day, and suddenly the pain returns to her in full force, this burning in her throat, so demeaning, what a trap for her was this miserable little room, with the peeling walls and mould on the ceiling, what a trap for her was this dreadful apartment, and now she's getting out of here, she'll cross the threshold and go, many years have passed, soon the carer will be arriving for her mother and she's going home, after all she has a home of her own, a family of her own.

Reverberations of raucous canned laughter are audible on the stairway of her house as she climbs up with an effort, floor after floor, you could be driven mad by this artificial laughter emerging from the neighbours' houses, the kind of laughter that actually makes her want to cry, to bemoan the increasing stupidity of the world, and she tries to insert the key in the keyhole but without success, apparently it's locked from inside. She rings the bell but nobody hears, and indeed how could she be heard. To her surprise she realises that the repellent gusts of mirth are coming from her own house, how can this be, it's so unlike Nitzan, and she takes her mobile from her briefcase and calls her, but the phone won't be heard either and she slumps down exhausted on the stairs, leaning against the door of her apartment, her fingers and hair stinking of puke and cheap soap, her clothes drenched in sweat. Open the door to me, Nitzan, she whispers, open up my dear girl, my sweetheart, my dove, my treasure, and miraculously it seems her whispers have been heard because the door opens suddenly and she tries to steady herself so she won't fall flat on her back with the abrupt removal of her support.

Nitzi, I was giving up hope, she says with forced jollity, luckily you heard me in the end, come on, give me a hand, she goes on babbling as if some miracle has happened, and already she's rising a little unsteadily, because the hand that her daughter extends to her is attached to a weightless body, not to be leaned on for more than a split-second; this hand is cold and lifeless, or perhaps loveless, and when she finally stands facing her daughter she sees her hostile expression, which ages her so much that she dares for a moment to guess how she will look in her dotage, and she tries to draw closer with a clumsy movement that doesn't work out well, how are things, my dear, has anything happened?

No, she retorts angrily, avoiding her touch and throwing herself down on the sofa, then pressing the remote to turn up the volume and Dina sits down beside her and caresses her bare thigh, what's up, Nitzi? Talk to me, turn the TV off, but the girl immediately moves her downy legs out of reach, stubbornly holding on to the remote.

Don't you feel well? Have you fallen out with a friend? Has someone hurt you? she presses her, thinking immediately of that boy who possibly left a strand of hair behind, as well as a lot of doubts in her heart, has he dumped her, and the primeval fear of rejection comes back to haunt her and she falls silent, but her daughter shakes her head and at once goes on the offensive, you, you're the one who's hurt me, and you have no idea how much!

I? She's baffled, what have I done to you? And when Nitzan doesn't reply and only juts out her chin defiantly, she puts out a hand to pull the remote from her fingers but the girl isn't letting go, and it seems this grappling is the closest contact she's had with her daughter for a long time, as the air leaving her lungs, warm and fragrant, is drawn into her nostrils, and the long honey-coloured hair tickles her face when she leans towards her, give me the remote, Nitzan, turn off the television and tell me what the problem is; she finally succeeds in detaching her daughter's fingers from the remote, and in the silence that reigns in the void of the house all that is heard is the wail emerging from Nitzan's throat, when she blurts out in an aggressive tone, Dad told me you want to swap me for another child.

Gideon, what a traitor you are, she clenches her lips, all methods are kosher when it comes to wrecking my plans, even exploiting your daughter! Usually he behaves with restraint until he feels threatened, and then he's capable of acting without any thought or consideration, blind to the damage he causes. I didn't know you hadn't told her, he will pretend innocence when she confronts him, of course you should have shared it with her and I had the right to speak out, and again the torch is lit in her chest cavity and its flame is rising to her throat, and she tries to put aside for the moment her anger at Gideon and concentrate on her daughter, but to her surprise she realises she's angry with her too, for siding with her father in such unequivocal fashion, and she wipes her face with the edge of her blouse, what are you talking about, Nitzan? Are you out of your mind? she says bluntly, what's this about swapping you? What utter nonsense!

You see me growing up and you want to trade me in, the girl insists, and not even for a kid who's really my brother but someone from another country who has no connection with our family anyway! And Dina is surprised by the clumsy way she's expressing herself, not like her normally fluent daughter, and she wonders which of the words belong to her and which have been planted in her by her father. Take it easy, Nitzi, she tries to summon up all her resources and convert them into reasoned argument, it's just a thought that occurred to me recently, and I mentioned it to your Dad. Nothing's happened yet and of course your opinion is important to me, and I was going to consult you about it. But Nitzan doesn't respond to this conciliatory speech and interrupts her with a howl, I'm not talking about things that have happened or not happened yet, it's the fact you're even capable of having such a thought! If you don't want me I'm out of here, I'll go and stay with one of my mates, you won't need to chuck me out that way!

I really don't understand you, Dina says, alarmed by the extremes of her daughter's vocabulary, since when did a new child in a family mean someone being thrown out? When Tamara's brother was born, did her mother want to get rid of her? When Naomi was giving birth to a new baby every two years, did she want to dispose of the rest?

But you want to adopt, and that's something completely different! the girl protests, and Dina says, why is it so different, really? It may be less natural but on the other hand it's more humane, at the end of the day a child is a child, but her daughter cuts her off, it's completely different, not a real sibling!

But you never wanted a real sibling, she reminds her with an incontrovertible argument, when I still could have given birth, you weren't keen on the idea, and Nitzan replies drily, why did you ask me anyway? Since when have kids been consulted about things like this? You shouldn't have asked and you certainly shouldn't have taken my opinion into account, you screwed up, she adds coldly, but you don't put one mistake right by making another.

So perhaps this time too I shouldn't be taking your opinion into account, Dina says, an unfamiliar hatred swelling in her, directed at her daughter, it's easy for you to talk, you're young and for you everything is open, the gates of the body and the gates of the mind, the gates of the future, and what do I have, what's left for me but to see you moving away, and Nitzan says, maybe that's the truth, you might just as well take no notice of my opinion, because you're not going to hear it, I won't be here, and Dina snorts, oh yes, and where are you going to be?

That's none of your business, she hisses, if you're prepared to destroy our family and bring into this house some fucked-up kid who isn't going to feel like one of us, and where are you planning to put this kid anyway? We don't have a spare room. You see, you're counting on using my room, aren't you, and Dina says, stop talking nonsense, your room is yours, stop inventing imaginary threats, since when have you needed proof of my love? You've had so much from me and I still have a lot to give you, more than you want to accept.

That's exactly the point, she yells, this is what makes the whole thing so twisted, it's because of me, because I'm growing up and this is tough for you, and Dina is quick to deny this, what a strange thing to say, I'm glad you're growing up and it isn't tough for me at all, I just feel I have a lot more to give to a child, so why not? and Nitzan is yelling again, her face reddening, because it's a fact that before I grew up it didn't suit you, and now because of me you're acting out of desperation, don't you see that?

Who's talking about desperation? Dina protests, it's an optimistic project, it's about belief in life, belief in myself, willingness to give, what's desperate about it? But this lame argument doesn't even convince her, let alone her daughter, curled up in a corner of the sofa, taking off her glasses and blowing her nose again and again, I'm not living here any more, she repeats, you bring in another kid and I'm out of here, and Dina shakes her head back and forth, how can you be so negative after all you've had from me? How can you not see my needs, the hopes invested in this child? I really don't know you, I thought someone who has had so much would be capable of giving something back.

I'll give to whoever I please! her daughter yells at her from the end of the sofa, my friends get a lot from me, believe me they're not complaining, and Dina stands up quickly and goes to the kitchen, pouring herself a glass of water with a shaking hand, an iceberg of cynical sobriety confronts her, immovable, it was all in vain, all those years, all that love, the absolute commitment. Chance remarks ring in her ears, overheard in hairdressing salons, bus stations, cafés: children are so ungrateful these days, you can't expect anything from them, just disappointment, and the older they get the worse it is, but she had always felt protected, she never imagined that Nitzan would round on her like this, hurling such vicious words at her. Everything was in vain, not only her relationship with the girl, if there was any chance of this surviving under all the pressure, but the person she brought up, turning out to be selfish and pitiless, how did this happen, and at once the accusing finger shifts in Gideon's direction, well, what did you expect, you weren't bringing her up single-handed, this is what he's like, this is from him, and at the same time she's struggling to believe her daughter's words; is this the girl who strokes and feeds any stray kitten in the street? Is this the girl who gives generously to every beggar, who can be moved to tears by any story of suffering or injustice? She doesn't really mean it, she's just testing me.

Only a few months back she told her about a crazy woman she saw in the street, running to and fro and cursing; I didn't pity her, she said with dignity, because pity means superiority, I identified with her, and Dina listened, deeply moved and grateful, and now she glances at her with a cautious eye from the kitchen, curled up silently in the corner of the sofa wearing an ultra-short denim skirt and a white T-shirt, her hair covering her face; what's hiding behind this crude reaction, which isn't typical of her? She must try talking to her rather than shouting at her, and she fills a kettle with water. Are you hungry, Nitzi? she asks in a businesslike voice, to show that even if harsh words have been exchanged, simple routine still goes on, mother and daughter, coffee and lunch, but the girl responds with a shake of the head and she rummages in the almost empty fridge, she has no energy for cooking and she takes out the dish with the remains of the yoghurt soup from yesterday, and although the memory of the whitish glob floating in the toilet bowl brings her a fresh twinge of nausea she cuts off the end of a dry loaf and dips it in the dish and raises it to her mouth and chews it, all this while standing before the open door of the fridge and composing a shopping-list. So many things are running short, she'll go to the shop this afternoon, the fridge will be filled, Gideon will come back, she'll cook pasta with a cream sauce and mushrooms, and the three of them will eat together on the balcony, perhaps she'll even find time to bake a cake, a cold cheesecake of the kind Nitzan loves, appropriate for the sweltering evening that lies ahead.

Would you like cheesecake, Nitzi? she asks, but no reply is heard and she closes the fridge door with a slam, why is she bothering anyway? Let it stay empty, who cares if there's no food, no home, no family, years have gone down into oblivion, weeks and months, and all for what: to keep Nitzan happy with cake and keep Gideon happy with wine, to make sure nothing's running out, to lay a cloth on the table on the balcony, to cover up and embellish, exercise restraint and absorb, why should she care about them if they don't care about her, let them eat on their feet in front of the fridge just like her, and while she's angrily chewing the bread she sees her daughter's eyes watching her through the locks of her hair, and for the first time since she was born she's taken over by such a deep sense of alienation from her, she's embarrassed to be seen eating in front of her, embarrassed to swallow, what an absurd spectacle, a woman of a certain age chewing anxiously while the wrinkles dance around her lips, a woman on the cusp of decay swallowing hurriedly and the muscles of her neck protruding, and it seems to her suddenly her daughter is recoiling from her, from her body, from her mannerisms, and absolute loneliness hits her so hard she throws the rest of the bread in the bin and escapes to the bedroom, leaving the strange creature in the corner of the sofa, a creature with glossy fur covering its hands and feet and no face, and perhaps, judging from her experience, no heart either.

Nothing has changed in the bedroom since yesterday, the made-up bed, the empty cup, and especially the closed shutter, which shows that Gideon didn't sleep here last night, as the moment he opens his eyes he rolls up the shutter with a flourish. What did he say to her back then, I'm addicted to the light, how can we live together, and she replied lightly, then we won't be living together. Did he sleep in his darkroom, did he sleep in the house at all, did he notice her absence, and when did he get the chance to see Nitzan and tell her the worrying news. It's possible to try and investigate all these things, and it's equally possible not to bother, and really it's all the same, and when she strips off her sweaty clothes she remembers how her daughter didn't even take the trouble to comment on this, just as she wouldn't tell a woman sitting next to her on the bus, a stranger, that she needed an urgent wash and a change of clothes, that's how far apart we are, and she goes to bed in bra and panties, under an empty quilt cover.

This is surely how that woman felt, the one who killed herself, she hears herself thinking, suddenly she stopped caring, suddenly she was no longer busy catering for the needs of her family, otherwise she couldn't have left them like that, left them guilty and damaged. How much power is latent in the absence of feeling, in the absence of that compulsion that drove her from place to place, all the time from them and to them, her two loved ones, to remind them they have a house, they have a family, she and she alone is the house, she is the family, the one who listens and reassures, who clothes and launders, puts to bed and wakes up, serves as chauffeur, all of this for the sake of being confronted by a heinous insult the moment that, for the first time, you're interested in doing something exclusively for yourself.

At one time she used to be in touch immediately after the end of the lecture to remind him to cut the crusts off the girl's bread, ask which picture the editor had chosen, but now she's walking in other worlds, these trite details that swamped her love for them don't interest her any more, she's letting go and releasing herself, as that woman did, her own age approximately, maybe a little older. What else did he say about her, did he explain why she did it? But that she definitely understands, understands so perfectly it seems she knows her well, as she knew only one other woman in the world, her best friend Orly, and all at once, with a swift movement of certainty like a shutter opening to the light of midday, it becomes clear to her that she is the one, she has to be Orly, as who else besides her would be capable of misleading her closest relatives year after year, devoting herself to them and then betraying them in one moment, and suddenly it's also clear to her how it happened: she didn't hang herself, she jumped into a cloud, clutching its branches.

She remembers how the two of them stood one winter evening on the roof of one of the university buildings, leaning on the rail side by side, and the wind whipped up their hair and lashed them together, and Orly fingered the matted knot and said, if I jump now I'll take you with me, and Dina chuckled in surprise, she loved her so much in these moments, even this was a pleasant prospect: the viscous air would rock their bodies in a giant cradle and they would sink gradually, hair entwined, and when the pain came they wouldn't feel it since at that precise moment their souls would be parted from their bodies, but not from each other, like their hair – interwoven for ever, with nothing to distress them any more, and that is why she chuckled in the face of it without fear, the wind pricking her exposed teeth. How successful she was in finding a delusional refuge among the most desperate and how painful was the break; in one night Orly went out of Dina's life for ever, leaving in the open void anger and blame, grief and destruction, and were it not for Nitzan, who had just been born, she might never have recovered, and here she is, coming back to her finally the moment Nitzan has released her grip, and she's tempting and menacing, I'll take you with me, and Dina wipes the sweat from her brow with the edge of the quilt cover, take me with you; suddenly she remembers how Nitzan loved being put into this cover as if it were a sack, in the garden at the foot of their building, and she would pull her around the lawn, as the girl's laughter came spiralling up from the depths. Red light! she announced, and then she had to stop, green light, left, right, guiding her with cries of delight, and Dina would fill her lungs with green air, and it seemed to her she had never been happier than in these moments, when she ploughed the lawn back and forth like a mule seeing only what was ahead of her, and even when her fingers froze from the grip and her back ached she didn't stop, so the girl's laughter wouldn't stop, and now the quilt cover shrouds her sterile body. In the warp and weft of the compressed cotton, are they still woven there, those moments of simple pleasure, are the sounds of triumph and joy still hidden there? We need so little, she remembers thinking then with pride, but even this little was short-lived, a festival that passed, and she rises from her bed, putting the cover over her shoulders like a cloak, and goes out to the enclosed balcony.

The heat hangs heavy in her watchtower, but her fingers hesitate before the sliding windows, if they are opened wide as the gates of the sky how will she resist the temptation, a wild and powerful impulse, to disappear completely, not to be any more, not to feel any more, not the sorrow nor the missed opportunities, nor the anger at them and especially at herself, for daring to be miserable when all is well, no disaster has happened, besides ludicrous pampering, extravagant expectations, no disaster has happened besides the one that will happen when she climbs on the low stone balustrade and from there steps out through the sliding windows, wrapped in her blue cape, flapping like a pair of primordial wings. How long will the fall last from the fourth floor? A few seconds before the sound of the impact is heard, and Nitzan won't even notice, the canned laughter will cover the thud of her body hitting the pavement.

The temptation is so strong it sets her whole body shaking in the sweltering void, like the compulsive eating, like the vomiting that follows it, she will vomit herself through the window, that's the most fitting end for her. She puts her forehead to the glass, the echoes of the raucous laughter reaching her ears distant and dim, the hated sounds of a world in which there's no place or comfort for her, and she knows this was precisely the way Orly felt before she did what she did, she always was braver than her, a step ahead of her. He was right, their professor, absolutely right when he decided to give her the post; she really was better qualified for it, quicker than her and more desperate and the wick of her life burned out first, the fact is, she won the race and now all that is left for her is to follow in her footsteps, and she breathes heavily, her hands stretched out to the glass and leaving moist fingerprints like a farewell salutation. A shudder spreads through her body, a twitch of temptation and provocation, and she clings to the glass, if weights were attached to her feet it would be harder for her to climb on the balustrade and from there to the window opening before her, when from the depths of her briefcase lying on the table her mobile rings, a forgotten sound from another world, and she pulls it out and peers at it with the last vestiges of curiosity. Perhaps Gideon has finally noticed her depression and he's trying without knowing it to keep her here, with them, but it isn't him, the number looks familiar but she can't place it, and she presses the button, just to hear the voice and not answer, and when the words come to her ears it seems to her she's already dead; this is the voice of her father calling her from the world beyond. There was always love in his voice when he spoke to her, but in this too she struggled to find consolation, since this was a conspiratorial love, contrived primarily to frustrate her mother and her brother, and even now she recoils, moving the phone away from her ear and bringing it back again at once. Hey, Dini, how are you? he asks, Shlomit told me you spent last night at Mum's place, are you all right? She never noticed before how similar her brother's voice was to her father's, and she shakes her head at the blind machine, her lips moving silently, no, I'm not all right.

When he arrives there deliberately late, to allow no room for banal conversations, enquiries, what are you really doing here, what's your connection with the deceased, the event has already started, from the stage far away a monotonous female voice is heard and he sits down in one of the back rows in the hall, which is filled to capacity, thoroughly scrutinising the audience. Shoulder to shoulder they sit in silence to pay their respects to Professor Rafael Allon, a mixture of lecturers and students, blond heads and dark, hairy and bald. He spots from a distance the golden head of the neighbour and bobbing beside her the golden head of the widow; apparently they went to the same salon and there was only one shade of dye available, an unnatural and provocative pumpkin colour, but the smooth black hair that he remembers so well he doesn't see anywhere, although his gaze wanders from woman to woman, and of course he knows that a woman's hair is a volatile creature, unreliable evidence, and colour and style are liable to change at a moment's notice, and for that reason he's also looking out for any pale profiles that may present themselves, registering some candidates and waiting for them to turn their faces in his direction, but one after another they are eliminated: it isn't her, not her either, and that one's a man . . . He bows his head and closes his tired eyes, the voice of the lecturer coming through to him, sounding muffled: when you look at the sky you always see what used to be, the stars of the past, she declares sadly, light years separate us.

She isn't here, he sighs, she didn't dare show her face here and he's never going to find her, this was his last hope, cherished these past weeks, after he gave up the idea of trying to meet her by the freshly dug grave, again and again he sneaked into the cemetery and lay in wait for her from a distance, standing like a mourner beside the grave of a young woman, with a pink headstone designed to resemble a party dress, and the inscription on it, rest in peace, beautiful bride.

Rest in peace, beautiful bride, he used to stand there repeating, but she never appeared, wiping her eyes with the paper tissue he offered her, and she isn't here either; it's clear to him now that it's all been in vain, all the cunning and resourcefulness and pretence and crossing boundaries. And he opens his eyes to the toecaps of his shoes, his hands massaging his nape, what is this grief that's rising in you for a man who's a total stranger to you, what's this compulsion to locate a woman who's a stranger too, what do you want to hear from her, what do you want to say, he's been so preoccupied with the project he hasn't given enough thought to what it's really about.

Does the universe remember its creation? the lecturer asks in her faint voice, at odds with the magnitude of the question, the fingerprints of creation are what we're looking for, primeval radiation that's steadily cooling, but if indeed it existed, some trace of it must be left, and when he sits up and looks for the first time at the small figure on the stage, a clumsy lectern hiding her body and only her head and neck visible above it, a gasp of astonishment escapes from his throat when he realises it's her, she in person, in clear view on the illuminated stage, exposed to all those present; how typical this is of him, searching in the dark, in secret, while the object of his quest is standing before him without mystery or evasion. She stands alone on the stage, a big portrait of the man hanging behind her and she's almost swallowed up by his big smile, and before her in the front row sit the wife of the deceased and his children, and in the back row sits the one who wants to console her, and she's so far away it's hard for him to discern her beauty; her face has become slightly leaner, and it isn't as pale as he remembers it, and her voice which he never really heard is sad and weary, but it remains steady when she declares, background radiation proves there was a point of beginning, before space and before time, and this, this is the memory of the universe, it is testimony to creation, even if it has continued to cool down. It is possible to calculate its energy on the basis of what we observe today, on the basis of the fundamental frequencies of the universe.

Despite the turmoil of his feelings, he forces himself to listen; it seems she's already approaching her closing remarks, and in a moment she'll dismount from the stage and someone else will stand behind the lectern and speak, since he has the impression it's him she's addressing when she says with a brief smile, I'm sure you all know the words of Saint Augustine, what did God do before He created heaven and earth? He created hell, to accommodate those who ask too many questions, and he's quick to nod and even to laugh aloud, so she'll know someone at least is listening to her and her words aren't lost in space, and he also claps appreciatively when she steps down from the stage, with a noisy enthusiasm at odds with the nature of the occasion, attracting astonished glances from those sitting close by and he smiles apologetically, a fascinating lecture, he whispers, who is the lecturer? The young woman sitting next to him hands him the programme, which reminds him in its design of the invitation to Anati's wedding and there he reads, Memories of the universe and of creation, lectures in memory of Professor Rafael Allon, with the first lecture to be given by Dr Talia Franco, and already the next lecturer is mounting the stage, as scheduled in the programme, while Talia Franco descends the side stairs and sits down at the end of the front row, after warmly shaking the hands of the widow Elisheva and the children Ya'ara and Avshalom.

It's easier to remember images than ideas or words, the voice of the next speaker booms out, a balding, tall and thickset man, and that's why we create palaces of memory in our minds, and then we go out to stroll in the spaces we have created, and Avner finds himself listening with interest, although his gaze is fixed on the second seat in the front row. Most of the time she's hidden from his view, depending on the movements and the limbs and the sitting postures of those in between, but occasionally she's revealed to him in full, and when he sees her bending down and wiping her eyes with the edge of her blouse, a movement seared into his memory, he knows, knows why he has been searching for her these days and weeks, as if his life depended on it, since this delicate feminine movement sets the roots of his soul shaking with the shudder of the universe remembering its creation and arouses in him a yearning for the primeval radiation that has been almost entirely eliminated from the face of the earth, and he stands up and manoeuvres his way through the seats, hurrying to claim the vacant place he's spotted a few rows ahead, determined to establish himself in her vicinity before it's too late, so she won't slip away from him at the end of the evening. First she'll be surrounded by well-wishers congratulating her on the lecture, and suddenly she'll disappear without knowing she has a comforter here, and he's sitting in his new place, and despite the disruption that he's caused so many people with his moving around, it seems that he's accepted there with good grace; after all, at an event like this people tend not towards impatience but rather towards brotherhood. They all come to pay their last respects to the dead, and they're all clinging to their lives and in a more complicated sense to one another, like passengers on a plane that has hit turbulence drawing reassurance from the presence of strangers around them, the surprising thought occurs to him, for some reason it seems to us that strangers are protected while we and our loved ones are exposed to all kinds of danger, and their very presence protects us too.

In his new and improved position he succeeds for the first time in studying the portrait of the dead man, looking straight into his narrow grey eyes, surrounded by lively laughter-lines. His face fuller than it was the morning of their meeting, but the expression is just as boyish and pleasant as he remembers, and his smile is generous and he finds himself smiling back at him with longing, at the friend he never had, because he never got to have a real friend. A barrier always stood between him and members of his own sex, the kibbutz children who loved bullying him, the smart kids in the new town who shunned him, a timid and dreamy vagrant from the north, and even during his few weeks of combat training he didn't enjoy much of the legendary comradeship; it was only in the course of his legal studies that he succeeded in finding colleagues in whose company he felt at ease, especially when facing a shared objective, applying for jobs or sitting exams, but at the end of the day there was none of the warmth created there that goes beyond circumstances, and now when he replies with a smile to the smile of the dead man he wants to say to him, don't worry, friend, you weren't mistaken when you entrusted your secret to me the last morning of your life, I'll take care of her, I know that's what you would ask of me if you could. Tears prick his eyes as he swears a silent vow, but when he shifts his gaze to her, to share with her the covenant that's being sealed in her interests, he's alarmed when he sees her leaning for a moment over the person sitting next to her and whispering in his ear, realising to his chagrin that the miracle of their coming together in one time and one place doesn't yet promise anything, very soon he is liable to discover that Dr Talia Franco came here accompanied by a partner, perhaps she simply doesn't need him and his condolences and the absurd covenants that he's stitching up behind her back with strangers and with the dead, and worse still, with strangers who have already died.

And for this reason he remains seated when all the others get up at the end of the third and final lecture, and even when he stands up finally he remains rooted to the spot, undecided and watching her. Around the family of mourners a dense crowd has gathered and she is a part of it too, also the one who was sitting beside her, a rotund and fair-haired man, and although he strains his eyes he can't tell the difference between the gestures typical of a couple and gestures of friendship, and he waits for the crowd to disperse into smaller groups which are easier to analyse, threesomes, pairs, individuals, who is giving whom a lift home, who is going home to the family, who is shaking off the grief and the remembrance of the deceased and the oppression of death itself and who is still carrying the heavy burden, and when he's left alone in the line he proceeds slowly, striving not to draw attention to himself and at the same time not letting her out of his sight for a moment, not risking losing her again. She's wearing a dark blue sleeveless buttoned blouse, and when he comes closer he notices white dots on the fabric, tailored blue slacks and a little leather attaché case under her arm, but he doesn't dare get in too close, and only when she detaches herself from the circle does he allow himself to move towards her. To his relief, the man who sat beside her is accompanied by another woman, as rotund and fair-haired as he is, and for the moment he's entitled to hope that if there's a couple here within this threesome she isn't part of it, and he follows in their wake towards the car park, where his car is parked too, but he bypasses them and keeps going, trying without success to eavesdrop on their conversation, until in a rare moment of wish-fulfilment he sees farewell gestures beside one of the cars and its doors open and the man and his wife are swallowed up in there, while she is left alone in the car park, as she stood alone on the stage, simply walking towards her car, her back erect, her heels clicking with an intensely lonely sound, and his heart goes out to her until without thinking he starts running towards her, ignoring the absurdity of his bouncing paunch and reddening face, as if he were a child in a green stripy shirt running across the lawn to his mother's arms, who will get to me first, but she won't open her arms to welcome him, won't even notice the commotion he's causing, and only when he catches up with her and stops running and the sounds of his heavy panting reach her ears, does she stop and turn to face him, with such a forbidding question that he can't even twist his lips into a smile when he pants out the syllables inflated with hot air: Talia, he says, pronouncing this name for the first time, not that it's particularly unusual but it seems he's never spoken it before, I loved your lecture, although there was a lot I didn't understand, and she replies politely, thank you very much, and already she's moving on but he has to stop her and he tries again, I wanted to say something to you, he hesitates, I wanted to ask if you remember me. How typical this is of you, waiting a whole month for this meeting and making no plans for it, not knowing exactly how you should behave and what you're going to say.

I don't think so, she says, studying his face and shaking her head almost apologetically, and he says hurriedly, of course not, I meant to say that I remember I saw the two of you there, in the hospital, I was sitting next to you, you cried and I gave you a paper tissue I had in my pocket, it's like in your lecture, this radiation you talked about, I remember that feeling, and then a faint look of relief rises to her face and she says, that's right, you were there with your mother, how is she?

How is my mother? he asks with a touch of rancour, still alive, he blurts out, if you can call it living, not the best decision on the part of the creator of the world – Rafael Allon dead and Hemda Horowitz still alive, but he hurriedly turns the conversation back to them, to expand and deepen that moment they shared, the single memory they have in common. You wore a red blouse, he tells her, you promised him he'd feel better soon and he believed you, he was calm and the two of you looked almost happy. I didn't understand it, I had never seen anything like it in all my life, and being unable to explain precisely what these words mean he falls silent, and she's silent too, staring at him with a rather bemused expression and then walking on slowly until she pauses beside her gold Citroën, identical to the one he's been trying to locate for ages, and he's baffled. Just a moment, is this car yours or his? – betraying in his haste the information he has gathered so far, and she replies with surprising candour, it's mine, we bought two identical cars, a silly thing to do perhaps, but we had to find oblique ways of feeling close to each other.

This was one possibility that had never occurred to him, and he wonders now where her car is usually parked and how close he came to locating it, and he tries to remember the list of addresses he obtained, the crumpled list that he carried around in his pocket day after day, but he has to pull himself together because she's already at the door of her car, and it seems she has no particular interest in continuing the conversation, even if she did accept a used paper hanky from him one morning. With closed lips she smiles a farewell at him, she has nothing to say to him and anyway it seems she's not a great lover of words; even on the stage they filtered from her mouth reluctantly, but he can't give up now and hastily he lays his strange request before her, would you be prepared to tell me about him?

About Rafael? she asks, but why? And he says, it's important for me to know him, I don't really understand it myself, perhaps if we could sit down somewhere you could tell me about him, and she stares at him in bemusement, as the yellow lamp lighting up the car park paints her skin the colour of sand. All right then, she concedes, do you want to come in? – offering him her car as if it's her home, and he approaches from the passenger side and opens the gold door; once more his car is going to be left stranded in alien territory, and once more he will have to retrieve it and invent some excuse, just so long as she doesn't slip away from him, the woman he's been seeking thirty days and nights, and not knowing why.

She drives in silence and he wonders about her, wonders about himself, stubbornly and impetuously he has been seeking her out, and now they are belted up and enclosed in one confined space, their inhalation and exhalation mingling together, and for this short time their destiny is shared, if she swerves suddenly out of her lane he risks injury too, although she knows nothing about him, and from her point of view it makes no difference if he goes on existing or stops, and the gulf between them is so huge it seems there's no way of bridging it, but isn't the gulf characteristic of the clash of presumption and indifference, he muses, after all the newborn baby is unaware of the scale of the expectations and the worries bound up in his entry into the world. Lacking opinion and information he goes forth, blind to his needs, and she is the same, driving in silence, she doesn't know yet how intently he's waited for her, nor how much she needs him and his condolences, and therefore it's incumbent on him to be as silent as she is. He's so used to verbose women, like his wife and his sister and most of the female lawyers he has come across, the words fired from their mouths with no effort required, and even when they are sweet they are hard and painful like the confectionary thrown at the bar-mitzvah boy, and it seems that sitting here beside him is a new and rare strain that he's examining with curiosity, taking care to look straight ahead to avoid embarrassing her, but giving her furtive sidelong glances, trying to follow her movements and glean as much information as possible.

Her hands holding the wheel are narrow and their skin slightly wrinkled, under her chin too he sees the beginnings of a dewlap, the signs of ageing are more perceptible in her than he remembers, or perhaps it's only this last month that her age has caught up with her. In the palaces of his memory she transcended time, made of marble and porcelain, and now her skin is set out before him in all its vulnerability, enfolding thin arms on the verge of decay, a long neck with delicate grooves scored in it like the footprints of birds. It seems that the moment she was deprived of the love of Rafael Allon she was exposed to the onset of time, but he is going to take her under his wing and protect her from it the way he protects his powerless clients, and for a moment he wants to tell her all about them and especially about himself, to boast, gather together all his past achievements and present them to her as a gift, the innocents whose rights he fought for, children whose education he fought for, women whose divorces he succeeded in preventing, the house demolitions he blocked, all the petitions, the judgments, the debates and the claims, all down the years.

Furtively he goes back to scrutinising her profile as she moves her hair back behind the lobe of her ear, in which a tiny earring sparkles like a distant star, her high forehead, lips bright with lipstick and the eye, its colour obscured from him by the dense lashes, twitching nervously, as he rehearses his accumulated data again and again as if he's still searching for her, his secret love, an unacknowledged widow with no rights, a mistress. Now she peers at him briefly, smiles a faint smile and presses a button, sighing as the vibrant sounds fill the void of the car, a low and melancholic male voice, a solo French horn, more and more wind instruments joining in and yet still it seems every note is lonely.

This is what Rafael loved hearing most of all in the last weeks, she says, as if remembering she's been asked to talk about him, do you know it? It's Mahler's Kindertoten Lieder, he didn't understand German but when I offered to translate it for him he refused point-blank, and Avner hesitates, wondering whether he should ask her to translate for him, or would this be a breach of trust, a subversion of the memory of the deceased, but before he has made up his mind, with an abruptness that seems to surprise her too, after all what is the point of driving for a long spell in silence and turning on the music a moment before the journey ends, she parks in a space reserved for the residents of an old stone building; he has no idea where he is, as if his eyes have been blinkered all the way, as if she was all that he saw.

When he steps out of the car and looks around him, scouring the dark and narrow street, he realises to his surprise how close he is to his home, and for a moment it seems to him everything is the exact opposite of what he has assumed; in fact she's the one who knows all about him, down to the last detail, and now she's driven him to his home and in a moment she'll be parting from him with a wave and continuing on her way, but she's already locking the door and signalling to him to follow her, along a side path skirting the main entrance, framed by a sparse bamboo hedge, and he wonders about her decision to invite him into her house rather than one of the cafés in the neighbourhood, a decision fated to answer straightaway certain questions that have obsessed him in recent weeks: does she have a husband, does she have children, apparently not, and the lack of balance between her and the dead man distresses him when he enters the dark ground-floor apartment, in an alleyway running at a tangent to the busy main road, and when he remembers the sumptuous house where the deceased used to live in the quiet garden suburb he feels for the little woman in the little apartment and all kind of impractical vows reverberate in him, and even when the light comes on to reveal the heartening sight of colourful curtains descending to the gilded floor and a cream-coloured sofa strewn with cushions, he's still feeling sad: who is all this for?

It's nice here, he remarks, and she says, thanks, it isn't quite finished yet, I only just moved in after the renovations were done, this was my parents' house, and he remembers the commotion of the construction work in this side alley in recent months, when he used to pass this way with Yotam in the pram, cursing because access was blocked by heavy machinery. And it was all for her benefit, as it's turned out, and apparently for his benefit too, as he has the pleasure of relaxing on the sofa and looking around him, at the tiles with the motif of blue diamond shapes like little fish, at the dining corner with the wicker canopy shading it, at the stormy landscape paintings, strong in colour and in expression, and as he's answering her questions, wine or coffee, water or lemonade, he notices a photograph on one of the bookshelves and gets up from his seat to take a closer look; it seems it was that very day it was shot. Arm in arm they are standing, leaning against the car, is that the hospital in the background? She's wearing the red blouse that he remembers so well, and he's in the grey cotton shirt, masking his fearful emaciation, there's no doubt they were photographed that morning, and he reckons if he strains his eyes he'll see himself peering at them from the hospital entrance, and he asks in astonishment, who took this photo? And it seems she's equally astonished by his question, saying as she pulls a cork from a wine bottle, we asked someone who happened to be passing, and he's almost offended at not being asked himself, how happy he would have been to immortalise them, immortalising them has been his sole obsession these last few weeks.

Did you know? he asks cautiously, did you know there wouldn't be another opportunity? And she says, yes, of course, as if talking of some fact easily digested, and he wants to ask, so why did you make that promise, why did you promise him, but then he sees another picture on the shelf, smaller and faded, of a girl and a boy arm in arm and leaning on the trunk of a tree. The boy he identifies at once because his smile hasn't changed, that's also the way he smiled the last day of his life, and it seems to him, to Avner, he recognises this look, a kind of pensive melancholia and overriding it, the smile that erases it almost entirely, but the girl beside him with the long black hair is harder to identify, since the indignant expression on her face is quite unlike her adult appearance, and he wonders aloud, is this you? although he knows the answer, and she nods, almost apologetically, have I changed that much?

Yes and no, he says, your face hasn't changed much but your expression has, and he holds the framed photo and moves it close to his eyes, smoothing it with his finger although there isn't a single grain of dust on it, gliding over the impressive porcelain cheeks, the outlined lips and the black, supercilious eyes, and he puts the other picture beside it; impossible not to try spotting the differences between them, some of them obvious and some of them concealed from the eye, a kind of game of superiority and inferiority which becomes clear to him at once, since in the youthful picture she's holding his hand in hers in a kind of supplication, and in the later picture it seems the supplication is hers but it isn't directed at him, and he slumps exhausted on the sofa, the pictures in his hand, as if he himself is compelled to bear for their sake the burden of the decades that elapsed between one picture and the other, the weight of lost opportunities, and in the meantime the table is filling up with cups and plates, a dish of purple grapes and bright cherries, a dish of nuts and almonds and a jug of iced water, but he can't let the pictures alone, like evidence presented in court they are set out before him, telling a closed and gloomy story until it seems there's no need to add anything. Is that why she isn't talking, working away in the kitchen in silence, taking a tray of cheeses out of the fridge, slicing bread, as if it was all set up in readiness for his arrival, and not only for him but for other guests too, calling in at the end of the thirty-day interval. Where are they, then? Why don't they come? And he's waiting for her to suspend her activities and sit down facing him in the flowery armchair, and then he will address to her the only question that can possibly be asked with those two couples looking on from the pictures: how did this happen, I mean, why? How did you miss your chance if you were together in your youth? Why didn't you marry and have children and set up a family? How has it come about that you're alone here in this doll's house while he's living with another woman, or rather dying with another woman, and yet in spite of that I saw you there, the last day of his life.

When she finally sits down facing him in the armchair and pulls off her high-heeled shoes he notices to his surprise that her toenails are painted black; he's never seen such a colour on the feet of a grown woman, is that how she expresses her mourning, and he wishes he could sit at her feet and wipe the black dye from her toes with his tongue, and in fact he doesn't want any more conversations, hearing or being heard, since there are only a few words that he wants her to whisper in his ear, words known from the outset, tomorrow you'll feel better;

in fact these are the only words that don't provoke him, that don't cause him almost unbearable pain, like the words she is about to say as she pours wine for both of them and raises her glass to him with a gloomy smile and drinks thirstily, her skin reddening as if it's the liquor colouring it from inside, and on her forehead beads of sweat are gleaming as she holds out her hand to him and takes the photographs back, studying them earnestly as if she hasn't seen them in a long time. This was his idea, she grins, indulging the tragic caprice, having our picture taken in exactly the same pose, he had all kinds of private jokes like that, she explains for his benefit, as if striving to comply with the wishes of the strange guest, and Avner hears himself asking, why didn't you stay together?

What business is that of yours, really? she asks, but there's no hostility in her voice, only puzzlement, and he tries to answer lightly, I myself don't understand this, but ever since I saw you there together I've been thinking of the two of you, your radiation goes with me, and to his relief she's satisfied with this, I left him, she says, her diction constricted and controlled as in the lecture she gave just a few hours before, we met at the university, we were together several years, Rafael wanted to marry me but I wasn't ready for it yet, the future he offered seemed too bourgeois to me then, and already she's refilling her glass with the dark and prickly wine, crossing her legs. I left him for some musician, she reports briefly, as if delivering some judgment which is almost superfluous, since the two of them have already learned that actions exist even without the words that accompany them, I lived for some years in New York, and when I came back to this country he was already with Elisheva and with two children, and everything was lost, for me at least, she concludes, and Avner finds himself listening to her with dropped jaw, why lost? he protests as if all this could still be changed, people dismantle families, people correct their mistakes, or make new mistakes, it happens all the time, although not to me, he hastily makes the exception, it happens to other people, and she agrees with him, yes, it happens all the time to other people, and already she's filling her glass yet again, and he wants to put his hand on her wrist to soothe the tense movement, but contents himself with a grape that he plucks from the bunch, sucking it in the void of his mouth. He never managed to do that, she says, when I left him he had a serious crisis and Elisheva helped him through it, he didn't dare leave her and he was afraid of hurting the children and afraid of putting his trust in me, and so the years passed.

And all this time you were together? he asks, and she replies, not all the time, and whenever we met we tried yet again to separate, excessive guilt on his part and excessive anger on mine, and it was only this last year after his children left home, our relationship seemed to have a future, he helped me renovate this apartment, we planned to live here together, he finally decided to tell Elisheva and leave home, but just then he fell ill.

And did Elisheva know? he asks and she says, there are all kinds of knowledge, it isn't unequivocal, and besides that we worked together, we had joint research projects, and just when he decided to tell her and leave her the disease was diagnosed, she repeats, and there was no point hurting her unnecessarily. I put so much pressure on him, she sighs, who knows if that caused his illness, I wanted him to myself and I ended up with a dead partner, perhaps if I'd been prepared to go on sharing him he'd still be alive, when you want too much you lose too much.

Don't blame yourself, he tries to reassure her, eager to be of service, this particular illness doesn't need any specific cause, who do we know who isn't ill? he asks as if they have many friends in common and she says, it's hard not to lay blame, although he himself wanted this very much, he wanted to live with me here, and she points weakly around the cherished little room, he was really into home improvements, she stresses again, it was symbolic for us because this was where we fell in love, I was living here with my parents when we met, we thought we would succeed in recreating the universe, what a foolish idea, she says, and for the first time he detects a hint of bitterness in her voice, and when she reaches again for the wine bottle he offers his glass, as if volunteering to drink on her behalf, but she isn't content with his glass and she fills hers too, with an alacrity he's not used to among his acquaintances, taking hasty gulps; the wine colours her teeth purple until her mouth looks as empty as his mother's mouth, and he flinches slightly, looking down. You see, her story is laid out before you, served up to you like the grapes and the cherries, is this what you wanted? Will the information satisfy you, or will you try now to dismantle the story into chapters, into its inflamed components? You wanted to know but where will you take this knowledge, what will you do with it now, when you have it in your hands?

So here's another life story, there are more bitter ones, another love story and there are sadder ones, what's he to you, what's she to you, how do their lives connect with yours? He's surprised that she herself isn't seeking further clarification, entrusting her life story to him without probing his motives. Is it because she's so steeped in her sorrow, she's stopped noticing him, or is this the way she normally conducts herself in the world, inert and wrapped up in herself, and apparently he can go now, this is the story and it isn't going to change, it's impossible to lodge an appeal or an objection, the verdict has been handed down, the case is closed, and a kind of emptiness spreads through him, a heavy emptiness indeed, a prodigious weight. You've got what you wanted, so what will you do now? Why not get up and go home, respond to the tetchy text message from Shlomit that's just come through, where the hell are you? Home is only a few streets from here, and you'll see this woman from time to time in the main street or in the grocery store and exchange pleasantries, wishing each other a good week and a peaceful Sabbath, have a happy New Year and enjoy the festival, what else can people say to one another, and as he's sitting back on the soft sofa that wasn't meant for him, it seems to him he has nothing to say to his wife either besides have a good week and a peaceful Sabbath, have a happy New Year and enjoy the festival, likewise to his children, his mother and sister and all his acquaintances, to be on the safe side just add, may you know no more suffering, and that really is everything. And he sprawls exhausted on the sofa, he doesn't want to go and doesn't want to stay; to be taken from here is what he wants, gathered by a mysterious and concentrated force with a stronger will than his, as Rafael Allon was taken from here, since suddenly it's clear to him that they came here that morning in the gold car, she brought him here from the hospital after she was told his hours were numbered.

There are people who prefer to die at home, the casualty nurse had whispered back then, as if letting him into a secret, but this man definitely preferred to die in this place where he planned to live out the rest of his life, and he lays his head on one of the cushions, the wine that he isn't used to drinking so copiously fuddles his consciousness and it seems to him he too has given up the struggle, his train of death is speeding too and he is inside it, from the place he was born to the place he will die, from the moribund lake bordering on the sea of death, via the ruins of Beit She'an and Jericho buried in the desert, to the city where since time immemorial members of his race have aspired to be buried. How well he came to know this long route, there were years when he recognised every thistle and every flower on the way, every station, but this time the train isn't stopping at stations, being meant only for him. Now and then they wave to him along the way, the single traveller changing from baby to child, to youth and adult, growing up from junction to junction, is he really travelling or are they moving away, after all time and space need to join together to create movement, like a man and a woman, whereas with him space is detached from time when he reaches the valley under the hills reddening in the east, between the bathing sites of the secret Jordan and the promises that were given here and will never be fulfilled; sparkling are the golden towers and silver turrets of Jerusalem, and he passes by the tents that are so familiar to him; stay with us, his ghostly clients will plead along with their wives and children, after all they're used to their pleas going unanswered, stay with us his children will plead, and he sits up all at once, his hands twitching and he looks around him in bemusement, his gaze meeting her eyes, which are red like the eyes of a rabbit, the wine glass in her hand and she's drinking in silence.

Sorry, I seem to have fallen asleep, he mumbles, I'm not used to drinking. How strange, in his own bed he has whole nights of insomnia, whereas here on a stranger's sofa he nods off in spite of himself. Perhaps he should ask her to lease him this sofa and he'll come here to sleep from time to time, they are neighbours after all, even if she doesn't know it, clearly she doesn't know and isn't interested in knowing, and suddenly he wonders about this almost with indignation: is it so obvious to her that strangers will be interested in her depressing story, she needn't bother to respond with so much as a hint of reciprocity, and he pours himself a glass of water, forgive my bad manners, he says, I've fallen asleep on your sofa and I haven't introduced myself. My name is Avner Horowitz.

I know, she says, raising her glass to him and drinking his health, and he's taken aback, really? How do you know? And she says, I saw you once on TV or in a newspaper, it took me some time to remember, you're the lawyer of the Bedouin, and for some reason she chuckles, and he nods his head, surprised and flattered. This unexpected recognition induces him to speculate: maybe the neighbour identified him, and the widow too, while he was pretending he was from the faculty of sciences. How absurd he is, he could yet be arrested for impersonation, but that isn't the main point; giving himself his identity back, he feels like a man walking the streets naked and eventually clothes are found for him and he puts them on, or perhaps it's the opposite, he's like someone wearing clothes that aren't his and getting stripped stark naked, one way or the other he's lost the freedom of anonymity but gained some recognition which inspires him with confidence. He's no longer a foundling picking up scraps of information, but a lawyer of renown who fights for the weak, even if his achievements have been fewer in recent years, and from this standpoint he looks at the woman facing him, her extinguished eyes and purple teeth and her head swaying a little, and he stands up and holds out both hands to her, come on, Talia, he says, you need to sleep.

To his surprise she obeys at once, holding his arm and rising to her feet, and he guides her before him to the adjacent room with its closed door, as if escorting a little girl who has been walking in her sleep, and meanwhile he's thinking she herself has never had a child to escort like this and now she's left it too late, and indeed when he lays her down on the broad bed, delicately unfastening the buttons of her blouse and pulling off her trousers, the body that is revealed to him in stages is slim and smooth and shows no signs of a pregnancy, her stomach is flat as if a living creature has never resided in its inner recesses and her breasts are small and solid as if they have never filled with milk, and she lets him undress her, obediently holding out an arm or lifting a thigh, arching her back, and while peeling off her clothes he wonders about her and about him, thinking that if her consciousness were to clear and she saw him leaning over her like this she would raise such pandemonium he would definitely be taken out of here an arrested felon, exploiting the grief and intoxication of a stranger to spy on her body, the last of the peepers, but it isn't vision that's the crucial thing so much as smell, since he finds himself kneeling on the carpet at the foot of the bed and sniffing her body, not the lower abdomen which is still encased in lacy white underwear, but the neck and arms and legs and feet, until she lets out a sigh and opens her eyes and he straightens up at once and spreads a blanket over her, a fatherly gesture. Sleep, Talia, he whispers, I'll bring you a glass of water, but when he returns she's already fast asleep, and he puts the glass down on the cabinet and leaves the room, his body in a whirl and her smell in his nostrils, the smell of bitter grapes, the smell of grief and disappointment, the smell of a man's woman without her man, after thirty days is there anything left of his smell, the smell of his love, of his sickness and death? Although his heart is beating tensely and his head is heavy and swaying he doesn't go yet but meticulously returns the tray of cheeses to the fridge, also the grapes and cherries, peering in meanwhile to see what else she has there, what she's eating, but the fridge is empty, the entire contents she put out on the table; there's not even any milk in there – more like a squat than a residence.

Moving quietly he transfers the dishes to the sink and can't resist sniffing them, then leaving them on the draining board, examining with fascination the new wooden cabinets and the still sparkling kitchen utensils, and while standing at the sink he notices another door opposite the bedroom and hurries over there, finding himself in a study evidently designed for both of them, as two chairs stand before the gigantic desk overlooking the garden, and there are two computers and an abundance of books on the shelves, and of all the rooms this is the one where the monkish scholar feels most like a trespasser and he hurries out on tiptoe to the front door, it's time to go, he tells himself, your time is up, but it's then he sees the keys in the keyhole, and he stands by the door wondering how he can leave when the hostess is in no fit state to lock up after him.

He really should go home, his wife has already left him another urgent text message, but how can he leave her here like this in her bed, in a deep sleep and exposed in an open house, where anyone could get in through the garden, which has only a thin bamboo hedge protecting it, and from there to the unlocked apartment and from there to the bed, and he agonises over what to do; he could lock the door from the outside and then at least she'd be safe, but how's she going to get out unless she has a spare set of keys, and the windows are barred and netted – two contradictory options and both unacceptable, one involving too much freedom and the other the denial of freedom.

Of course he'd be happy to stay here and doze on her sofa, but he's afraid of her waking up and being scared, or misinterpreting his presence, and he goes out into the garden as it seems this is the only realistic option he has, to defend her from outside as if he's the watchdog of this house, like Casanova of the enigmatic smile, and that was also the way he sniffed at her, eager and desperate, satisfied with little, and he looks for a place to lie down, the garden isn't completed yet and there isn't even a deckchair to sprawl in, nor a bench nor a hammock, but his fatigue is so deep that he collapses in the porch and rests his head on the coarse doormat, bearing the word WELCOME in big green letters, and this reminds him to text a message to his wife, don't worry, I'll be home in the morning. All the arrivals are welcome, the people leaving are welcome too. Even more abject than his low-lifers who sleep in tents, without a blanket or a roof over his head, a dog without a kennel, and yet in spite of all this his mind is at ease, and when he drifts into sleep it seems to him that beyond the bamboo hedge he can hear the footsteps of Shlomit taking Yotam to the nursery; where's Daddy, he hears the clear and ringing voice, where's my Daddy?

Chapter Nine

From a distance she recognises her sister-in-law pacing along heavily, with a child in a pram, a dark tent-style dress covering her body, and she avoids her, slipping into a cool alleyway which the sun hasn't yet succeeded in dominating, and there she stands, leaning on a bamboo hedge and putting her shopping bags down, panting as if she's been rescued from danger. Why does she feel so threatened by a woman she has known since they were both children, or is it for precisely this reason; it seems to her she embodies more than anything else the very scale of the change. If this is indeed the bashful and thin-limbed girl who used to caress her brother's arm so delicately, hanging her admiring eyes on him; after all any change is possible, including the change that befell Nitzan, and her as well, if it's possible that the transmigration of souls takes place during life and not after death. Her body is cumbersome, her face coarse and her voice grating, and for some reason she turned against Dina too, as if she were to blame for her brother's deficiencies, and even the birth of her miracle baby did nothing to temper her wrath, and it seems she's claiming the little boy as her exclusive property, isolating him so he won't connect with any other person but her, as she tried to do with Avner and almost succeeded; he was indeed separated from his sister but he didn't cleave to her, and perhaps the separation came about because they never bonded as siblings.

They were the children of the same parents, their bone and flesh, but how insignificant was this fact for them, growing up with their contemporaries and not with their family, and it was only after they left the kibbutz that they were presented for the first time with the opportunity to infuse some meaning into this blood relationship, when they found themselves living for the first time in one apartment, in two adjacent rooms. She chose the smaller one for the landscape views it afforded, and he the larger, overlooking the car park, and like a pair of migrants they were offered the chance to bond together, and she remembers suddenly how insomnia, the family curse, used to unite them in the kitchen at night, how she used to boil milk for the pair of them in a small saucepan, and how her heart was opened up to him in the middle of the night, to this handsome, slightly eccentric youth, who was awarded the love that belonged to her but also paid too high a price for it, and at times she was even happy for him, she forgave him for the theft.

Behind the backs of their sleeping parents they succeeded in becoming acquainted for a few hours, the mother's son and the father's daughter, and it seems to her now that those nights they tasted for the first time the relaxation of true fraternity, a welcome respite from loneliness, and she would return to her bed calm and reconciled, her heart overflowing like the milk spilling from the pan; it was spilled again and again because they were deep in conversation and they didn't notice it, but the fragile covenant that was beginning to be sealed between them Shlomit soon shattered with her constant visits, demanding his attention with bashful insistence, and Dina would lie awake at night hearing the friction of their limbs and their whispers, convinced that she herself was doomed to eternal loneliness, and she was especially shocked by her brother's behaviour, giving up so easily, as if he had nothing to lose, not only on her, his only sister, but on himself as well.

When to her relief she sees her sister-in-law walking away, she notices a colourful poster on the electricity pylon facing her, a new day-care nursery opening in the neighbourhood, luxurious and spacious, she glances round to be sure no one's looking, she tears off a piece of the notice giving the phone number and alongside it the logo of a baby's dummy, and on her way home this morning, carrying heavy bags of fruit and vegetables, she finds herself lingering by every notice she passes, and reading it intently: apartments for sale, music lessons, yoga and self-defence, and by the time she arrives at home she has stuffed away in her briefcase three advertisements offering the services of dedicated carers for babies and two advertisements presenting day-care nurseries of quality, filling her with emotional satisfaction, as if the very action of tearing off a scrap of paper establishes an incontrovertible fact, a first stimulus of the process in the practical world.

And of course she knows this is the tiniest of steps, the most marginal of activities, again and again she reads the stories of her new friends and colleagues who are unaware of her existence and yet are giving her more help than any of her relatives, and more and more she's understanding how much is required of her if she's to come closer to her goal, and the sheer scale of the obstacles and dangers, but now with the adverts in her pocket, giving her child some kind of validity, she dares to act, and she's barely arrived home and she's already on the phone checking out the location of the new crèche, how many children and how many carers, recording the details avidly and straightaway she contacts another and compares the data – one is closer and in the other there are fewer children, which should she choose? And when all the information has been assembled she drops the phone and covers her face with her hands, you're crazy, you're crazy, and she goes from room to room to check the house is empty and there's no one here to witness her insanity, and so perhaps she'll dare to contact one of the agencies recommended to her by her new friends on the net, and she hears her voice, anxious and impassioned, we want to adopt a little boy, what needs to be done?

But the clearer the picture becomes, the scores of documents needed, testimonials to health of body and mind, solvency and honesty, information regarding the prospective adopters and the stability of their relationship, places of work and ownership of property, photographs of the house and its occupants, financial checks and assurances of the patience and determination required to face the risks and complications, those before and those after, while all her papers are filling up with exhausted scribbles, to be hidden away hastily among the books on the shelf, she realises how firmly her hands are tied so long as Gideon isn't on her side, how dependent she is on him; without his consent she can do nothing and even with his support their prospects of success would be slim. There are many abandoned children but the way to them is long and arduous, strewn with obstacles as in the fairy stories she vaguely remembers about princes and princesses kept apart by hopeless tasks, condemned to fight dragons and monsters and defy natural forces in their quest to return to their kingdoms or fulfil their destinies.

In this country their age will preclude them from obtaining an infant, and abroad there are few states willing to hand children over to their unstable part of the world, and there's an infinite number of foreign bureaucracies piling up endless difficulties supposedly in the interests of the child, and she has to hurry, as the obstacles become ever more formidable, but how can she hurry when her hands are tied between difficulties outside and difficulties inside, and again she immerses herself in stories overflowing with sincerity, innocence, warm-heartedness, look at this woman for example, calling herself Dew Drop and telling us that her husband had reservations and was opposed to adoption, but how happy he is now with his daughter and how happy they are together; or alternatively here's Amazona, who went through the whole process by herself and that's the way she's going to bring up the little boy too, and she finds herself envying her: how wonderful it would be now if she had no partner, as then she could go ahead, arrange meetings, impress and be impressed, clarify and elucidate and most important of all, she could hope, because it seems to her without this hope her life isn't life.

You're not normal, Dina, you've gone right off the rails lately, Naomi scolds her when they're sitting after work in the café near the college. Adopting a little boy? I can't believe this is what you want to do! You know how hard it is? My friends adopted a girl of three some years ago, and you can't imagine what they've had to put up with, poor things, and you'd only get an older child anyway, because of Gideon's age, and by the way, is Gideon backing you in this insanity?

Not really, she admits, the truth is, not at all, at the moment I'm on my own in this but I'm thinking of looking abroad, that way there's a chance of getting a child of around two, and Naomi slams her cup down on the table in consternation, abroad? Do you know how expensive that is? Where will you get the money from? And how will you know they're not conning you? All those agencies are corrupt, they'll give you a chronically sick child and tell you nothing about the genetic history, you want to spend the rest of your life in and out of hospitals? You couldn't stand that, Dina, believe me, it's putting a healthy head in a sick bed.

I'm not sure the head is that healthy, she grins, asking the waitress for another glass of water, as once again she feels a ferocious flame rising from her gut, and her face is covered in sweat, haven't your hot flushes started yet? I feel like a dragon breathing fire, and Naomi smiles complacently, not really, because I had my brood at a later age and it seems my clock has been turned back, and Dina sighs, what a fool I've been, why didn't I realise I needed to produce another child, I can't get a hold on this, what could I possibly have done that was better?

That's enough, Dina, don't get worked up about it, what has been has been, Naomi waves her hand as if to ward off an irritating fly, the question is, what do you do now? What about egg donation? It's much simpler than adoption and cheaper too. Lots of women do this and at least you know who the father is, but Dina shakes her head, that isn't right for me, she says, what's right for me is to bring up a child who's already in the world and needs a home, I prefer to adopt.

You reckon you prefer to adopt because you're living in a fantasy, Naomi persists, you have a romantic vision of a sweet blond baby boy who'll be glad you've rescued him, but in reality you'll be bringing up a difficult and problematical child who's going to be testing your limits all the time and making your life a misery, and he'll always be different and never belong to you, and that's hoping for the best and assuming he's healthy.

How can you be so sure? That isn't what I'm reading in the blogs, she protests in a broken voice, people tell me such lovely stories about their kids, and even if there are difficulties they tackle them with love, and Naomi bites hungrily into her sandwich that's just arrived, obviously, what do you expect them to say? I made a bad mistake with this child, they cheated me? Of course they love their children and strive to see the best in them, but don't forget these are people who don't have children of their own, they have no yardstick for comparisons.

In your case it's a shot in the dark, you have no idea what surprises are liable to pop up.

And biological children don't surprise us? Dina grumbles, anyone would think you know everything about your children. If you'd told me a year ago that Nitzan was going to change the way she has, I'd have said you were raving, and Naomi asks, what's really going on with her? How is she reacting to this insanity? and Dina sighs, very badly, she has no empathy at all, she's threatening to leave home if it happens.

You see, her friend utters a snort of triumph, so there's nothing to discuss, if you have no support at home and only opposition you have to give it up, don't be angry with them, they're saving you from making a terrible mistake. You'll get over it, you'll see, it's just menopause madness, calm down and everything will be fine. If you feel like it, volunteer for part-time work at the nursery, and that will be the end of the story. She brushes the crumbs from her hands, yet again, I've eaten too much and you haven't eaten anything, she complains, I'm not sitting with you in cafés any more, *yalla*, sweetie, get out of this, you have no choice, you'll get over it and you'll thank God you've had a lucky escape.

How can you be so sure? Dina mumbles while her friend takes a crumpled note from her purse, saying leave it, I'm paying, after all I ate your share too. I'm absolutely sure, she announces as they leave the café, what is there to doubt here? Adoption is a dangerous gamble, and don't forget your age.

But Naomi, why is it, when you get yourself pregnant for the fourth time at the age of forty-four it isn't madness, but when I want to adopt at forty-five it is madness? Explain to me what's so different about it, she almost pleads, and Naomi looks at her sadly and opens the car door. How come you don't see this, Dini? You really worry me, don't you realise adoption is Russian Roulette? Doesn't Gideon's opposition count for anything? He doesn't want another child now and never has, you think he's going to join you in bringing up a kid who isn't his, with no end of problems?

He won't have to do any of the bringing up, I just need his signature, I'll do all the caring and nurturing myself, Dina says, and I don't want to hear any more scare stories, anyone would think all biological children come healthy in mind and body, and Naomi snaps, listen, it's impossible talking to you, you're not balanced, you're incapable of rational thought, you need to go to a shrink, or better still a gynaecologist, that will be a lot quicker, he'll prescribe hormone treatment and that will be the end of it, problem solved.

I can't believe you're saying this, she leans on the door of the car, painfully aware that her voice is cracking up, how come you've taken in all that male mythology? Any unconventional aspiration on the part of a woman has to be down to hormonal imbalances? You should be ashamed of yourself!

Well, that can't be helped, sometimes it's the right answer, Naomi takes her seat in the car, looking up at her with her doughy face, sometimes hormones do lead us astray and this needs to be dealt with, and in my opinion that is what's happening to you now, you're moving into a new phase of your life and you have to cope with it, go forward and not back. Sorry to be so hard on you, but you need to understand the situation you're in, a good friend should tell the truth and not give blind support to every idiocy, *yalla*, I have to pick up my Ro'i from the nursery, we'll talk again soon, and already she's revving up and driving away; like her, the car is short and dumpy but a light mover, and Dina watches her go with a look of hatred, holding on to the trunk of a desiccated cypress. It seems to her, to her alarm, the tree is tottering, but she's the one who's unsteady on her feet, she who has eaten nothing all day, she whose best friend hasn't given her even a morsel of warmth and support, maybe she's right, maybe she will thank her one day, but not today, because today she feels abandoned and betrayed, today she feels she'll never want to speak to her again, to her best friend since the link with Orly was broken, and when she remembers her, her teeth chatter as if the temperature has suddenly plummeted; Orly would definitely have supported her, she was feisty, original, not a square-minded conservative she-bear like Naomi, but where is she now anyway, did she really leap into the abyss, to her death; even if she is still alive she might just as well be dead for her; Orly will never forgive her, that's the kind of person she is, feisty and original but also vengeful and vindictive, how could she forgive someone who betrayed her trust, who destroyed her life? When she crosses the street, her mind elsewhere, a car pulls up just short of her with a squeal of brakes, so close she can feel the warmth of the motor on her skin like moist breath, and the driver yells at her, watch out, psycho! If you want to top yourself go ahead but leave me out of it! And she stares at him, puzzled, how does he know who she is, does he too think it's madness to adopt a child, and it's only then she realises she's crossing the street on a red light and yet she carries on going, as a heavy motorbike has to swerve to avoid her and when she finally reaches the pavement she finds herself wondering about the fragility of the life force, the sudden abolition of the most basic instincts. It seems everything that's been done over the years almost in a state of distraction, without thought or intention, has been cast into doubt, the preservation of the fruit of our lives, keeping the wick from burning out, and suddenly she wonders if there's any justification for the mundane effort of crossing the road with care, of looking to right and left and checking the way is clear, and what's it for, really; she personally for example, Dina Horowitz-Yarden, lecturer in medieval history at the training college, soon to be forty-six, married with a daughter, this sweltering morning when her teeth are chattering in the cold, will raise no objection if one of these monsters of urban traffic will help her to settle this dichotomy that seems insoluble, between the voice of the heart and the voice of logic, between her voice and the voices of her husband and her daughter and her friend, and she imagines herself walking in the street without a white stick or a guide dog, just she and her will to live, which is dwindling from moment to moment, entrusting herself into the hands of fate; will the hands of fate be colder than the hands of those closest to her?

Exhausted, she slumps down on a bench at the end of the pavement, covering her face with her hands, she needs help, she needs help and she has no one to turn to, how has this suddenly come about: there's no one who can help her, and she's lost the taste for life and it seems to her only a child will restore it to her. What's this child idea all about? Since when does there have to be a child? After all she's never been one of those broody women who worship babies wherever they are, on the contrary, such women always repelled her, from her superior vantage point she looked down on them, and what has happened to her now in the middle of life?

Naomi is right, Gideon is right, and so is Nitzan, she should be rejoicing in her lot, how repellent is this bitterness that has sprung up all at once like nettles in a regimented flowerbed, that's why no one is supporting her, that's why even the cars on the roads are trying to harm her, and that's why she has to stand up and get into her car and drive home, immerse herself in her doctoral thesis, cherish her little family and not disrupt the course of routine life, and this she will do, but when she tries to rise she's gripped by such a powerful wave of giddiness she slumps back again on the bench, hands twitching convulsively, and she shakes her head, this isn't making any sense, a serious internal contradiction is taking shape here, because if indeed she has a home, why is she sprawled on a bench at high noon like a homeless vagrant, if indeed she has a family, why isn't she in touch with one of them now, asking to be picked up from here and taken home, where they will feed her and give her something to drink, and she fumbles in her bag for her mobile, she'll call Gideon; not long ago he did a series of photographs of the homeless, come and take my picture too, she'll say, but even the thought of the digits that join together to make up his number repels her, those annoyingly asymmetrical figures, there's a seven and a one and a three and a five and a nine, and besides this she hasn't the strength to cope with his cold looks of reproof, she needs warm consolation, overflowing, like a steaming mug of milk in the middle of the night.

How calm she felt going back to bed after night conversations with her brother, almost happy, so many years have passed since then and the alienation between them has burgeoned, and yet there is one memory she has and it's a tangible one; she fiddles with the mobile and brings up the name, Avner Horowitz, for some reason she took the trouble to key his surname in too, as if to emphasise the distance between them, a distance they both made a point of preserving and cherishing, as if it were a precious possession, Avner, come quickly, I need you.

What's up? he asks, has something happened to Mum? I'm rather busy just now, and she says, no, Mum's all right, clearly her entire existence has been condensed for him into a conduit of information about their mother, and she's already regretting contacting him, she doesn't want him to come to her under duress but out of good will, out of love, but where will this love suddenly spring from, something out of nothing, and already she's backtracking, it doesn't matter Avner, leave it, I'll be OK, but he perks up at once, where are you?

To her surprise he arrives in a taxi, and sooner than she expected, just as she was preparing herself for a long wait. She stretched out on the bench with legs drawn up, and the sun spread a golden blanket over her, and for a moment this was as pleasant and relaxing as anything she had felt in a very long time, a baby in the playpen, gazing at the tops of the eucalyptus trees bowing down towards her, and unconsciously she covers her eyes with her fingers and plays hiding and revealing games, moving away and coming closer, how familiar to her is this movement from her mother's stories about the red berries of the pepper tree; she was always irked by her mother's childhood memories, intended as they were to arouse her compassion, but now her heart is drawn to this one story of an overgrown baby who doesn't dare walk and lies day after day in the playpen and controls with her fingers the sights of her eyes, exactly as it is now. Around her life goes on, the heavy and dirty traffic streams on, people pass by, their knees powering back and forth, leaving behind fragments of conversations, indifferent to her existence, but this urban alienation doesn't bother her; she's waiting for her brother, and the expectation is pleasant because there's nothing demanding about it. That's the way she waited for him to be born, so he would be hers, and stand beside her, and make everything right, and here is a taxi stopping close by and the man stepping out of it in a crumpled black suit is her only brother and she is his only sister, and she's happier welcoming him to her bench than she ever was when inviting him into her house, and she gathers up her legs and makes room for him, thanks for coming.

What's up? Not feeling well? he asks, and adds unnecessarily, my car's been stolen, I left it in the university car park and someone nicked it, and she looks at him in surprise, how different he looks today; his face is thinner and his expression has changed, an anguished concentration dominates it now, instead of the haughtiness that he used to radiate, towards her at least, and when he sits down beside her she sees his attention is distracted and his lips trembling slightly and he's all agitation, and it seems to her this bench under the eucalyptus is a kind of tiny raft adrift in the heart of the lake, tossed by the waves, and although adrift it is their only hope, survivors as they are from a ship hijacked by pirates, a brother and sister needing the help of Heaven.

I've brought you some water, he says, taking a cold bottle from his lawyer's briefcase, and she puts it to her forehead and moves it slowly over her cheek, and when she finally takes a sip it seems to her the most wonderful thing she has ever tasted, you have some too, she hands it to him, and he tilts his neck with a sharp movement that reminds her of the time of his infancy, reclining in his pram and drinking from his baby's bottle, his pretty blue eyes fixed on the sky with such intense concentration that all who saw him were looking up, wondering what he had found there, and now too she gazes up at the treetop blazing in the fire of midday, and the white sky rolling above it like smoke, but his eyes return to her and he asks, so what's happening, Dini? What's going on with you? I contacted you a few days ago but you didn't answer.

I felt unwell suddenly, she hesitates, as if I was about to faint, I couldn't even get up from the bench, and he appraises her with a quizzical eye, you're looking terribly thin, are you eating anything at all? Have you eaten today? And she says, no, I have no appetite, and he opens his case again and takes out a bulging sandwich, of dark nutty bread with tomatoes and lettuce leaves peeping out from the edges, here, have some of this, and she fingers the sandwich, impressed, some sandwich this, do you make yourself one of these every morning? And he grins, no, not I, and she tries again, does Shlomit do these for you? He says, no, this isn't her style, and Dina peers at him with curiosity, peeling off the plastic wrapper and biting into the fresh bread, the soft goat's cheese, and a raging hunger is aroused in her as she eats, the mysterious hands that sliced the bread and cut the cheese and vegetables for her brother are indirectly consoling her as well.

Like some coffee? he asks, I see there's a café at the end of the street, and she says, no, I was in there before, let's stay out here, I've nearly finished this for you. She hands him the remains of the sandwich and he chews in silence, watching the slices as they disappear until his hands are empty, and he takes a tissue from his pocket and wipes the crumbs from his lips. She notices how his cheeks, usually so smooth, are covered with dark stubble that accentuates his eyes, looking almost transparent in the dazzling light of midday. Tell me, she asks, do you remember how we used to meet in the kitchen at night? What did we talk about? I remember we talked, but I can't remember what it was about.

About our insomnia, I think, he says, you found it very hard to cope with, and she's surprised, really? More so than you? and he says, definitely, you used to say all the time you wished you were dead, at least that way you'd get some sleep. I remember you really scared me, I was a kid and I didn't know how to help you.

So did you tell Mum and Dad? she asks, and he says, no, I gave it a lot of thought and in the end I decided it was your decision, if you wanted to tell, if you wanted to live. I had resolute views of the world back then, he grins, I wish I'd held on to them until now, and she sighs, so it seems I've changed less than you, unfortunately, even today I wanted to die, or nearly, she qualifies it, lately it's seemed to me I'm already dead, my life is over, it's a terrible feeling and I can't get rid of it.

How did it start? he asks, it must be connected with some circumstances, right? and she sighs again, maybe it's age, or hormones, I don't understand enough about this, but I feel I've suddenly been left alone, and everything I thought I had has evaporated, and because he doesn't respond but confines himself to nodding gloomily, as if in corroboration, she adds, I've had an idea which everyone thinks is crazy, meaning that I'm crazy. There's something I want to do with what remains of my life, but this apparently isn't going to happen.

What is it? he asks, and she hesitates, leave it, you'll think it's crazy too, I know I'm supposed to forget all about it and be happy with what I have, but I can't do that, and when he chuckles she asks, what's funny? and he says, since when have members of our family felt what they're supposed to feel? She smiles, relieved, I didn't think of that, the truth is, I'm not used to seeing myself as part of a family, we were always so divided.

So what do you want to do now? he asks, go to India for a year? Take a young lover? And she says, I wish those options were right for me, believe me it would be a lot simpler. No, what I want is something more basic, she pauses, but also much more complicated, I want to adopt a child. That probably seems to you absolutely psychotic, most men don't sympathise with this, and the truth is most women don't either, she adds acerbically, nor girls, young women I should say, meaning Nitzan, and when her voice breaks and her head gravitates almost unconsciously towards his shoulder he puts his arm around her. Dini, he says, I don't know why you're apologising so much, in my eyes this is a beautiful thing, what could be more beautiful?

But it isn't because of the beauty that I want to do it, she admits, her eyes moist, it's for my sake, you understand, because it's what I need, I'm no saint, and he says, why do you need to be a saint? And what difference does it make anyway, what your motivation is? Do you know how many different motives induce people to bring children into the world? You need a child and you'll find a child who needs a mother, what could be more logical?

But Avni, it's a fantasy, she blurts out to him all the words said to her these last weeks, it's just a romantic fantasy, we're talking about difficult children, with lots of problems, and he grins, so what? Difficult children don't need a mother? Of course there are bound to be problems but you'll cope with them and in the meantime you'll be rescuing a kid, and she weeps on his shoulder, it seems it's myself I'd be rescuing, they all say I need to treat myself some other way, take hormones or go into therapy, or just be happy with what I've got, and I can't do it.

Of course you can't do it, he says, handing her his used paper hanky, how can you suppress a desire that runs so deep? I'm afraid even to think of the price to be paid for such suppression, but she interrupts him, I have to give it up, I have no choice, Gideon isn't prepared to help under any circumstances, and I can't do this alone, and he says, so I'll help you, I'll travel with you anywhere you need to go, and she shakes her head, you don't understand how complicated it is, I can't destroy a whole family because of my obsession, I have to get over it and find other things to take an interest in, I'll give therapy a try, I'll take up yoga, I'll find some institution where I can volunteer to help out, just to feel needed.

Oy, Dini, he grins, you're lucky you're not in my profession, you'd never win a single case in all your life, the way you're running yourself down all the time, hush now and let me represent you, and she falls silent gratefully and listens to him with sparkling eyes and thumping heart, sitting on the bench under the blazing treetop and thirstily drinking in his words, because it seems he's talking about some other woman, not about her, a brave, generous woman, the kind she'd be happy to know, a woman whose mother didn't want her and who, in what remains of her life, is seeking to take into her house and into her heart a little child whose mother didn't want him, and raise him with love.

She's late again, and again the reproachful, malicious looks will accompany her, what's the matter with you, Hemda, late in the classroom again, both as pupil and as teacher, late in the cowshed, in the chicken coops, dreaming among the vegetable plots, advancing slowly, inadvertently challenging their sacred cow, the sacred cow of work, which they worshipped intemperately in those years. Who is first arriving for work, who has not missed a working day, whose hands are the most diligent, whose baskets are filled more quickly with the hard, bitter olives, who is milking more cows, who is catching more fish, who hoes weeds with the dexterity of a pianist – while she of all people, her father's daughter, is always late, and always last in line, her baskets empty.

He was their conscience, their conscience and their compass, but she was marooned on the periphery of this dispensation, with its prickly edges. Everyone gives according to his ability and receives according to his needs, he used to drum it into her, it isn't equality we aspire to, equality is a sore evil, but how will you know what your ability is, and how will you believe in your needs? Exhausting himself, grinding his teeth, because all must give according to their abilities, and it always seems they can do more, and what do you deserve? Nothing, is the honest answer. That's why he's content with the very least; in his rare hours of leisure he's teaching himself English, filling notebooks with his small and neat handwriting, reading works of philosophy, reading Tolstoy, reading Brenner, and she is crushed before his eyes, crushed before the eyes of all in this transparent pressure-cooker, surrounded by scores of critical eyes, what are they saying about you, what did they say yesterday, what will they say tomorrow?

What didn't they say about her? She's lazy, she's spoilt, she dreams instead of working, she exploits her workmates, how could such a daughter be produced by such a father? Well, what's so surprising about it, have you forgotten she has a mother too? No wonder if you have forgotten; she's forgotten she has a mother, poor girl, and the mother has forgotten she's a mother. Have you seen her? Only just returned and she's off again, to America this time, for a year, on a fund-raising campaign, while we are stuck here cultivating the blisters on our hands. This is the sour fruit of the mother who wears stylish dresses and travels to the centre on a Sunday and returns to the kibbutz on a Thursday, that's assuming she's in the country at all. Poor girl, poor husband, and how can he let her do this, as if he doesn't mind being left alone all the time, a grass widower. But she was so proud of her mother; choking in her admiration she listened to her stories about training farms that she set up in Poland years ago, and the importance of training up young Jews in manual work, so when they arrive in the country they can be integrated straightaway into the kibbutz system, and the importance of meeting the Jews of America and persuading them to contribute to the funding of the settlements, so we can build ourselves up here, so we can defend ourselves, don't worry, Hemda, the time will soon pass, in less than a year I'll be back and you can write me long letters, you write them so nicely, and Hemda would part from her, all her energy drained, knowing she too was giving according to her ability, she was giving her mother, and this was more than she could afford.

And even in adult life she was late, by a minute or two that would ruin the whole day, who ever heard of a teacher who's late? Teachers were suspect anyway, because they didn't do manual work, only when their turn came round or they were conscripted, and they were always looked at askance, all the more so a teacher who didn't arrive on time, who didn't force her pupils to do homework, who didn't believe in exams or awarding marks. Even the pupils who benefited most from this used to betray her, informing on her to their parents, but she abhorred competition, detested authority and recoiled from discipline, she wanted them to learn willingly and not under compulsion since the wounds of the coercion inflicted on her had not yet healed, and how could she enforce it on others? Teaching itself was almost forced on her, what choices did she have after the war? Dairymaid, poultry-keeper, cook, nurse? Obviously teaching was preferable, but she wanted to teach literature or Bible studies and they forced her to teach agriculture, with nature study in the more junior classes. She never forgave them for compelling her to rip away the mysteries surrounding her own nature, it was too close and too precious to her for its precepts to be taught and turned into a burden for her and for her pupils, a resented imposition, as the routine of her whole life had rapidly become. How disappointing was adult life, did her father feel the same, did her mother feel it too? Apparently not, since she was immersed in other questions entirely, how mankind should behave, rather than how life should be perceived.

But that's the way her adult life seemed to her then, constantly contracting just like the surface of the lake, between the steel monsters digging into it, between the western channel and the eastern channel, sinking with the declining water level. Under sentence of death the lake wasted away before her eyes year after year, but unlike her it wasn't giving up so easily, heaping more and more problems on the engineers with their sophisticated machines brought in from America. Again and again it drove them back, again and again work was suspended because the lake refused to go quietly; it blocked the drainage channel, disrupted the ploughing of the first furrow, and even at the last and the most terrible stage of all, when they removed the steel joists of the dam, and the place was buzzing with crowds of the distinguished and the curious, all eager to see the spectacle of public execution, as they had been promised it would be emptied within a few hours, they were forced to go back the way they came, since the lake held out stubbornly for many long weeks, until the winter came and flooded it all over again. Every time she believed it had finally succeeded in outwitting them, but they came back with alternative solutions, until she realised these were only the dying spasms. They weren't giving up, determined to offer it as a sacrifice and even call it a new act of creation, as they were determined to call the stubbornness of the lake sterility, and fertility when it finally came they called a blessing, although only a few years after the subjugation of the lake the blessing disintegrated in its turn.

What was all this, she sighs, and for what, and why is she the one who has carried on so long, outliving her lake, outliving her parents, outliving her husband? Even for the job of dying she's late, snatching another moment of idleness, daydreaming, and there they are, all of them, obedient labourers in their working clothes, cultivating the ruined fields, harvesting the hollow olives, drawing black milk from the corpses of cattle, gathering the fossilised eggs of dead chickens, going out in the evening to catch the skeletons of fish, so much toil and all in vain, after all the dead need no nourishment.

So much toil and all in vain, that's exactly the way she feels even today, as there's no taste to all of this, no taste to the food, no taste to the olives, to the fruits since they weren't picked with love but with hatred, with arrogance. How arrogant they were then, adults and children too, convinced this was the superior style of life, everyone giving according to his ability and receiving according to his needs, but why the relentless scrutiny, how is the other one behaving, who is exploiting whom? It seemed to her that even in her sleep she was being tested, her bed surrounded by judges and lawmakers growing more severe from hour to hour, and even now she wakes up in fear, she's late again, looking around her almost apologetically, hoping no one will notice, after all she has to set a personal example, the precept her father drummed into her.

Are you awake, Grandma? she suddenly hears a voice she hasn't heard in ages, she mustn't be late this time, she needs to be present in time and in place, probing her gums to be sure her teeth are where they should be, is that you, Nitzi? Yes, I'm awake.

How are you feeling? the girl asks, and Hemda holds out her hand to the warm breath, her eyes still closed; most of the day they are masked by the lids, like blinds which there's no point in rolling up, and now it seems her brain is incapable of contriving even this simple movement. Between her fingers is a clump of hair that reminds her of her mother's hair, when she used to dry it in the sun after the Sabbath shampoo, her hands caressing the fragrant cloud and her eyes fluttering with the effort. Are you all right, Grandma? the girl asks, her voice a little anxious, and Hemda hurriedly says, yes, don't worry, it isn't hurting as much now, as an orange light penetrates her eyelids and sends beams of honey spreading from the top of her head to her toes, how sweet this girl is, but how little she knows about her, as if she's really dead, and how happy she was when she was born, and longed to be a part of her upbringing, but Dina froze her out, allowing her no foothold in their love. Just once, when they went to Venice and left the girl with her, she tasted this sweetness, which was soon taken away from her, and she hoped that when the girl grew up she would liberate herself from her mother's intermediary role and draw closer to her, but even when she grew up Nitzan was always a little reserved, as if she had no need of her, has she really not needed her until this moment?

Now her eyelids lift and her eyes open to the pale, slightly freckled face, its transparent, inward beauty stealing slowly into her heart, who does she resemble? More and more it seems that she sees reflected in her the features of her Elik in his youth, let's just hope she doesn't turn out as hard as he was, she'll succeed in retaining her sweetness. She still looks like a little girl, she hasn't changed much since she was six years old and stayed with her for a week, and she remembers how she wanted to sleep in her bed so she could hide in her heart, so she said. Hide from whom? she asked and the girl replied, from the separation, and so they experienced seven nights of tranquillity, how simple this was, for the first time in her life, simple to sleep, simple to love, a little girl who isn't her own, and she says, how nice it is to see you, it seems years since we met each other, have you come here alone, without your Mum?

Yes, Mum's at work, Nitzan replies, I haven't even told her about coming to see you, and Hemda asks, and how are you, how are things at school? – trying to find some hook to hold on to because in fact she knows nothing about the life of her granddaughter. She remembers how old she is, knows she enjoys reading and painting, maybe photography too, and not much more than this, but Nitzan immediately interrupts this fumbling conversation, there's no school, this is the long vacation, and in a gloomy voice she asks, tell me, Grandma, can I come and move in with you?

Of course, why do you need to ask? she replies, are Mum and Dad going abroad? And the girl says no, I just don't want to live at home any more, and Hemda ponders her words, feeling suddenly very tired, any moment now her eyelids will fall, taking with them the clarity that is slithering like an elusive fish in the lake of her consciousness, she must try to catch it with the ploys familiar to her, the trawl-net opening in a circular movement, white durra by the handful, oars beating the water, get away, get out of here, and now the whistle is heard from far away, must hurry back to the shore and drag the boats on to dry land, the waves are rolling slow and long until they turn on their backs, spouting white foam. Don't go to sleep, it isn't your turn to sleep yet, her father rebukes her, and she shakes herself, staring at the figure sitting beside her. Don't go to sleep, Grandma, stay with me, and she moistens her lips with her tongue, they taste of blood, what did you say? And Nitzan sighs, I said Mum doesn't want me at home any more, I'm interfering with her plans, and Hemda asks again, what did you say, what's happening to your mother? An ugly satisfaction sweeps over her.

Tell me, Grandma, supposing you've got an old pair of shoes that you've worn for years and you don't need them any more, what would you do with them? she asks, and Hemda smiles, well, you know what we were like on the kibbutz, we wore our shoes until they fell to bits, my father was proud that he never threw away a pair of shoes in his life, and the girl interrupts her again, but these days it's different, these days you throw them out, right? You put them out beside the bin until someone who needs them picks them up, right? And Hemda nods, I suppose so, why do you ask? You've found some shoes you want to pick up and your Mum says no? And the girl answers in a cracked voice, don't you believe it, Mum's throwing me out now like an old pair of shoes.

Throwing you out? She's bewildered, what are you talking about? Your mother loves you very much, but the girl protests with a strange kind of snort, you don't know what's been going on, Grandma, she doesn't love me at all, not any more, and she grabs a tissue from the box on the medicine table and wipes her nose, laying her head on the old woman's shoulder and sobbing sporadically.

That's enough crying, she caresses her hair sadly, she's heard all this before, more than once, what's going on in that family of theirs, sitting around the fire of love and tirelessly measuring the height of the flames, what strange kind of torture is unfolding for them from generation to generation, how has such an implausible idea popped into her head? Of course she loves you, she insists, you're her daughter, her only daughter!

It isn't like that, the girl yells, she wants to adopt a new child, do you get it? She's suddenly got the idea of trading me in! And Hemda is stunned, what do you mean, trade you in? Oddments of words, fragments of conversations, she stitches together with a clumsy hand, who said what to whom and when, it seems the mouths are changing, the tongues rolling, but the transparent spool of memory is still in her hands, she must not let it fall again, what's this about trading you in, I loved the pair of you equally! Fragments of words, oddments of conversations, and still her granddaughter is moaning on her shoulder, for as long as I was her sweet little girl she loved me, but now I'm bigger and not as much hers any more, she's finding this hard to cope with and she's come up with a simple solution, to give me up and take another child in my place, so I don't intend to get in her way, I'm moving out and leaving her alone with her new sprog.

What's this story you're telling me, she mumbles, and for a moment there is such a clear picture in her mind, she must put words to it before they are erased, this is her opportunity and perhaps there won't be another, one more step, Hemda, don't fall down now, and she says with an effort, you and your mother, you're not a married couple, it's true that in a couple a new partner may replace a former one, but a child? Think of your cousins for example, when little Yotam was born did he replace Tomer?

This is completely different, Grandma, you don't understand, the girl detaches herself from her grandmother's shoulder, takes off her glasses and puts them down on the oval table, she wants to adopt, she wants to bring a child home, a total stranger from the other side of the world, and Hemda says, every child is a stranger until he comes out into the light of the world and sometimes even afterwards, but a child is a child, there's no real distinction here, it isn't that different from pregnancy.

The fact is she didn't want to be pregnant! And another fact, she didn't want another child when I was younger! It's only now she's suddenly remembered, and that means her love is conditional, and the moment I'm not giving her what she wants she's looking for someone else, and it's all my fault, she wails, I was horrible to her, and she couldn't cope with it, and now she's punishing me by deserting me the way I deserted her, she's stopped loving me and I deserve it, and Hemda takes the trembling girl in her arms again, as she carries on without a moment's pause, I didn't mean to, it just happened, I don't understand it myself, suddenly things have changed and I've started going round more with my friends, and every time I came home I found Mum waiting for me with this really depressed look on her face, and so I preferred sleeping over at my friends' houses, and even when I wanted to be with her and tell her things, the words just didn't come out right. Suddenly I was angry with her and saying bad things to her and then I was angry with myself and taking it out on her, is it my fault I've grown up? Only dead children don't grow up!

That's enough, Nitzi, it's a wonderful thing that you're growing up, she whispers in her ear, and it's natural that you're moving away from your mother, and it's good that you feel capable of saying unpleasant things to her and being angry with her, I wish I had been capable of being angry with my parents when I was your age, but her granddaughter protests, what's good about it? How has it helped me, being angry? I hurt her and that's why she's going to bring in another kid who won't hurt her, and what will happen when he grows up? Who is she going to adopt then? And Hemda strokes the fragile shoulders, that's the way Dina used to besiege her bed with all kinds of complaints, but how much easier it is to calm things down when the complaints aren't directed at you, since revealed to her now in the hinterland of her consciousness are all the words she couldn't find for her daughter, like the objects discovered on the bed of the lake after it was drained, the shaft of a plough, the mast of a ship, lost nets. Look, Dini, see how non-existence exposes existence, she wanted to say, see how the stories of make-believe are engraved in the memory of reality, how loves unconsummated wander from generation to generation, a voice unheard turns to an echo, the voice of the woman who longed for fruit in her womb and she bathed every day in the waters of the lake, and he said to her, I shall be your son, I shall be your baby, and he flooded her with his waters until her womb was filled and her belly swelled and she gave birth to a water child. You see, Nitzi, when I was a little girl I had so many stories to tell, but in my stories there wasn't enough love, too late I understood that the more people love, the more love there is for everyone, it's a kind of wonder, like the miracle of the cruse of oil; when I was your mother's age I already wanted to be left alone, your mother wants to be needed, you want both of these things, and anything's possible.

Not true, nothing's possible, the girl insists, if she gives up on this it will be terrible and if she doesn't give up it will be terrible, and Hemda shakes her head, you're mistaken, you're so far from the truth; she imagines she sees the truth on one bank of the stream and the girl on the other bank and she needs to bring them closer together with her fingers, covering her eyes with her hands as before, under the branches of the pepper tree, how sweet was the game of the fingers. So much she has to say, what has she been thinking of all these years if not of this, mother and father, mother and daughter, mother and son, but the simplest way of all is without words, moving finger towards finger, give me your hand, Nitzi, see how everything approaches and goes away, in our family things happen too late or too soon, it isn't down to you.

Oh, but it is, she sighs, I never wanted to have a little brother, I was happy with the way things were and I always felt sorry for my friends with their irritating brothers, I always told my Mum they shouldn't even dare to think about it, and now because of me she needs to adopt some fucked-up kid from the ends of the earth, and Hemda strokes the damp cheek with her finger, I too was an only child and I so much wanted brothers, she says, we had a little boy on the kibbutz whose mother died giving birth to him and I so much wanted my mother to adopt him, I think it's wonderful when you can take a child who already exists in the world and give him a home and love.

What kind of home and what kind of love will that be with a mother who's totally insane and a father who doesn't want to know? the girl complains, he told me if this happens he's going to walk out and leave her alone with her lunacy, but I'll be here with you, Grandma, I don't need to watch this happening, and Hemda sees before her eyes the scrawny legs of her daughter at three years old, how she snatched her baby brother from his cot and ran with him as if possessed by a dybbuk, this is my baby, I'll be his good mother. It's true this is an extreme act, she says, but it doesn't seem insane to me, on the contrary, there's a lot of strength in it, a lot of hope.

I'm so tired, Grandma, can I sleep in your bed with you? she asks and Hemda lifts the blanket, of course, come and sleep with me and hide from rejection, hide in my heart, and when the girl snuggles against her she watches the rays of light softening between the slats of the shutter, it seems evening is approaching and pangs of hunger rise in her for the first time in weeks, the carer will be here soon, she'll ask her to cook porridge for both of them, hot porridge with honey and cinnamon. Tell me, Grandma, the girl whispers inside her heart, do you think if my twin brother had been born Mum would be happier now? Would that be enough for her? You know he was the only one I wanted, he was the only genuine brother for me, and Hemda says, yes my dear, I know. It's a pity we haven't talked enough all these years, the girl sighs and Hemda whispers, it isn't too late, I promise you, we'll have plenty of time to talk, and she wraps her in the blanket and lays her hand on her shoulder, and that's how Avner finds them when he arrives in the night at his mother's house in an overwrought and feverish state.

Chapter Ten

Again and again he's up before the judge who changes her face every night. Sometimes it's his wife with her square features, her eyes flashing rancour and resentment at him, and he presents her with scores of documents, some of them already crumbling from repeated use. I did the best I could, he's trying to argue, give me the benefit of the doubt, don't blame me and I won't blame you, we both made a mistake, got hitched to each other too soon and didn't dare separate, come on, let's salvage what remains of our lives. I disappointed you and you disappointed me, I hurt you and you hurt me, and I really believe all this was done in innocence, the innocence of children who have no awareness of what changeable creatures they are, and I've realised something recently, he wants to tell her, at dictation speed of course, so the stenographer can type it all and not miss a word, I've understood something about myself, I've realised that I don't want to live without love, or more to the point, die without love, even if I'm fated to discover that to love and be loved is too much to ask for in this life, I'll be content with one of those, and with us there's neither one nor the other, we both know, so let's cool things down, the children will benefit too, we'll share their upbringing, relieve them of the burden of the struggle between us.

Why didn't we think of this before, he wonders at times; in fact he thought of it constantly, but with the kind of defeatism that renders any turnaround impossible, and now that this has been removed as an ugly stain is excised from the retina of the eye, the sight is precisely the same sight but vision has changed, and even if he reminds himself again and again about the pains of separation, the unhappiness of the children and the stress of holidays, the fear of loneliness and the dread of old age, still sight is as clear as an equation to which there's only one solution: he won't and can't and is under no obligation to try, living alongside a woman who does nothing but scowl at him and mock him in front of his children, and all her aspirations are focused on the project of proving to him that he's her inferior, belittling his achievements and exaggerating his shortcomings, and if he exerts himself some of these nights when she's sleeping beside him and tries to remember the good times, he can barely find isolated moments in recent years, perhaps during her maternity leave when she used to come with the new baby in the pram to meet him at Sheychar, but how fragile all this was, since one moment of distraction on his part was enough to arouse her bitterness, and as for him the same applied, if the truth be told: it didn't take much to make him recoil from her, one crude gesture on her part was enough to send him back into his personal exclusion zone, and now as he is more and more obsessed with death it's becoming ever more clear to him that this isn't the way he wants to die. For the purposes of living this would be almost tolerable, apparently, but he wants to die with another woman beside him, kind and noble-spirited, who even if she doesn't love him will consent to receive his love from him, and even if she doesn't consent she won't be capable of wresting it from him; sometimes he sees her there, sitting in the judge's chair, and he lays his appeal before her, Talia, let me do for you what the dead man didn't succeed in doing, let me leave my wife and my sons, redeem you from your loneliness and perhaps thereby redeem myself too, let me console you for an injustice that I didn't cause, let me teach myself to love, because more and more he is realising to what extent love is detached from its object, and he certainly realises this where she is concerned, in her well-kept apartment, which he has visited almost every day this past month on some excuse or another, and he'll always find her there alone, planting flowers in her little garden, sitting in the armchair with a book in her hand, or busy at the computer, and she'll always smile at him her hesitant smile, and he'll always feel how the void in his heart is being filled by her heart, heavy with love, and he understands that just as her love for the dead man continues to exist even after his death, so his love for her can also exist without any response from her, as if she were his dead lover.

Again he sits facing her and tells her what he's been doing, about his visit to the Bedouin school in the heat of midday, just unbelievable how overcrowded they are, he says, but so eager to learn, perhaps some time you'd like to come with me, see the place for yourself, and she listens with interest, speaking little; since she moved into her parents' house her main concern has been with them and pictures of her childhood are returning to her in full vigour, and sometimes she shares with him a little of the confusion she feels; in particular she's focused on the dead man, and when she talks about him in her restrained way it seems to him again it's him he's falling in love with, and he wonders if this is really the only thing that unites them, but for the most part he doesn't try to clarify anything, preferring to concentrate on the sweet delight that he feels in her company, a delight familiar to him only from his own company and that only on rare occasions, and when he parts from her he kisses her cheek, which is slender as a fallen leaf and doesn't say when he'll be back and she doesn't ask, smiling at him the same reserved smile on his arrival and his departure, such that he doesn't know which of them makes her happier, if at all, and it seems to him sometimes this blank tablet of hers allows him for the first time in his life a degree of relaxation, since he isn't responsible for her pain and her desires aren't aimed at him, he has nothing to offer her, only to himself can he offer the love that at the moment is turned towards her, but maybe one day it will be perfected and polished and elevated to the point where she feels she can turn to the other person who genuinely wants her, since the more powerless he is when confronting her, the more he feels arising in him an impulse of manly emotion, such as he never knew before except in youthful fantasies, a mysterious and comforting strength when facing up specifically to the grieving woman, who doesn't want anything from him.

And yet sometimes it isn't she who is there in the black pleated robe but his mother, and to her too he presents papers yellowing with age, pointing to them in silence, and the stenographer waits for his words, while his opposite number is quick to deride him, what is the matter with my learned friend, why the sudden lapse into silence, has he not prepared for this case, I will not agree to another adjournment, and he mutters from a parched throat, the facts speak for themselves, the witnesses have testified, I have nothing to add to my former submission.

My learned friend is holding this court in contempt, the lawyer sneers at him, why are we gathered here if he has no new evidence, and suddenly he notices it's his sister Dina, her hair dyed raven-black and her face carefully made-up, before their mother they stand so she may judge between them, the three of them in black gowns, like a family of bats, but in front of their eyes she is ageing fast, already her mouth is agape and her head slumped, her skull almost bald and her eyes closed, and he wants to say words of valediction to her, but only a babyish whimper emerges from his throat, and he wipes his eyes with the edge of his gown. What am I to do with your love now, Mother? he mumbles, I always hated it, it constricted me, it drove me away, how dangerous was your love, combined with the full force of your loneliness and your misery, which I of all people am supposed to be assuaging, and here he is awakened by his plaintive voice, fearing lest all this has already happened and he's finding himself alone, without wife and without children, in an alien and neglected rented room, and he tries to snuggle up to Shlomit's body in the sticky night. Relax, nothing's happened, just thoughts and since when have thoughts changed reality. Your wife is here with you and despite all her shortcomings you're committed to her, and she's the mother of your children, and you share an address and so it will be for ever. In your imagination you go the full distance, but will we see you daring to say to her one single word from all the speeches you are formulating here, he challenges himself and stands by the ventilator fan, which blends all their breaths into one giddying blast, and agrees with himself that thought is much easier than action and dream much easier than speech, and for the time being he should avoid taking any hasty steps, but when she sits beside him in the car in a black evening dress on their way to Anati's wedding – as usual they're running late, the clock on the dashboard shows 6:55 and the wedding starts at 7:00 and they're still stuck in traffic jams on the outer city bypass – he knows tonight it's going to happen, he feels in all his limbs and extremities the itch of imminent change in the offing, as if his body were the rickety track for a train that's already set out on its way, even if he wanted to he'd be incapable of stopping it, all the more so when he doesn't want to do that.

You should have driven through the forest, she reproaches him, at this hour all the exits are blocked, and he retorts, oh, really? So why didn't you mention that before, you're such an expert in hindsight, and she says, I was sure you knew, I didn't think you were stupid enough to fall into this trap, and he hisses back at her, if I was stupid enough to fall into your trap and get stuck there for the rest of my life, why are you so surprised, and she says, no one's keeping you here by force, as far as I'm concerned you can get up and go, we'll all be better off without you, and he flexes his itching fingers irritably, unintentionally hitting the wheel with his hand and setting off the horn, annoying the driver in front, who signals back to him with a lewd gesture, and she grins maliciously, why are you hooting? What exactly are you expecting him to do? He's got wings and he's going to fly over the obstruction? And Avner pants heavily and opens the window, there's no air in the car, she's gobbled up all the air with her hatred of him, but a sweltering and polluted vapour comes wafting in from outside and she's rebuking him again, close the window, what's the matter with you?

He stares at the rapidly rising glass, sealing in the air-conditioned space, and for a moment he wants to insert his fingers in the gap, get them crushed, why not, the pain spreading through his body will ease his resentment, and he growls, that's all right then, I might just as well get up and go if I'm so superfluous to you, turning her and the children into a single entity, for his convenience, and she's quick to pinch his vulnerable spot, sure, we've heard all about you and your heroic exploits. How exposed are the partners in a long-term relationship, he sighs, everything is known and remembered and kept and will be exploited to your disadvantage until the day you die, and already he's thinking about the day of his death, will she regret all the harsh words she's thrown at him over the years; they won't be forgotten either, like his youthful failings, but from this moment, Tuesday afternoon, late August, to the day of his death is still some distance, who knows if it will be long or short, and on this journey he doesn't want her beside him, and he shakes his head this way and that, the classic refusal gesture of Yotam when they're trying to feed him against his will, grinding his teeth and closing his eyes tight.

Why aren't you driving? she nags him, the blockage has cleared at last and you're still standing here? He pumps the accelerator pedal abruptly and nearly collides with the car in front, which is making the transition from stationary to mobile at an appropriately gradual pace, and his wife mutters, maybe I'd better drive if you still want to get to this wedding alive, it's too dangerous to let you drive, and he feels his blood bubbling; it's as if a dam has been breached and is flooding his brain, this woman is dangerous to me, and he pulls up at a flickering green light to the sound of the protests of the driver behind, by all means, you drive, he snaps and steps out of the car and for a moment he wants to leave her there and carry on walking, wander for ever amid the islands of traffic like one of those tramps. With deliberate slowness he circles the car and gets in, not sitting beside her in the front but in the back, beside Yotam's safety seat, and he sees her lifting her bum over the gear-stick and moving laboriously into the driving seat without leaving the vehicle, and he reckons he detects a faintly sadistic smile on her face; she's driven him out of his mind, and she takes pride in being a woman who can show that her husband is still drawn to her, as a wave of nausea shakes him, how shameful it is, what an insult to arrive at a wedding like this, spreading the spores of an unhappy marriage, endangering public health.

They are certainly accustomed to quarrels and yet here he identifies that leap from a higher to a lower step on the staircase, since this time there's no pain in their hearts, only perverse pleasure, and that's why he's suddenly so alarmed, sitting in the back seat, his whole body full of revulsion and his whole being crying out for change, and again he says, I'm getting up and getting out, I'm leaving the house, but she doesn't hear, at that very moment she's turned the radio on, looking for traffic bulletins, and from time to time he catches her eyes in the mirror and notices a deep groove of concern etched between them and on both sides of it an unhealthy flash, but most of the time he's looking out at the cars alongside them, all determined to overtake the slowcoach. His eyes wander over the passing travellers, couples sitting conventionally in the front seats, bickering like them or deep in relaxed conversation, and for some reason this evening he's no longer convinced they're all happier than he is, this evening he skips without interest over the faces of the random couples, as it's the lone drivers he's looking for, the lonely travellers with no one sitting beside them or behind them, to whom no one turns in conversation, just themselves they are transporting from place to place, and when he sits like this in the back seat, harnessed by the safety belt that's stretched tight across his paunch, he realises how this evening is different from all other evenings; in his own eyes at least he is no longer a partner in a couple.

He has always loved weddings, and even now he's gripped by childish relief that in spite of everything they haven't missed the ceremony. How slender and pure are the moments preceding it, while the banquet afterwards always seems to him insipid and crude. They should finish the wedding the moment they're done with the canopy, he tells himself, just shower a load of felicitations on the happy couple and go, and there's no point saying any of this to his wife, since they've seized the opportunity to argue about it a number of times before. It just shows how unreal you are, she used to mock him, that's your problem in a nutshell, you're trapped by romantic conceptions, you're expecting the whole of life to be as radiant and glamorous as the canopy and anything less than that disappoints you, and now once again he wanders disconsolately on the lawn, her thoughts attacking his thoughts even when they are both silent, yes maybe she's right, it's his expectations that leave him always dissatisfied, a destructive blend of guilt and unease. But in the meantime he can enjoy the wide open green expanses and the vista of the Jerusalem hills. White cushions are strewn liberally on the lawn, there are low wicker tables and some Spanish tune warbling in the background, the skies are soft with a smattering of white clouds, almost transparent, and it's a long time since he saw such a harmonious match between heaven and earth and this has to be a favourable sign for the young couple. He looks around for the bride to share this thought with her; perhaps this portent will resolve her doubts, although he doesn't even know if they have persisted. Since that evening she hasn't been sharing her personal concerns with him, it seems she resents him for all the advice he showered on her so hastily, advice based solely and entirely on his own experience, with no recognition of her or of her partner, and she has avoided intimate conversation with him as if he were doubt personified. He has tried to find opportunities to qualify his words, but he himself has been involved in other urgent issues, and he hopes that she no longer needs this portent, that even without it she is whole and her heart full of happiness and love as his heart has never been, even on his wedding day. When he takes two glasses of wine from the tray and hands one to his wife he remembers the woman now sitting alone in the garden of her house, a glass of red wine in her hand and her teeth already turning purple, and he wishes he were sitting there beside her, the flimsy bamboo fence insulating them from the hubbub of life; although he wants everything from her and she wants nothing from him, only at her side is he content.

In silence she takes the glass of wine from his hand, but her silence no longer oppresses him, silence is fine when there are no pleasant words to be said, and he peers at her, standing stolidly with the glass of wine in her hand, slightly ridiculous in the evening dress tailored to her measurements, with the transparent chiffon sleeves, and her unpractised attempts at self-titivation, the lipstick applied with a clumsy hand and missing the line of the lips, the eye-pencil which has drawn a thick ring round one eye and a thin ring round the other, high-heeled shoes pinching her reddening feet. She'll always look like a countrywoman dumped in the big city, but none of this would have bothered him if only she were by his side and not against him, and perhaps it's his mistake, for years he's wanted a partner more impressive than her, and even when he stood beside her under the canopy he felt disappointed and frustrated, and if he felt that way, he must surely have shared this with her in some indirect fashion, even though the words denied it, and for this he should apologise to her. Better for her too if he hadn't married her, but she pressured him into marriage and threatened separation, and he didn't dare lose her and hoped things would change for the better. He had only just lost his father and he needed a handhold.

Distractedly he surveys the few guests, to his surprise he doesn't know a single one of them, some of them are sitting on the cushions, little plates in their hands, some of them wandering this way and that, deep in conversation, in thought, and it seems the same sweet anticipation grips them all, from the largest to the smallest, anticipation that the new couple due to consecrate themselves in this place will bestow on all those present the light of hope and change, grace and truth. A pleasant breeze stirs the hair, blending scents of perfumes and soaps, selected foods and drinks; like angels the white-clad waiters bestow abundant victuals upon the small congregation, and he samples the delicacies and wonders at the choice of this extensive site for a gathering of this size, have most of the invitees ducked out of it, and why?

He sees Shlomit glancing at her watch and turning to him with a look of indignation, as if he's responsible for this delay too, and he shrugs his shoulder at her, already nearly eight and where is the couple and where is the rabbi and where is the canopy? Have the doubts that she mentioned to him come back to haunt her, and is she weeping now in the decorated limo, unable to make up her mind? And perhaps at the last moment she's decided to heed his advice, to learn from his experience, perhaps the wedding has actually been cancelled and they haven't had time to tell everyone, and that's why they are so few, and he takes his mobile from his shirt pocket and checks to be sure he hasn't missed any new messages, absently picking up another rolled and spiced vine-leaf, while Shlomit moves away from him and stretches out on one of the cushions, as if washing her hands of the whole event.

In the diminishing light the lawn turns black rapidly and the pillows are grey and her form can no longer be broken down into constituent parts, a solid mass of humanity compressed by angry memories, and he finds himself remembering the evening of their wedding in the kibbutz, nearly twenty years ago, what an orphan he was, he never felt his orphanhood as powerfully as then when he stood a long time in the shower under the stream of hot water, knowing that even now white cloths were being laid on tables outside the dining hall, in the houses nearby people were putting on their best clothes, and some were coming from far away, and soon they would be showering him with hugs and good wishes, while all he wanted to do was run out of there, grab the cloths from the tables and ditch the flowers, cavort naked and wet on the lawn yelling like a newborn baby, scaring the guests away with his antics, bringing disgrace on his family and on his bride, and already he's convinced this is what's going to happen here this evening. Not for nothing had he felt such a strong and sad sense of intimacy with her since the day she turned up at his office, an intimacy which he misinterpreted at first and took for attraction, an intimacy which will soon be demonstrated when she fulfils his old dream and rushes naked across the lawn, her heavy breasts bouncing this way and that, crying and yelling with the last vestiges of her strength, and running behind her the angry groom and her glowering widower father, and even when he sees her finally appearing among the cushions in a simple wedding-dress, arm-in-arm with her groom, he still believes that what he saw in his mind's eye is more valid than anything happening now in plain sight, since her puffy eyes and flushed cheeks, likewise the deep pallor of the groom, tend to back up his worrying interpretation of the delay. Suspiciously he scans his face, jutting chin and narrow lips giving him a stern expression, within a few years his authoritative and demanding streak will come to the fore, and what will become of her then, the girl who lost her mother at the age of eight and ever since then has talked of herself in the third person, and he observes them from a distance, leaving his wife behind and clearing himself a path towards them as if he were the rabbi himself, the one person without whom the marriage would be invalid, being drawn further into the innermost circle around the couple. There is the father of the bride, now revealed as a giant of a man with a stern expression, and beside him a young woman who looks about the same age as his daughter, and the parents of the groom, elderly and tense, and although he presses towards them eagerly, not wanting to miss anything, he's not sure he wants the bride to see him there and so he stays behind the broad back of her father, and there he will be when the canopy is unfolded almost above his head, under the sudden light of the full moon, and he skulks in the shadow of the stranger, hidden from her eyes but fully exposed to the crowd gathering around and the astonished stare of his wife, and he retreats slowly from the place he pinched for himself with so much effort, and without taking his eyes from what's happening under the canopy he finally stands by her side.

What a charming couple, she whispers, trying to conciliate him while the rabbi is intoning; *Soon to be heard in the cities of Judah and in the streets of Jerusalem will be the sound of merriment and the sound of joy, the voice of the groom and the voice of the bride, blessed art thou O Lord who makes the groom happy with the bride*, and Avner is stunned by her short-sightedness. What's so charming here? Can't you see their unhappiness is crying out to the sky, but when the groom gently lifts the veil and hands her the goblet, the bride's pretty eyes are seen to be calm and her face is radiant with the light of sheer bliss, all of which tells him that his wife is right this time; the Divine Presence, no less, has come down to this lawn to make the groom happy with the bride and the bride happy with the groom, and the change that he sees in her face is the finger of God sent down from on high to erase all doubts, whereas in his case the miracle didn't happen. He himself went under the canopy and came out of it precisely the same person, and so too did the woman who stands beside him now and gazes with envy at the newly-weds, and he sighs, man and woman, woman and man, what are they without the intervention of God, tormented creatures consumed by fears and regrets, and it seems to him that once again the pain of orphanhood has been laid on his shoulders, that double orphanhood, orphaned of both his father and progenitor and of his father in Heaven.

When the crowd that has thickened around them surges forward and besieges the couple with blessings, he clutches his wife's hand, come on, he says, there's nothing else here we should be looking for, and to his surprise she doesn't argue and doesn't demand an explanation, sitting beside him in silence in the car that's still warm, looking straight ahead at the winding road with pursed lips. Has she too realised something this evening of incomparable importance? Even when he says to her a few minutes later, after they've arrived at home and relieved the babysitter, I won't be here tonight, I'll be staying at my mother's apartment, she glances at him with a defeated look and doesn't say a word.

He has never looked at her like this before, as if she were dangerous, and not only he, it seems the entire universe, between the treetops and the stars, between roofs tinted pink by the sun, the windows, the shutters, is peering at her with scores of suspicious eyes, tracking her activities. Even when there's no one there beside her she's subject to unrelenting scrutiny, like now, for example, when she's standing on a chair and reaching up for the top drawer of the cabinet, where she keeps Nitzan's childhood clothes, and some toys which a child might still enjoy playing with: building blocks and dolls and battered furry animals. One after another they tumble down from the cupboard, a deluge of toys, a cataract of sweet memories, and she sits on the floor, glancing around her again to be sure no one's there and eagerly emptying the bags, as if it's in the power of these ancient objects to carry her far away from here, to other days.

Here's a grey velvet kitten, with a gloomy look on his face; she bought it her as a present for one of the festivals, and together they made up a story about the kitten who lost his mother and nearly died of hunger but then was rescued and taken into their house and became a happy little cat, and they really were convinced his expression had changed for the better too, but the long years of confinement in the cupboard haven't been kind to him, nor to the other creatures which have lost their vitality, like her in fact, but now she has good news for this hopeless company, a child will be coming soon, a little boy who will cuddle you in his arms, let you sleep in his bed; it's possible, she talked again today with some people, pleasant voices answered her, explained things in detail, she knows what she has to do and she will do it, the moment she's confident enough that things will work out, she feels this power, strong and inexorable as the very laws of nature, she feels it passing through her at times, checking her capacity to contain it; is she capable of turning into an unstoppable person?

Meticulously she examines the toys, it seems every one of them is telling her in its own way a simple story of love and intimacy, and that's what she longs for, love and intimacy, these are her needs and she sees no reason to apologise. There are some who need freedom, achievements, excitement, whereas her need is different, but no less profound, and although at the moment it's still hard to achieve it, this doesn't mean the idea is flawed, and she gather the toys in her lap and buries her face in the fur. You are witnesses, she whispers, you are the only witnesses to those days, long days of love and intimacy that I believed would last for ever, and it seems to her they are sighing at her until she hears his cold voice at the end of the sigh, good, I see you've decided to clear out the cupboard at last.

Not exactly, she mumbles, dropping the furry animals from her lap, what's happened? You're home early, and he sighs again, I don't feel well, my head hurts, and she gets up hurriedly, have you had enough to drink? Maybe you're dehydrated, it's terribly hot today. You're telling me? he grumbles, I was taking pictures in the valley. On his sweat-soaked T-shirt is the image of a man's face, and he too is looking at her askance, as if detecting some dangerous illness in her, and she asks, who is that on your T-shirt, and he replies, just a face, I think, stretching it and looking down into the ever more distorted features, while she puts the toys back in the bags. I'm going to the territories this week, he says, I can take that stuff with me and hand it out to the kids.

Come and lie down on the bed, she suggests, I'll get you a drink of water, and he takes off his shirt, only one pair of eyes staring at her now, and he's never looked at her like this before, I need a shower first, he says, and she's shocked, seeing the state of his chest, how thin he's becoming these days, and she watches him with concern as he disappears into the shower. This is her fault, she's the one who's disturbing his peace of mind with her crazy ideas, that's why he doesn't feel well, that's why he isn't eating, she's imposed too heavy a burden on her little family and the results haven't been slow in coming. Nitzan is spending the night somewhere else, and Gideon is getting weaker, they need her more than she realised, need her to be steady and calm so they can live their lives, ignore her in other words, and she ties the laces of the bags and then changes her mind and retrieves the grey velvet kitten, yes, by all means, take it all away, she says to him although he isn't listening, I have enough for one, and she strips off her clothes and gets into the bed, laying the kitten on the pillow beside her, what a cruel contest this is, Gideon, my need against your need, my happiness against your happiness, what a mistake it was to assume they were identical.

Are you asleep? he asks, stretching out on the bed beside her, his skin smelling of pungent herbal soap, and she lays her head on his chest, talk to me, Gideon, we hardly ever talk, you're so distant from me, and he grins, I'm distant? I'm always in the same place, you're the one who's suddenly changing with this new lunacy of yours, look at yourself objectively for a moment: a radiant and attractive woman, with a successful family, who suddenly needs to bring up another child, just at the age when most people reckon they're through with the responsibilities of childcare, sometimes I think we need an exorcist to uproot this crazy demon of yours.

Don't exaggerate, she protests, it's true it sounds extreme but in the end it's a simple story, even an ancient one, a woman wants a child, no more and no less, and he straightens up and leans against the wall, taking off his glasses, the question is how far is she prepared to go, this woman who wants a kid, in most cases it's the degree of the obsession that counts, that's the difference between sanity and madness. It isn't every woman who would endanger herself and her family to fulfil this aspiration, and if you don't even see the danger, it proves there's something about you that's fatally flawed.

Of course I see the danger, she says, leaning on the wall beside him, sending out the words without checking them first, but I also see the prospects of happiness, and the danger of giving up I see as well, and he interrupts her, giving up, what are you talking about? How can you mourn for something that doesn't exist anyway, that you never had? I really don't understand you.

I did have, she mumbles, that is we had, another child who wasn't born, have you forgotten him? And he groans, oh Dina, really, why is that relevant? No child you give birth to or adopt can compensate you for what you lost then, it's twisted logic, can't you see that? And she protests, why are you choosing such harsh words, that really isn't what I need now, and he says, sorry, I can't give you what you need, I've already told you, maybe you need a new man and not a new kid.

I don't need a new man, she hisses angrily, I want you the way we once were, there's no longer any warmth between us and no intimacy, that's what I miss, perhaps if we'd been closer I'd have found it easier to give up, and he grins, what is this, cosying up to me this time, are you? You're always complaining I'm too cold and hard, I can't be your baby, and I'm sorry about that, but I'll be very happy if you bring me a bottle of water, and she gets up from the bed and goes to the kitchen in bra and knickers. It's hopeless, completely hopeless, he'll never give way on this, and he's right, from his angle, he can live without her, the threads binding them together are steadily unravelling. When she returns to him he's lying there with his eyes closed, how vulnerable he looks without his glasses, what does she expect of him, it's not in his power to give her what she wants, and she sits beside him at the end of the bed, have a drink, she says, how's your head? And he says, no change, and opens his sunken eyes to her, I'm tired, I don't have the energy for your dramas, I've worked hard all my life and I'm not looking for new challenges now, I'm sorry, if you're incapable of letting it go we'll have to separate, and you must decide if it's really worth your while, dismantling your daughter's family for the sake of some caprice.

I don't want to dismantle anything, I want to build, she protests, why do you make everything so negative? Since when has a new child dismantled a family? A child means life and love, but he cuts in at once, no, a child means worry and exhaustion, and that doesn't suit me now, I want a quiet life, and she mutters, in your grave you'll have all the quiet you want, I promise you, your approach is so depressing, as if at our age a quiet life is all we have to look forward to, I don't want to live like that.

So don't live, he throws back at her, I'm speaking only for myself, this doesn't oblige you, just don't force on me extreme changes that don't suit me, and she counters with, aren't you forcing your quiet life on me, when that doesn't suit me? And he says, maybe, but what I want is more conventional, I'm following the natural course of life and you're the one trying to do something abnormal.

Since when have you been a paragon of normality, she complains, being left with one child isn't such a normal thing either, and he snaps, why do you think I came home early, I wanted to rest and you're doing my head in again, there's no point in talking about this any more, I'm telling you, it isn't going to happen, and now I need some sleep. She says, wait a moment, let's agree on something. I'm prepared to let it go, but only after you've given it serious consideration. Let's meet some people who've adopted, or just read about it in the blogs, after that you can decide, and he says, Dina, I'm not meeting anyone, I'm not reading anything, I'm not the one who's agonising about it, I'm not interested, end of, and she clutches his hand, but how can you dismiss outright something so important to me? You owe me this much at least, to look into it before you decide.

Tell me something, he straightens up and sits beside her, pushing her hand away, if I announced I wanted us all to convert to orthodox Judaism, would you agree to that? Would you agree to run a kosher kitchen and cover your hair, move to a religious neighbourhood and teach in a religious college? Would you be prepared to look into it, or would you kill it stone dead? What you're trying to force on me and Nitzan is much more extreme, don't you see? I have nothing to look into, do you hear?

How can I help hearing when you're shouting, she says softly. I really believe I would do that for you, perhaps not all the way, but I'd find some compromise that would allow us to stay together, and he grins at this, well, thanks very much, really, but what kind of a compromise can you make with a kid, be half a dad? A child means absolute commitment, either it's there or it isn't, and she says, I believe it is possible to find a solution and that's precisely what I'm talking about, oy, Gideon, lighten up a bit and come with me along this road, at least let's look into it together, and again he shoots her a glance of intense hostility. Listen, he yells, waving his arm at her, you're so detached from reality you don't understand what people are saying to you, I'm not interested, subject closed, find yourself another partner for this adventure, and he turns on his stomach and pulls the blanket over his head, leaving her without air, without hope, shaking her head this way and that.

Oy, Gideon, she mumbles, I understand you completely, but what's to become of me, this cold taciturnity of yours is killing me, and she stares resentfully at his coiled body, a heap of lifeless bones; in spite of everything the thought of leaving him has never occurred to her, it seems he's succeeded in keeping her by his side with precisely calculated measures of frustration and satisfaction, keeping her busy with the effort to extract warmth from his iciness, to identify cracks in his shell, not to miss out on moments of grace, which never depended on her but which he was always happy to share with her, and he manipulated her with the ploy of really not asking for much, just the opportunity to live according to his lights, to sanctify his freedom, expressing himself not in grand gestures but in the very simplest ways.

If he had been warmer and more enthusiastic towards her, she wonders, if he had offered her the delights of married life more generously, would it have been easier for her to give up on the idea of the child? Perhaps so, although it's always been the notion of the threesome that appealed to her, she and he and the child, the reflection of love, as it was in the early days with little Nitzan, when the warmth that he lavished on the girl rubbed off on her too. Is this the focus of her desire for a child, the need to rekindle his love? No, she says aloud, such things are bonuses and minor ones at that, the focus isn't there, but in the pulsations of life and the beating of the little heart, that's what she wants and how can he prevent it, how can he stand between her and her objective. It isn't logical and it isn't decent, the Moloch of marriage isn't supposed to demand such huge sacrifices, sacrifices of life almost, as he's expecting her to sacrifice for him the child who's waiting for her in the distance, and if she refuses she'll be forced to sacrifice their small family. Nitzan will never forgive her, and so she has no choice, she must choose the real and living girl over the little boy she's dreaming of; there's only one way open to her and that's the way of capitulation, not with bitterness but with love she has to capitulate, and not expect anything, as they won't thank her for it or show any appreciation of her self-denial.

Yes, with love and resignation she must make her way through the world, join the column of obedient ants. She's received her portion of happiness and there won't be any more, she's left it too late, there's no one who makes no mistakes, and now she must pay the price of her mistakes, and again she scrolls back the sequence of the years, when was the mistake made? Again and again it was made, a necklace of black and flawed pearls, all those nights when she could have conceived, so intent she was on preserving her treasures and incapable of realising they would be lost anyway, and now how hard it is to set things right; so many new mistakes she will have to make to correct one old mistake. It seems to her one of the doors is opening and she perks up but there's no one there, maybe it's just the memories of the house misleading her, its cravings teasing her, or maybe these are the cravings of the cat, who emerges from Nitzan's room and leaps on their bed, and she gathers him to her and presses her cheek against the fur. Rabbit, you'll help me, won't you? There's nothing the cat can do to change the past, he's even more helpless than she is and yet she intones her appeals into his ears as if he were some ancient god, as if it were in his power to give her a sign, Rabbit, Rabbit, what shall we do?

This is my brother, Nitzan used to cavort around him, the bestest brother in the world, offering him little presents on days she decided were his birthdays, or special festivals for cats, spools of sticky paper, used shoelaces, toy mice, what a lot of cat-worship goes on in this house, Gideon used to laugh, aiming his camera to immortalise the ritual. Me and my Rabbit, we don't want another brother or sister, she used to announce at times, and it seemed it was easy to go along with her, at least in the early years. It was only later that it began to bother her, towards the age of forty, and that's when the conversations began, in this very bed, or in more spacious beds on weekends in the north or the south, by the light of scented candles. Come on, let's have another baby, Gidi, this is the last opportunity, otherwise we'll regret it for the rest of our lives, but he stood by his refusal and she wasn't forceful enough; she let it go and tried again, lying in wait for propitious moments. He was an expert at the art of applying pressure to her sensitive points: Nitzan needs you, you have such a special bond, do you know how this will affect her when suddenly you're busy all the time with a baby? It isn't appropriate, Dina, believe me.

It isn't the same thing, she would protest, not the same thing at all, but again she retreated, we'll wait a few more months, it's not so terrible, these days women give birth at a much later age, she used to promise herself, and the months turned into years, and so long as she was talking and striving and waiting for agreement she was already a different woman, stronger than her, capable of bringing three children into the world, until around two years ago the doubts coalesced into an anxious certainty, and faced with this Gideon eased off a little, which had the unfortunate effect of showing her that in fact it had all been dependent on her from the start, and he had been responding to the needs of her body on the appointed days with a patronising smile, as if pandering to the whims of a charming and spoilt little girl, but the months passed and she wasn't pregnant, and when she started knocking on the doors of doctors' surgeries it was made clear to her it was too late, because this fruit of fertility, the mysterious and volatile fruit, menacing and miraculous, had rotted and withered away, earlier than expected, and what has been cannot be undone, and now as she's lying under the ceiling with its old damp stains, the cat licking himself beside her, the remains of her life are sketched out before her eyes, sharp and clear. A beggar for love and affection she is destined to be, picking up scraps of wood at street-corners, never again in her life will she see one great and vivid flame blaze up but only random twigs that will flicker and light up the darkness for a moment, and with this she'll have to be content, perhaps in this she will find a remedy, and she turns to stare at the sliding windows of the enclosed balcony, at the yellow sky reflected back to her. What would she not give now for a sign and symbol, a whisper to emerge from there and show her the way.

If only she could turn to a rabbi, a guru, some kind of necromancer, but she was always a sceptic, and a private omen is what she's looking for, revealed only to her, without intermediary, and she gets out of bed and sits down in front of the computer. No, she's not going to immerse herself now in the heart-warming stories of her new, anonymous friends, she'll never go in there again, she's not joining their fellowship, she's not as brave as they are, or perhaps not as desperate as they are. She has something to lose, and that's why she's returning to the doomed community in Spain, on the verge of destruction but not aware of it yet; Valencia, Cordoba, Toledo, Seville, the end was coming upon them, even though it wasn't the Jews themselves that Don Fernando and Donna Isabella wanted to uproot from Spanish soil so much as Judaism, it seems they didn't realise just how deeply ingrained in Jews Judaism is, to the very marrow of their bones, and so it may be said that not only did the expulsion edict fail to achieve its objective, a mass conversion of Jews, it also engendered the phenomenon of the secret Jews, much more subversive in the eyes of the establishment. She rereads these words from the preamble to her doctoral thesis, dealing with the roots of the strange phenomenon of Judaism without Jews, since that's what she's supposed to be concentrating on now, not motherhood without children, and aroused in her again is the perplexity that has accompanied her for years, how come you didn't assimilate in your masses? Were you not tempted to stay in your homes and your cities, rather than boarding unseaworthy ships and travelling to strange lands, endangering those dearest to you?

Is it possible to understand this choice in our generation? she asks, and turns her attention to the first chapter of the thesis, a chapter which she succeeded in finishing and even publishing some years ago, in an article dealing with the heinous blood-libel named after the holy child of La Guardia, of whose murder the Jews stood accused, although it turned out the entire story was pure fabrication – until the mobile on her desk starts vibrating, and she hears her brother's voice: hey, Dini, I'm at Mum's place, you'd better get over here, and again she's gripped by the terror of orphanhood, what's happened to Mum? And he says, nothing, she's fine, don't ask questions, just come.

I've just sat down to work on my thesis, she mumbles, but the briefcase is already in her hand, of course she'll come, for the first time in years his voice instils calm and confidence in her, little brother, her first baby. She loved him so much and he too was stolen from her, she wanted to clasp him to her heart, fasten him to her skin, but her mother snatched him away. Perhaps she was afraid her daughter would harm him, perhaps she just wanted him for herself, and not only she, it seemed the whole system united to keep them separated, and even he himself, her pretty baby, found it easy to abandon her, without a word of protest.

I'm coming, little brother, she says, excitement gripping her as she stands before the mirror, fringing her eyes with black and her lips with bright lipstick, make the most of your quiet life, she mumbles to the inert assortment of limbs curled up on the bed, maybe I won't be coming back, since it seems to her, her brother is waiting for her with news, and who knows, maybe there will be a rebirth of their old and yet immature family, which never ripened fully, perhaps there, between him and her mother, in the tiny apartment sweltering in the afternoon sun, she'll find her redemption.

And yet nothing could prepare her for the surprise that awaits her when Nitzan opens the door to her, wearing one of her grandmother's dressing gowns that reaches to her ankles, her hair untidy and on her face a rather solemn smile, as if it's a grown-up and responsible thing that she's doing, and already she's in her arms, clinging to her in that miraculous and incomparable fusing of limbs so familiar to both of them, the girl's head nestling in the dip of her shoulder and her lithe body held tightly. How complete is this integration of inward and outward curves, of the body and the spirit, how serene is the calm that envelops her, everything will be restored to its rightful place, she feels suddenly, restored peaceably, holding her breath for fear of defiling the sanctity of the moment, afraid to move so much as a fingertip lest their embrace be broken, lest she be deprived again of her daughter's love, which breathes life into her limbs. It seems to her that hour upon hour they've been standing there thus without moving, it seems the sun has already set and in a moment it will rise again, it seems years have gone by, retreating back into the hinterland of the past, pushing forward the secrets of the future, what was and what will be, life and death, old age and adulthood and infancy, all these things are virtually the same when measured against the absolute substance of their love, when measured against the beauty of the soul accustomed to drawing out from within itself such strong and concentrated emotion, and in the seconds and years of their tight embrace she realises no one can take this beauty from her, not even Nitzan herself, since the beating heart of her existence she feels inside her own body, and all the delight they have showered on each other since Nitzan was born to this very day, nothing has been taken away, nothing has disappeared into oblivion, and for this reason she will never be grieved again, knowing that without the cold and sterile burden of regret over both past and future, every future, it will be easier, and perhaps that is the purpose of this confession of love that her daughter is offering her, to dissolve the blocks of sorrow that have fastened to her limbs till they slide down her body like melted snow, and a sudden sense of celebration will flicker in her over the joy of her daughter's existence, even if she's far from her, as in fact it is her existence that confirms all the charms and wonders they have experienced together.

This was no fabrication but an aspiration substantiated in full, and this past no one will steal from her, and therefore she's suddenly calm, therefore she can now lay foundations, one by one, build the wall between what was and what will be, block the baleful intrusion of the predatory beasts that roam the inner deserts, between the twilights of time, diffusing danger and desolation. It seems to her this work is well within her capabilities, to mark out the boundaries brick after brick, and only then can she stand up and face up to the mysterious continent of her desires and analyse her actions, read the signs and the symbols. Thank you, my darling, she whispers, smoothing the soft mop of hair with her fingers, and Nitzan nestles against her, Mummy, she says, in her most melodious tone, I'm so glad you came, and she takes her hand and leads her with rhythmic steps, as if in some ancient ritual, to the hated room of her youth where her brother Avner sits in the armchair, his face very thin with hints of his former beauty still perceptible there, and in the bed, with eyes closed under wrinkled lids, her aged mother, on her lips a thin, satisfied smile.

It's great that you've come, Dini, her brother says, we've talked a lot about your plan, the three of us, and she's surprised, really? What have you said? And her brother says, we agree that you're very brave, and she's quick to protest, brave? I haven't done anything yet, it's still just a dream, and her brother says, even dreaming takes courage, and I know you well enough to be sure it will end in action, and I don't think there are many bigger and more beautiful things that can be done in this life, even if it leads to problems with those closest to you. And his eyes shift to Nitzan; he's never looked at her like this before, he's never looked at her at all, and Nitzan often used to complain that the only uncle she had wasn't a real uncle, he took no interest in her and wasn't kind to her, and Dina retaliated by treating his children the same way, but now his look is warm and encouraging, and her daughter responds to him at once. We talked about this a lot, Mummy, she says, I understand you better now, and if it's so important to you, you mustn't give it up, certainly not on my account, and Dina smiles at her, deeply touched, thank you, my darling, it's so nice what you're saying, and it means a lot to me, but I'm part of a family and I don't want to damage anyone's interests. I was hoping we'd all do this together.

That apparently isn't going to happen, her daughter says softly, the question is, is this a good enough reason to give up, I'll need time to get used to the idea, but I withdraw my opposition, perhaps this isn't enough but it's all I can say at the moment. If you really want to adopt a child don't give it up on my account, and Dina nods her head in bemusement, her glance lingering for some reason on the oval table covered with packets of medications. How bitterly she had wept in the shop, when she wanted to buy the table but her mother wasn't so keen, it seemed to her that with this object the room would turn into her room, the life would become her life. What have you done to my daughter, she asks her brother with a chuckle, and what are you doing here in the middle of the day? And he says, I'm living here now, I've left home.

He enjoys saying these words, although sometimes it seems to him he's lived here all his life, sleeping on the narrow single bed in the room overlooking the car park, his few clothes stowed in a rucksack at the foot of the bed.

I've left home, he reminds himself when he wakes in the night and listens to his mother's moans, the keening of a baby who refuses to be soothed by any means, bottle, hug or dummy. We are both mourning the passing of our lives, Mother, and it comes so naturally to him he finds it hard to understand why he never did this before. You spend a whole lifetime agonising, fearing, striving, regretting, promising, and in the end this happens in an offhand sort of way, without thought or intention, and this is natural and even small in scale, how small the deed is in the final analysis, and perhaps death itself is the same, shrinking upon its arrival after being feared throughout life.

I've left home, he reminds himself in the night, I took a few clothes and some books, the laptop and the mobile, I didn't even kiss the children in their sleep, went down the stairs as if I was just taking out the rubbish and I'd be back directly, got into the car and not for a moment did I think of her, of her astonishment and her anger, and I didn't calculate the resentment of the years passed and the dread of the years to come. No, all tabulations and computations have been left behind, in the grey zone of inactivity, while I have been at the heart of the action itself, trapped in it and energised by it, the little deed: one man goes in the night to his mother's house, to sleep in his youthful bed with its faded linen, to be again, to live again, before he dies.

I've left home, he reminds himself again, home, he's careful to say, and not Shlomit, because the abandonment of a woman may be interpreted as an act of betrayal, whereas leaving a home sounds like a sacrifice, giving up something precious for a worthy objective, but what is this home and was it really mine, was it precious to me, and he finds himself thinking more and more about the house, about its furniture and fittings and odd corners, the balcony overlooking the street, where he sometimes took a chair and sat in the sun, a book in his hand, but instead of reading he tended to watch the passers-by, trying to catch snippets of their conversations, jealous from the outset, wondering in his usual way, is it possible they're all happier than he is? And he thinks of the corner of the lounge and the old leather armchair facing the TV set, where he loved to stretch out and doze although it was usually occupied, and the cramped kitchen where he always felt he was in the way, even when he was cooking or washing up; he was responsible for the bigger items and she for the smaller – in fact he hardly ever felt comfortable in his home. On rare occasions he found himself alone there, and that wasn't particularly enjoyable either, but normally the house was the least secure of pastures where he was hunted relentlessly, caught and subjected to her implacable scrutiny, always a disappointment, always guilty. No, he didn't like being at home and that's why he feels no sorrow repeating the words, he even enjoys the sounds they make, the surprise they put on the faces of his audience – his mother, his sister, Anati, who has come back after a short honeymoon, a few of his friends – and in a triumphant tone he goes on proclaiming his achievement, I've left home, as if he's defeated an enemy in battle.

Big hero, he mocks himself at night, victor over a woman and two children, over a helpless old biddy, since the very idea of staying with his mother he's suddenly no longer afraid of, for so many years he has feared finding himself alone in her company, any excuse to avoid close contact with her, while now he almost enjoys living with her; most of the time her eyes are closed and she's in a state of quasi-sleep, laid on her back and not asking him for anything, her face has withered and her cheekbones protrude, giving her a new kind of dignity.

When he turns to her she shakes herself with an apologetic smile, I slept a while, I'm late, she mumbles, opening one eye with an effort as if winking at him and a moment later she's fast asleep again, and between sleep and wakefulness a few words emerge from her mouth: even if he could interpret them they would remain of dubious relevance.

Who do you love, Avni? she asks him from time to time, and he avoids the question, what does that mean? I love my children, and she ignores the answer and asks again, who do you love, it's impossible to live without love, and it's not only her questions he's evading, he's ducking some questions of his own: why did you leave home and on whose behalf, how is your life going to look, and your old age, how are you going to live alone and how will you cope with heartbreak, that's bound to happen, if it hasn't already; it seems to him he's holding his heart very carefully in both hands, like a cracked vessel that the slightest careless movement could shatter, so he has to avoid disturbance of any kind, proceeding ponderously, at a slow and hesitant pace, and for this reason he makes a point of not meeting Talia, although he passes by her alleyway from time to time when bringing the children back home, and he leans against the bamboo fence, trying to catch brief glimpses and slivers of conversation but not going inside, returning to his mother's house and going to bed early, or sitting alone in the bar in some local pub, revising his plans once more, what will he say to her and how will she respond? Will there be any link at all between what he has to say and her response, is there any way of inducing her to react differently, to accept him in other words, to love him in other words? There's no such way on the face of the earth, so it's best she doesn't even know he's left home, his wife and his children, he's done for her what the man she loved was incapable of doing, better she doesn't know; it would be clear to her then just how simple and straightforward was the deed, and her resentment would be redoubled and her grief magnified, knowing it wasn't done for her by the right man at the right time.

Perhaps all the same my love will succeed in arousing her love, he sometimes thinks, but at once he hastily erases the hope, since when did things like this happen in reality, what are you, an adolescent? Have you not yet learned the simple rule of the chain of unrequited loves, that every person falls for the one who doesn't want him? There are times when he does indeed conduct himself like an adolescent, much to his embarrassment, wild and impetuous in imagination; the charm of life beginning is roused in him and sparkles, all the things he never allowed himself to feel, the power of falling in love and its truth, its riddles and traumas, it seems all these things are redoubled within him since it's by himself that he experiences them, without her, since he's as lonely in his love as a bachelor at a wedding, lonely as a pregnancy without an embryo, and absence intensifies the sensation that no one can set boundaries before you. So she will go on with her transformation into a supernatural and superhuman being, a goddess of love who's come down to the earth and there she walks about barefoot and sad, a goddess of love who has only been elevated by virtue of her suffering. Now she's tormenting others, a goddess who needs to be pitied and guarded against, as she's more vulnerable than most mortals, and if she is injured then love is liable to leak from the hearts of human beings like water from a broken vessel, and how bitter and hollow they will be without it, bitter and hollow like the woman he has left, whose face is contorted with hatred and who seems to loathe even her children.

Was her devotion to the children really meant to prove to him her superiority over him? His departure signalled the end of the competition and apparently as a result of this she lost interest in them, he sees this in their clothes, in their faces, their movements, their diet, and his heart goes out to them and is aroused to make up the deficit. Where shall we go today? he asks Yotam, who's waiting for him at the garden gate, climbing on the fence like a little monkey, fancy an ice cream? Pizza? The zoo? And the little one responds enthusiastically, usually choosing the last option on the list, but he hears his distress at the end of the joyful whoop. In vain he will stuff him with sweet and sickly distractions, he'll be content with the modest local playground, just so long as afterwards they go up to the house together, to the reassurance of routine, and he knows there's only one way he can appease them, only if the break-up that he's forced on them through no fault of theirs will ultimately give them a better father; it's up to him and he owes it to them, however hard it proves to be, less so with the cheerful younger one, resembling the baby he himself once was, more so with Tomer and his perpetual scowl.

He must work hard to forge a way through to him, to exploit this time of opportunity, when Shlomit loosens her grip, seeing that in this land it's very short and circumscribed, the time fathers spend with their sons, and when he's finding it hard to sleep at night, his thoughts skip from his mother, who whimpers like a baby, to the mother of his children and the one who will now never have children and he finds himself thinking more and more about his country. It seems his sense of belonging to her has strengthened since he uprooted himself from his home, he clings to her and wonders about her and her destiny with growing trepidation, sometimes with malicious pleasure when he reflects on the ways she has so sorely disappointed him, and then he counts her mistakes and her blunders, and sometimes it's her sufferings that are revealed to him, choking him with grief, she's as close to him as his mother and his sister, and like them she is complex, and like them she is flawed, and like them she is precious to him in her distress, and he bemoans her fate as if it's already been decided, so many years the state has existed, and before growing up she has grown old, and before ripening she has decayed, and he contemplates her death as he would contemplate the death of human beings, the anticipated death of his mother. How will this happen in the final analysis, which is the organ that will decide the outcome of the battle, what calamity will scourge the state that hasn't done enough to endear herself to her citizens, the state that will yet force her citizens to betray her and abandon her, exactly like Shlomit; it seems to him he's gone out of his mind when he conducts nightly conversations with his country, reproving her and delivering moral homilies, his heart beating fiercely when he thinks of her intolerable demands, a country dependent on so many of the dead, trusting them to continue holding her up with raised and enfeebled arms. Tens of thousands of the young dead, children almost, lifting their arms while she lies with spread-eagled limbs, unbearably heavy, lazy, foolish, greedy and sacrilegious.

Wear sackcloth and ashes and fast, he berates her, perhaps you will yet succeed in saving yourself, if not for the sake of the living at least for the sake of the dead, but she laughs in his face, a resounding laugh, who are you to preach at me? You who weakened me and betrayed me, because of people like you I fell sick, and now I am sick, sick, she shrieks in his ears, and her tirade blends into his mother's moans, the weeping of the baby from the apartment next door. Don't cry, Yotam, he mumbles, it's just a bad dream, Daddy's here with you, Daddy's looking after you, but of course he isn't with him and if he calls he won't hear, and what's left of being a father if he doesn't hear his son crying in the night? He must find an apartment, and soon, and fix up a room there for the children, but in the morning, as he grinds through the traffic-jams between his mother's suburb and his office in the centre of the city, he relaxes the pressure on himself, it's too soon to get established, it's all happened so abruptly, without thought and without planning. It's necessary to think, this being the case, after the event, to plan for the future that will follow the event, which he will not necessarily regret. The possibility of returning home he finds nauseating, but it's another home he's thinking about day and night, a little apartment in the middle of the alley, with a fragile fence separating it from the passers-by, who would never imagine that so close to them, in the heart of the tumult of life, the world to come is quietly residing.

He peers between the yellow and interlacing branches, is there a light in the lobby, can he hear voices emerging from the interior, is that a fleeting movement he sees at the window? How flimsy is the fence, and yet so impervious, just like her; at times he feels a sudden surge of hatred for her – how can she be so indifferent to his absence? It's been a long time now, more than a month, and nothing is omitted from her regular routine with which he's so familiar: in the evening she'll park her car close to the alleyway, go down the main street to buy some groceries, she'll cook herself a light supper, vegetables, cheese, bread, glass of wine, put a CD in her sophisticated sound-system, opera again; for someone who doesn't like words, she's strangely addicted to opera, and then perhaps she'll stretch out on the sofa with a book in her hands, or sit down in front of the computer and correspond with colleagues abroad, and it seems nothing will grieve her any more or gladden her either, nothing will shock or shake her. Just a sterile old woman, he thinks irritably, women like that used to be called aunts, this is Auntie Talia, he'll tell his children if he ever takes them to her house, and at once he's appalled by the intensity of his hatred. What does he expect of her, what does she owe him, he was the one who suddenly latched on to her while she was in mourning for her life, burdening her with unrealistic expectations and having the nerve to be angry when they're not fulfilled, and he drags her feet away from there. At the end of the alley he notices the gold car that wasn't parked there before, and at the sight he feels suddenly weak and his knees buckle: she's here and she can save him, she's here and she'll never save him, and he leans helplessly against the car, its engine still warm, pressing his cheek against the roof, and the body of the car responds to him as he strokes the smooth paintwork with his fingers, how long had he been hunting for her, criss-crossing the streets of the city as the summer was just beginning; now it's coming to an end and still he's as far from her as ever.

A sudden tremor shakes him, bringing with it a choking sensation, what's happening to him, are his eyes closed or has it suddenly gone dark, can it be sunstroke, the sun must be setting by now, suddenly he can't see, can't see anything at all, but he can hear, and he hears a pleasant voice asking if he needs help, and he hesitates before answering; he certainly needs help but what exactly, and from whom, help is a complicated business. Would you like some water perhaps? the voice goes on to ask, and a bottle is pressed to his lips and he takes it gratefully, he hadn't realised how thirsty he was, his eyes are thirsty too and he splashes water on his face until his vision clears and he sees a tall woman standing there, her body bony and her face sharp, her hair long and damp. There's a virus going round, she says, fever and convulsions, I only just got over it myself, I know exactly how you're feeling, and he replies with a groan, really? How long does it last? And she says, not long, a day or two. Do you need help getting home?

And he answers, no, it's all right, I live here, and he points to the bamboo fence.

Come on then, I'll give you a hand, she offers, taking his arm and letting him lean on her, a pleasant autumnal smell wafting from her hair, and he tries to extricate himself, thanks, there's no need, I'm OK now, thanks a lot – how complicated things get when you start telling lies. How can he explain to her why he's standing outside his own house without a key, about to ring the bell hesitantly like an uninvited guest? Are you sure? she asks and he hastily says, yes, I'm sure, and when she continues on her way he calls after her, thanks, you rescued me. From behind she looks like a young girl, in tight jeans and a long white blouse, and suddenly he wants her to come back, and he waves to her with the bottle in his hand, although it's empty, although she isn't looking. Hey, your bottle, he shouts, as if she's entrusted him with something valuable, but she's too far away and he puts it to his mouth and tries to draw the last drops from it, as a savage thirst attacks him again, and he imagines himself crouching down and lapping up water like a dog, drinking from puddles and gutters, his tongue growing longer and longer until his mouth can no longer contain it, grabbing every drop of moisture that comes its way. His tongue is so heavy it's weighing him down, as long as a tail and wagging incessantly, and any moment now it will lay him out flat almost on her threshold, and in a panic he gropes for the bell, so he'll have time to sound a sign of life before he collapses on the asphalt, giving her one last opportunity to take him into her house and into her bed, secretly wipe away a tear with the edge of her blouse and promise him all will be well, he'll be feeling better soon.

Her touch stings him when she lays a hand on his forehead, you're running a temperature, she says, you should go home. Is it because she hasn't seen him in so many weeks that her hands are so cold, has she been waiting for him all this time? Reluctantly, she opens the gate to him, wearing a faded red dress and hair gathered up in a bun, her hands brown with mud and a hose pipe wrapped round her body; apparently she's been watering her little garden, apparently she saw him leaning on the fence and was in no hurry to open up, perhaps she heard him telling that woman this was his house. The smell of wet earth arouses a vague longing in him, when he says, I've missed you, Talia, I don't feel well.

Come inside, I'll make you some tea with lemon, she says, filling the kettle with water as he stretches out on the sofa, exhausted. I can't go home, he growls, I've left home, flinging at her words heated in the acrid vapour of his mouth, not as he had planned it, casually and offhandedly, and she retreats a few paces, driven back by the impact of his new dream in collision with her old dream; how she had longed to hear these words but not from his mouth. Really? she asks, why? He's never spoken to her about his wife, confining himself to uneasy sidelong hints, and now, clumsily, he's going to offer her his special present, and he repeats her question, why? What a strange question, he rebukes her with sudden anger, it can't be answered anyway. There are many reasons and there's no reason, and she says, you're right, I meant to say I'm sorry to hear that, and again he's angry, why is she sorry, as if he's shared his misfortunes with her, there's a prospect here too, and hope, for too long he's waited, too much preparation, and now their conversation isn't going well, he should have come here the night of Anati's wedding, when the course of action was burning between his fingers, come to her vibrant and passionate, overwhelming her with the power of the moment, and not like this, sick and weak, rotten with flawed thinking. How severe her expression is, it seems she's repelled by what he's done; after the death of Rafael Allon, who never quite managed to leave his home, did she think no man on earth would dare do this, let alone before her very eyes?

She's washing her hands now in the kitchen sink, wiping the touch of his skin from her fingers, and when his glance wanders over the bookshelves he notices the two photographs, the pivotal points of her story, aren't there any more, is she too expecting to start again? And once more he feels a sudden surge of pique as if he's the one she's shutting out; after all it was only the dead man who forged the precarious link between them, with his thin and morbidly yellow fingers he gripped their arms, held them together. Where are the pictures? he asks, and she replies, Elisheva was here yesterday, I took them down not wanting to hurt her and I forgot to put them back, and he's amazed, Elisheva was here? What did she want? Once again he's swept almost with alacrity into her familiar story, our story almost, he thinks, we're not getting another one.

To talk, she says, leaning on the marble and facing him, to listen, to fill in the picture, and he asks, how was it? And she sighs, it was sad, what would you expect of a meeting between widows, and he's taken aback by the pride he hears in her voice, is she now recognised as a widow by the official widow, what an awesome achievement, and he wants to shake her, life is running away, Talia, as agile as a rabbit, cunning as a fox, isn't it enough that you've given up the first half of your life for this man, are you going to sacrifice what remains of your life too, like those Indian widows who throw themselves on the funeral pyre, and you're not even a widow.

Your tea's going cold, she says, drink it, I put in a slice of lemon from the garden, and he says, your life is going cold, and she turns to him with a suspicious look, sitting in the armchair facing him, very erect, and he imagines her body, solid and impervious as the body of a doll, tiny breasts without nipples, genitals without aperture, what are you trying to say? And he avoids her glance, how will he offer himself to her? Don't be offended, Talia, obviously it's none of my business but I care about you and I was glad to see you coming back to life.

You're making too many flawed assumptions, she says, I've nowhere to come back to because I've never been a part of this life that you're talking about, and I never wanted to be a part of it, I didn't want a family, I wanted Rafael, that was all, she continues in a monotonous voice and she remembers how she stood alone on the stage, dominated by his smiling portrait, people confuse love with family, children with lust, and that has never suited me, not when I was young and definitely not now. Her mobile, on the table between them, emits a brief squawk and she reads the incoming text avidly, I hate what's happening to women here, this enforced servitude that they accept so willingly, she says, her eyes still fixed on the screen and for a moment it seems to him she's quoting from it, apparently they're liberated from their husbands but they're still in thrall to their children, they stop being women and turn into mothers, I didn't want that. Only yesterday I realised how much I had gained from him not leaving home, I got the best of him, we had a sacred kind of love, not a secular one.

But do you really not regret not having children? he asks, for some reason protesting on behalf of his own children, as suddenly he misses them and wishes they were here beside him now, and she replies, I always knew I'd have no children, I don't like mixing things. What does that mean, mixing things? he asks and she explains, when I was a little girl I loved painting but I hated mixing colours, I loved the beauty of the primary colours, most kids mix them all together and end up with incoherent splodges of paint, and he listens to her and remembers his sister. You know, my sister, he starts and at once breaks off, he really doesn't want to bring up the saga of his sister, deciding suddenly that without a new child her life is no life, he looks at her and wonders about them, about women, putting her on one side and his sister on the other and his wife in between them. It seems to him nothing links them other than their reservations towards him, deep and fundamental reservations, with various and even contradictory motivations, is this what unites the whole of womankind on this earth? Even his intern has recently launched a campaign of crude hostility towards him, but who knows, maybe it's all about an aversion that radiates from him, as it seems to be expanding to the point where he can't look at her, and he turns his attention to the meshed window with its view of the inner side of the fence, shadows quivering between the interlaced branches. Is it because she doesn't need him that he's suddenly recoiling from her?

A big yawn crumples her face and she apologises, I didn't get any sleep last night, Elisheva stayed until the morning, I'm so tired, and he says hurriedly, I'm going, Talia, don't worry, I don't want to put pressure on you, believe me, from the first moment I saw you I wanted to help you, and now that seems unnecessary, in fact I'm more in need of help than you are, can you imagine it, just now a woman in the street, a stranger, was helping me to walk, and she smiles at him with sealed lips; only the delicate twitch in the skin of her cheek tells him she's smiling. How fragile is this skin, he thinks, when she grows old it will crack rather than wrinkle.

I'm grateful to you, she says seriously, help is a complicated business, you must see that in your line of work, I wish you could help me, I wish I could help you, and she bends over her foot and peels a thin layer of mud from her ankle, as if unwrapping a bar of chocolate, but perhaps after all I can help you with some advice, she hesitates, you must go home, and he listens to her with pain, the void of his body already foretelling emptiness, how do you know? You have no idea what my life is like with my wife, and she says quietly, true, but if it's carried on until now it can't have been that terrible.

What has it really been like up to now, he wonders, it seems to him he's done nothing in his life, never married a wife or brought children into the world, knocking again and again on a locked door, his gift not accepted, again and again and at the same time never, never has he allowed himself to become so committed, his skin scratched by the thorns of missed opportunity, the void of his body already feeling the emptiness that will dominate him when he's forced to uproot her from his life, and he stares at her, her hands absently massaging her ankle, the black varnish has gone from the toenails and they are pale, almost invisible.

What do you want, Talia? What's to become of you? he asks, and she says quietly, I've planted cyclamens in the garden, holding out her hands by way of proof although the mud has just been washed from them, and I'm waiting to see them flower in the winter, I love cyclamens, I love my work, I've just received a grant for new research, my parents lived small lives here and now it's my turn, and he thinks about his family, with us it was always big stuff but only in the imagination, that's the most fatal combination, big dreams and meagre achievements. In our family we create myths, he wants to tell her: his mother's dying lake, the consummate kibbutz society of her parents, his father's lost Europe, he himself is the champion of the downtrodden, and now his sister has devised an ambitious and desperate myth of her own, reckons she can save a child and thereby save herself, what do we know about growing cyclamens? What do we know about small lives? But he so much wants to be there with her in the winter, when the cyclamens will bloom in their soft pink colours, to sit with her in the garden while his sons play with a ball on the burgeoning lawn, and when the cold sets in they'll go inside and he'll make the hot chocolate, and this will be simple and glorious, an event so tiny in the annals of humanity, but sensational for him because it will happen before her eyes. Before her eyes he will embrace his children, before her eyes they will pass their tongues over their chocolate-sweetened lips, and perhaps this thing is so sensational precisely because it won't happen, it will never come about, he knows and she knows, even the children dozing on their beds know, and his wife who burns with anger like an eternal flame and has no consolation, and therefore he must uproot himself from this doll's house in which even the most modest of dreams aren't going to materialise, but before doing this he needs to touch her. This isn't lust but a deep and ancient yearning which stretches from the soles of his feet to the top of his head, a yearning born before him that will outlive him, like the yearning of the universe for that primeval radiation which in the beginning accompanied its creation.

Now she stands up and walks to the bedroom, and he watches her movements tensely, will she signal to him to follow her? She returns with an armful of white bedlinen and a pillow, you can sleep here tonight, she says quietly, you can't go walking the streets in that state, and he stands up heavily and watches her smoothing out the sheet like a chambermaid, plumping the pillow, and all of this for him, and yet she won't be sorry if he says to her now, thanks all the same, Talia, I'll sleep at home, that is what he's supposed to say, that is what he's supposed to do, and yet the words emerging from his mouth are quite different. Thanks, he says, I don't feel up to driving, I'm staying at my mother's place in the suburbs, he adds unnecessarily, while taking off his shoes and putting them on again immediately, worried about the sweaty smell, but she doesn't seem to notice, handing him a pair of blue pyjamas, decorated with yellow stars. When you look at the sky you always see what used to be there, the stars of the past, light-years separate us.

Rafael liked pyjamas, she smiles, he said with pyjamas he could sleep much better, like a little boy, and Avner grins, really? Did he have a teddy-bear too? and he holds on with interest to the fabric which smells of soap, as if recently laundered. I wear these sometimes in my sleep, she admits, I wake up with them in the morning and don't remember putting them on at all, and for some reason he lets go of the attractive garments, maybe he wants you to wear these, he suggests, no thanks, I'll manage without them, I always sleep naked, he adds, wondering about the dry intimacy that's unfolding here, could we have been lovers twenty years ago, twenty years in the future, since now the time isn't right, the night isn't right.

Good night, she says, from close up her face looks thin and tired, the shadows under her eyes doubling their size and he whispers, good night, Talia, acute misery pricking his flesh at the thought of not seeing her again, he knows this for a fact when the bedroom door closes behind her; he will see her just once more, when the little reading lamp beside her bed is turned off and the footsteps in the alley fade away, and the rustling of insects in the garden grows louder, and the soughing of the lawn as it tightens its grip on the ground, and the whisper of the cyclamens budding between the onion beds, and he'll stretch out on the sofa fully clothed, his body aching and his loins aching, he'll put the pyjama top over his face and sigh heavily. Hot words split like chestnuts in the incandescent void of his mouth, his desire mounting and no outlet for it, how deceptive is her proximity, a few paces separate them tonight and it seems there's no woman in the world as far away from him as she is, even the woman who gave him the drink of water and disappeared is closer to him than she is, and he puts a hand to his loins and straightens up, he has to go, he has to escape from here, but before this he must take his leave of her in his own way, how can you be separated from something you never had?

By the light of the full moon that shines on him through the windows her face is dark, ageing, and for a moment he sees her at his mother's age, with slender wrinkles pointing to those that will deepen still further, when he won't be there, when no one will be at her side. An expression of concentration on her face, as if a bitter thought has been oppressing her and she's been turning it over and over until she fell asleep, and with a shaking hand he pulls down the neckline of the white nightdress. Rest, beautiful bride, he remembers the inscription on the tombstone in the place where he used to stand and wait for her, rest easy on your bed, he mumbles, staring breathlessly at the pale nipples, the flat, decisive stomach. She's barely stirring in her sleep, raising a leg slightly and exposing a boyish thigh, you too will not be exploited, he whispers to the thigh, but for the moment it's tempting and forbidden, and he takes a deep breath, it seems to him that steam vapours are erupting from his throat, any moment now the whole room will go up in flames, ignited by the heat of his breath. Trembling and sweaty and calm nevertheless, like someone in whose heart the decision has been taken to take his life in his hands, he bends down and presses his lips to the milky skin of the thigh, he know she won't wake up, he knows even if she does wake up she'll pretend to be asleep, she'll let him complete the ritual of valediction, this is a ceremony after all, the sacrilegious version, idolatry included. On her ankle a stain of crusted mud remains and he gathers it with his tongue, tasting the taste of death, these clods of earth are waiting for him and for her, for his mother and his sister, his wife and his children, a deep and strange taste but familiar enough to him, as if everything he ever put in his mouth had been seasoned with this taste, and he goes down on his knees at the foot of the bed, linking his hands together. Give me life, he mumbles, not with you but without you, give me another chance before I'm buried in the dust, you're a woman who never gave life to anyone, give me back my life, give me an answer, and this entreaty he brands on her skin with white-hot words, on the skin of the ankle, the inner thigh, her pubic hair and belly and nipples, on her neck and her shoulders and her arms, all her parts arouse him in equal measure, those concealed and those revealed, and he inscribes his plea on them, give me life as if I were a bulb of cyclamen, give me what was stolen from you, swaying on his knees in prayer this way and that, his lips moving and his voice unheard. Down his body a cascade is tumbling, springing from the top of his head, shaking his chest and turning his stomach over, rattling his loins and springing out into the world bitter and painful as the blood-letting of the importunate soul, and he groans at her feet, see, her lips are parted in a wayward smile and her hand stretched out to his face as if his gift has been accepted, and he straightens up slowly and with cautious movements, like a father holding his newborn son for the first time, he dresses her in the pyjamas, lifting her body and pulling her arms and swathing her in yellow stars, her body lost in the voluminous folds of fabric and her face pale against its dark ground.

The breeze of a first autumn night filters through the open window, cooling his limbs, and he looks up at the full moon, transmitting to him an intimidating and familiar smile of leave-taking, exposing long teeth. Is this not the smile of the dead Rafael Allon, and he rises from his place hurriedly, his knees painful after the prolonged kneeling, clutching at the wall and shaking convulsively, and before he has time to regret it and fling himself down on the sofa with its sheets and pillow, he goes out and closes the door, which locks itself behind him with a newly installed mortice, and then the gate which closes with a brassy metallic click, and again he finds himself in the alley leading to the main street, leading in turn to his house, where his wife and sons are sleeping, and he strolls towards them like a dreamer, something that hasn't been logically computed he wants to say to them, to share with them the revelation revealed to him this night concerning what remains of his love.

Chapter Eleven

Forget your dream, it isn't going to happen, only when you come to terms with that can you decide if adoption is right for you. Forget the dream of a sweet baby snuggling in your lap, forget what you experienced with your own daughter. You want warmth and softness, you're missing the sweetness of the early years, but the odds are stacked against all of that. You're not going to get a baby but a damaged kid who's already been through a lot, who's liable to reject any kind of warmth, liable to bite and kick you rather than hug you. I'm not saying this to frighten you but to prepare you. I wasn't sufficiently prepared and I had a terribly hard time.

Really, what happened? Dina asks in a weak voice. She was expecting encouragement, not scare stories, she's heard plenty of those, from all sides, but this woman sitting facing her in the café in the city centre has practical experience of it and that's why she needs to listen to her. In the blogs she calls herself Thumbelina, but to Dina's surprise she's met by a tall and heavily built woman, with a blunt and candid style of speech, flaxen hair and a somewhat florid complexion. I'd had ten years of fertility treatment, she says, my son was twelve years old and I so much wanted another child, I couldn't accept the idea that it was over, I'd never again have a baby of my own. Ten years of treatment before I threw in the towel. My husband wanted another child too, but not by adoption, too much of a shot in the dark. What battles I had with him, it took me a long time to persuade him to adopt. The whole process was horrendously long, until they finally offered us the little girl, and then were the journeys, the tests, the legal technicalities, you need such strong nerves for all of this, but the hardest part begins the moment you're done with the bureaucracy, when all the external elements move out of your life and you're left alone with the girl; overnight, by the decision of some foreign court, you've become her mother.

And what happened then? Dina asks, again this pain between her ribs, making it hard for her to concentrate on the details of the answer. I got a two-year-old girl, underweight, bald, pale, and frightened, in the children's home she'd been treated like some kind of doll, or a pet, and I was worried, I reckoned she was too apathetic, but the moment we took her out of there she changed completely. She became hyperactive, running around and creating havoc all the time, when I tried to cuddle her she ran away. My husband, who had reservations about it from the start, never got tired of saying I told you so, and something about her just wasn't right. In the night she used to wake up with nightmares and it was impossible to calm her down, whenever I came near her she would scream and kick. I felt I was part of her nightmare and our lives were turning into a nightmare too, and the worst thing about it was, there were no gradations. Not like a child born to you that you bond with at a leisurely pace, and all difficulties arise against a backdrop of familiarity and love. What you have here is total alienation, and with the best will in the world, the girl is a stranger and there isn't yet enough trust and confidence to cope with this sensibly, and of course this is entirely mutual, she has no trust and confidence in us. You need masses of patience, these kids are like prisoners released from captivity, and you shouldn't overburden them with love. Love can be oppressive too, and you shouldn't overburden them with expectations either. They need to be treated with delicacy and restraint, and given time to adjust.

How long did it take? Thumbelina repeats the question previously asked, covering her arms with a broad woollen shawl, it's turning cold suddenly, she says, the winter is early this year. How long? It hasn't really finished yet, you know, this is a confrontation with no end to it. But the first year was the hardest. It's a tough age anyway, and she was inquisitive, everything was new to her. She ran around the house and pressed every button she could lay her hands on, the computer, the television, radio and dishwasher. She threw food on the floor, slammed doors, and all the time I was having to tell her to stop. She was testing the boundaries from the moment she woke up. It was so different from what I imagined it would be. Instead of kissing and hugging and reading stories and building things with toy bricks, I was having to chase her round the house telling her not to do things, not that she really heard my voice anyway. Suddenly you understand these concepts, testing boundaries, emotional blockage. You'll find that a child with blocked emotions isn't the child who's going to respond positively to the love you have for him, on the contrary, he isn't used to love, it threatens him. It took months before our little girl settled down, before she even consented to sit on my lap and listen to a story, and these are just the little problems. From the start I was sure something about her wasn't right, the genetic mystery was driving me crazy. She used to beat her head against the frame of the bed, harm herself and damage her toys, she bit us all the time. My son used to say, I'd rather have a dog, why didn't you get a dog instead? He really wanted a little sister, but not one like this. And all the time the conflict with my husband, who couldn't resign himself to having no more children of his own. After a year he moved out. These days he's very attached to the girl, but in the meantime he's married again and so he has new children too. Where does your husband stand in all of this?

My husband isn't really on board yet, Dina admits bitterly, but I hope I'll be able to persuade him in the end, and she says, yes, it's harder for men than it is for us. It damages their ego, it's the obsolescence of their personal seed, and with them bonding is usually slower too. They'll compete with a child, and take offence because they're not enough for us, but don't kid yourself, this isn't the biggest problem. It's reasonable to expect him to agree in the end, somehow, the question is, how are you going to cope with this assignment, seeing that the responsibility will be yours, and all the hard work will be on your shoulders, and Dina nods dejectedly, looking out at the street, crammed with bulldozers and workmen. What a shame it is, they're tarting up the centre of the city, she really liked the old shabbiness. Even when the terrorist attacks were at their height, she dared to wander round here now and again, peering into the second-hand bookshops, in search of reality, memories, here she used to sit with Orly, drinking frothy coffee and marking exam papers. One day Emmanuel came by, apparently by accident, and she immediately got up and left them to it. The siren of an ambulance alarms her for a moment, but there's only one, thank God; one is a personal disaster, more than one is a national disaster, meaning it could be hers too. There is so much negotiation to be done with disaster: if you take Nitzan I'll take my own life, that's the advantage of an only child, just don't take me from her as long as she needs me. Now she needs me less, and so the fear has diminished too, and perhaps it's better like this, but if I wasn't prospecting for more of this bonding, at almost any price, I wouldn't be here now.

And how is she now? How old is she? she asks, she's feeling the cold too but she forgot to bring a sweater, and anyway no garment will ward off the cold wind that's blowing inside her, and Thumbelina replies, she's already eight, a charming girl but still not easy to get on with. Proudly she holds out her mobile, decorated with the picture of a fair-haired girl wearing thick glasses, only yesterday when I told her to go to bed she yelled at me and said her real mother was better than me and she'd let her do anything.

Really? Dina asks, disappointed, and how do you respond to that? And she says, I try not to be hurt, although that isn't easy, I explain to her that it's natural for her to feel this way, but I'm the one who's raising her and she has to do as I say. Lately she's been obsessed with her biological mother, asking a lot of questions, how could she leave her this way, desertion is a deep wound, a wound that lasts for life.

But she loves you? Dina persists, a little abashed at exposing the shady motivation, the demeaning need for love, and the woman facing her smiles broadly, of course she loves me, and we have wonderful times together and I love her dearly, but it's important to me that you understand it's not like having an ordinary child, it's much harder and more complicated. You have a daughter of your own, just don't expect an adopted child to be the same, I don't want to scare you, just warn you.

Thanks, Dina mumbles, wondering what she will do with all this information, feeling as if her guts are being skewered, and she sips the coffee that's rapidly going cold. At a table nearby a young couple is sitting down with a baby, immediately taken from his pram and dandled in the arms of his beaming mother, how young they are, barely more than children themselves. Well, this isn't coming back, not this age and not the gentle, decisive fusion, and she needs clarity to determine whether she has the strength to face all these difficulties, and how will she know? How will she know if this is the right reply to her aspirations? It's obvious that bringing up a child is fraught with problems, obviously it's wrong to set conditions, but she yearns for that wondrous combination, that whole and empowering love. It isn't coming back, and it will be different, if it happens at all. Persuading Gideon is expected to be the easy part of the assignment, and that too is liable to fail. For weeks they haven't spoken about this, and he probably assumes she's dropped it, and he's making an effort to approach her with sensitivity, as if she were a post-operative patient with stitching still fresh, coming home earlier, occasionally sharing his professional issues with her. Years ago they used to bow their heads over the developing trays, waiting to see his photographs emerge, and now they sit together in front of the computer in the evening, but the supposed similarity is uncomfortable for her, proving to her how much has been lost, and maybe it was never really there, but in the past she had been armed with hope, with a future, with a young daughter, whereas now what's left between them is so paltry.

Most of the time he's wrapped up in himself, and she has neither the power nor the inclination to ignite a flame in him, he is the way he is and he's not going to change, she's the one who needs clarification, not he, and she peers at him, reading in the fading light; novels he has no time for and only philosophical and scientific works interest him, like this book by a scientist who died recently, someone called Rafael Allon, until the book falls over his face and he dozes. Nitzan used to clamber all over him and wake him up with tickles and little kisses, and that's something else that isn't coming back, how can she force on him a damaged, aggressive child, and she gazes at the book covering his face, and from the back cover the portrait of a handsome man looks at her, a sensitive smile on his face, and she smiles back at him and thinks of other men she has known, full of *joie de vivre*, the kind of men who would have backed her enterprise enthusiastically, seeing it as a meritorious act, and most of all she thinks about her Eytan; looking back at him today she can appreciate his qualities, and while still surveying Gideon's recumbent form in the armchair she sinks into a fantasy about the death of Eytan's American wife. After all, people of their age are leaving the world, regrettably, like that scientist for example, and she who abandoned him twenty years ago will come to him for the seven days of mourning, and will stay there, devotedly nurturing his four children, compensating him for his old sorrow and comforting him for his new one, and Nitzan will join her, she has a kind heart and her compassion will be kindled for the poor orphans, while Gideon will barely notice her absence, she explains with a twinge of conscience to the face smiling at her over his face, and his routine won't be affected at all. After all his needs are modest, and who can say he won't find himself, in that typically offhand style of his, consorting with a new woman and subsequently acquiring a new child too. This part of the fantasy appeals to her less, and she feels a surge of anger at him and jealousy aimed at that woman, but what's enviable about her; after all she too will be forced to accustom herself to the chilly blast blowing from him, and yet in spite of all this there's something still left in the man that she isn't ready to jettison just yet, even though she has difficulty explaining why; the moment his eyes turn to her and his face softens, her joy is so overwhelming that she can't remember what it was that upset her before. It's moments like these that she's waiting for, and she won't give them up easily, even if they are becoming increasingly rare, she'll be describing a disagreement with one of her colleagues, or trying out an idea for an article, and it seems to her he isn't even listening, and suddenly he's on the case, resolving some contradiction at lightning speed, surprising her with a kind of natural, effortless empathy, and maybe this isn't much, it definitely isn't much, but these things are close to her heart, and now she wonders if she can give them up, and if she can be content with them, and it seems one option is impossible and so is the other, there is no middle way, and meanwhile no one's mentioning the abandoned child who's waiting for her somewhere far away, until it seems he's been deserted again, again his hopes are fading.

Nitzan peers at her now and then, admittedly, but doesn't ask any questions, and she's just glad she seems more relaxed, more inclined to share her daily concerns with her, help me get ready for the test, she sometimes asks, handing her a book or a printout, or showing her what she's written, and Dina is flushed with pride, how clever the girl is, how beautifully she expresses herself, and at once a backwash of regret will accompany the pride, what a mistake it was, what a waste, not bringing another child into the world. She still keeps some distance from her, not conducting long and intense conversations with her, sometimes emerging from her room with moist eyes, but Dina, her stomach constricted by the prolonged fast, has learned to be content with modest portions, she observes her behaviour tensely and tries to keep calm. There's no need to worry; the girl's eating normally, sleeping well, keeping up with her studies, meeting her friends, not drinking and not smoking, and overall she seems to be getting through this age unscathed – more than could be said for her, she who spent her adolescent years crouched over the toilet bowl forcing herself to throw up, the bitter reek of puke accompanying her wherever she went – and it seems to her the pair of them, her husband and her daughter, are appealing to her in their restrained manner, be content, be content with us despite our shortcomings, be content with yourself despite your shortcomings, no one is complete, no one will ever be fully satisfied, and she makes an effort to remember, what did she say to her then, in that miraculous conversation in her mother's house, did she say don't give up, or did she say don't give up on my account, was this just her way of evading responsibility?

Long hours she sits in her watchtower this premature winter, while a small electric stove thaws the air in the little room with its glass walls, serving only to reinforce its reality: sweltering in summer and cold in winter. A slow and incessant movement is discernible to her, the quivering treetops, clouds floating in the sky like dead fish, birds on bustling wings, and the view is reflected in the glass door opening to the bedroom, until it seems to her she's surrounded on every side by spasms of life, and apparently they're all addressing to her the silent plea, stop, compromise, give up. Even the cat, springing into her arms, is purring rhythmically, give up, compromise, stop, you're not going to get what you're after, your life from now on will be a patchwork of resignations and compromises, big disasters and small delights, that's the way of the world and who are you to turn it on its head?

Perhaps she really should be looking for partial solutions, she thinks, plucking up her courage and contacting a refuge for children in danger, offering her services as a volunteer, but to her disappointment she's greeted with suspicion and asked what skills she has. No, I'm not good at creative projects, she's forced to admit, and I've no experience of music therapy either, or P.T. What can I do with children? Read them stories, she mumbles, play simple games, give them love. At the other end of the line they say they're recording her details but they don't get back to her, and she's embarrassed by the exposure of her delusional and desperate efforts to belong, looking for love and offering love, perhaps it is a man she needs after all and not a child, but for years she hasn't encountered a man who aroused her interest. The only one she thinks of, now and then, is Eytan, who loved her so much, and one day when her lecture has been cancelled again she travels to his settlement, feeling some excitement as she drives up the winding roads of the Jerusalem hills, how green are the hills after the first rain, even the cyclamens are showing their pink buds among the rocks.

At the entrance to the settlement she asks for the Harpaz family and receives a civil answer, and so there she is, looking from a distance at the massive house. He married a rich American, they told her, but they didn't tell her how beautiful she was; within minutes of her arrival a sophisticated-looking jeep pulls up outside the house, and a small and light-footed woman, her golden curls piled up casually, emerges from it, picks up a baby and goes inside, a fair-haired toddler of around three years old bounding at her heels, and Dina watches them with an ache in her heart; she looks perfectly healthy, much healthier than her and younger too, in a hurry and happy, she has no time to stare at the houses of others, to observe lives not lived. There isn't much that's wrong with the way she's living, in her spacious house thronged with children, with a devoted and warm-hearted husband, and yet you didn't want him, she reminds herself, his aspirations bored you, even then he was already talking about a house in a settlement and a big family, and you were rolling your eyes at him in protest, you spurned him, you spurned his love and in the end you abandoned him for a man you didn't know at all, who ran away from you when you were pregnant, and even when he eventually returned, he always kept himself to himself.

You wanted an inspirational life, you wanted to write books, to lecture at international conventions, she reminds herself, you should respect the person you were then, frustrated hopes and all, and she gets out of her car and approaches the house, a stiff breeze tangling the heavy cloud of her hair, how cold it is here, much more so than in the city, the raindrops are bigger too and she's already soaked to the skin. Maybe she'll knock on their door and ask if she can come inside, just for a little warmth, how big the house is, there's bound to be a temporary room for her, or perhaps not temporary, perhaps they'll agree to adopt her and she'll be their elderly grey-haired little girl. She'll behave herself, she won't bite or kick or mess around with electrical appliances, she'll just sit by the stove and keep still; as that's the way she always felt with her Eytan, she didn't need to lift a finger because he'd take care of everything, whereas with Gideon the roles were reversed; in fact it was thanks to what he denied her that she learned to live in a fuller sense, since it seems that every couple is allocated a limited quantity of vitality, and it's only the distribution that varies, with one taking less of it and the other more.

Hey, Gideon, she texts him a message on the way back, where are you? My class was cancelled, so if you're shooting anywhere around here I'll be glad to join you. Once she had enjoyed accompanying him on assignments, looking at the world through his eyes, and sometimes she even managed to help him, creating strange diversions so he wouldn't be noticed, suddenly starting to run or stripping off her shoes in the middle of the street, and meanwhile he would be snapping away undisturbed, but now he doesn't reply and she goes back to the empty apartment, her throat sore, stretches out on the sofa and covers herself with a blanket, and when Gideon comes she wakes with a start, shivering in the cold, what's the time? Where's Nitzan? And he says, I've booked us a place on the Dead Sea at the weekend, a room with sea views, for your birthday.

Really? She's taken completely by surprise, that sounds lovely, I'd forgotten all about my birthday. His efforts touch her heart and she holds out her arms to him, come here, Gidi, I'm cold, I'm wet through, and he moves closer to her gingerly, sitting at the end of the sofa beside her. Where were you, why didn't you answer me? she asks, and he says, it's been a crazy day, I didn't even see your message until I was on my way home, so how are things with you? And she says hastily, I'm all right, I just fell asleep suddenly, his hand is on her hair and suddenly she's embarrassed by its drab colour; a man's sunburnt hand on a greying head, a woman's wrinkled hand on a lean and ageing chest, how we have changed.

Should I dye it like everyone else? she asks and he says, no, to me it looks fine the way it is, I like the natural texture, and she says, maybe for my birthday I'll dye it, maybe it will do me good, and he smiles, no problem then, if it's going to do you good, and it seems on account of the momentous nature of the issues that stand between them they're incapable of saying anything to each other besides banalities such as these. Come and lie down beside me, she suggests, you look tired, and slowly he takes off his shoes, bending down from the sofa and she asks, do you remember when I used to do weird things for you while you were shooting?

Yes, he says, that was a long time ago, and she grins, I did something weird today too, and he asks, what did you do? His voice sounds distant and she stops herself, no point telling him where she's been, she knows him, again he'll say she's out of her mind, again he'll suffer by comparison with Eytan. Have you seen my book? he asks, it was here on the sofa, and she says, it's still here, between the cushions, how does it work, outside you see it all and when you're at home you can't find anything? She hands him the book, the work of that dead scientist, and when he settles down to read it, instantly engrossed, she leans against the back of the sofa and stares up at the ceiling, it seems to her an invisible eye is peering down at them from on high, a man and a woman, a man and a woman and nothing else, their skin raddled and beneath it the calcium draining from their bones, what are they really capable of doing for each other? Will she strain her neck and kiss his lips, and what's in it for her, kissing lips that are tightly closed, hermetically sealed, and again his proximity arouses bitter tension in her, a pale imitation of the proximity of mother and child.

Man and woman, what's left for them to wait for? Two years from now they'll be escorting Nitzan to the army recruitment office, ten years from now most likely they'll escort her to the wedding canopy, and some day one of them will escort the other on his or her last journey, and in the meantime the creases between their eyes will deepen and their height will diminish, and in the meantime they will exchange words, the oral and the corporeal ones, eat their meals face to face and sleep side by side, dreading the disease that will fling one of them down and force the other to prove his or her devotion, and although this is a depressing thought, their situation is better than that of many couples who are doomed to separate or make each other's life miserable, but this isn't enough for her, and the fact is becoming ever clearer to her. She needs to achieve something, she needs a little boy, even if it's as hard as Thumbelina described it, she won't be afraid, she prefers to confront his difficulties rather than her own, thus at least she'll bring him consolation, while herself she'll not succeed in consoling.

She won't be afraid because she hears him calling her, she know he's waiting for her, she believes she can be more useful to him than to this one who's lying curled up beside her. It wasn't by chance he offered to take her to the Dead Sea, to mark her birthday with a room overlooking the Sea of Death. The death of their love is what he's trying to make tangible for her, and even this isn't such a big deal, even if it happens with most couples they apparently have more distractions than she has, or secret loves, and when she sees him reading with taut lips she almost hopes for his sake he has some secret love that's bringing him joy and excitement; it isn't only her little child who mustn't be overburdened with expectations, mutual bonding within couples can't bear too heavy a load either, like the moon whose light is borrowed, it needs radiation from outside, children, friends, events, while they, who were always content with lesser quantities of all these, were left looking out over the dark desert, over their Dead Sea.

What's the point of a luxury room in a hotel, it isn't this that she longs for, but to pack a suitcase and go to her child, the one person in the world to whom she can still bring happiness. Even if the first year is difficult and the second too, even if he is cold and suspicious, aggressive and menacing, she will believe in him because she will know him; after all this is exactly the way she used to be herself, and still is to this day.

From moment to moment the air is warming up and her hopes grow stronger, he won't refuse her on her birthday. It seems they have left their gloom behind in the rainy city and they're passing through the gates of another country where everything is possible, if in the middle of winter her bones are thawing and she's shedding garment after garment, left with only a thin vest, perhaps the strata enfolding his heart will disintegrate in the face of her appeal, for you too this will be good, if you don't fight it, giving a home to a child who has nothing, have you anything better to do in your life? And when she looks at his handsome, still boyish profile, with the charm wrinkles around his eyes and running down his cheeks, it seems to her he's already agreed, their journey has really begun and it's painting this very day in colours of hope and significance. It isn't for the purpose of dining and resting and enjoying themselves that they have crossed the thirsty desert but to take the child to their bosom, and this man beside her in the driving seat is destined to be the father of the child and thereby her love for him will be deepened, she already feels this with all her body, with all her years, the wondrous awakening to greet the future, sometimes you have to create the future if it doesn't create itself, and this she does, and this she will tell him, I've prepared a future for us, come and join me, you can always leave.

From moment to moment her love for him grows, since the mysterious and so painful strength inherent in his absence now confers a miraculous grace on his presence by her side, turning them momentarily into the children of gods, and her love fills the void of the car, her love for him, for life itself of which she had almost despaired, for their daughter, for the child who's waiting for them, it seems that if she opens the window her love will stream away and kiss the mountains that sprawl side by side, kneeling submissively like a train of camels. Soon they will be roused from their repose, parched lips gaping, but the more they drink so the flow will be increased, as she gives more so her stocks will be replenished, it's the wonder of existence, that the very thought of the child gives her legendary strength, set to increase as the sights surrounding them lose their substance.

Can it be that the sight I'm seeing, the mighty pillars, the iridescent sea, the rosy vapours rising from it and swallowed by the sky, can this be the way the next world will look? But for the time being it's the energy of this world that she feels, demanding of her that she act before her life is over, and that is why the moment they arrive at the room assigned to them, she will turn to this man with whom she's chosen to live her life and tell him of her final decision and ask him for his backing.

Is this the hazy air that's quivering before her, filtering in through the open window, or is she the one who's doing the quivering, so fragile is the moment, like thin and polished glass, and everything she sees through it, the good and the bad, blessing and curse, and although she knows that life generally takes the middle way between these extremes, it seems to her this time there is no intermediate option, soaring to the heights or crashing to the ground, acceptance or divorce, and that's why she's quaking by the open window, but when she pulls a sheet over her naked body she is enfolded by a happy certainty. It's going to happen, at the end of the day it depends only on her, and therefore she's entitled to relax for a while and make room between them for that delight, delight of the heart and delight of the body, and for a moment she wonders about this word, the name that never suited her mother, nor the time and place she was born into; what were her parents thinking of, saddling her with that combination of letters?

Poor Hemda, not much delight in her life, she says aloud, and Gideon, coming out of the shower with a towel around his waist, asks with a smile, what did you say? Oh, nothing, she replies, smiling back at him, because now she wants to be light and jolly, sink into the depths of the moment and feel its pleasures in full, she wants to love this man at this moment, she wants to love his body and her body, which today celebrated its forty-sixth year, and even if it can no longer bring life it can still love, and this ability time will not steal from it and perhaps it's the opposite, perhaps with the end of fertility the heart is eager to make up the deficit, because she loves his little and slightly twisted smile, and the precision of his movements when he aims the camera at the mysterious haze in their window; it seems everything will be revealed there when it clears, even her mother's lost lake.

On her birthday she always thinks about her mother; of course it belonged to her first and foremost and years were to pass before the birthday was removed from the purview of the parents and placed at the disposal of the children as a first sign of adulthood, Mazaltov, Mother, even though you never learned how to enjoy me, and Gideon turns the lens of the camera towards her, what is this, all the time it seems to me there's someone else in the room with us. There's always other people with us, she says, those who bore us and those we bore and those who weren't born, and he grins and presses the button, just don't start again with your lamentations, but she isn't offended, she likes being photographed like this, sitting on the end of the bed with her shoulders exposed, apparently she's still beautiful in his eyes, as he is in hers, and she takes the camera from him and puts it to her eye, wait a moment, don't move. Like a couple on whom a painful separation has been imposed they photograph each other, but the picture she takes of him won't come out well, as at that precise moment he advances on her and grasps her chin and caresses her shoulder and pulls the sheet away, and when her back arches to accept him she knows they're no longer a veteran couple trying to rekindle burnt-out embers, but a man and a woman on the verge of change, and even he who doesn't yet know it is changing before her eyes, in years she hasn't seen him like this, eager and committed. Does he too understand that at this very moment the embryo of a decision is taking shape between them, a spark of love for the child of whom they know nothing yet other than that he belongs to no one, the child of no one who will become their own?

This is a moment of conception, and through its energy their desire is redoubled and their intimacy intensified, from the tips of her toes to the crown of her head she rejoices in the tactile, the touch of the soft sheet and the touch of the warm breeze, and the touch of his hands and his lips and the touch of her hands along his thighs. She can no longer tell between his body and hers, as it seems to her she feels his delight as well, ever since the moment she flung her heart wide open she has been seeing him as he is, fearful for himself and for her, flustered by the change, and she can forgive him his tightly sealed heart, and even her mother she can forgive today, suddenly seeing her as a sad and neglected girl, like the mother of the abandoned child.

It seems to her this is what the child is asking of her, to forgive her mother so that in the fullness of time he can forgive his mother, and she will do this for his sake, for his sake she will forgive and for his sake she will take pity and for his sake she will indulge herself, send out through the open window a sigh of bliss and longing, a sigh that will skim across the heavy waters of the Dead Sea to the further shore and from there climb and hover on a northward course until it reaches the child laid in a small wooden bed in an overcrowded room, surrounded by children likewise abandoned, some weeping bitterly and some already asleep, and others beating heads on bed-frames, and only he will turn his eyes to the window and on his lips a smile will spread because her voice has come to his ears, and he knows he will soon be gathered in, soon it will be said of him: this is my beloved son in whom I am well pleased.

Her hands shake when she interweaves her fingers with his and her head rests on his warm chest, her right hand clutching his left arm and her left hand his right, and when she stretches her arms out sidelong his arms are extended too, as if he's been lashed to the bed, and she says, Gidi, I've decided, I'm going ahead with this, and perhaps she didn't say it but only meant to say it, because he doesn't respond, so she says it again, in a louder voice, and still there's no response, and she adds nothing and takes nothing back, no explaining or justifying, urging or threatening, proving or promising, all these things she's already done and now on her birthday all that's left for her is to tell him what she's decided, and wait for his reaction, which is taking its time. His arms are outstretched, his face she can't see and the rising and falling of his chest are all that she feels, apparently he too understands that their words are rationed, and so he pauses, choosing his words with care. I'm sorry you've made that decision, he will say finally, his voice hoarse and muffled as if it's travelled a long way over deep water, I can't be a partner in this enterprise, and she will straighten her neck and look him in the face; he will be pale, almost transparent, and his eyes will avoid her eyes, and she will lay her head on his chest again, despite the rebuttal the mood of intimacy hasn't dissolved, and she'll place her legs on his legs and her thighs on his thighs, ribs on his ribs, covering his whole body with hers and her lips on his lips, and she'll whisper, I need your presence, I need your signature, and once that's done you'll be free, I'll make no more demands of you, and he will reply with a choke in his throat, very well, so be it. How fragile is the moment, as he's about to disrupt the little tableau that she arranged with such care and he'll extricate his fingers from her fingers and his body will wriggle out from under hers, he'll dress quickly and put his glasses on and hang the camera round his neck and throw his possessions into a suitcase like a fugitive from a disaster zone, and when she asks him sadly, what are you doing, he'll say, I'm going home, are you coming? And she'll give him a long look and reply, no, I'm staying here, this is my birthday.

He didn't see her progressively declining, losing a third of her body weight in the last third of her life, he didn't see her skin rusting over the internal organs which had shrunk like withered fruit, the rotten fruit of a long and empty life, he didn't see her sagging breasts and hairless genitals, her chin sprouting such a crop of bristles there's no telling if she's man or woman. Alone she has grown old, alone, and she has not been spared his suffering but he has been spared hers, and for this he would surely be secretly grateful, if he knew, and he would always keep it a secret, not wanting her to stop compensating him. Would he be capable of caring for her today, slicing tomatoes for her and feeding her with a spoon, changing the soiled bedding, did he do her a favour leaving her by herself during the onset of her old age or was this another vindictive desertion, maintained until it was too late to start a new life?

Really too late? Today she's no longer sure of this, after all, this wasn't about age but it was her interpretation of the passage of the years. Again she chose a strategy of avoidance, as before when she fell on her back in the dining hall, in a hurry to give up from the start, to cleanse her life of reality and leave only the unavoidables that always disappoint – the children, the children – and what else was there: hiking on summer evenings and private tuition for the local kids, who became more stupid from year to year, demeaning fantasies at the window, and her empty notebook, and all the things that must not be recorded there.

Perhaps you should go back to the kibbutz, her children suggested after their father's death, and one after the other they collected their meagre belongings and left the house,

Dina with Eytan, Avner with Shlomit; why don't you come home now, delegations from the kibbutz used to urge her, visiting her from time to time, what is this city to you, how can you live in such isolation? The children who grew up with her, who scampered and cavorted while she still lay in the playpen, who mocked the stories about her lake, would arrive in an old van bringing apples, avocados, eggs, what do you have here? There's nothing for you here, but she stuck to her new life even if there was nothing in it other than the denial of her former life. Her husband she did try to forgive at the end of his life, but she struggled to forgive the kibbutz even in its death-throes, angrily watching as the dream disintegrated, short as the life of man, shorter than the life of man, and all of it holes within holes, pinpricks on pinpricks. So this is your great story, she used to grin, remembering one of the few times her mother tucked her into bed, and when she asked her to tell her a story she refused and said, since I came to this country I've forgotten all the stories, Hemdi, because our story here is the biggest story of them all, all legends and fables are pale by comparison.

So tell me this story, she urged her, and her mother replied, but there are no words in it, only actions, the deeds of our hands are our story, you, the kibbutz, the land, and she accepted her answer with painful love, as she accepted her absences with painful love, accepted her untimely death from a recurrence of the kidney disease which this time subdued her easily, while Hemda was busy with her newborn baby, wondering how it came about that in her life in particular, birth and death were so closely connected, like twins.

One after the other and almost in their prime her parents left this world, setting in their own way a personal example, refusing to be a burden, and since she was allowed no opportunity to tend them, she tended her sick husband with devotion, seeking to prove to them she was capable, seeking to share with them her sorrow that they didn't rely on her and didn't believe in her, were ashamed to be seen before her in their weakness. It was only after he fell ill that she realised she should have lived beside him like this from the beginning, as if he might die tomorrow, and it was only then she understood how deceptive is the supposed life-expectancy of human beings, and she lamented this too as she cared for him assiduously, committing herself to the order of the day as dictated by his disease, adhering to one clear objective, although he didn't know how to be grateful to her and he continued to complain and fling accusations at her almost until his last day, blaming her for both his sickness and his pain. It was only then it occurred to her that even if you're accused incessantly it doesn't necessarily mean you're guilty, and she was almost grateful for this revelation which breathed new strength into her, and now she remembers the night of his death; there was a heatwave and she lay beside him on the bed and held his feverish hand, listening to his breathing. That night she washed his hair which was still dense, ash-gold and grey, and it gleamed above his tormented face and diffused a dazzling brilliance. A rhythmic grunting emerged from his throat, his mouth was open and threads of blood sparkled between his teeth, and she pressed against him and took deep breaths for him, till she fell asleep briefly and when she woke up he was no longer grunting. Late again. Reverently, she caressed the body at her side as it cooled, and the colder he became the more pleasant and reassuring was his touch, and she stroked his forehead and cheeks and lower neck and protruding collar-bones. His skin was turning solid from moment to moment like polished marble and she couldn't take her hands from him, leaning her forehead on his chest as if it were a prayer-wall.

His body was never as pleasant to her as that night, when he couldn't return her touch, and she nestled against him, refusing to be parted from him. Her children were still asleep and she didn't rouse them, they would do him no good, and anyway she wanted to be alone with him for ever, but a sudden ringing was heard at the door, she forgot she'd asked a technician to come in and repair the television set facing his bed, and the technician came into the room and opened his bag of tools and started working, stealing a glance from time to time at the motionless recumbent form. She didn't say a word, standing in the doorway and gazing proudly at her handsome husband, who looked remarkably young in the strong morning light, his glass-blue eyes open and staring out of the window, and long minutes passed before the technician came to her and asked with a shudder, excuse me, is he dead? She nodded drily, as if this were a routine occurrence, but the man picked up his tools and fled in a panic saying, sorry, I'm from a priestly family and I'm not allowed any contact with the dead, and she called out after him, but what about the TV, forgetting that he wouldn't be needing it now, you can't leave me like this, she chased him down the stairs weeping bitterly, it isn't fair, you take ages to arrive and then just go!

How young he was when he died compared with her today, how young her parents were, who would believe she would be a pioneer in this of all things, the first in the family to attain grey old age, not letting death dominate her, and sometimes she thinks that because she hasn't lived she won't die either, and if death is a wake-up call for the living, how can anyone who hasn't been asleep be awakened? Does this mean that in her life she has died and in her death she will live, because sometimes she sees him in a higher form of life, life without body, and so perhaps from the beginning she has been fated to die, after all as far back as she can remember her body has been a burden to her, ever since her father beat her for refusing to walk.

I'm fated to die, she mumbles, my fate is to die, and sometimes she longs to experience the separation from her ever-diminishing body, from day to day she is shrivelling, light as a ghost, so it seems to her the force of gravity has no influence over her, it's only the weight of the blanket that's holding her down on the bed, and the moment it's removed she'll be out through the window, hovering with the migrating storks. She hears them calling her name, Hemda, are you really the one who waited for us in the blue autumn, amid the papyrus reeds? How perverse you are, you humans, compared with the birds! The passage of the years makes no impression on our feathers, whereas on your skin every year is inscribed. Is it awareness that emphasises the weight of the years?

Poor Hemda, aged child that you are, they nod to her with a flurry of wings. Even then you had nothing but your lake, so we named it after you, Lake Hemda. Soon you too will be flying in the sky, you'll circle around your loved ones, you'll no longer be capable of reminding, testifying and warning, time is running out, Hemda, tell them the story now, tell them the history of your father and your mother, tell them your history, tell them their history.

Hurry up, you'll be late, she whispers to the flock of storks conversing with her, winter has come early this year and you still have a long way to go to reach the warm countries, and they answer her in ringing chorus, you need to hurry too, Hemda, your winter is cold and it's the last one, you won't have another, even if you haven't lived you shall surely die. Tell what has been entrusted to you, things no one other than you knows, and she sighs, who shall I tell, for years I've been trying and no one wants to listen, and they answer, tell the child, the new child who will arrive at the end of the winter, when you won't be here any more, he'll need your story, he'll long for your testimony, and it seems to her she hears other voices suddenly rising from the interior of the house, voices of a man and a woman bound closely together. Is this her mother and her father coming to collect her? Just a moment, she tries to call out, her heart pounding, I haven't yet found the first word, my notebook is still empty, but when the voices come closer she recognises her son and her daughter, hears them conversing in whispers in the kitchen next door. How warm their voices are, in her body she feels this and in her blood, she's never felt them so close, she's never felt herself so much loved, after all if they love each other their love will pass through her body, which gave them life, so much loved she can almost take her leave, but not before she has her notebook in her hands, pulling it out with an effort from under the pillow. Dina Horowitz, Class Eleven, History, is the inscription on the cover, written in blue ink. Her father hated waste and was always checking her exercise-books to make sure she was writing on both sides of the page and not leaving empty spaces, and she too was in the habit of checking her children's homework from time to time and scolding them for their extravagance, until one morning Dina angrily threw this notebook down in front of her and it became her property.

With an effort her finger caresses the hollow lines, sees them filling up with blue words like rivulets from a spring, as it will not only be stories of the lake written there but stories of its tributaries too, her children who have grown up, and her parents like mountains casting a shadow over the dying water. I'll start and you carry on, she will say, looking around at the room that suddenly seems vast to her, so spacious her eyes struggle to take it all in, has it really grown or is she the one who has shrunk? This is the smallest room in a minuscule apartment, but now as she is confined to her bed from morning to evening it seems its dimensions have expanded, it would take her hundreds of paces to reach the window, hours by the score, who knows if she'll live long enough.

Chapter Twelve

He hears a knock on the door and his heart pounds as he's aroused from his sleep in the narrow bed in the room of his youth in the long night, the days contract and the nights are drawn out, bound by the colourful chains of fabricated stories. He has never before slept so absolutely, acquainted with his sleep and craving it, waking again and again to enjoy the prospect of more slumber awaiting him, going to bed early, although it isn't weariness that sends him to sleep but desire. No, he isn't weary any more, it seems the heavy fatigue that's accompanied him in recent years has melted away in a single moment, and that's why in his bed he strays time and again to that moment, how he returned to his house in the dead of night and entered silently like a thief, coming not to take but rather to give, although his hands were empty, empty and cold, when he walked into his house and found three people asleep in three beds, one small and one medium-sized and one large, and more than anything else he longed to plunge into their sleep, a diver submerged in the depths, sinking between them in silence, a dance without movement, a song without sound.

This was the longest night of his life, longer than his whole life, since this was when everything nearly happened, he nearly got the woman he wanted, and he nearly got his wife back, and his children and his house, and he nearly wrapped himself up in his early life, an ancient disguise, but in the end nothing happened, and it seems to him now that within this nearly, in the space narrow as an infant's footstep between action and inaction, his entire life has been crammed. He stood and stared at his sleeping wife, leaning weak and worn-out on the wall facing her, and lusted so intensely after her sleep, longing to blend with her into one sleeping body, forgetting and remembering in turn why he came and what he wanted to say to her, until he sat down beside her, stroked her hair and whispered in her ear telling her not to grieve, she shouldn't weep for her youth since time is cyclical, even if its trajectory is clear, and therefore youth is diffused over the whole of life, exactly like old age, while the gift of love is waiting around unexpected corners, and it isn't too late, sometimes one moment of love is weighed against many years, or the memory of love, and sometimes it's possible to be content even with expectations, and when he came out of there in the blue light of dawn, leaving the house buried in sleep as it had been when he entered, he felt in all his bones, shaking in the cold of the winter morning, the state of being bereft of everything, the depth of failure attending on all his actions, and it seems to him there's always a woman involved in this, how easy it is to depend on women, and has been so since the dawn of history, but evidently the time has come to exist without women and this will be his time, even if it lasts months and years.

His aching knees as he descended the stairs reminded him of his age, all the years that had been snatched away, chewed up and discarded, but all of these did nothing to dilute the good news that adhered to him that early morning, some weeks ago, and even now they're hurting as he rises, still half asleep, from his bed, and gropes for the wall and shuffles towards the door. Who can it be, nearly midnight and he isn't expecting anyone, he put the children to bed in their house and Shlomit seemed relaxed about it, almost appeased, anyway she's not going to leave her home at a time like this and Dina's having a weekend break by the Dead Sea, it must be a mistake, but when he peers through the spyhole he sees her and hurriedly opens the door, what's going on, where's Gideon? Didn't you go to the Dead Sea?

We did, she says, but he didn't stick around, and I wanted to visit you and Mum before my birthday was over, and she holds out her arms to him and walks into his embrace, his arms enfolding her, and he's astonished to find how thin she is, he's used to Shlomit and her chunkiness, and he probes the slim back with curiosity, also the vertebrae protruding like little nuts, since when have you been so thin? he asks, you weren't always like this, do you remember how you used to make yourself sick in the bathroom to keep yourself slim?

What, you knew? she asks, surprised, why didn't you tell me you knew? And he replies, I didn't want to embarrass you, and she sighs, what a pity, that would have helped me, and he remembers the thin woman who offered him a drink of water in the street, if he had held on to her he would no doubt have felt the same direct pulsation, bone against bone, without the guile of the flesh, how fascinated he is suddenly by this close contact with bones, and he holds her hand and leads her to the kitchen, come on, Dini, let's make you a proper birthday.

What will you drink? he asks as she takes her seat on the backless chair and she says, hot milk, and the lips that smile at him are pale and beautiful and her skin is lustrous, and he comments, it's done wonders for your complexion, the Dead Sea, did you bathe in the sulphur? And she says no, we hardly went out of the room, it's this pale light that does it, Mum's economy bulbs, and he says, I don't know, you look different, and he boils the milk in a pan and pours it into two old yellow cups.

Good health, Dini, he clicks his cup against hers, happy birthday, sister, and she looks up at him with her deep and damp brown eyes, and he remembers how exactly thirty years ago they sat like this, his sister at sixteen and he nearly fourteen, a few days after they left the kibbutz, the apartment was still full of packing cases and their parents were arguing in the bedroom. All that day the house had been in uproar, because in the morning their mother was notified that the teaching job she had been promised in the local high school had been cancelled, and their father was yelling at her incessantly as if it was her fault. We should never have left the kibbutz, he shouted, what are we going to live on now? You think my salary from the bank will be enough? And if they sack me too? I warned you over and over, this is no age to be starting a new life! And with all the commotion and the anger Dina's birthday was forgotten, but when he got out of bed at midnight he found her in the kitchen, so clearly he remembers this now, wearing a long-sleeved nightdress with a motif of grey flowers, her dark hair combed, drinking milk and eating the plain biscuits they brought with them from the kibbutz.

For a moment she recoiled when she saw him approach, but then she moved her feet from the chair opposite and signalled to him to sit and said almost apologetically, it's my birthday today, as if only on a birthday were eating and drinking allowed, just once a year, and he well remembers that he wanted to hug her because his heart went out to her, but with a typically clumsy adolescent movement he jolted her arm and the cup she was holding was shaken and the milk spilled on the table, and she scolded him and mopped up the milk in somewhat slovenly fashion, letting it drip on the floor, and he hurried back to his bed, embarrassed and chastened, but he couldn't get back to sleep and then he heard her shutting herself in the bathroom. At first he didn't understand what they were, the sounds emerging from there, the coughs and choking sighs, for a moment he was afraid someone was attacking her, and when he realised what was happening he was furious at the waste, they sacked Mum today and we have no money and there'll be no food, and you're puking up biscuits.

Only now, thirty years later and at midnight, is he capable of expressing an opinion of that girl who crouched over the bowl in her flowery flannel nightie on her birthday and tried to purge her gut of biscuits dunked in milk, and he looks at her sadly but to his surprise she's beaming and she says almost apologetically, my world has turned upside down, I should feel terrible but I feel wonderful, and he asks, what happened? Did you quarrel over the adoption? And she says, more or less, we didn't really quarrel, I just told him I wasn't giving up on the child and he said it's out of the question as far as he's concerned, but he's agreed to do what's necessary and not spoil it for me.

So what's going to happen? he asks and she says, I'm going ahead with this, as soon as he left I contacted the company and arranged a meeting, and he persists, you're really prepared to dump Gideon? And she draws the flattering purple sweater more tightly around her body and shrugs her shoulders, I don't know, but that isn't the main issue, I simply can't give up on this child, and if to him this constitutes grounds for separation, he has that right, of course, but it isn't my decision.

To tell you the truth I completely understand his apprehensions, he says, when Shlomit wanted another child I was really scared too, I suppose our function is to be afraid and your function is to ignore our fear and thus reassure us, it's a kind of unconscious test that's supposed to prove to a man that his wife is strong enough. Obviously, in the case of adoption it's much harder but essentially they are the same thing, he'll change his mind, you'll see.

I'm not so sure of that, she says, her long fingers gripping the cup emphatically. It seems to me, all that Gideon really wants is a quiet life, he's never been especially family-minded and this kind of adventure just doesn't appeal to him, and Avner says, when you're together he may think that's what he wants, but he's not going to give you up for the sake of a quiet life, he needs you more than you know, perhaps even more than he knows. Thanks Avni, she sighs, but I'm not sure of that any more, it was convenient for me to believe all these years that even if Gideon didn't make a big display of his love I could still rely on it, and yet he left me there today, and when I was pregnant he left me too.

But he came back in the end, and he's a wonderful father, Avner finds himself speaking up in defence of a brother-in-law he never really liked, there's nothing you can do about it, pregnancy is a threat to most men, theoretically we're programmed to want to inseminate, but it seems the average male of today has lost the basic impulse to procreate, he reckons the seed is taking his place, it's cancelling out his existence, and not giving him validity, as is the case in nature. I felt exploited when Shlomit was pregnant, I only wanted a child who came out of love, I had the fantasy of a couple producing a child from desire alone, without recourse to ovulation tables and biological clocks, but apparently there aren't many love-children in this world, perhaps great love isn't necessary where procreation is concerned.

Love is too elusive a creature for me, Dina says, leaning her elbow on the formica tabletop, it's like clutching at the wind, and children are so real, especially when they're young and need constant attention, their corporeality is reassuring in its certainty, and very often it stabilises the bond, it did us so much good, the birth of Nitzan, and he says, apparently there are no recipes, in our case the children have only added to the tensions and the frictions which are not their fault, even little Yotam couldn't bring us closer together, perhaps a bit at first, but very quickly we reverted to our old ways, we're just a lost cause.

And she isn't trying to get you back? Dina asks, and he replies, not any more, I'm glad to say, in the beginning she tried, for better or worse, and this was the most depressing part of it, to see her pleading, but very quickly she stopped, it seems she too found it easier to separate than to stay together, and even the kids haven't reacted too badly, the moment they realised this way they're going to see more of me they calmed down, but even as he speaks doubt assails him again. Why are you putting such a positive gloss on your divorce, he asks himself, you're vilifying your marriage and embellishing its breakdown, since in spite of everything, when he tucks them into bed he can't ignore the entreaty in their eyes, stay, sleep with us, even on the sofa in the lounge or in our room, live with us, Daddy, what kind of a father doesn't live with his sons, and what kind of an argument is it, saying, I don't love your mother, and she doesn't love me. Anyone would think you can measure love the way you measure heat, or put it on the scales, or perhaps the two of them will go one morning to the clinic and hold out their arms for the needle, and the blood extracted from the vein will be taken to the lab for analysis and within a week the results will be in, such and such a percentage of love in your bloodstreams – you come out as borderline normal, and this report you're going to show to your children like a document presented in court? The dimensions of love are like the dimensions of divinity, hidden from the eye.

And yet, when he leaves that house, after the bedtime stories and the kissing and the hugging and the reassurances, his legs are light and his gait confident; the very thought of the evening that would have been in store for him with his wife is profoundly depressing: that demeaning mud-wrestle and alongside it the expectation, the hunger for total acceptance in spite of everything, evening after evening, week after week, year after year, he can't handle it any more. I can't handle it, he tells himself every evening to the rhythm of the quick paces to his car, where are you going in such a hurry? Not to the café or the pub where lonely people tend to congregate, it's his mother's house he's going to, to the narrow bed in the room of his youth, to his rendezvous with sleep, how will she appear tonight, as gentle mother or affectionate mistress, impetuous lover or the love-child who may yet be born to him? And even now he can't wait any longer and he suggests, don't you think it's time to go to bed, Dini? I'm in court tomorrow and I need to prepare for it in the morning.

Yes, of course, she says, is it all right if I stay with you for the time being? And he waves his arm, taking in the whole apartment, this is yours as much as it's mine, and they both know it isn't a question of legal rights, but the possibility of making space for her in what was once the impregnable fortress of that inseparable duo, mother and son, son and mother. Your room is taken, he says, will you sleep in the parents' room? Although their father died in this room more than twenty years ago, they still call it that, and she nervously opens the door and turns on the light, I always hated my room, she says and he smiles, I hated mine too but now I really like it.

Perhaps it's because you have another home, she suggests, and he says no, I no longer have another home, and she looks at him sadly, oy, Avni, I have no doubt you're doing the right thing, but doing the right thing at the wrong time can cause a lot of pain, and he sighs, yes, at our age there are no easy choices, there's a heavy price to be paid and it just gets heavier, and at this point another sigh is heard in the empty shell of the apartment and Dina whispers, you see, we've both come home to Mum and she doesn't even know, she can't even be happy.

Or be sad, he says, good night, Sister, as it seems to him the sleep that's waiting for him will be angry if he delays any longer, her limbs will cool and her embrace won't be warm and devoted, so he leaves his sister standing irresolutely beside the double bed and hurries to his room, sweet tranquillity descending on him. Here they are again, the three of them, as if only now their father has died and left them like this, but then they were separated and dispersed, whereas now they are clinging, each to the other's mistakes, and he lies on his back and smiles at the ceiling, time plays games with us, isn't it absurd to feel the soothing presence of the first family for the first time at the age of forty-four, in mid-life, and when he wraps himself in sleep between his mother and his sister he's overwhelmed by sentimental gratitude, he's returned to them from a long journey of twenty years, returned to them finally without fear of their love.

Next morning when he gets up they're still asleep; between his mother's fingers he's surprised to find a silver pen, and when he tries to pull it from her hand she grips it firmly, and he lets it go and boils water for coffee in the dimly lit kitchen, the two yellow cups in the sink raise a smile to his lips, some birthday party that was, a milk party, a party without cake, without flowers or guests. There's no milk left over for coffee, but here comes Rachela, her gait as vigorous as ever and her hands laden with shopping bags, and the fridge soon fills up. Like some orange juice? she asks him, pulling oranges from the bag and putting them in the basket.

No thanks, I'm in a hurry, he replies, noticing with some bemusement that she's dressed all in white, a lacy long-sleeved white dress and white court shoes, standing there with her fruit like a kindergarten girl bringing her contribution to the festival of Weeks, and he's impressed, that's a very nice dress you're wearing! Is there a festival today, and she smiles awkwardly, not an official one, but just for me, it's my son's birthday.

Mazaltov, he says, how old is your son, and she answers, eighteen, and he asks, how are you going to celebrate? Her voice retreats when she replies, after work I'm taking him for a pizza and then to the cinema, her eyes are avoiding his and he's a little puzzled by the choice of entertainment, more appropriate for his twelve-year-old son. Which film? he asks, and she answers hesitantly, *All about my mother*, and he buttons up his dark woollen jacket, ah, I didn't get to see that one myself but I've heard it's powerful stuff, you'll enjoy it, and he's already on the stairs and doesn't see her hands taking an orange from the basket and squeezing it, her attention distracted, until it splits and the juice sprays her dress, but Dina, who will hear the exchange of words while lying awake in her parents' bed, will leave the room and take the dripping orange from her hands and embrace her, don't cry, Rachela, and don't be too hard on yourself, you made the biggest of sacrifices for his sake, you gave him up so he would have a better future.

I should have rehabilitated myself for him, she wails, laying her head with its raven-black hair on her shoulder, what good did it do me, getting my life sorted out after I'd given him up, and Dina says, but the fact is, you couldn't have done otherwise, and you shouldn't judge yourself in hindsight, there's no sense in that. He'll definitely be in touch soon, he'll see the file and come looking for you, and Rachela mumbles, I hope so, I'll compensate him for everything, we'll make a fresh start.

I'm sure it's going to work out for you, Dina says, her fingers caressing the smooth parted hair, and she moves on to the subject uppermost in her mind, a little boy who's going to be needing the services of a childminder a few months from now, perhaps not the easiest of children to handle, someone who will demand lots of love and patience, would she be interested, and Rachela looks up at her with a lively expression, yes, gladly she says, when your mother gets better I'll be needing a new job and I really love working with children.

Getting better? Is that the way death will reveal itself in the future, the life that is evaporating through the pores of the skin, is that really our disease? So I'll be counting on you, Rachela, she says, those are lovely oranges, we'll cut them into small segments, the way we used to do it in the kibbutz, and as they stand at the marble worktop, slicing orange after orange and putting the segments on to the plate, to Dina these resemble little orange boats that aren't going anywhere, scores of mouths gaping in the wet and toothless smile of the extremities of life, the beginning or the end of it.

Strange, how cagey she was telling him about her son's birthday, he thinks while clawing his way through traffic jams, but then it isn't that much of a surprise really, after all the eighteenth birthday means the army isn't far away, and that's the moment parents start dreading the day a male child is born, and right on cue there's a newsflash on the car radio, a soldier seriously injured in an incident in the south, and very soon that could be her son, a few years from now it could be his son, and he switches off the depressing report, it's all becoming so personal, the newsflashes and the bulletins, the gloom-laden accounts that always arouse in him a feeling of personal failure, as if it's his family that's in the news. He didn't try hard enough, the responsibility was his, he was the favourite son and the biggest disappointment, and he remembers Anati telling him yesterday she needed to talk to him urgently, her face was hostile, and he disappointed her too, walking out on her because he thought she wanted to update him on her precocious pregnancy.

It pains him to watch the accelerated changes taking place in her personality, it seems that everything he experienced in twenty years is happening to her in the space of a few months; her irritating enthusiasm has melted away, its place taken by defeatism. We can't help them anyway, she mutters from time to time, so why even try, and when he thinks of her while searching for a parking space in the congested streets, he feels in his flesh the pinpricks of unease. What does she want from him, what's the meaning of the accusing glances she's been fixing on him lately, as if he's been leading her astray, but he warned her from the start that in this office there would be more frustration than satisfaction. Did she fall in love with him the day she arrived, and ever since she's felt rejected? But that isn't rational, he's many years older than she is, things like that do indeed happen, but not to him, although something had happened to him. How strange that the night of her marriage was also the night of his bid for freedom, it was she who marked the change in his life even if she wasn't in any way involved in it; why had she aroused an irksome craving in him from the moment he first saw her on the threshold of his office, a heavy-set girl, nice eyes, trying hard to impress?

Good morning, Nasreen, he hears her voice as he enters, no, Attorney Horowitz can't take this brief, I handed him the material the other day and the answer was negative, no prospect of winning this one, and he interrupts the phone conversation, bewildered, what is this, Anati, which brief are you talking about? I don't remember you giving me any new material recently, and she puts the receiver down and says drily, like I said, no prospect of winning, we've had cases like this before and we haven't succeeded in halting the expulsion, and he asks, what expulsion is this?

Another mixed couple, he's from East Jerusalem with a blue card and she's from a village near Ramallah, brother a terror suspect, and they put out an expulsion order on her, the usual story, and he's repelled by the tone of her voice, there are no usual stories, he reproves her, every story is single and unique, and I don't understand why you're turning people away in my name without consulting me, has this been going on in the past?

Not exactly, she says, and he warns her, don't you dare do this again, because if it ever happens again, but she interrupts the threat, don't worry, there won't be any more opportunities, that's what I'm trying to tell you, I'm leaving, I want to start a new internship in a commercial office, I'm fed up with human rights, that's the department for fantasists who always lose, I'd like to win now and then.

Always lose? he protests, this mindset isn't unknown to him but her vehemence shocks him, since when have we always been losers? And she says, as long as I've been with you at least, you've achieved nothing. Steven was awarded a few coppers as an ex gratia payment, hardly adequate compensation for the damage to his face, the Bedouin school is finally facing demolition, those building permits will never be granted, not even for toilets, and if they build without permits the authorities will slap an eviction notice on them and send the bulldozers in to obliterate the toilets, and the best you can expect to get is yet another interim order to delay the demolition. It's nice that you've managed to return a few goats to the Jahalin and they admire you for it but what have you done since then, more and more interim orders? I don't know how you can carry on like this.

A few goats? he retorts angrily, what about all the people I've helped, resisting their eviction orders and getting their prison sentences reduced, you think all of this is worthless? And she says, fine, so you've done some good, but the harm you're doing outweighs it. You go along with the establishment script, pretending there's some real legal process operating here, when you know it's all a game and the results have been rigged, don't you see that your very presence is giving legitimacy to agencies that aren't legitimate?

So what do you suggest, we stop trying? Abandon people to their fate? He raises his voice and she hits back at him, perhaps yes, in times like these it's preferable to do nothing, or at least try not to make things worse, and perhaps out of this a solution will come. Don't make those pious faces at me, you know I'm right, here and there you succeed in helping some poor sod, but on the big issues the state is screwing us and you accept the verdict with perfect resignation, as if secretly you find it reassuring to have it proved for you, how much stronger the establishment is than you.

Reassuring? he yells at her, it distresses me, it breaks me! And she's quick to turn his words against him, so that's it, you're broken and I'm not blaming you, but this doesn't suit me, I'm still at the beginning of my career and I want to get on, make money, I'm fed up with delusions, don't you see that again and again you're duping your clients? You failed to prevent the deportation of Halla to Jordan, why do you expect to succeed with Nasreen? And he turns to stare at the window, breathing hard, suddenly he can't stand the sight of her, when were you thinking of leaving? he asks, and she says, a few weeks, not until you find another intern and he says, I want you to go today, if you have somewhere to go.

I've approached a few offices, she says, and I'm waiting for an answer, and he's shocked, you applied to other employers without talking to me? I don't understand this, his voice is hoarse and it seems to him his teeth are chattering out of anger and disappointment, take a day's holiday, Anati, I want to be alone here today, and he sits in his chair and watches her movements impatiently; how long does it take her to disappear, putting a file on the shelf, stacking papers on the desk, hunting for her mobile in the other room, violating his holy of holies. There was always a good atmosphere between him and his interns, he thought this was his real, exemplary family, uniting around the same goals, everyone giving according to his or her ability and receiving according to his or her needs, the founding principles of the kibbutz movement.

Here too I shall need to start again, he sighs, peering at her morosely, at her clumsy gyrations in a black jacket several sizes too small for her, everything she wears is too tight, and when at last she picks up her briefcase, the jacket rides up too and over the waistband of her low-cut trousers a fold of white puppy-fat is revealed, and suddenly he feels sorry for her. Why didn't you talk to me first? he asks, you didn't give me an opportunity to change your mind, and she says, you've been out of touch for months, you don't answer my calls, even when you're in the office your mind is somewhere else all the time, I feel you've been avoiding me and anyway, maybe I didn't want you to change my mind, don't take this personally, I just can't stand it, I'm sorry, and he says, don't be sorry, it's better if these things are revealed in time, just like in a marriage, there are mistakes that can be avoided if they're foreseen.

When she goes out with downcast eyes he's gratified to find he can identify the number of the previous caller, and he makes contact at once. Attorney Avner Horowitz here, he says mildly to the sullen female voice that answers, you tried to contact me this morning, and there was a misunderstanding, and straightaway she's complaining, our attorney abandoned us, left us in the lurch, and you're our last hope, Ali told me only you can help us, and he asks, what's your connection with Ali? and she replies, he's my uncle, my father's brother.

When can you come to see me, he needs to know, and she says I can be there in an hour, and he paces up and down the empty office, staring at the ugly tree outside, stripped bare as a skeleton; it must be tough losing everything every year, but then every year it grows back, whereas we just lose. A long time since he's been alone in the office, a long time since he's given it his full attention, just he and his wretched files. Maybe she's right, small rewards compared with the frustrations and yet, the flocks were returned to their owner, is that too trivial for her taste? and the toilets are still standing, is that too trivial? Yes, I fight for toilets and flocks of sheep, since that is where the honour of mankind resides in a war zone, and he stretches out on the sofa facing his desk, suddenly uneasy; for many years he's felt that if he tried very hard there would be changes, has he not tried hard enough? Could he have done more? There's no doubt he's been defeated, but in a war such as this even defeat is something to be proud of, and believe me, it isn't a war against you, he says quietly, resuming his nightly dialogue with his country, like a dream carried over into consciousness, you never understood me, you always suspected my motives, and as for me, I was concerned for your future too, as you tried to be concerned for mine, so we would succeed in surviving here, all of us together. In the process of defending oneself it is necessary to reduce the points of friction and enmity, emphasise the fundamental and minimise the trivial, this was what I wanted to do and over and over again I aroused your ire, and sometimes I think you're more innocent than I used to think, prone to fear, committing yourself readily to anyone who promises to watch over you. Is it possible to fight fear without creating fear? Is it possible to defend oneself without attacking? I believe this is hard but still possible, and you have no answers, you always look for them in the same stupid and violent place, and it seems to me you haven't tried hard enough, and that's why I'm so disappointed in you, but I'm not giving up on you and I'm not giving in to you, it's a blood-tie, impossible to unfasten, since this anxious rhythm is beating on the panel of your heart and I ask you to listen to it, and at this point he jumps to his feet and hurries to the door, sure enough, an hour has passed and here she is, how like Ali she looks, with those attractive features, slightly masculine in profile, dressed in European style, dark tailored trousers and a red sweater, big sunglasses covering her eyes and when she takes them off she reveals the downcast expression that's so familiar to him.

So Ali sent you to me? he asks, wanting to hear the comforting words again, and she says, yes, he said from the start if anyone could help us it was you, but my husband wanted to engage a lawyer from the east of the city, someone who would speak our language, and he hastens to reassure her, that isn't a problem, you did what you thought was right, so now tell me where things stand, and she unfolds the story before him once again, a story beginning apparently around the time she married her husband, a resident of Siluan, and went to live with him in the choicest segment of the land, but in fact it began many years before she was born, a story with many beginnings at various points in time which could evidently have ended at various junctures over the past hundred years, but people have been born into this story and are dying within it, not to mention those who have died because of it, and still it has no end, and it seems to Avner he has never seen such a consistent dichotomy between individuals and the whole, since these individuals, like for example the young woman sitting before him, want more than anything else the well-being of their families and hence the well-being of the whole region, and he wants this too, for himself and all his family members and relatives, and Ali as well, and yet it seems that the whole which is composed of these individuals is dissolving them with the energy of contrary aspirations, jealousy and violence, and in every generation it's possible to lay the blame on one figure or another, but accusations change easily, and new culprits appear, and nothing changes, and it seems a wild and unruly force like primeval radiation really would be capable of obliterating simple human aspirations and dragging the masses into a reality devoid of hope.

Perhaps scientists should work on this dispute and not statesmen, he thinks, perhaps they'll succeed in devising some formula, since this contradiction between individuals and the whole is extended in this part of the world over generations, and these are the smaller sacrifices; this young woman who is being evicted from her home although her husband is a citizen of the state, and she must separate from her family or take them with her to her village of origin because her brother is a member of a hostile organisation and she therefore apparently constitutes a security risk, even though she hasn't seen her brother for years, and of course there are bigger tragedies than this, he himself has handled much tougher cases, after all she's entitled to take her husband and children with her to her natal village outside the frontiers of the state, but their lives will still be adversely affected and it's these effects that he's determined to prevent, and to this end he will gather together all the details, examine them all from the lightest to the heaviest, when did she last see her brother, what kind of relationship does she have with her family, and what is her brother's relationship with the rest of the family, and how much does she know about his activities, and he's so tense and attentive, time being short as the hearing has been scheduled for the beginning of next month, he doesn't notice it's time to pick up his son from school, and he ignores the ringing of the phone until it's repeated.

Where are you, Dad? his son asks, I've been waiting for you half an hour, and he leaps up from his seat, oy, I'm sorry, Tomer, I'm in a meeting here and I didn't notice the time, I'm on my way now, and he hastily takes his leave of Nasreen, I'll go over the material and contact you, he promises her, and her lips quiver as she asks him her question, do you think we have a chance? And he hesitates before answering, remembering the words of his intern, you always lose anyway, so why deceive them?

That depends very much on the judge and on all kinds of factors, he says, but I have a good feeling about this, and it accompanies him all the way to the school gates, a good feeling such as he hasn't felt in a long time, he's not going to allow her eviction, that simply isn't going to happen. But when he takes his son into his car with a mouth full of apologies, the feeling rapidly dissolves, he looks at him with such bitterness, accustomed as he is to being insulted and overlooked, and again Avner wonders where he's going to take him, it really is time to find an apartment of his own near his old home, no point taking him now all the way to Grandma's house, and he remembers Rachela and asks, a pizza OK for you? Knowing that his son will stare coldly at him, as if to inform him that no gesture will compensate for the insult, but he isn't opposed to the idea.

When they arrive at the neighbourhood pizzeria, its roof covered in nylon but with sunshades over the tables as if it's still summer, for some reason he looks around for Rachela in her white bridal dress with her son, and glances angrily at his watch as if he arranged to meet her here and she's running late. The city is full of pizzerias, why this one and why now, and what do you need them for anyway, is it to defuse the tension between you and your son? Why not do that by yourself, but how? It seems it's already too late, and he orders pizzas and grape juice for them both, waiting at the counter and humming along absently with the muzak, Yes, I'm falling in love with you again, he intones, falling in love one more time, caressing with his eyes the ludicrous sunshades, the crowded and charmless concourse, full of hairdressing salons, flanked by a patisserie and a greengrocery. No individuality here, it seems, one more suburban mall in one city in one state, and yet some heavyweight questions are hanging from the tatty nylon roof, we're all of us residents of a live-fire zone, even if it is full of hairdressing salons. Let me fall in love with you again, he hums, picking up the tray with its fragrant load, love renewed is deeper than love that's new, let me fall in love with you again, he whispers to his son, who accepts the pizza with an air of studied reluctance.

What have you been doing with yourself? Not far from here there's a boy of your age who's threatened with deportation, he almost flings at him, but at once seals his lips, what's it to him, how can he know when you've never told him, Shlomit always silenced him: not in front of the children, I don't want you upsetting them, or planting doubts in their minds about the rectitude of the country they were born in, for which they'll be fighting one day, but even when he tried to share work issues with her alone she always found excuses for shutting him up, champion of human rights, she used to scoff, and what about my rights?

Was she jealous of his clients, of his wholehearted commitment to them, of a kind she never enjoyed, did she envy the satisfaction and success that had been his lot for a number of years? She always suspected him, ridiculed his motives, until he stopped telling, and his work, Daddy's work, became in the eyes of all the household a kind of hostile agency, although they were all nourished by it, and he didn't protest, but now, facing his son, who is moving his square jaws in a mechanical and dejected sort of way, he lets the words roll out, and to his surprise they flow so naturally, they could have been waiting years for this moment, the moment he would sit facing his firstborn son and say to him, I'm really sorry I was late, Tomer, I forgot to look at my watch, a woman was with me who really needs my help, they want to expel her from the country.

Why do they want to expel her, what has she done? his son asks, putting the pizza down, and he unfolds the whole story for his benefit, in the process drawing attention to other cases he has handled, other people he has succeeded in helping, and his son interrupts him now and then to ask pertinent questions, full of compassion and empathy, and his interest enlivens Avner's inclination to go on talking, and as he talks he is overwhelmed by a surge of pride such as he never felt in the past, setting out his world before his son. Yes, Tomer, it's true I put on a sour face and argued with your mother, it's true I wasn't always tolerant and attentive, it's true I couldn't give you everything you asked for, not even the most important thing of all, and yet I have succeeded now and then in doing the right thing, opposing injustice, and for this I'm entitled to feel some satisfaction.

Eat up, he says finally, the pizza's going cold, but his ever-hungry son has lost interest in it, it's his father's words he wants to eat and drink, and in the end he looks at him thoughtfully, running his hand through slightly greasy hair, if I were the judge, he announces in a grown-up tone, I'd ask her to swear not to meet her brother again, not ever, if she meets him, that could perhaps be really dangerous, but if she promises I would let her stay here, and only then does he take a slow and contented sip of his juice, and lost in admiration Avner says, you really could be a judge, Tomer, it's great that you're capable of seeing both sides, and his son smiles awkwardly, I got used to that at home, with you and Mum, seeing both sides so I could carry on loving both of you, and Avner rises from his seat and pulls him into a tight embrace, my boy, my dear boy, he can't find any other words, and again and again he kisses the sticky quiff and savours the smells wafting from it, the supper-time omelettes, the morning toast, Yotam's nappies, the liquid soap scented with mandarins, fabric conditioner, home in other words, home for better and for worse, here is home, in this embrace of theirs, without walls and furniture, my boy, my dear boy, I'm proud to be your father, he mutters.

Perhaps you can take me with you to the trial, Tomer suggests, and sure enough three weeks later he picks him up at the front door of the house in the morning, seeing to his surprise that he's wearing a white shirt under his coat and blue trousers as if he's on his way to a memorial ceremony, and he's calm and solemn, excited to be meeting face to face the heroes of the story that fired his imagination and awakened his sense of justice. Does Mum know you're coming with me? he asks and Tomer replies, oh yes, I told her, and she said I should dress up smartly for the court, and Avner is pleasantly surprised by the unobtrusive cooperation, and he puts on his gown and strides confidently down the corridor, his excited son beside him. Nasreen comes running to meet them, her hair gathered up neatly and her face tense, introduces them to her husband, a short and rotund young man, and their firstborn son, who peers curiously at his son, and because he no longer has an intern he sits Tomer at his side, signalling to him to stand when the judge comes in, a new judge whom he doesn't recognise, young and sensitive-looking. Do it for the sake of the kids, he mumbles, his eyes roving from his son to Nasreen's son, as if he's strayed into a house of prayer rather than a courthouse, the presence of the children gives him a forgotten sense of power, and when the state attorney announces that the woman's brother is an active member of a terrorist cell, implicated in acts of violence, and therefore her presence here threatens the security of the state, he rises to his feet immediately and says it is inconceivable that rational judgment will not be exercised here, for more than ten years she has held a residential permit and throughout that time she has had no contact with her brother, and there is no security risk involved in granting an extension of this permit, furthermore the decision to expel is unfair and disproportionate and a violation of the legal right of the husband and the children to maintain a family life in the state of which they are citizens. My clients are people of peace and integrity, he proclaims with heartfelt passion, let them refute the suspicions raised against them.

To his satisfaction, the judge is giving the state attorney a hard time too, is there any evidence that she has actually met her brother? And what precisely is the extent of his involvement? And Avner glances at the small, silent group of spectators, at Nasreen's son standing close to his father. It seems everything is happening over the heads of those involved, as if the officers of the court were surgeons presiding over the anaesthetised and ventilated body in the operating theatre, where the patient has no hand in his fate, and they are even removed from the courtroom while the state attorney briefs the judge on the classified material, and when counsel for the security services arrives, looking strangely similar to the husband, Nasreen clutches her son and wails, what's going to happen, the judge doesn't believe us, I have nothing to do with my brother, nothing, he was a gambler and a thief, he stole money from me, he stole from all the family, no one wants any connection with him.

Don't expect the verdict to be given today, he reminds his son, who is looking with concern at the distraught woman, they'll fix a date for another session, and Tomer says, this really is a tough problem, Dad, I believe her when she says she hasn't been in touch with her brother, but if he turns up in the middle of the night and asks for help, won't she help him? If your sister asks for your help, you'll give it, won't you? And he sighs, I prefer not to ask, Tomer, I know the answer, but I still wouldn't expel her on those grounds, there are risks that have to be taken. But it's obvious this isn't a simple problem and that's why the case is liable to drag on for months, he says, and how surprised is he when immediately after the recess the judge delivers the verdict in a resolute tone and instructs the Ministry of the Interior to restore to the claimant the status of temporary resident, with a provisional permit which may be extended to allow permanent habitation, since the security risk represented by the brother isn't an exclusive consideration but one of several which the security services are entitled to probe, and furthermore the classified evidence has confirmed that she did indeed sever all contact with him as stated in the petition, and it is therefore appropriate to continue giving the claimant temporary residence rights, unless a new body of evidence comes to light, and when they all rise he looks on with admiration as the judge leaves the courtroom, it's been a long time since he stood up at the end of a case feeling so fulfilled, so steady on his feet. Perhaps there is still hope, not only for this family but for the state as well, if the people who grow up here are capable of seeing the totality of considerations, and recognising that the security consideration isn't the only one, and Nasreen hugs him in gratitude, I'll tell Ali he was absolutely right about you, she cries joyfully, you know he wanted to be here today but he was held up at the checkpoint.

Dad, I'm really happy for them but a bit worried too, just imagine if her brother succeeds in carrying out a terrorist attack, his son says to him as they walk out into the rainy day, and Avner replies, I'm not comfortable about this either and believe me, if that happened there's no way I'd ever defend him, unlike some members of my profession, but I want to believe that in the end legal processes like this one move danger further away rather than bringing it closer.

The very next morning he goes to a letting agency near his office. I'm looking for a three-room apartment on a long lease, with a garden or a large balcony, he announces, and he specifies the neighbourhood he wants and the rent he's prepared to pay; following his recent success he feels confident enough to offer a little more, and the heavily made-up agent wrinkles her brow as she stares at the computer screen, at the moment I have nothing in that locality, she says, would you consider compromising on the area, the further out you go from the centre the more choice there is, and he shakes his head, no, not under any circumstances, being close to his children is critical, he wants them to be within walking distance, so Tomer can get there easily, without a lot of tiresome advance planning, sorting out clothes and school-bags ahead of time.

Tell me if anything turns up he says, disappointed, and turns to the door, it really is urgent, and she stops him, wait a moment, I was offered an apartment in that area just this morning, but I haven't seen it yet, three rooms with a garden, fully furnished. And he asks, which street? and she says, we can't disclose precise details at this stage, once I've seen it I'll update you.

Perhaps I could come with you, he suggests, and she says no, that isn't the way it's done, we don't show apartments before we've seen them ourselves, but he insists, I'm free this morning and that doesn't happen very often, I need to find an apartment urgently, I've nowhere to take my kids, and immediately it turns out she too is a divorcee with children, and his predicament touches her heart and she relents, locking the office door and offering him a seat in her car. The owners of the property are academics, she says derisively, smoothing down her hair, dyed a dazzling peroxide blonde, they're off to New York for two years at least, term starts soon and they're in a real hurry, I hope they'll be flexible on the price, and having exhausted the topic of the apartment they haven't yet seen, she tells him about her divorce, I pleaded with my husband to live close to us, it's so important for the kids, but he's always thought only about himself, and he bought an apartment in a military compound, the children can only go there at weekends and even that isn't a lot of fun for them, they're missing out on so much, and well done to you, putting their needs first, she adds in an admiring tone, I'll do everything I can to find you an apartment close to them, where did you say they live? He names the street again, just as she's parking her car not far from his former home.

From the point of view of location it's perfect, she says, I just hope the apartment itself is suitable, sometimes people describe a palace and when I get there it turns out to be a ruin, unfit for human habitation, you have no idea how cheeky people can be, and that's why I always check first. I never bring a client in until I've seen it for myself, but he's no longer listening to her words because her quick footsteps, her stiletto heels drilling into the tarmac, are turning now towards a narrow and chilly alleyway that's so familiar to him he could have constructed it himself between the cramped buildings and he wonders, is it just for a short cut she's brought him this way, or is the apartment somewhere round here, and if so this is something he can't possibly accept, resigning himself to living so close to her, to see her coming and going, opening the gate and closing it at once, he doesn't need this niggling torment and his throat is dry when he tries to put a question to the agent, who's talking incessantly, and just as they pass the closed gate she takes a note from the pocket of her coat, concealing it from him and following the house numbers.

I left the documents behind in the office, she says, you can sign for me later, and he whispers, if it's in this alleyway it really doesn't suit me, but she isn't listening and already she's moved ahead and her sharp red-varnished fingernails are pressing the familiar bell-push, and before he has time to retreat the door opens and he sees her, so pale by comparison with the flamboyant agent, a blurred image of herself in black and white, wearing a long and dark golf sweater, her close-cropped hair damp and sticking to her skull, giving her the appearance of a miserable and neglected urchin, and the agent says hastily, I'd like you to meet my client who is genuinely interested in renting this property, and this lady is the householder, coaxing them as if they were shy children who need to be pushed into making friends.

Should we go inside? she suggests, since both of them are rooted to the spot, hurt and embarrassed and unable to move, as if they've collided with each other and the force of the impact has paralysed them, and there's no one to be angry with because it's no one's fault, and yet anger fills the air between them and the agent is already hurrying inside, invading the little garden and leaving them there, facing each other, until a faint smile rises to Talia's lips, why didn't I think of you, she says, what a pity, we could have saved the middleman's fee.

Those are the words that accompany him all that day and the days to come, when he paces the familiar rooms, when he signs the contract without even reading it, jolted for a moment on seeing his name beside hers, as if it's a marriage contract that has been drawn up, we could have saved the middleman's fee. It all happened so suddenly, she said, just a week ago she received the offer, and overnight she took the decision to go, she needed to get far away from here, and he packs his few possessions which migrated with him to his mother's house, what a pity, we could have saved the middleman's fee, that's what she said to me, he tells Dina who's carefully folding his clothes and putting them into bags, again you're leaving before me, she smiles, again you're leaving me alone with Mum, I thought we were going to live like this for ever, the three of us, and he says, but then I left too early, and now I'm leaving too late, and she looks at him thoughtfully, I'm not sure, Avni, it seems to me this timing is exactly right for you.

And the first evening, after he's left his clothes in the ornate and solid oak wardrobe, among her clothes, left there with his agreement, alongside some of the dead man's clothes, I'll come round in the summer and sort everything out, she promised, he stretches out on the sofa on which Rafael breathed his last breaths, and a joyful pain fills him, a painful joy, I didn't know such a combination could exist, he reflects, who knows what else I am going to discover, and in the night on her bedlinen, experimenting with her double downy woollen blanket, so many things she left behind there, towels and kitchen utensils and books, there was barely any room in the house for his possessions, he thinks that since the two of them, she and the dead man, are absent from the house in precisely the same incontrovertible way, and yet their clothes are present there in an incontrovertible way, perhaps they are existing together somewhere far away exactly as they dreamed, perhaps they went away together and together they are destined to return and he is left here like the priest in a sanctuary, keeping the flame alive for them, or perhaps the two of them have died, died together, the painful gap has been erased and he is the last who has survived to testify to their love, as if he were their only son, the fruit of their longing and desire.

I too shall yet have such a love, is his prayer between the white sheets. It seems he's grown accustomed to the hard bed in his mother's house and suddenly he feels he's sinking into the softness of pillows and blankets and mattress and he shudders, clutching the sides of the bed, echoing in his ears are his mother's stories about the marshes bordering on the lake, how they used to crawl like crocodiles so they wouldn't sink, is he not crawling too, and has been year after year, but how tiring it is, time perhaps to pack it all in. Between sleep and consciousness he lets go of the sides of the bed, and a strange delight sweeps over him as he's swallowed up by the moist softness of the marshes that were drained before he was born, and in the morning he's almost surprised to find himself awake, I still exist, I exist still, exist I still, he turns the words over, and when he leaves the apartment and sets out for his children's house to walk to school with Yotam, locking the gate behind him, he will see in his mind's eye the tall and girlish woman who offered him water when he collapsed at the end of the alleyway, I told her I lived here, he will remember, and this is where she will find me if she wants me, she believed me, although I was lying, and the lie has now become the truth.

Chapter Thirteen

The timescale allotted to her will be equivalent to the duration of pregnancy, in nine months from now you will have a child, they promised her the day she signed the contract, perhaps even earlier, there are pleasant surprises too. She has already been pleasantly surprised, realising to what extent the anticipated change is gathering her in, tightening her days. No more idle distractions and wasting time, suddenly every free moment is devoted to them, to those scattered communities in Spain, standing on the verge of annihilation, to those Jews who will be forced to choose between expulsion and conversion, between poverty-stricken exile and abandoning the faith of their ancestors. Can the faith of the ancestors really serve as a substitute for home, homeland, security, it is stripped of love after all, and yet there are those who will say faith and faith alone is the one and the sole security, fragments of families, fragments of communities, setting out broken-spirited for unknown lands, anything rather than abandon their faith. What was the role of the holy child of La Guardia in this cruel choice that was put before hundreds of thousands of human beings? A child who never existed and never was born, whose body was not found, whose disappearance was reported by no one, succeeded in whipping up a storm that led to the drafting of the expulsion order imposed on the Jews of Spain, since in spite of conflicting testimony and in the absence of any evidence, the Jews of La Guardia were accused of a horrific ritual murder. The stories that circulated described how, when the boy was bound and his heart ripped from his body, the earth shook and the sky turned dark, it was also said he was stolen from his blind mother and the instant his soul left his body the light of her eyes was restored to her. Was this blood-libel an exceptional event, or part of a systematic campaign to prepare the ground for the impending expulsion? She pondered this question in the first article she published, nearly twenty years ago, the article that was praised so fulsomely by the dean at the bus-stop, when she was broken, and told her story.

But this time she isn't letting any concern unravel the thread of her concentration, and there is certainly no shortage of concerns, impossible even to count them: who will the child be, the one allotted to her, is she really sure she can cope with the difficulties he'll bring with him, how will Gideon react and how will all this affect Nitzan, is her little family heading towards disintegration, and the toughest question of them all, is this really an act of lunacy, with drastic consequences that will not be slow in coming, and every one of these concerns splits into scores of secondary concerns, and yet she succeeds in setting them all aside, as she did many years ago, when she used to sit for hours in the library, engrossed in her work, writing the first dissertations, and it seemed her way was clear before her. How happy those years were, had she not longed for this as long as she could remember? To study, amass knowledge, cling to solid facts like stakes in the ground, dates, processes, not morbid imagination, what could have been, what was not, but what was and was so, what was real.

As then she sits facing her books, and it seems for the first time since the action that threw her off course she is towing behind her a sturdy rope that will not be easily broken, and only now and then when she gets up from her seat to stretch her bones does she look around her and for a moment wonder where she is, or more to the point, when she is, because sometimes she's a girl studying for the baccalaureate in precisely this room, in the cramped lounge of her mother's house, and at times the months of pregnancy reverberate in her, how alarmed she was when Gideon left her and only Orly was by her side, ostensibly supporting her and at the same time intensifying her isolation with her forbidden stories, with her supercilious glances at the distended young belly.

I'm not bringing any children into the world, she used to promise repeatedly, I don't intend to look after anyone, I've had enough trouble bringing up my younger brothers, and it's because of them I haven't had any kids, I just want to look after myself, and Dina would listen to her, thoroughly perplexed. Perhaps she's right, perhaps it really is perverse, this absolute obligation, from now until death to care for someone else, someone she doesn't even know, the fact that he's been a temporary resident inside her doesn't mean she's going to like him, and she's on her own, if only Gideon were with her, enjoying her and her pregnancy, she would certainly feel encouraged, but he's left, he left even before he knew that the creature which had doubled itself had reverted to single status, and she looks back now at those days with tolerant bemusement, how little we know about what's in store for us. She struggled so hard back then to endure the thought of the little person who needed her, while now she can't endure the opposite thought, that there won't still be on the face of the earth a little person who needs her, and to reach him she'll turn worlds upside down, and who knows, perhaps she's got it wrong again, wandering blindly in the labyrinth of her life, precisely as she used to then, and perhaps what was good for her then isn't suited to these days, but the moment the doubts intensify she kicks them brusquely aside, not now, the war is still in full spate, in the heat of battle you can't begin to doubt its urgency, you need to wait for the moment of truth, follow Gideon's example. She knows that's what he's waiting for, only a few days ago he said to her, surely you're not going through with this, I know you, at the moment of truth you'll get cold feet, when you're confronted by the child and you're asking yourself what he means to you, and if you really want to commit yourself to him from now until the end of your life.

Sometimes within the stream of time that advances and recedes, sending up sticky foam, she misses him, the early days of their love which are imprinted in her indelibly, what was there that anyone could consider unacceptable? She remembers her mother trying to dissuade her, how can you give up Eytan, any woman would love to have a husband like that, you're making a dreadful mistake, and the harsh words she found immensely gratifying, she'd succeeded in driving her dreamy mother, always wrapped up in herself, to the point of losing control. What do you know about it anyway, she answered her, what do you know about love, because Eytan's good qualities lost their powers of attraction the moment she met Gideon, and she knew her mother was watching the turnaround tensely, after all she had made no secret of her amazement that such a paragon of masculinity was taking an interest in her daughter, and now she watched their parting with sorrow and scowled at the stocky and introspective man who took his place, but she herself was ecstatic for months on end. She loved looking into his eyes, narrowed one moment and the next suddenly bursting into life, she loved listening to him, again and again she would wipe away a tear when he talked about his mother, who died in her prime and left him alone with his father, a dour and depressive Holocaust survivor who was constantly telling him how sorry he was, even apologising for giving him life. If it was up to me you wouldn't have been born, was his steadfast reassurance, but your mother insisted and now what, she's died and left me with you, forgive me, son, for bringing you into this terrible world, and he used to go down on his knees and plead, and his little boy would forgive him yet again, and Dina loved stroking his arm as they talked, side by side on a thin mattress, pine trees lowering above them, perfuming the air with a sticky smell of resin, and it seemed they were inhabiting a higher plane of existence, and normal life taking place down below on the ground wasn't touching them at all. Down below were her mother and her brother and Eytan and a few friends, but up on the roof amid the treetops everything was vivid and sharp, pain and pleasure and intimacy, she loved feeling close to him in a way she had never known before, he didn't put pressure on her and didn't steal anything from her, when he was silent she too was present in his silence, and when he spoke she was always surprised to hear him choosing the same words she would have chosen, but he didn't exert himself at all, didn't strive to curry favour. She loved having it proved to her again and again how comfortable he felt in the world, mainly because he didn't need its approval, he was comfortable in his squat and muscular body, comfortable inside her, when her thighs were wrapped around his body and she clung to him, so there would be no partition between his skin and her skin, and yet there always was, and the effort to eliminate it imbued days and nights with a pungent and feverish taste which lingered a long time, over so many years, and from time to time it cropped up again even afterwards, and surely it was this that set the process in motion.

What kind of thorny project is created by the vacuum seeking to be filled, she thinks, and we yearn for what will starve us, not what will satisfy, but it seems to her that recently this mysterious mechanism has been spoilt, from the moment the balance was disrupted and the non-existent covered the existent almost entirely, like an eclipse of the sun, and even if at times she longs to return home in the dead of night, and creep naked into their bed, roll aside the stone of controversy and concentrate on love, or invite him to come to her, she's reluctant to contact him, there's no point to it, it will only weaken her, and perhaps he won't want her at all, she doesn't know what's going on in his life, better not to know. When she passes news-stands she occasionally sees a picture he's taken on a front page, recognising from a distance his fresh vision, that somehow he's managed to preserve all these years. So it seems he's working normally, and he wakes Nitzan in the morning and takes her to school and comes home early to be with her in the evening, he does the shopping and cooks the meals and makes sure she goes to bed on time, all this she hears from her daughter, who describes to her with some amusement her father's record as a single parent, awesome, she says generously, sharing his efforts with her mother and not a word of complaint, but beyond this she knows nothing, who is he talking to, who is he seeing, what is he planning to do, does he miss her; of course these aren't questions she can ask her daughter, who to her surprise doesn't seem perturbed by the change that's taken place or by the one that's coming.

Almost every day she visits her there, at Grandma's house, after school, and it soon becomes evident that shared lodgings in themselves don't encourage close contact, while hospitality affords time that is clear and purged of surprises. A long time since they spent so much time together, Dina realises, astonished, there are moments when it seems to her they are drifting apart, and that is why they have seen fit to devote so much attention to each other, both understanding that something incomparably precious is coming to an end. Is this childhood? Is this their individual existence, mother and only daughter, only daughter and mother? And of this they hardly ever speak. She does try from time to time, but Nitzan is evasive, let it go, it's between you and Dad, I already told you, if it's so important to you, go ahead and all the rest will sort itself out somehow.

Sometimes she pokes gentle fun at her father, describing his failures in household management, he turned all my clothes pink, she grins, and his pasta is a disgrace, he never takes it out in time, and when Dina comments cautiously, it must be hard for you like this, living alone with him, she says, that's enough, Mum, don't suddenly turn psychologist on me, I know this is my time and it really isn't that hard, it's nice to change colours now and then, and I have a life too, you know, she chuckles, but she doesn't talk about that either, occasionally her mobile chirps and she texts hurried messages, her fingers dancing on the keys, sometimes going aside and conversing in a low voice, and Dina watches her with curiosity, it seems it's been easier for her since she left the house, and apparently a new relationship is growing up between them now, relaxed, ventilated, healthy perhaps? Is this what health is like, distant and lacking weight?

It's like a lunch-club here, she laughs sometimes when she arrives, I eat and do my homework and then go home, and she sits down on the floor of the lounge and takes books and exercise-books from her briefcase, all this history homework they've given us, she grumbles, by the summer you'll have finished with your shenanigans, right? I'm counting on you to help me prepare for the exam, and Dina smiles at her, of course, I've been waiting for this for years, though I reckon you can cope easily enough without my help, and sure enough before long she stands up and stretches, that's it, I've finished, she says, I'll go and see how Grandma is.

What's going on, why is she sleeping so much? she complains when she returns to the room, I wanted to talk to her, and

Dina says, the important thing is, she looks relaxed. She's dreaming, making up stories, that's what she likes doing the most. So perhaps we should go for a stroll, Nitzan suggests, it's really nice outside and by the time we get back she should be awake, and Dina says, good idea, I need some air, I haven't been out of the house yet today.

No shortage of air round here, Nitzan grins, and sure enough the wind is stalking them, lying in wait among the housing projects, whirling around the mock-archways, playing havoc with their hair until they find themselves almost entangled together. Come on, let's jump, Orly said to her that time on the roof, let's die together. Her hair is caught up in Nitzan's honey-coloured tresses, and she looks at her in wonderment, how beautiful she is, a short black sleeveless coat is wrapped around her, a sweater coloured bright turquoise sets off her regal pallor, and she grips her round the shoulders as they arrive at the fringe of the development, where terraced houses kiss the desert. Look, it's starting to rain, she says, we should go back, and Nitzan protests, not yet, it's only drizzling, you remember the first umbrella you bought me? I liked it so much I walked around with it open even indoors, and Dina says, an umbrella wouldn't do us any harm right now, see that black cloud overhead, and when she looks up she sees a woman coming out to the balcony opposite to get the washing in, is it because she's just been remembering Orly that she thinks it's her; sometimes when you think of somebody you come across that person in reality, on the second floor, on a roof-balcony crammed with flowerpots, a full-bodied, beautiful woman, with bronze hair stirring in the wind, gathering up the laundry and hurrying inside, is this her? In the early years she imagined she saw her everywhere, red curls would arouse her hopes, guilt and longing too, again and again she tried to locate her, to glean information about her, without success, is this her? Of course you could examine the mail-box, even ring the doorbell, but you prefer to keep on walking; if not here then somewhere else, where a black cloud is shedding rain, in another house, in another country, does she remember her too on windy days?

This is the wind she now wants to swallow, let it blow inside her, shake her roots, life moves in giant circles, sometimes the life of a human being is insufficient to complete the circle, and those who come after him are incapable of understanding, and in fact she too is far from comprehending the meaning of things, repeating the simple facts is all she's capable of, something that was and was so, even if today she would have behaved otherwise, and she hugs her daughter and the two of them stride along as the wind frolics about them, trying to blow them into the desert.

I must tell you something, she contacts Gideon in the night and he's surprised, since her birthday they've hardly spoken, you remember Orly? she pants, I think I saw her today in my mother's neighbourhood, and Gideon isn't impressed, yes, I know she's back in the country, I bumped into her in the street a few months ago when I was taking Nitzan to her ballet class, she was waiting for some girl, but I don't think she lives in Armon Hanatziv. Where then? she asks, stunned by the load of information landing suddenly on her head, and he says, I don't remember exactly, somewhere outside the city, she was doing some kind of professional survey, she manages a hedge fund if I understood it right, I don't remember, it was a long time ago. So why didn't you tell me when you could still remember, why have you hidden this from me? And he says, it's such a sensitive topic for you, I didn't know how you'd react, and indeed how will she react, what is this information worth in her life, come to me now, Gidi, she whispers, perhaps this is how she'll react, and he says, how can I come, there's a little girl here whose mother has left home, I'm a single parent.

Your little girl is quite big now, she laughs, you can leave her alone for an hour or two, and he grumbles, an hour or two, is that all the time you're allocating to me? Supposing I want more? A light and mischievous wind blows at them, from those days, from their history, a little comma in the chronicles of the nations, but nearly twenty years out of their lives, and she remembers how he supported her back then, you've done the right thing, stop blaming yourself, you've been done an injustice, this job should have been yours, and she asks, does she have a family, does she have a husband and children? and he says, she was talking so much I couldn't take it all in, but she definitely had a child or two with her.

And what's a hedge fund anyway? she asks, and he chuckles, is it urgent for you to know that right now? And she says, not really, I can wait until you come round here to explain it to me, and he says, sorry, Dini, there's no point, the day you say you're giving up I'll gladly come to you, but this child of yours is driving a wedge between us, it's either me or him, and she tries to steady her voice, good night, Gidi, and he sighs, good night, and she sees him lying on their bed, reading without spectacles, the book close to his eyes and sinking over his face when he sleeps, and the little lamp is still on, she doesn't want to lose him, a last spark remains precious to her heart, a slender reading light, but she can't give up the child either, and she leaves the bed and wanders round the house, peering into her mother's bedroom; she's lying on her back with eyes closed and hands folded on the blanket, her limbs in exemplary order as if arranged in readiness for the coffin, and again she wonders about this new phase in her mother's existence, she's turned over the past year into an almost supernatural being.

At a time when most old people of her age are concerned exclusively with their aches and pains, burdening the members of their families with their ailing bodies and soon-to-be-vacated minds, her mother of all people is succeeding in hovering above the needs of her corporeal existence, she doesn't ask for anything and doesn't complain, letting Rachela wash her limbs and change her nappies, munching obediently and swallowing her medications, and beyond this she is barely present in reality, and yet, in a few moments of lucidity she surprises them with clear and rational observations, until it seems to Dina she's only pretending to be asleep, she's listening to them as attentively as ever, monitoring their activities as if wanting to know how they will run their lives after her death, located in a kind of third form of existence, which isn't life and isn't death, isn't growing and isn't static.

How simplistic is this crude distinction, her mother is trying to say, as it seems the very qualities that made her life difficult are good for her in her latter days, there are those who live well and those who die well, and indeed, how well her third form of existence suits her, a new nobility is perceptible in her features, oy, Mum, in the very place where all are withering you are flourishing, she says aloud, and her mother opens her eyes and smiles a mischievous smile at her, and she has no idea if there's deep understanding in it or utter detachment, and she flops down, exhausted, in the armchair facing her. How do they know what's the right thing to do? How do they know where the mistakes lie? After all, only with the passage of the years does the full picture become entirely clear, and although her mother is silent it seems to her she knows the answer, knows there is no answer, apparently most things aren't absolutely right or absolutely wrong, the question is what are we to do with them, and again a smile rises to her lips and her fingers move on her arm in circular patterns as if she were holding a pen and writing, and Dina sprawls in the armchair and in some implausible fashion she feels protected, more so than she has ever felt before. How can this moribund old woman protect her? What a comical thought, and yet firm and enduring, and it seems to her if she falls she'll catch her, and her grasp will be as soft as this blanket that she pulls from the open wardrobe and wraps around herself and thus she falls asleep, sitting in the armchair facing her smiling mother, just as well Gideon didn't come, she thinks, nights with him have become more of the same to me and a night like this hasn't happened yet, and nor will it, because everything's bound to change.

In the morning the ringing of the phone wakes her, and she's just a little bit excited seeing his name on the screen, perhaps he regrets refusing me, perhaps he'll suggest he comes round tonight, but he's being hard and practical, Nitzan came home early this morning and since then she's been lying on her bed in floods of tears, crying incessantly, he reports, she won't tell me what's happened. I have to leave soon, so you'd better come home and relieve me, she can't be left alone, and she says, of course, I'm on my way, dressing hastily and saying goodbye to Rachela, who's already busy in the kitchen, humming some mournful tune. What's happened to her, what can this be, only yesterday they parted company and everything was fine, it must be that boy, only the pains of love drive girls to take to their beds, and when she enters the building Gideon is already on the stairs, nearly a month since she's seen him and her heart goes out to him, so you didn't have a girl at home last night, she remembers, you could have come to me.

Let me know if you get anything out of her, he cuts her short and she says, of course, will you be back by four, I'm teaching this afternoon, and he replies, no problem, and already he's disappeared, and she stands on the threshold of the apartment, which looks to her suddenly spacious in comparison with her mother's house, surprised to find just how well the apartment is functioning without her. Clean and orderly it's all set out before her, the sink empty of utensils and the fridge full, the cat dozing on the sofa, sleek and pampered, and she goes into Nitzan's room, the curtain is flapping vigorously over the bed, a cold breeze is blowing and she hurries to close the window, but a sharp cry from the bed stays her arm, don't close it, I need air, I'm suffocating.

What's happened, Nitzi, she sits down beside her and tries to draw the fragile form towards her, but her daughter recoils from her touch, leave me alone, she yells and throws off the blanket, face flushed and eyes swollen, and Dina coaxes her, tell me what's happened, let me help you, and her daughter shakes her head tearfully, I'm beyond help, I want to die.

Relax, sweetheart, that's how you feel now but in a day or two you'll feel better, she promises her, what's happened, has he left you? and Nitzan peers at her in astonishment through the tangled mass of wet hair, who? and after a moment of confusion she asks her, how do you know? And Dina says, I saw you here together a few months ago, I still don't know why you needed to lie to me.

Because he's older than me, Nitzan wails, I was afraid if you knew how old he was you wouldn't let me see him, he's nine years older than me, and Dina says, that really is a huge gap at that age, amazed to hear how much authority her daughter attributes to her, the power to separate a pair of lovers. So all this time you've been together? she asks carefully, and Nitzan sits up and leans against the wall, wiping away her tears with the back of her hand, not exactly, she says, he really wanted that but I was scared, it took me a long time before I started trusting him, and now I regret it so much, she groans again, pulling the blanket over herself, and Dina asks, what is it you regret?

On Sabbath I had the house to myself, she whispers urgently, Dad wasn't here, so I invited him and we were together all day, and in the end you know what, it happened, for the first time, because I always wanted to wait, I felt it was too soon for me, but on Sabbath we were having such a good time together and I thought well, why not, I love him so much and he loves me, and then he didn't contact me but I wasn't worried, I reckoned he was busy, and yesterday I went to his house after I'd been at your place, and he was kind of cold, like we were strangers. And suddenly he said he was already moving on, he's met up with his ex and decided what he really wants is to go back to her, and that was after we slept together, I'll never go with anyone again as long as I live, and Dina absorbs the painful information in silence, her body tensed and the words thumping her with clenched fists. This hasn't happened, why did it happen, she'll make sure it doesn't happen, but it's already happened, the moment came and she was incapable of doing anything to help her, how bitter is the total powerlessness of the all-powerful mother, how easy it was to cheer her up when she was little, a sweet on a stick, an ice cream tub, the moon in the sky, and now what, on the very threshold of her love-life she's been dumped, and she feels she could happily rip that boy to shreds, how dare he violate her youth, like twins in the womb they lay on that bed, half-clothed, how shocking the sight had been, did she see the desertion there between them, this was exactly the way her twin brother abandoned her on the very threshold of her life, leaving her to tremble alone in the dark like a frightened rabbit.

I'm sorry, my darling, she sighs, cautiously caressing the scrawny arm, it really is terribly hard but everyone goes through it one way or another, the main thing is not to take any blame on yourself, don't let it damage your confidence, and Nitzan interrupts her, oh, Mum, it must be my fault, I disappointed him, and that's a fact, if he wanted me so much, how come everything changed? And Dina protests, that's nonsense, there are some men around who lose interest once they've got what they're after, and that's their problem, how can you blame yourself? There's poison in that way of thinking, steer well clear of it.

Has this happened to you too? Nitzan whimpers, and her first impulse is to invent for her some truly horrific desertion stories to serve as consolation. Not really, she admits, but it didn't happen to me only because I was so afraid of rejection I preferred to stay by myself, can you imagine it, I had my first boyfriend at twenty-four, and even him I was with mainly because he wanted me, and Nitzan sighs, maybe it's healthier that way, at least nobody hurt you, but Dina interrupts her, what's healthy about it? I hurt myself, nobody can hurt us more than we hurt ourselves.

So were you with Dad only because he wanted you? she asks, and Dina says, no, with your father it was different, the love I felt for him was stronger than the fear, apparently, but believe me I've been through all kinds of desertions, Nitzi, anyone who hasn't been deserted has never been connected, and if you're not connected you're not really alive, no challenges, no growth, I'm sorry, my darling, this is the price of living, of daring, just don't give up, as you once said to me yourself, don't give up on what's important to you, and Nitzan interrupts her, that's enough Mum, all this pathos! and for the first time a smile appears on her puffy face, and Dina is embarrassed, I really believe in what I'm saying, and Nitzan says, of course, but why does it sound as if you're moving away from me?

Returning to her car after the lecture she soon finds herself on the road leading to her house, and it comes as no surprise to her, her hands and her feet guiding her this way; after all this is what coming home is like, like the leaving of it, almost casual, without proclamations and promises, and so when the three them sit down together round the table for the first time in weeks, and eat supper, this too will be low-key, and perhaps when the invitation comes to meet the child, it will be the same: here is the little boy, do you want to be his mother? Here comes the moment of truth, can you stand up to it? I know you, he said, you'll get cold feet, you'll run away, and what if he's right, because this evening for example when she sits between the two of them she feels she's lacking nothing; Nitzan is tucking with great gusto into the fried eggs that Gideon served up, dipping fresh bread in the yolk, and apparently feeling much better, and Dina marvels at the way the consoling power of motherhood is gradually returning to her. It never occurred to her that her mother could help her in a time of adversity, on the contrary, all she could expect was the admonitory finger wagging at her, I told you, I warned you, and only now, when she can hardly speak and there's no knowing if she understands, it seems to her she's supporting her, and even this is a straw she's prepared to clutch at, the straw of an embrace from those desiccated arms, and who knows, maybe this is the reason Nitzan is stronger than me, she reflects, if I were in her shoes I'd be weeping bitterly day after day, not stuffing myself with fresh bread and fried eggs but throwing up my stomach contents, scraping the skin that he touched, I'd be inconsolable, inconsolable, while she's already taking her seat on the sofa in front of the TV. Mummydaddy, she calls them with a sweet smile as she used to when she was little, come on, let's watch a movie together! It's been ages since we've done that. And they too smile at her in the old style, how endearing she can be, little rabbit, cute and lively squirrel. How they used to enjoy those mock-arguments, which does she resemble more, squirrel or rabbit, and what do we give her to eat, carrot or nuts, and now she's been dumped, but her fingers are already on the remote, flicking through the options, and she's calling out the titles of the films. We'll find something we'll all enjoy, she announces, with such strange exuberance that Dina begins to suspect, and even to hope with all her heart, maybe the whole of this crisis was staged for her benefit, a ploy to bring her home, and she turns to Gideon with a question in her eyes. Leave it, he grimaces, you'll never find a film we all like. How taciturn he is this evening, digesting her presence in silence, keeping his distance, where was he last Sabbath? Who was he with?

Give over, Dad, you're always spoiling things, Nitzan complains. Look, this is a movie my friends recommended, come on, let's roll it, and Dina is already sitting beside her on the sofa, what difference does it make which film they see, just to be together, the three of them like this, in the forgotten intimacy of a domestic evening, but Gideon is grousing as always, what's this about? You know I hate melodramas, let's watch a documentary, and Nitzan reproaches him, oh, what a misery-guts you are, this is a really cool movie about a teacher having an affair with his pupil and she has a baby and gives it up for adoption, and then it all gets complicated.

You can bet it gets complicated, Gideon mutters, turning to Dina with an icy glance and she avoids his eyes and knits her fingers together hard, and Nitzan asks, what's going on? Is it because of the adoption? Woops, how sensitive everyone is here, come on, get over it, you're grown-ups aren't you, and already she's turning off the light and sitting with legs folded, laying her head on Dina's shoulder, and she for her part is stunned by the rapid and inexplicable turn of events, in the course of this day and also on the screen before her, where the child is given up for adoption by his biological father, who doesn't know anything about it until his pupil comes back into his life, and then a loud snort is heard from Gideon's armchair, and Dina wipes away the tears that have flowed unchecked this past hour, what a nightmare, Nitzi, what a terrifying film, and Nitzan whimpers in her arms, you're right, I don't know why my friends raved about it so much.

We're surrounded by enigmas, Dina sighs, large and small, her temples pounding and her head aching, what's her daughter trying to tell her, what's this evening trying to tell her, how confusing the signs are, and when Gideon emits another snort Nitzan bursts into laughter, and at once her voice breaks, oh, Mummy, I love him so much, I can't believe it's over, all my life I've never loved anyone like that, and Dina presses her to her heart, time will soften it, my darling, every day will be a little easier, and there will be many more loves, I promise you, and she caresses her body slowly, the new-old love that the girl is lavishing on her suddenly, the memory of their close contact, memory of her childhood, this exists, it's yours, perhaps this is what you'll understand at the moment of truth, this was and therefore it exists, even if it never returns but only flickers from time to time in what remains of your life, this isn't the sun but memory of the sun, distant rays of warmth, most people are satisfied with this, what about you?

I want to sleep, Nitzan wails, I want to sleep and not wake up, how can he stop loving me? And Dina escorts her to her bed and spreads the blanket over her, the heating's already been turned off and cold spreads through the house. The love that you've experienced won't be taken from you, Nitzan, it's yours, both the love with which you've loved and the love with which you've been loved, it's stored up inside you, we're like cyclamens, like all plants with bulbs and tubers, we have mechanisms for storage and renewal, do you hear?

Yes, Mummy, the girl mumbles agreement with eyes closed and turns on her side, and Dina leans over her and kisses her forehead again and again until her breathing steadies and she falls asleep. No reason to worry, she's sleeping, she's eating, she'll recover. I wish I could take the pain from her but she'll get through it, she has strengths, and she gets up and goes cautiously into the master bedroom like a trespasser, checking out the double bed which is arranged in meticulous order, for some reason it seems no one has slept in it for a long time, I'm returning to my house, to my daughter, so why does it seem to me this is a separation?

One week later precisely the phone will ring after midnight, while outside the rain is teeming, with thunder and lightning, and she responds in panic, sure this must be her brother calling to report her mother's death. Mum, Mum, her heart pounds as she fumbles for the phone in the dark, but an animated voice with a heavy Russian accent is calling her name, Dina? This is Tanya from the institute, I told you there are pleasant surprises too, and here it is, we've been offered a little boy, you can come and see him. I'll send a picture and details via email and you can give me your answer tomorrow.

Really? How is this is happening so quickly? she mumbles, stunned, and Tanya hesitates, I'll tell you the truth, we offered him to a different family some way ahead of you in the queue, and they made the journey but didn't bond with him and they turned him down, once there's been a refusal it's harder to find someone who's willing, so I thought of you, with you the time factor is critical because of your husband's age.

What does that mean, they didn't bond with him? she asks, thoroughly alarmed, and Tanya says, I don't know exactly, the chemistry wasn't there, if you ask me they're making a mistake, but perhaps their mistake is to your advantage, so let me know tomorrow, goodnight, and Dina's close to hyperventilating, wait a moment, Tanya, tell me about the boy, how old is he, what's his name, what's known about his background?

He's two years old, Tanya replies impatiently, I'm sending you via email all the details known to us, a medical file and a picture. Don't be too scared by the medical file, they sometimes insert bogus illnesses because it's illegal to take a healthy child out of there, and Dina asks, so how do we know his real state of health? and Tanya says, I'll explain to you tomorrow, we know these codes, I promise you the boy is all right, more or less, so don't miss this chance, if you refuse it will take a long time and in the meantime the law may change to your disadvantage, and Dina stands up from the bed in a whirl, her heart pounding ferociously, sending shock-waves around it, all of her body is a giant heart, and the whole building is swaying and tossing in time to its pulsations. This is the moment of truth, this is the beginning, it's starting now, at midnight, as the heavens crack open above her head and she goes out on to her translucent balcony, the cold is intense but she doesn't turn on the heater. To shiver in the cold is what she wants, to hear her teeth chattering, she wants to watch as the fields of the sky are blasted by electricity, she wants electricity to strike her too, she's pleading for a sign, for a signal, since this is a great moment and she's staggering under its weight, it's come too early, before her preparations are completed, more frightening than she expected, since this is what encounter with destiny looks like, although the truth is such encounters take place every moment of a human life, and here we're speaking of a frontal encounter, of known intensity. Is this the possibility of choice, is it the lack of support, the magnitude of the responsibility, the magnitude of the gamble, the magnitude of the distance, to travel to Siberia this week, in the middle of December, to meet a little boy of two years old, can you be his mother, and she turns on the computer, make it so I know, she mumbles, so I'll see the picture and know this is my child, so I'll look into his eyes and know this is my beloved son in whom I am well pleased. Her hands tremble over the keys and she stares at the letters, as a ferocious light floods the balcony, followed immediately by the roll of thunder and to her dismay the computer screen goes blank before her eyes, the light of the street-lamp is extinguished too, it seems the last lightning bolt knocked out all the circuits. Most residents of the street are unperturbed, fast asleep in their warm beds, while for her this is unbearable, she's waiting for the child, she believes when she sees the picture she'll know, she's expecting a dissolution of doubts but this is slow in coming, and perhaps this is the way it's meant to be, saying yes without knowing anything, without seeing anything.

The street-lamp comes back on and with it the computer, my boy my boy my boy, she mumbles, what a long journey you've had to make to reach my mail-box, here it comes, arriving at last, just open the file and you'll meet him, and here he is, filling the screen is a little boy standing with a book in his hands, his hair blond and sparse, his face long, eyes dull and set close together, looking at her without smiling, his forehead high and his lips tightly closed, he's serious and gloomy, he's a stranger. He's not like Nitzan, as she hoped he would be, and he doesn't look like the lost twin who lives in her imagination, not like her or Gideon. He isn't sweet, isn't captivating, he isn't trying to please, he's not asking to be taken, it seems he's resigned to the betrayals he's suffered, apparently he's saying, even without you I can sort out my life, he isn't making it easier for her, not giving her a sign.

Again she'll study him from head to toe, he's wearing red girly sandals and white socks, light coloured trousers, almost tailored, like those of a miniature man, and on his chest is a striped shirt with short sleeves, too big for him, in drab green and white. A bitter smile stretches her lips when she remembers her brother's shirt, is this the sign she has been waiting for? Here he is, her handsome brother in the striped shirt, running into their mother's arms on the lawn and his laughter rolling, while she stands to the side, observing their love with hard eyes, how frozen is his stare, did she stare like that at her mother and her brother? Does he know how to smile, has he ever smiled?

She never saw a child like this, he isn't a child at all, he's a miniature man, a homunculus, sceptical and severe. He's the one studying her, he's looking for a sign and she squirms under his scrutiny, since that's what a moment of truth is like, only when you stand up to it will you understand what a mistake you're making, what challenges await you. Only then will you understand the distance between reality and your dream of warm and tender co-existence, I know you, you don't have the strength for this, and she detaches herself from the picture and opens the second file, the documents laden with expressions most of which she doesn't understand, a meticulous record of countless tests and diagnoses, immunisations and hospital treatments, and when she tries to interpret these through internet searches the results are even more frightening and she returns at once to the picture, which after the brief separation already looks familiar to her. Who are you, young man? All these details say nothing at all about you, on such and such a date you were immunised and on such and such a date you were examined, but who are you? And my fate is in your hands as much as your fate is in mine, and she looks at the book he's holding in his little hands, on the cover is an illustration of a majestic white cat, one forepaw black and the other brown, exactly like their cat, how could she have failed to notice this before? Is this a sign? Is it possible to be satisfied with such little signs when the task is so huge?

In the glare of the lightning flash it seems to her the child is paler, and she puts a cautious finger to his cheek, the thunder's coming soon, she whispers, but don't be afraid, Mummy will look after you, because it seems a change has been taking place since the beginning of the moment of truth, a change she wasn't expecting and is still finding hard to understand. No, it isn't for the purpose of getting from him the tenderness and warmth that she deserves to receive from her daughter that she's taking him in, but the opposite; it's actually by virtue of the abundance that she has received and is giving, that she'll be capable of bringing up this boy, because it's there, stored up inside her, as she promised her daughter, even if it doesn't come back. This isn't the sun but memory of the sun, no one can take it from her, and suddenly the deed takes on a different face, the hard face of the boy, which suits him better this night, with the rain drumming on the roofs, and she opens the window and pokes her head out of it, to the cold rain that's lashing her neck and tugging at her arms.

Her teeth chatter as she gropes her way to the darkroom, where Gideon has slept since she came back home, her hands smarting as she creeps like an alley-cat towards his bed. It seems to her the tips of her fingers are encased in ice, is this the Siberian cold that has suddenly arrived, along with the child? What's up? he murmurs, his arms enfolding her with sleepy warmth, as if he's forgotten they're not supposed to be touching, barely on speaking terms, and she's emboldened by his embrace and lays her damp head on his chest. Gidi, listen, they've found us a child, we need to go there, come and see his picture on my computer, but to her dismay he pushes her away and sits up, what? What are you talking about? I'm not interested in seeing a picture of any kid, I'm not going anywhere!

But you promised, you promised! she cries, pulling his arm and he rebuffs her brusquely. Calm down, you want to wake

Nitzan? I didn't promise you anything, for months I've been telling you over and over again this isn't what I want, and you've ignored it the way you ignore everything you don't like to hear, and she's not giving up that easily, you promised you'd come with me, they won't let me see him if I go by myself, by law you have to be with me.

I didn't really promise, he mumbles, I didn't think it was going to happen, I thought you'd get over it and I wanted to gain time, and she whispers hoarsely, you wanted to gain time? You didn't really promise? It seems to her that her bones are cracking under the impact of this fusillade, and she stares at her arms, externally there's no movement but under her skin everything is falling apart. How will she stand on her feet and get out of here, how will she hold out her arms to the child, like a snake she'll crawl on her belly across the snowy steppes to faraway Siberia, and perhaps she's already there, she's so cold, she never felt cold like this, spreading from the centre of her body, from her severed umbilical cord, with scissors they cut her from her mother's body, with scissors they cut Nitzan from her, they cut the boy in the picture from the mother who rejected him, a pair of sharp scissors is roaming the streets, detaching partners from each other, decreeing isolation. Gideon, she whispers, I'm begging you for just one thing, come with me on this journey, do what's necessary under the law and then you're free, you have no obligations towards this little boy.

Are you insane? I'm not going to Siberia in the middle of winter, even Stalin took pity on geriatrics like me and didn't send them to Siberia in the winter, maybe in the spring if there's no other choice, and she clutches her throat, gasping, we have no choice, no options, they've offered us a certain child now, if we refuse we lose him, we've already lost one child and I'm not going to let that happen again, and all the time it seems to her he's listening to their conversation, peering at them with his lifeless eyes, and she must go back to his picture to take care of him, so he won't lose hope, and she moves away from the bed and steadies herself against the wall, standing on the threshold and staring at the shadow of her husband's impervious body, sharp scissors cut her from him, and thus it is decreed, tomorrow morning I'm ordering two tickets, her voice as cold as her fingers, if I have to drag you there forcibly, we're going.

But in the morning reality arrives and kicks her with its heaviest boots, we're going, are we? The pressures exerted by the institute don't inspire confidence, the bogus ailments and the genuine ailments, what is really wrong with him, just how sick is he? Why did they refuse to take him? The missing documents, the delayed translations, the savings plan prematurely aborted, she needs to buy tickets and doesn't yet know if she's going, if he will join her. When she woke up this morning he was no longer there, and nor was Nitzan, independent and laconic the pair of them, behaving as if she hasn't come home, only the kid was waiting for her patiently, looking at her with his penetrating eyes.

He stares straight at her, and takes her still further away from the dream, she has to remember again what she learned in the night, according to the law of love it is all one-sided, she will learn to love him as men and women over the generations have learned to love those allocated to them, for she has no choice, he's already there, living in her computer, he has no other home. Inside the computer he is changing and developing, in the morning light his eyes are brighter, but their expression is more severe, she's never seen such a serious child, as if the face of an adult full of years and disappointments has been transplanted on to the body of an infant.

Who are you? Your name wasn't translated for some reason and appears only in Russian, this month two years ago you were born, three days from now will be your birthday, on the very day we're supposed to be seeing you for the first time. Will we bond together? Will you accept a mummy and a daddy, or just a mummy if the truth be told, and a big sister, and a cat, this isn't perfection but it's not at all bad, I hoped things would be different but that's no reason to throw in the towel, you should go with the flow, Nitzan says, even if the river is frozen, even if you're liable to drown, anything's preferable to retreat just now. And here's Tanya from the institute, in touch again, I'm waiting for your final answer, you'll have to present yourselves at the adoption centre three days from now and then go on to the children's home to see the boy, and Dina finds herself trying to play for time, it's hard to get everything sorted at such short notice, we need a few days to make arrangements for our daughter, and I'll have to talk to my employer.

It's Russia, Dina, not Israel, Tanya rebukes her, over there a day means a day and an hour is an hour, you'll need to leave here tomorrow evening to be there on time, and she feels a surge of panic, tomorrow evening? We haven't even got enough warm clothes, she imagines them stepping off the plane and turning on the spot into pillars of ice, and who will look after Nitzan, and who knows if he'll even get on the plane, if he'll use the ticket she's about to order for him. It's a short journey, Tanya tries to reassure her, you arrive, see the little boy a few times and then decide, if your decision is positive you have to go the court once more after about a month, I've explained the procedure to you.

Yes, it's clear, Dina mumbles, who would have thought it would happen so quickly, in her imagination she still had time to talk Gideon round, in her imagination they sit side by side before the picture of the winsome child with the sweet smile of entreaty and hope, in her imagination they're preparing for the journey in the early summer, Gideon happy at the thought of the new landscapes awaiting his camera, the adventure in store for them, and she confident in their love which will flourish like the love of the child, but it didn't happen like this and she doesn't even have time for regrets. She'll buy the tickets and pack a case for the pair of them, if he refuses to come she'll go without him, she has no choice, if she believes in herself she'll believe in the boy, and if she believes in the boy nothing can stand in her way, and again she approaches the computer, who are you, little man? Suspicious, deflated, domesticated, and yet at the same time solid, upright, sturdy, what have you been through since you came into the world, what awaits you, what awaits us, together? Exhausted, she slumps over the keyboard, again her strength is draining away, again her heart is fluttering between her ribs, one moment she's all-capable and the next she longs to go to bed and stay there for ever, but before doing this she'll contact her brother: Avner? Listen, we have to travel to Siberia tomorrow, I don't even know if Gideon will agree to come with me, the kid is wearing your stripy shirt and I have nothing to wear, have you got any warm clothes? Coats, hats, gloves? Can you come?

To Siberia? he'll ask and she'll say no, here, I need your help, and Avner, just about to leave his house, will retrace his steps, listening to her with a dry throat. Don't worry, Dini, I'll go to Siberia with you if Gideon won't. I'm not letting you travel alone, and I'm not letting you bring the kid up alone, I believe in what you're doing, I believe in love, that's what I've discovered recently, I know it sounds absurd. Don't worry, Dini, you've got me, you've got my kids, all of us together will make a family for the newcomer, and while trying to reassure her he's rummaging in the full wardrobe that Talia left him, moving the hangers along the rails until he finds a pair of heavy-duty ski parkas, and on his way to her house with his hands full, he's intrigued by the thought of his sister and her husband wandering around snowbound Siberia in the clothes of the dead man and his lover, short and stocky Gideon will be covered from the thighs upwards by Rafael Allon's black parka, with Dina the winter bride in resplendent white, a baby in her arms.

On the very cusp of their deaths people cease to be mortal, with the departure of their souls they will be turned into gods, mystical heavenly knowledge will enfold them, they will drop the past from their hands and cling to the future, no more accusations and injustices, fears and regrets and sins, but the abstract future with its host of possibilities will reveal itself before their eyes like scores of colourful carpets set out for display all at once. From the high towers of their ending they look down, everyone who dies has a tower of his own on the hills of destiny, everyone who dies has his secret future and the future of his loved ones to the end of all generations, and she too, Hemda Horowitz, daughter of Ya'akov and Rivka, who never succeeded in drawing from her life the fullness of their qualities and their exploits, who dipped her fingers in the honeycomb only to have them come back to her dry, who was content with hints, with exegeses, with repressed longings and inexplicable joys, surely deserves now, in her last hours, the consolations and the blessings denied her all her life, yes, for the first time in her life she attains absolute knowledge, and with its power she will accompany her only daughter on her fateful journey, give her a parting gift, and over distances beyond measure she holds out a transparent hand and touches her forehead. Let me draw out all your fears, my dear daughter, I am with you, though we will never meet again, I will be with you, and since we will never meet again, I shall be where I am, a clear winter day on a snowbound slope, in the whispering vestiges of the night, on a baby's cheek, the shadow of a bird among the pine needles, there you will catch a glimpse of me, and Dina who is resting her forehead on the window of the plane will suddenly feel the miraculous touch of the clouds surrounding her, and it seems to her this is the touch she has longed for all her life, chilling and yet consoling, enfolding but not oppressive. She's held in the arms of the clouds like a bride led to the canopy between her father and her mother, and a sense of utter calm overwhelms her, secret and mysterious, and she gives no thought to the momentous encounter awaiting her or to her husband who's sitting beside her with a sour look on his face, a can of beer in his hand, drinking in hostile silence. Until the last moment he didn't let her know he was coming with her, he went out to work this morning without saying a word to her, he didn't reply to her messages, only an hour before the time of departure he came back, stood before her pale and tense. I'll ask you one more time to abandon this madness, he said, you're dragging us towards disaster, and she bent down in silence over her suitcase and fastened the strap holding it together. These are the last words you'll ever hear from me, he said, I'm going with you only as an escort. I don't intend to speak to you ever again, I'm not interested in seeing the kid, and when we get back I'm moving out, and she dragged the suitcase to the door, thank you for escorting me, she said to him quietly.

These were just words, dust motes in the air, it's actions that count, she tried to keep calm while parting from her daughter with countless warnings and prohibitions. That's enough, Mum, there's no need to make a fuss, it's only three nights, the girl protested, Shiri's sleeping over here and everything's going to be fine, don't worry about me, and have a good time, she added with a mischievous smile, completely ignoring the purpose of the journey, as if they were going away for a romantic weekend, when in fact they had never been so far apart. It seems the whole plane is filled by the painful tension between them, the floor covered with fragments of shattered aspirations, the air seeping poison, the poison created by two people constantly at odds over conflicting needs, and she watches the stewardesses, impressed by their confident gait when pacing the gangway, and the passengers surrounding her, one reading a book and another working on a laptop, and nobody squirming yet from the effects of poisoning, and only her hands are shaking and her breathing laboured, and she lays her aching head on the window pane, seeing the clouds racing towards her with arms outstretched, taking her worries from her and carrying on their way, and suddenly she doesn't care that he isn't going to say a word to her even when they land in Moscow, and all the hours they'll be waiting at the airport for the connecting flight to Siberia, and when they finally arrive in the grey and remote city where the little boy was born and where he was abandoned and handed over to the children's home, even then he won't say one single word to her, as if he too, like all the people around them, doesn't speak her language. Silence is good for times like this, there's no point in holding trivial conversations and as for the issues that stand between them, they've already discussed them ad nauseam and beyond, and not been brought a hair's breadth closer together as a result.

This is the hour for action, the hour of mysteries that brings the living close to the dead and human beings close to gods, this is the hour when destiny speaks and we are silent, quietly absorbing the illusions of space, the barely perceptible transition from one land to another. Even at the airport in Moscow, similar to every other airport she has known, it's possible to sense the change, the soft and rolling sound of the language, the expressive faces, the beauty of the women stepping lightly on stiletto heels, in flamboyant furs, is one of them his mother, the girl who bore him? Again she takes the documents from her briefcase and checks the year of the mother's birth, and it's only now, when she has leisure to peruse the sparse information, she realises that the girl who today is not yet nineteen was exactly Nitzan's age when she gave birth to him two years ago, and she gasps with the pain when she sees her daughter before her eyes and the secret cleaving her body. Don't worry, little girl, she wants to say to every young woman passing by, don't worry, it seems you couldn't have done otherwise, you're still only a child yourself, a child of Mother Russia with her many faces, her acquaintance with grief, the eternal mother whose flesh the upheavals of history have scored mercilessly and almost without respite.

Between grey deserts of ice the plane lands in the evening, and when they step out the cold takes their breath away, a stone smites your heart and what can you do, a memory of old stories rises to the surface of her mind, children sliding on toboggans and their laughter suddenly freezing, Nikolai, Sergei, Andrei, Yuri, put cloth over your lips or else you die! The waggoner and his horse are waiting desperately for the morning, is it nearly morning? Aha, the clock reads midnight, sealing their fate, they're not going to hold out, hungry soldiers trudge through the snow, their boots in tatters, growling like bereaved bears, they were all children once, Nikolai, Sergei, Andrei, Yuri. The cold mocks the quilted parka she borrowed from her brother, the matching gloves, the hat, how could anyone survive here, even a handful out of the millions of exiles and deportees? The deep freeze could kill you in a few hours, and she looks around her at the flat and forbidding landscape, how much suffering has this great plain seen, how much cruelty, mothers torn from their children and sent here by train, people torn from their identities, confessing to crimes they didn't commit, convicted of murder and executed by murderers whose own fate would catch up with them in the end, how much injustice has been piled up here like the snow stacked at the roadside; its radiant beauty is long gone and yet even in its ugliness it is impregnable.

A tall young woman, wrapped in a black fur coat, is waiting for them in the desolate terminal building, its floor wet from the melted ice, on her face a confident and almost disdainful expression, a local woman amused by the anxieties of foreign visitors, fear of the cold, of the open spaces, of the magnitude of the event, and she holds out a manicured hand. Welcome, I'm Marina, how was the flight? she asks in slow, hesitant Hebrew, and Dina answers briefly, it was fine. How to describe the fierce currents of air that swirled around the body of the plane and her body too, the currents of hope and presumption, the sharp and frightening sounds, what am I doing here, what witchcraft brought me here? A person thinks a thought, a person is filled with desire, and through the strength of this thought he suddenly reaches another star, and it seems to her it was her desire that kept the plane aloft and her fear that sent it into a dive, and if indeed it was through the power of thought alone that she reached Siberia, who knows what else she is capable of doing, and now she's surprised to be reunited with her suitcase that was packed, it seems to her, many days ago and by a different woman, and Marina takes it from her and shows her the way, outside again, into the cold that's almost solid.

My car is close by, she says, but Dina has to struggle to take even two steps, and she clutches the arm of the strange woman, in the throbbing darkness, at home it's midday and here it's already evening, Nitzan will be coming home soon, heating up the soup she left for her, spicy lentil soup, a recipe she got from Orly nearly twenty years ago, and it seems to her there's a close connection between these things although she's unable to identify it, between that soup and the smooth ice under her feet, forcing her to walk very slowly, heel to toe, like the shuffling gait of her elderly mother since that nasty fall she had, her face turned down towards the malicious frost, that's busily sowing pitfalls in her path. Only when they reach the car does she dare stand up straight for the first time and she's astonished to see that Gideon, who has jealously guarded his silence, so much so that even the effervescent guide hasn't attempted to strike up a conversation with him, has taken his camera from his back-pack and is immortalising the icy car park, the silhouettes of grounded planes in the distance, the low chains of mountains, the darkness coming down silently like black snow, and this action, the first thing he's done voluntarily since they set out, gives her some reassurance as she sits back in the front seat and makes an effort to move her frozen toes.

Throughout the journey he carries on taking pictures, and through the twilight of the drowsiness that enfolds her she hears him asking the guide animated questions about the history of the city and its sites of interest, about the river and the great dam, as if he's nothing more than a keen tourist, he doesn't ask any questions about the child, and nor does she, although this woman has seen him in person and taken his picture for them, and what would she ask, is he the one destined for me? In his little hands that hold the book he's holding my destiny too, what is there to ask. In her clean and archaic Hebrew, conserving a different reality, she answers him, when have they ever had a conversation like this in their own country, with its crises and the alarming speed of changes? Her dainty hands are clamped firmly on the wheel as she drives on into the snowy wastelands. Occasionally a low house appears beside the road, lights dimmed, was the child abandoned there? How far away they are from home, how far they have come, the distance between this city and Moscow is greater than the distance between Jerusalem and Moscow, and she listens to Marina explaining in detail what they can expect tomorrow, a short meeting in the adoption centre in the morning, then a drive to the children's home, first encounter with the child, with the doctor and the social worker who will give details of his condition. And what then? For some reason she doesn't go on, and what would she say? Then your world will be turned upside down? Then your life will be changed for ever? And then you'll be facing the hardest decision of your life? If you refuse like that other couple you won't get another chance, and what's worse, he probably won't either, and if you decide to take him to your bosom and into your hearts you're in for a massive upheaval, but of course all of this she doesn't know. She doesn't know that this couple, the squat and sturdy man with the black balaclava covering his face and the taller woman in the white parka, won't be going anywhere together ever again, but will be crushed under the weight of constant disagreement, that this couple, whose aspirations have collided frontally, painfully, can indeed live the mundane life in relative equanimity, but can't handle the big issues, that these two people, whom she's extricating now from her car and leading to a small and surprisingly pleasant hotel, won't be exchanging love in the bed with its clean white quilt or defusing the tension with words of sympathy and solidarity, and even when they sit face to face in the overheated hotel restaurant, where stunningly attractive waitresses in micro-skirts – could one of these be the mother? – serve them freshly roasted river fish and green beans in an aromatic sauce, they will still be avoiding eye-contact and she won't dare, as she usually does, dip her fork in his portion to sample it, as if the overcrowding in this restaurant has forced her to sit with a total stranger and she has no choice but to look on with embarrassment as he chomps away noisily, the powerful jawbones hard at work, and she reminds herself not to think too far ahead, not about the imminent separation and the upheavals in their lives, just about the little boy, whose photograph is in her handbag, and she glances at it from time to time. Tomorrow we're going to meet, kiddo, tomorrow the chapter will be over that began back then, who knows when exactly, and the start of a new chapter, a new book, or rather an old book in another language, to be written by another woman, after meeting you I can't go on being the same person.

The television suspended on the opposite wall is broadcasting an endless series of short clips interspersed with adverts, a cacophony that there's no escaping from, likewise the aggravating heat, only a little while ago she had been longing for warmth and now it's really bugging her and she strips off layer after layer, down to the tattered blouse which wasn't meant to be exposed, while all the other women are dressed in such provocative style, and she notices Gideon's intoxicated eyes studying them appreciatively, yes, anything could happen yet, despite his age he's still attractive and his name is quite well known, he could easily get himself a woman many years younger than him, younger than her, and a stab of resentment raises her to her feet, I'm going to the room, she says, forgetting that they're not supposed to be speaking, picks up the parka and the two sweaters and the scarf and leaves him there to finish his beer, or order another, and in the bedroom she strips off her heavy shoes and stretches out on the bed in her clothes, in a moment I'll get up and take a shower, she promises herself, and I'll impose some order on this day, that began who knows when and will end who knows when, a day without boundaries, but she's incapable of standing up from the bed, although the sound of a choking cry comes to her ears, little boy, she sighs as she drifts into sleep, is that you crying in the distance, and are you calling me? From moment to moment time scrolls backwards and she mumbles, Gideon, Nitzan's woken up, can you bring her to the bed? Her breasts are full and leaking milk, and now she's in the children's house in the kibbutz, every night someone cries and sets all the others off, and tonight it's her turn, Mummy, my Mummy, she wails, come to me, Mummy.

A few hours from now, when she wakes in agitation to the milky light, she'll hurry to the window, how strange the sights are, how touching, a spacious and picturesque ruin of a house abuts on the hotel, and in the distance, in the space between one building and its neighbour, she sees the main street of the city and people walking briskly, wrapped up from head to toe, bent against the cold, trying to shelter from the wind, the snow isn't falling, it's been absorbed into the air, although the few trees are already covered with it, and she carefully opens the window and the cold takes her breath away, a stone smites your heart and what can you do. She hears Gideon sighing in his sleep, tossing the blanket away and sleeping in his underwear, as if this is an Israeli summer, and the sight of his body hurts her, he isn't hers any more, she has no right to wake him with caresses for acts of love, not even the love of strangers meeting by chance at the end of the world, it's over, wound up and sealed; her love for him isn't wound up and sealed, but she broke the rule and for that he won't forgive her, and even if she changes her mind at the moment of truth her offence won't be wiped away. He expected her to give it up for his sake, take account of his legitimate demands, and she refused and that's why she's here in Siberia, and that's why for him she'll always be staying here, exiled from him, even when they return home, with or without a child in tow, and she stands at the window and strips off the clothes she last wore years ago, one evening in Jerusalem, how strange to be naked when the others are wrapped up in layers of clothing. It's the way of the world, one feels hot and the other feels cold, even if only a few paces separate them, even if they are married to each other according to the law of Moses and Israel, and she steps into the shower, pity she can't take a ritual bath before meeting the child, bathe in the river that flows beneath the layers of ice, only then will she be purged of doubts, only then can she see him as he is, and as she tries to blend hot with cold water she's amazed once again that's she managed to sleep at all, night after night she's been kept awake by thoughts of what lies ahead, and now, just a few hours before the event, she's slept soundly, she didn't even notice Gideon coming into the room and into the bed, and suddenly she remembers the fantasy that used to help her sleep in the children's house, her mother hearing her cry and coming to her, walking briskly into the room, climbing into her bed and enfolding her in warm and protective arms. It was only after some time that she realised to her horror why her imaginary mother was periodically leaving sticky stains on the bedlinen, and yet the revelation didn't spoil her memory of the feeling of safety, at the time when she was in fact at her most vulnerable, so now even when they go down in silence to eat their breakfast before the chattering television set, even when they're picked up by their guide and crammed into her car, heavy and clumsy in their multifarious strata of clothing, she feels safe and protected, listening attentively to the final instructions, what to say and what not to say under any circumstances, and she looks out calmly at the reddish suburban houses, the snow piled up like garbage at the sides of the road, women encased in fur coats and hats and looking like colourful birds, the monotonous streets, without storefront windows, almost without signs of any kind. From time to time, springing up amid the desolation, some remarkably attractive wooden houses appear, relics of another era, and over there is a young man leaning on the wall and smoking, his breath freezing along with the snot that's running from his nose, is he the father? A few drunks stagger along by the roadside, one of them sinks down on a heap of dirty snow, Nikolai, Sergei, Andrei, Yuri, they were all children once, is this the future he can expect if she turns him down?

At last the river comes into view, and when they cross the massive iron bridge spanning it her heart suddenly swells, she's being led to her destiny, they are being led to their destiny, grey and majestic is the river, sending up plumes of vapour, spiralling like phantoms, icy trees on the banks, the landscape of the moon wouldn't be stranger to her than this landscape, but they've crossed the river and on the other side the little boy waits, and before being allowed to see him they now have to leave the car and go into a long building like a train carriage where a woman waits for them, heavily built and for some reason familiar to her, looking remarkably similar to one of the kibbutz veterans, as she remembers, and for a moment it seems to her it's all being treated as a joke. In rolling Russian she relates the child's life-story and Marina translates casually, turning long sentences into short, what's she leaving out? And then they are asked why they are so keen to adopt and Dina looks nervously at Gideon, afraid he may trip her up with a rude awakening, but he stares in silence at the window and she explains in a whisper that they have just the one daughter and they are eager to have another child, and they want to share their good fortune with a little boy to whom life has not been kind, as has just been described to them in detail, and it seems this explanation satisfies the questioner, although this is just the first of the many hurdles that stand between them and the delivery of the final judgment, and they are sent from there to the nearby children's home. Again and again she hears his camera clicking in the back seat but doesn't turn to look, focusing only on the way ahead, on the heavy trucks hissing on the icy roads, the gigantic and ascetic urban squares, the gloomy estates, to the yellow-painted house with the snow-covered tiled roof, and again she clutches Marina's arm on the slippery steps, and once more they are greeted in the entrance hall by oppressive heat, but this time it's accompanied by a heavy and bitter smell of closed rooms and suffocation and urine and sweat, is this his smell?

In the long and green-painted corridors women are pacing in white gowns, and they too are solemnly asked to insert their shoes in nylon bags as if they're on their way to an operating theatre, and when they climb the stairs she's mystified by the silence, it's as if there are no children in this building, though she knows there are hundreds, some of them allocated for adoption and some who will never be part of a family, on account of legal restrictions or the simple fact that no one wants them, and she looks around her tensely but for some reason isn't concerned, she will know, she will know, this is the hand of knowledge that is suddenly at her side, heavenly knowledge, mysterious and yet maternal. When Marina steps forward and knocks on the broad wooden door, she looks round and sees Gideon turning his back on them and walking down the stairs like a fugitive, I'm not looking at the kid, he told her then, but she's already inside, ignoring the inquisitive looks of the guide, studying the spacious room. A colourful carpet covers the floor and there's equipment there for games and exercises, a few bicycles, ladders with ropes hanging from them, a rocking horse, on the shelves a selection of toys, and everything so clean and orderly it looks like a optical illusion, and she touches one of the teddy bears to check that it's real and not painted on the wall for show, do the children really play here from time to time, and where are the children, why are we not hearing their voices?

In the middle of the room stands a Christmas tree, bright with its mass of coloured decorations, and around it scores of little chairs arranged in concentric circles. A heavy-bodied woman greets them and goes on arranging the chairs, and Dina looks apprehensively at the door, in a moment it will open and the little boy will appear in the arms of one of the nannies. She's read so many descriptions of this moment. Sometimes the child is reserved, not making eye-contact, sometimes he's sullen and slow, sometimes he's friendly, even too friendly, he may present any one of many different faces, and meanwhile her eyes wander to the colourful chairs, there are so many of them, and on every chair an abandoned child will sit, a child of no one, staring from a distance at the decorated spruce tree, and suddenly she sees on a chair in the corner of the room a tiny boy sitting in silence with a book in his hands. Her eyes open wide in wonder and she clutches Marina's arm, is he here? Is that him? she asks, because the image presented by the photograph is deceptive, it's as if he's gone back in time and shrunk, and she replies calmly, yes, it's strange they brought him in early, wait here, the doctor will be arriving any moment, but she's already advancing towards him with silent tread, as if approaching a kitten that's scared of human company.

He's wearing the familiar stripy shirt and mustard-coloured tailored trousers, his hair cropped short almost to the skull, and he sits with head bowed, not moving hand or foot, and when she sits down beside him he turns his face to her and peers at her earnestly and at once looks down again and she sees he's clenching his lips to stop himself crying, his body tense with the effort and his face flushing, and she whispers, you can cry, little one, it's all right to cry. She's become so used to his appearance in the photograph she's finding it hard to adjust to his live presence, he's smaller than she expected and fairer than she expected, his look wise and restrained, he won't sit on her lap or move into the arms that she holds out to him, he's a frightened and damaged miniature version of a man. He drops the book and picks it up hastily and she puts out a hand to his hand, will he take her finger? He doesn't, but neither does he recoil from her touch, my little boy, she whispers, gently caressing the hand that holds the book, and also, unconsciously, the fur of the cat depicted on the cover. Again his face reddens and he looks old, an elderly infant, alarmingly serious, is this the child she's been waiting for? His efforts fail and he bursts into tears, the nurse in the white gown comes hurrying towards him to quieten him down but Dina forestalls her with a gesture, let me, let me, because I too want to weep with him, this is the child even if he isn't what I prayed for, he's the child even if he'll never be mine, I shall be his, and as the two of them sit weeping side by side in the little chairs facing the Christmas tree she hears the door opening and looks up to see the doctor coming in to update her about the child, fill in all the details and promise her that he's healthy, although she doesn't want to hear anything, she's seen him and that's enough, but to her surprise this isn't the doctor but Gideon, it seems he was in such a hurry to arrive he hasn't taken off his big black parka, and with his gloved hand he's holding something out to her. What's that in his hand, for a moment she doesn't understand, what's she supposed to do with his mobile? She doesn't want to talk to anyone now and that's why she switched hers off, and she stares at his outstretched hand, what's he doing here? He didn't want to see the kid, and now the kid is there in front of him, withdrawn and sullen, just as he is, how similar they are in reality, and he says, Dina, Avner wants to talk to you, slivers of ice have stuck to his stubble and they're falling as he speaks, and she stands up and goes quickly to the corridor. Avner? she whispers, I've seen the boy, he's so tiny, for some reason she can't find any other way to describe him, and Avner says, listen, Dini, but she interrupts him, I can't leave him here, Avner, he needs me.

Dini, Mum has died, her brother says, and she cries out, why? and then, when? And he answers, just now, a few minutes ago. In her bed, it seems she didn't suffer at all, and she sighs, oh, Avner, this is so strange, and he asks, when are you coming home? Can we say the day after tomorrow for the funeral? We'll bury her in the kibbutz, right? Beside her parents?

I suppose so, she says, this is so strange, and he says, OK, we'll talk later, there are so many things to arrange here, and she puts the phone in her pocket and goes to the window. What is so strange about it? The snow here piles up without you ever seeing it fall, it springs from the earth and not from the sky, now that is strange, and she returns slowly to the room, pacing the corridor, on both sides there are closed doors, where are the children? Are they here, in the closed rooms, so quiet, institutionalised, like him, and yet for a moment he wept, he hasn't given up hope of making his voice heard, and she wipes her eyes with the edge of her blouse and opens the door. The doctor is already there, holding a thick file of documents and talking to Marina, who calls to her to join them, but she fixes her gaze on the corner of the room, where to her amazement she sees Gideon sitting in the seat she vacated and the little boy beside him, and the two of them holding the closed book. The little boy points to the cat and makes a strange sound, an indistinct syllable, and she hears Gideon say to him, that's right, it's a cat, or it's a rabbit, that's what we call him, a cat called Rabbit, it's confusing but you'll get used to it, and her knees are quaking as she approaches them, it seems to her she's crossing a narrow and precarious bridge, one careless movement and she'll fall in the river. Very slowly she'll advance, and on reaching them she'll say in a soft voice, to avoid distressing the youngster, my mother's dead, and Gideon will say, I know, and she will lay her hand on the cropped head and say, we'll call him Hemdat.

A NOTE ON THE TYPE

Linotype Garamond Three – based on seventeenth century copies of Claude Garamond's types, cut by Jean Jannon. This version was designed for American Type Founders in 1917, by Morris Fuller Benton and Thomas Maitland Cleland and adapted for mechanical composition by Linotype in 1936.